Praise for Tracy Brogan

Crazy Little Thing

Wall Street Journal Bestseller

RWA RITA® Finalist, 2013, Best First Book

"Heart, humor, and characters you'll love—Tracy Brogan is the next great voice in contemporary romance."

—Kristan Higgins, *New York Times* Bestselling Author

"Witty one-liners and hilarious characters elevate this familiar story . . . Readers will love the heat between the leads, and by the end they'll be clamoring for more."

—*RT Book Reviews*, 4 Stars (HOT)

"Brogan shows a real knack for creating believable yet quirky characters . . . The surprising emotional twists along the way make it a satisfying romp."

—Aleksandra Walker, *Booklist*

"*Crazy Little Thing* by Tracy Brogan is so funny and sexy, I caught myself laughing out loud."

—Robin Covington, *USA Today*, *Happy Ever After*

"Tracy Brogan is my go-to, laugh-out-loud remedy for a stressful day."

—Kieran Kramer, *USA Today* Bestselling Author

The Best Medicine

RWA RITA® Finalist, 2015, Best Contemporary Romance

"With trademark humor, lovely, poignant touches, and a sexy-as-sin hero, *The Best Medicine* is Tracy Brogan at her finest. Charming, witty, and fun."

—Kimberly Kincaid, *USA Today* Bestselling Author

Love Me Sweet

RWA RITA® Finalist, 2016, Best Contemporary Romance

"An upbeat, generous message about finding yourself, standing up for yourself, and living an authentic life . . . A sexy, slightly kooky romance that should please Bell Harbor fans."

—*Kirkus Reviews*

Jingle Bell Harbor: A Novella

"Brogan's hilarious voice and word play will immediately ensnare readers in this quick but satisfying small-town romance."

—Adrian Liang, *Amazon Book Review*

"*Jingle Bell Harbor* is a fun, funny, laugh-out-loud Christmas read that will surely put you right in the mood for the season."

—*The Romance Reviews*, 5 Stars

"This was an incredible read! I was definitely surprised by this book and in a great way."

—*My Slanted Bookish Ramblings*, 4.5 Stars

"*Jingle Bell Harbor* by Tracy Brogan is about discovering what you want, deciding what you need to finally be happy, and rediscovering a love of the holidays. It's a quick, easy read filled with laughter and enjoyable quirky characters. If you're in the mood for something light and funny, I would recommend *Jingle Bell Harbor* by Tracy Brogan."

—*Harlequin Junkie*, 4 Stars

"This is a really cute, uplifting Christmas novella. It's quick, light, and gives you warm fuzzies just in time for the upcoming holidays. There is plenty of humor to keep you entertained, and the quirky residents of Bell Harbor will keep you reading to see what else is in store."

—*Rainy Day Reading Blog*, 4 Stars

Hold on My Heart

"Successfully blends a sassy heroine and humor with deep emotional issues and a traditional romance . . . The well-developed characters and the sweet story with just a touch of heat will please readers looking for a creative take on romance."

—*Publishers Weekly*

"Launched in hilarious style by an embarrassingly cute meet, this delightful romantic comedy will keep the smiles coming."

—*Library Journal*

Highland Surrender

"*Highland Surrender* features plenty of action, romance, and sex with well-drawn individuals—a strong, yet young heroine and a delectable hero—who don't act out of character. The story imparts a nice feeling of 'you are there,' with a well-presented look at the turbulent life in sixteenth-century Scotland."

—*RT Book Reviews*, 4 Stars

"Treachery and political intrigue provide a well-textured backdrop for a poignant romance in which a young girl, well out of her depths, struggles to reconcile what she thinks she knows with what her heart tells her. *Highland Surrender* is a classic sweep-me-away tale of romance and derring-do!"

—Connie Brockway, *New York Times* Bestselling Author

MY KIND OF YOU

Other Books by Tracy Brogan

Bell Harbor Series

Crazy Little Thing

The Best Medicine

Love Me Sweet

Jingle Bell Harbor: A Novella

Standalone

Highland Surrender

Hold on My Heart

MY KIND OF YOU

A Trillium Bay Novel

TRACY BROGAN

This is a work of fiction. Names, characters, organizations, places, events, and incidents are either products of the author's imagination or are used fictitiously.

Published by Montlake Romance, Seattle

www.apub.com

ISBN-13: 9781503943247
ISBN-10: 1503943240

Cover design by Rachel Adam

Printed in the United States of America

For Webster Girl and Tenacious D. You are my everything.

Chapter 1

The Wawatam County Municipal Airport had all the charm and amenities Emily Chambers had expected, which, unfortunately, meant none. The terminal building, aptly named because its pale beige paint and jaundiced lighting made it appear to indeed *be terminal*, was the size of a parking space and boasted four dingy, mustard-colored plastic chairs on which to wait. A hand-painted red, white, and blue sign adorned one wall while glossy lacquered trout, mouths gaping wide in one last perpetual gasp for air, clung to simple wooden plaques above each doorway providing the only hint of décor, if one used the term *décor* as loosely as possible, of course.

"Mom, that airplane is not legit. It's nothing but a soup can with wings."

Emily's twelve-year-old daughter gazed with practiced consternation out a long, narrow window at a seven-seater plane sitting on the gravel tarmac. It was an astute assessment of the decrepit, duct-taped aircraft, but instead of agreeing, Emily did what any good mother would do under those particular circumstances. She lied.

"It'll be fine, honey. It's a short flight."

Chloe tossed red-gold hair over one slender shoulder. "A short flight? I'm sure it will be. I doubt that thing can stay in the air for long. Where'd you get these tickets? Podunk Airlines? Deathtrap.com? Fly the deadly skies?" Chloe bore an air of perpetual disdain that only a preteen girl could truly master. It was a new skill that Emily did not find particularly endearing, but she didn't have the energy at the moment to point that out, and in Chloe's defense, they were both exhausted. They'd been traveling toward Michigan since five o'clock that morning, starting back home in San Antonio, Texas. Two quick layovers meant no time to eat, and Chloe had devoured their stash of granola bars and grapes before the first plane had even left the ground. Now it was dinnertime, and here they were, stuck in this rustic wasteland waiting for one more plane to fly them over the lake to their final destination. Trillium Bay on Wenniway Island, Emily's hometown, and a place she hadn't returned to in seven years.

"Honey, I know you're not thrilled about spending the entire summer on the island, but I really need you to be a good sport about this. Your great-grandmother has hired me to renovate one of her rental properties, and it's going to take a while." That was essentially the truth. Not the entire truth, of course, but a reasonable facsimile of it, and it was the version that protected Chloe from having to worry about things no kid should have to worry about—like, for instance, how to pay the rent—because, not to put too fine a point on things, Emily was broke. Flat, busted, nothing-but-lint-in-her-pockets kind of broke. On the rather colorful list of questionable decisions she'd made in her lifetime, her most recent blunder had landed them in this cash-strapped predicament, but Chloe had no idea how dire their circumstances were. No one in the family had any idea except for her grandmother, Gigi, and Emily wanted to keep it that way.

"Gigi is so excited to have us stay with her, and Aunt Lilly and Aunt Brooke can't wait to see us, and there will be all of your cousins. And Grandpa Harlan, too, of course." Her voice stumbled on that last bit. She had no idea if her father was looking forward to their visit. Chief of Police Harlan Callaghan did not radiate warmth, nor was he the type to forgive lightly, and since Emily had given him quite a few things to be upset about, not the least of which was running away at nineteen to marry a boy she hardly knew, there was just no telling how he'd react to seeing her. She'd come home just twice since marrying Nick, but both times she'd left the island feeling worse than when she'd arrived.

Still, Gigi had promised Emily that this visit would be fine. Just fine. Enjoyable, even. She'd promised that Harlan would be nice. Quite nice, and that everyone from Trillium Bay was thrilled to have Emily and Chloe stay for a nice, long stretch. Simply thrilled. And even though Emily knew that Margaret "Gigi" O'Reilly-Callaghan-Harper-Smith was a master manipulator who would say just about anything if it served her purpose, Emily chose to believe her. Not that she had much choice.

"It's going to be fun, Chloe. I promise. You had fun the last time we were there, right?"

"I was five, Mom. I don't remember anything about it." Another flip of the hair.

"Well, see? You were just a little kid then, but this time you'll be able to do so many more things, like hike and bike and ride horses with your cousins. There's the big Lilac Festival, and fireworks and a parade. And fudge. You like fudge. Right?" Emily nodded, as if agreeing with herself made it that much more true. For them both. Emily knew this trip wasn't going to be fun. It was going to be hard work interspersed with periods of elongated denial and punctuated by acute dysfunction.

Ah, family reunions.

Chloe turned back to the window with an overzealously dramatic sigh and stretched out her arm to take a pouting selfie. "Sure, I like fudge," she muttered. "I just didn't want to give up my entire summer to have some."

Emily paused, letting that teachable moment on the meaning of gratitude pass, mostly because she understood exactly how her daughter felt. She hadn't wanted to give up her entire summer, either. This was so not part of Emily's grand plan, but then again, most of the stuff that happened in her life had not been part of any grand plan. Her life was more like a series of tattered Post-it notes with hastily scribbled goals written in dull pencil. Some of them stuck. Lots of them didn't. Like her marriage to Chloe's father. That one definitely did not stick. Other than Chloe, nothing good had come from it.

Emily had started to worry that her business venture into house flipping wasn't going to stick, either, although it had started out promising. She'd participated in a dozen or so successful flips with her friend Jewel, but their most recent project had spiraled out of control. A disaster wrapped in a catastrophe sitting on a pile of misfortune. A Calamity-ville horror plagued by mold and termites and a faulty foundation. Every day had brought them more bad news, more issues that cost money to fix. Now Emily was up to her earlobes in debt, and this financial drama had forced her to make a deal with the very devil. A clandestine deal with strings attached that were like fishing lines. Invisible yet impossible to break. And in this case, the devil didn't wear Prada so much as she wore a pink nylon tracksuit, polka-dotted bifocals, and answered to the name Gigi.

Yes, Emily had been reduced to borrowing money from her own grandmother. Gigi had been her last resort. Oh sure, Emily could have asked Nick for money, but since he never even paid his child support, she wasn't likely to get any additional support from him. He was a *last, last* resort. And there was Harlan, of course, but if the strings attached to her deal with Gigi were fishing lines, any loan from her father would be wrapped in barbed wire. Electric barbed wire. He was her *last, last, last* resort, so technically, Gigi, her seventy-five-year-old thrice-widowed granny, had come in third from the bottom of Emily's last resorts. There was little comfort in knowing that she could have sunk even further.

Emily bit back her own sigh, wishing she could indulge in feeling sorry for herself. In that moment, she wanted nothing more than to fling herself onto one of those incredibly uncomfortable plastic chairs and weep—delicately and beautifully, of course. Not the ugly cry. No one ever wants to indulge in the ugly cry. Maybe she could just whimper a little and have a single tear run down one cheek. But she had to put on a brave face for Chloe. Plus, she was wearing her very best and most expensive business suit. It was white, and those chairs looked none too clean. So her fainting and weeping and whimpering would just have to wait.

She stepped over to the dinged-up vending machine instead and jabbed at a few buttons without much optimism. The vintage contraption was held together with duct tape and only took coins. No dollar bills or credit cards, which meant no snacks for them. She tapped hard on the glass, gazing with pointless longing at an ancient bag of pretzels, hoping it might fall on its own. No such luck. If a bag fell, she'd have to give the pretzels to Chloe, of course, but maybe she could just eat the salty bits at the bottom of the bag. Damn, she was hungry. Her stomach growled in response. She tried again. Tap, tap, tap. The bag stayed solidly in place.

Hoping to score some loose change at the very bottom of her purse, Emily dug a hand inside her bag just as the door next to Chloe burst open, pushed by a strong wind and man in a navy-blue business suit. A red tie hung loosely around his neck, and he hauled a shiny black suitcase with one hand while pressing a phone against his ear with the other. An overstuffed computer bag hung from his broad shoulder and caught on the door handle. He tugged it free with an impatient huff and continued on inside.

"No, I'm not there yet, Bryce. Your secretary booked me on the worst flights imaginable, and don't think I don't know you put her up to it. Next time I'm flying charter." He walked over to the chairs, somehow not seeming to notice either Emily or Chloe in spite of how small the area was. "Yeah, very funny, jackass. I just landed in Outer Effing Mongolia. Someplace called . . . Wigwam, or Woebegone, or . . ." He glanced at the sign. "Wawatam. Yeah, that's it. Wawatam. Wherever the hell that is."

Emily bristled at his obvious disdain of the place since she'd grown up near here, but he wasn't wrong. This airport was one D-list operation. The check-in counter was nothing more than a folding table in front of a doorway leading to an office barely spacious enough for a gray metal desk littered with papers. A crooked old man had been playing solitaire in there with an actual deck of cards when she and Chloe had arrived. Emily estimated his age to be somewhere between eighty-five and infinity, and come to think of it, he hadn't moved in a full fifteen minutes. Emily peered at him a little more closely, suddenly wondering if perhaps his old soul had wandered off to that big airport lobby in the sky. Great. She seriously hoped he wasn't dead. If he was, she was really going to regret not spending the extra money and flying through the Pellston airport. It was much nicer, and the people there, to the best of her knowledge, were younger and healthier.

The man in the power suit set down his luggage, taking up one of the premium chairs with his computer bag, and continued talking loudly. "I'll do my best, Bryce, but I'm sure you're worried over nothing. This is Dad we're talking about, and he's certainly not going to just up and marry some bimbo that he hardly knows. That's your area."

Bimbo? Emily's attention shifted from the elderly, potentially deceased airport worker to the oblivious phone-talker, taking a quick inventory of his various attributes. He was tall, maybe six-two, with dark brown hair, cut short. Not marine sergeant kind of short, but short enough that it didn't take much fussing other than to style the front upward. Square jaw, big hands. Power suit. Good looking in a *Corporate*

America, I'm King of the World kind of way. She knew the type. He oozed confidence and an *I must win* demeanor.

As a house flipper, most of the guys Emily dealt with these days were subcontractors who wore tool belts and cargo pants and suffered from chronic ass-crack reveal. Or they were prospective home buyers dressed by their wives in a dad-bod uniform of khaki pants and golf shirts. Unlike those guys, though, this one didn't sport a beer belly, a bald spot, or a wedding band. Emily offered up a short, silent sigh at his businesslike hotness. Never underestimate the allure of a man in a well-cut suit.

Emily cleared her throat and went to sit down in one of the other chairs. He took note of her then and gave an awkward *I'm on the phone here* kind of nod. His eyes trailed lower, and she noticed him noticing her legs. Millennia of evolution took a backseat to the primordial part of her that felt validated by his subtle appraisal. Sure, she was a girl-power feminist all day long, but it was still nice to have someone notice your legs. Out of curiosity or boredom or just pure feminine empowerment, she repositioned herself on the chair, slowly recrossing her damn fine legs to her best advantage. Chloe frowned at her from across the tiny room. *Really, Mom?* Emily was quite accustomed to that look.

"Yeah, okay," the man said, turning away after another glance at Emily. "I'll call you when I actually get to the island. I'm assuming they have cell service over there. If not, watch for a carrier pigeon."

As he turned away, Emily crossed her arms and tucked her legs under the chair. So much for captivating him. He kept talking, and his loud voice was too big for this space. She wished he'd hang up. Her head was starting to ache from the day's traveling, her lack of sustenance, and the knowledge that her next stop would deposit her right into the clutches of Gigi and the rest of her family.

"Carrier pigeon," the man repeated with his outside voice. "Not an owl. Why the hell would I send you a letter by owl?"

Chloe burst out laughing, and he looked up at her quizzically.

"Harry Potter," she said to him, as if she were part of the conversation.

He moved the phone away from his ear. "What?"

"Harry Potter. In the Harry Potter books they send mail by owls, not carrier pigeons."

He looked at her for another moment, offering up one slow blink as his expression went blank. "Okay," he finally said, then pressed the phone back to his ear. "I have to go, Bryce. I'll see what I can do about Dad, but I'll have my own work to deal with. Yeah, I'll call you later." He tapped his thumb against the surface and then slipped his phone into the pocket of his jacket. He leaned back in his chair, stretching a little, manspreading. Then he adjusted his computer bag so *it* would be more comfortable in *its* chair. Finally, he looked back at Emily and nodded, a positive assessment in his dark brown eyes. He was very attractive. She couldn't deny that. Nick had been very attractive, too, and although it was a gross generalization to say that all attractive men bore a sense of entitlement and tended to be assholes, Emily had done a fair amount of personal research over the years, and all the data she'd collected seemed to support this theory.

"Fly through here often?" asked the Man with the Red Tie.

Case in point. That was the best he could come up with? Attractive men didn't have to try very hard to capture a woman's attention. They didn't have to be particularly witty or clever or original. This one was clearly accustomed to making the ladies swoon with just a wistful smile and a soulful gaze. And while a wistful smile and a soulful gaze had their place, Emily had no time for this.

"Hardly ever. You?" She paired his cheesy line with a dry-as-merlot tone of voice. He didn't seem to notice.

"Never. Never even heard of this place." He rose from the seat abruptly and crossed to the window near Chloe, as if his energy just wouldn't allow him to be still. He was going to be a joy to sit next to on the tiny seven-seater plane.

"Wow," he said, leaning forward and squinting out the window. "Looks like we're taking a Cessna Flying Coffin."

Chloe's eyes widened as she stared up at him. "Is that really the name of it?"

He laughed. "No, but it might as well be. That ride looks fifty years old."

Chloe redirected her distressed gaze toward Emily. "Mom?"

Emily shook her head. He might be handsome, but he was an idiot. What kind of guy said something like that to a little girl? Okay, so Chloe was tall for her age and looked much older than twelve, but still. He was an idiot.

"It'll be fine, honey. These small planes fly back and forth from the island all the time."

"Not today they don't," called out the very old but apparently not yet dead man from the office. "We're having technical difficulties." He stood up and shuffled over to the folding table as Emily rose from her chair.

"What do you mean, not today?" she asked.

"Sorry, folks, but Bertie just called me from the hangar." Emily imagined the hangar was what they called that rusty carport leaning against the side of this building. "She said that the what-cha-ma-hootchy in the airplane needs replacing, and she has to go pick up another one. She can't install it until tomorrow, though."

"The . . . the what-cha-ma-hootchy?" Red Tie Guy's voice had gone up about four octaves. Emily could not agree more. They both stepped forward.

"Yeah, you know," the old man said. "The thingamajig. The doo-hickey that makes the dealy-bobber in the engine work. I don't know all them technical terms for airplane parts. I don't really work here, you know. I'm just filling in for Ned on account of he's off to the doctor's office to have a mole looked at."

"But this is serious," Emily said.

"Naw, it's just a mole. He'll be fine. The thing has been there for years."

Her jaw clenched for a moment and loosened only enough for her to say, "No, I mean this is serious that the plane can't fly to the island until tomorrow. We need to get there today."

The old man scratched his head without removing his John Deere hat. "Well, I guess you could, you know, drive on up I-75 for about two hours and take a flight from the Manitou airport. Course you'll never make it there in time because that airport closes down at five p.m. and it's already past that now."

Emily's impatience doubled, fueled by frustration, exhaustion, and low blood sugar, but she held it in remarkably well. She didn't want to start yelling at this old man and scare him into having a heart attack, although in reality he appeared to be quite relaxed about the whole situation. "Sir, if we had a car to drive on up to Manitou, then we could just drive that car the forty miles to Michlimac City and take a ferry instead."

Father Time nodded. "Eh, yep. I guess you could do that, too. Problem solved."

She placed her fingertips on the folding table, resisting her urge to pound on it, even just a little bit. "Our problem is not solved because we don't have a car. That's why we bought airplane tickets."

Wenniway Island sat in Lake Huron just a few nautical miles east of the mainland, and the only way to get there was by plane or boat. Very old plane. Or very slow boat.

The old man looked off into the distance for a moment, as if contemplating her words. Then he crossed his scrawny, crepey-skinned arms. "Well, that there is a conundrum, missy. I'll be very interested to see how it all works out for you. In the meantime, I'm going home to have some meatloaf with my bride. Seventy-two years young, my Doris is, and still a looker. You folks are welcome to spend the night here in the terminal. Somebody will probably be back around eight or so in the morning. If you do make other travel plans, would you kindly turn out the lights when you leave? I promised Ned I'd be sure to turn off the lights."

"But there must be other planes," said the Guy in the Suit, his voice dropping back down into an authoritative range. It was deep with a kind of husky quality to it. The kind of voice that probably got him just what he wanted in the boardroom. And the bedroom. As if Emily had the time or inclination to dwell on such a thing. She shoved away that thought in favor of dealing with this problem right here in front of her.

The old guy, who was not Ned, and not yet dead, nodded his John-Deered head. "Oh yeah, sure enough. There's lots of planes, but none of them are here. Plus, Bertie is the only mechanic who knows what parts she needs, and she just left for the Walmart."

Chloe gave a little gasp. "She's buying airplane parts at Walmart?"

The old man's patronizing smile was nearly hidden beneath his shrubbery-like mustache. "Now don't be silly, little miss. You can't buy airplane parts down at the Walmart. She went there to get some lady loot for the women's restroom. Apparently we're out of them-there sanitized napkins."

He adjusted his hat and winked at Chloe, who proceeded to turn every shade of red before turning her back to the rest of them.

"Sir," Emily said again, "are you sure there are no other planes and no other pilots who can get us to the island this evening?"

"None that I can think of. Most of our planes already left for the island on account of the Lilac Festival. Now, Billy Cornwall can fly, but he doesn't have a license anymore, ever since he landed a plane in Mrs. McGurty's alpaca pasture, so I wouldn't feel right about you going with him. And Cody Faraday is in county lockup right now on account of he was jaywalking."

"They locked him up for jaywalking?" Emily asked.

His voice lowered as he leaned over the table toward her. "Well, he was naked, mostly. If it weren't for he was wearing his cowboy boots, he'd have been completely naked."

Emily turned to look at the Guy in the Suit. The Guy in the Suit looked back at her.

"You think there's any chance in hell they have Uber around here?" he nearly whispered.

"What's an Uber?" the old man said loudly, as if to counterbalance their hushed tones.

"It's like a taxi," Emily answered.

"A taxi? You need a taxi? Well, why didn't you say so? Number's on the wall right there near the pay phone." He pointed to the wall, and sure enough, next to the window was a beat-up old pay phone, and next to that, attached with the ubiquitous duct tape, was a sheet of yellow legal paper with a phone number scrawled in fat black marker.

Wawatam Taxi Service. Thank goodness.

~

Ryan Taggert had wondered if this day could get any worse, and now he knew.

The answer was yes.

Yes, it could.

He'd already puddle-jumped across the nation, wasted three hours in a hotel bar in Minneapolis drinking watered-down vodka tonics, and now here he was stuck in Sticksville, Michigan, facing the next leg of his journey. What was supposed to be a forty-minute plane ride, on an admittedly frighteningly out-of-date plane, was now going to be an hour-long taxi ride followed by half an hour on some ridiculous ferry. A ferry? Who the hell was he? Huckleberry Finn?

"I assume you're headed to the island, too?" asked the honey in the white suit. She was the one surprising perk to his day. What was a beautiful woman like her doing in a dive of an airport like this? Too bad this trip was all about business and not pleasure. Plus, the kid had called her Mom, and he was pretty sure that no woman traveling with her daughter would be looking for his sort of extra-curricular vacation activities. They were going to Wenniway Island, not Fantasy Island.

"Yes, Wenniway Island," he said. "The sooner the better."

"There won't be many taxis around here. As you can imagine, there aren't a lot of evening activities nearby that require public transportation." She rolled her shoulders, tilting her head from side to side, and he recognized the universal stretch of another weary traveler. Ryan lived out of his suitcase most of the time, and travel was an unavoidable nuisance. The crick in his neck was pretty much permanent.

"I would imagine all the evening activities around here require either a pickup truck or a tractor." All he'd seen on his flight in were fields and trees. Not another building or town in sight. There did not appear to be many people, either.

"You'd be correct. If we get lucky, there will be some kind of car available that can get us to Michlimac City, but the ferries only run until eight p.m. this time of year. So we'd better get there fast. That being the case, I suggest we share a ride. Unless you were planning to spend the night here."

Ryan looked over at the hard plastic chairs and the grimy, soiled floor. He'd slept at an airport or two in his day, and on a few dirty floors after one too many shots of Patrón, but this would be more like sleeping in county lockup, and he didn't have the benefit of being sloppy drunk. Since this woman seemed to know her way around, he had no issue with sharing a cab, as long as she and her daughter didn't want to chat. He was too tired for chatting.

"Sure. Yeah, that would be good. I'll call for one." He pulled his phone from his pocket and stepped closer to the sign taped to the paneled wall.

"Good luck, you kids. Don't forget to turn off the lights," said the grandpa in the John Deere hat, and then he shuffled out the door and was gone. So much for customer service.

As Ryan made arrangements with a raspy-voiced woman on the phone, he took note of how many bags his new traveling companions had. A lot. He was scheduled to stay on the island for two months while he worked with his father, and he'd managed to get everything into one suitcase, so what on earth did they bring? Probably shoes. In his experience, women always brought too many shoes. Impractical shoes, like the ones the woman was wearing right now. She had on high heels with lots of straps and even a pointless little zipper on the heel. They looked good, of course. Damn good, but those were not traveling shoes. They didn't seem much like mom shoes to him, either. And that wasn't a very practical suit she was wearing, come to think of it. It was white. Who the hell wore white to travel in? Besides the pope?

"Better make it a van," he said to the woman on the phone. "We're going to need it."

He hung up and turned back to the strawberry blonde and her mini-me. "The cab will be here in thirty minutes. That's going to be cutting it close for making that boat you're talking about."

"Well, if we can at least get to Michlimac City tonight, there are lots of hotels. Even with the Lilac Festival starting on the island, we should be able to find some rooms. Better to spend the night in one of those than on the floor here." She gestured toward the uncomfortable chairs.

He nodded. "Agreed."

"There had better be some restaurants open, too, Mom, because I am literally ravenous. Like I can literally feel my stomach starting to cave in on itself. We haven't eaten in like ten years." The kid pressed clenched fists against her flat belly to demonstrate just how long ten years was to have gone without food. He sensed a career in the dramatic arts might suit her.

"Maybe I can get into that vending machine," Ryan said before her mother could answer. "I'm Ryan, by the way. Ryan Taggert." He walked over to the machine, circa 1970s, and began pulling at the duct tape. "Hope the food in here is fresher than the technology, but at least it's easy to break into."

The door swung open, and the young girl squeaked with gratitude.

"Ohmygosh, thank you! I am seriously legit starving right now. I'm Chloe Chambers. Nice to meet you." She shoved her phone into her pocket, shook Ryan's hand, and then started pulling candy bars from the machine.

"I'm Emily." She extended her arm and gave him the hint of a smile. The kind that said *hello* and *I'm not interested* at the same time. No wedding ring, though. He was a details guy, and he noticed things like that.

"Chloe, only take a couple of things," her mother said. "We still have to pay for that, and I only have a few dollars in cash."

Ryan pulled a twenty from his wallet and slapped it down on the folding table. "Nice to meet you, Emily. Chloe. Dinner is on me." He smiled back, friendly and casual. She probably got hit on all the time, and even though he loved a challenge, he reminded himself, again, that this trip was strictly business.

"Thanks. I can pay you back once we get to the island, or if we find an ATM," she said, pulling out a tiny bag of cheese crackers.

"No worries."

They helped themselves to crackers, pretzels, Hershey bars, and gummy bears. Not the best dinner he'd ever had, but given the circumstances, he was pretty damn happy to have that. Emily found some Styrofoam cups in the little office and filled them with water from the bathroom sink.

"Thank you for the feast, such as it is," she said, handing him one of the cups.

"You're welcome. Such as it is."

She took a drink, then pointed at his computer bag. "It's not going to be much of a vacation if you bring all that work with you."

He shook his head and pulled a mini-pretzel from a foil bag. "Not a vacation at all. I'm heading to the island to work with my dad."

"And to rescue him from a bimbo?" Her gaze was innocent as she popped a cheese cracker into her mouth.

"How did you . . . ? Oh, I guess you heard me on the phone." Awkward.

Her smile might have been patronizing were it not for the tilt of her head that went with it. "Sorry. Kind of hard not to."

Ryan swallowed the excessively dry pretzel and washed it down with some water. "I get kind of loud on the phone. Bad habit. Anyway, yeah. My dad's been on the island for about a month now, and according to my brother, he's fallen under the spell of some gold-digging bimbo." Ryan didn't believe that, though. Bryce was full of shit most of the time, and even though their father had been a widower for the past eight months, it wasn't as if he was suddenly single and ready to mingle. Just the thought of his conventional, buttoned-down father in the arms of some woman after forty years of marriage to Ryan's mom made him shudder. "I'm sure it's nothing, though. Bryce is easily excitable, and my dad is much too smart to fall for some femme fatale."

"Siri, what's a femme fatale?" Chloe asked her phone.

"It's a dishonest woman who uses feminine wiles to manipulate men," Emily responded just as the phone replied, "It's a woman considered to be dangerously seductive."

Emily offered her daughter a satisfied smile. "See. I know stuff."

"Dangerously seductive? How is that different from all women?" Ryan's joke fell flat on this audience, and his skin prickled with embarrassment. "Anyway, I'll be there for the next several weeks, and I'm sure I'll get it all figured out."

"Several weeks? What kind of work do you do?" Emily had taken off her jacket, and the pale pink sleeveless shirt she wore was just sheer enough to give a hint of lacy stuff underneath. She had a whole naughty librarian thing going, and it was as sexy as it was innocent. He slid his hands into his pockets and paced a bit to remind his body where they were and what they were talking about. What were they talking about? Oh yeah. His dad getting distracted by a woman. How ironic.

"I'm a consultant." Ryan knew that answer usually stopped the conversation cold. No one ever really wanted to know what a consultant did, and he wasn't at liberty to explain it anyway since his father's company, Taggert Property Management, usually worked confidentially behind the scenes with their investors and clients. Time for Ryan to change the subject. "Do you know much about the island?" he asked.

"You bet she does. She grew up there," Chloe answered, standing up and walking into a beam of fading sunlight to take another picture of herself.

Ryan looked back at Emily, feeling the surprise that must have been registering on his face. "You grew up there?"

She nodded. "Born and raised."

"Really? Wow. I assumed native islanders were like four-leaf clovers, you know? Everybody says they've seen one but no one really has."

Emily chuckled. "Well, I've never seen a four-leaf clover either, but I do know lots of people who grew up on the island."

"That's very cool. What was it like?" Ryan grew up in Sacramento, with sunshine year-round and every convenience nearby. He could not imagine living someplace so remote.

"Probably a lot like growing up in any small town. Close neighbors, lots of gossip, lots of people to turn to when you need help. Lots of people telling you how to live your life. The usual stuff."

He still couldn't imagine it. "What about in the winter? Were you trapped? It's got to be like *The Shining* with all the snow."

This time Emily laughed right out loud, sincere and unguarded. And sexy. He started pacing again.

"We had pretty much everything we needed," Emily said. "Plus we weren't really trapped. Other than about a month right in the middle of winter where there's too much ice for the ferries to run but the lake isn't frozen enough to snowmobile over, we could almost always get to the mainland if we wanted to."

He stopped pacing to stare at her. "Snowmobile? Over Lake Huron?"

"There's an ice bridge," Chloe said, stepping toward him. "My mom's told me all about it."

Ryan turned to the kid. She was cute, a younger version of her mother, and he was pretty sure she had a gummy bear in each cheek. "Oh yeah? What's she told you?"

"She told me that her boyfriend could make it from the island all the way over to the McDonald's in Manitou in six minutes flat. But one time when my grandpa was young, he tried to go over the ice when it wasn't solid enough and his snowmobile went in the water and sank right to the bottom."

Ryan turned back to Emily. "He did? Was that your dad?"

She nodded but seemed wholly unconcerned. "Yes, that was my dad, but he's so cheap he went right back out onto the ice the next day with some ropes and some hooks and tried to pull the thing back up."

Ryan chuckled, relieved that the story hadn't turned tragic. "Did he manage?"

"No, but he got his name in a few local papers for being fool enough to try." She shook her head as she spoke, making the red-gold strands of her hair shimmy a bit. The industrial florescent lighting in this airport lobby was universally unflattering, yet somehow her hair still shimmered like something from a shampoo commercial. He wondered how it would look in the sunshine. Probably pretty good. Probably look pretty good spread out on a pillow, too. That thought caught him right in the throat and choked him. He coughed and picked up his cup from the folding table to take a gulp of water. "Dry pretzel," he explained. "What were you saying?"

"I was saying that now my father is the chief of police on the island and stops people from doing foolish things like that," Emily answered.

"Chief of police, huh? Impressive."

"I guess." Her expression was enigmatic, but it didn't take a genius to figure out there was something left unsaid. Not that it was any of his business, and not that he had any chance to ask her about it because a car horn honked outside.

"That's our ride, Chloe," Emily said. "Grab your stuff and let's go."

Chapter 2

"I promise, Gigi," Emily said into the phone as she watched the last boat leave the ferry dock—without them on it. "The plane broke down, the taxi was late, and we just missed the boat by five stinking minutes. If I could swim to the island with all our luggage, I would do it. We will be there first thing in the morning."

She should have known they were going to miss the boat. On the list of all the things that could go wrong, missing the boat was most certainly on there. Now she was going to have to spend money on a hotel room for the night and find Chloe some real food. Those cheese crackers and gummy bears had left her daughter with a stomachache and a bad attitude.

"I'm starving, Mom. Totally legit starving this time. And I've only got eighteen percent battery left on my phone. If I don't get a charge soon, my world goes black."

If Chloe's world went black, so would Emily's. She'd been on the bad side of a dead battery before, and it was not pretty.

"Food. Charge. Sleep. I'm on it." Emily was trying to put a bright spin on things, but she was just as hungry and tired as Chloe must be. Still, she was the grown-up. Mostly. She needed to be the one to hold it together.

Ryan stood next to them, staring after the boat as if it had personally betrayed him. "I don't think I'm going to like it here," he muttered.

"There's a motel right there. That's where I'm headed. Come on, Chloe. Grab your suitcases." Emily reached for hers.

"Here, I got them." Ryan managed to hoist several of their bags over his shoulder and offered his rolling bag to Chloe. "Lead the way."

Emily hesitated. She was more than capable of carrying her own bags. She'd been a single mother since Chloe was five years old, and realistically much longer than that since her ex-husband had never been much help to begin with. She'd learned to do things by herself. She prided herself on it, but tonight, she was tired, and there was nothing wrong with letting someone carry your bags once in a while. "You'd make an excellent pack mule," she said to Ryan.

"Are you saying I'm an ass?" he whispered, and Emily bit back a chuckle.

The three of them crossed the parking lot and walked into the dark, wood-paneled lobby of a generic motel that looked like virtually every other motel in Michlimac City. Paneled walls covered with cheap oil paintings of ducks and geese and views of Petoskey Bridge. At the check-in desk, a gum-chewing, plaid-shirted young woman greeted them with a friendly smile, and Emily was happy to discover this place had everything they needed. Cheap rooms, a bar that served food for another thirty minutes . . . and free Wi-Fi. Perfect. That was pretty much all she required. Ryan got a room, too, and soon they were making their way down the narrow, dimly lit hallway. The carpet had a camouflage pattern, and the walls were papered with scenes of a forest with deer and bears and bunnies wandering around.

"After we drop off these suitcases, Chloe and I are getting something to eat. Feel free to join us, if you'd like. I owe you dinner since you split open that vending machine for us," Emily said.

"Thanks, I'd like that, but I have a dozen phone calls to make first. If I miss you, I'll just see you on the ferry in the morning." Ryan readjusted that overstuffed computer bag on his shoulder.

She felt a twinge of disappointment at his answer. Heaven knew she wanted this day to be over and she was very much looking forward to her lumpy hotel bed, but traveling with Ryan Taggert, the Man in the Nice Suit, had made their misadventure a little more exhilarating. A little more memorable. Subtly flirtatious conversation in the fading light of the cab while Chloe snoozed in the other seat had stirred up in Emily a lovely case of the tingles. A mild case. A very mild case, because she wasn't interested in Ryan, of course, but it was always nice to stretch those charm muscles once in a while. She wasn't quite ready to say goodbye to that, but apparently he was.

Okay then. If he didn't care, then she didn't care.

"All right. We're taking the very first boat in the morning, so if we don't happen to see you again . . . well, it's been interesting."

He laughed, and she noticed how impeccably straight his teeth were. Someone had an excellent orthodontist. And a personal trainer. He was in good shape. She felt a second twinge of disappointment but tried to chalk it up to nothing more than fatigue and a misplaced sense of connection from having survived that airport debacle together. Surely that's all it was.

Ryan nodded. "Yes, very interesting. Thanks for helping me. If it wasn't for you, I'd probably still be sitting at that airport."

"Mom, can I have the key? We're here." Chloe pointed at the brass number on the brown wooden door, then took the key from Emily's outstretched hand. She hauled a couple of suitcases through the opening, dragging them into the room. "See you around, Ryan. Don't forget to try some moose tracks fudge. It's the best. Hope we see you over on the island." She waved and was gone, the door clicking shut behind her. Ryan had stopped walking when Emily stopped, and now they stood awkwardly in the hall, a florescent yellow light buzzing overhead.

"Moose tracks, huh?" he said.

"Rocky road is my favorite, but it's fudge, so you know, it's all pretty good."

"Right. Fudge." He seemed distracted for a second but then said, "Listen, maybe we could connect while we're over there? You know, maybe you could give me a behind-the-scenes tour?"

His suggestion seemed innocent enough. She couldn't tell if he was hinting at anything other than what was on the surface, but either way, she felt a little better. Even if this was the proverbial *I'll give you a call sometime*, at least he was making an attempt. Pride was a funny thing. Even though she didn't really *care* if she saw him on the island, she at least wanted him to make the effort.

"Yeah, sure. Text me your number."

He set down the other bags he was carrying, and they both pulled out their phones. "What's yours?" he asked, thumbs poised and at the ready.

She told him, and they said goodnight, hesitating just long enough for it to feel awkward again, and then he turned and continued down the hall while Emily quickly entered her room. Once inside, she leaned against the solid wooden door, feeling stupidly girlish about having just given a man her number, or maybe those flutters in her stomach were just from hunger. Yes, that was probably it. Just hunger.

"What's up with you?" Chloe asked. She was already lying on the bed, and her stuff was strewn all over the room. How had she made such a mess in the ninety seconds Emily had been out in the hall? It was a real gift that girl had.

"Nothing is up with me. I'm just tired and starving. Let's get something to eat before it's too late."

"I think he's cute, too."

"What?"

"Ryan. He's a hottie. I mean, for an old guy. You should totally hang out with him while we're on the island."

Emily pushed herself away from the door and kicked off her high heels. They'd been a terrible decision and her feet were killing her, but she'd expected to arrive on the island today and wanted to look nice.

And successful. Mostly she wanted to look successful, because as far as her family was concerned, that's what she was. A successful businesswoman, and it wasn't that she wanted to be dishonest, she just didn't want to add *penniless moocher* to her résumé. If anyone discovered her current state of money troubles, there'd be whispers, and then there'd be roars. Some people would want to rescue her, while others would enjoy seeing her fail. She just didn't need any of that right now.

She didn't need Ryan Taggert, the Good Looking Guy in the Nice Suit, either. Even if he was interested, he'd just be a messy complication to her already messy life. Plus, he'd told her he lived in Sacramento, which was too far from San Antonio to be workable anyway. Said the cart as it looked back at the horse.

"Ryan seems very nice, Chloe, but this trip is about family and work. That's all."

"I wouldn't mind, you know."

"Wouldn't mind what?" Emily pulled the ends of her top out from the waistband of her skirt and crossed over to the bathroom.

"If you were dating somebody. I mean, it seems kind of like you should be dating people. You haven't had a boyfriend in forever, and I'm going to start dating people eventually, and then what will you have to do?"

Emily looked over at her daughter, her sweet daughter with the sleepy eyes, curled up on a bed and looking very much like the little girl Emily saw her as. But Chloe was right. She was twelve, and in a handful of years she'd be dating. Heck, she'd be driving. And then, really, what was Emily going to do?

Chapter 3

The first thing Emily noticed as she got off the ferry at Wenniway Island and walked with Chloe down the short dock to Main Street of Trillium Bay was the wonderfully familiar aroma of fudge, lilacs . . . and horse manure. An earthy-sweet mixture that sent her mind scampering right back to childhood summers. Their last two visits had been in December, just fast trips back for Christmas, and long after all the flowers had wilted away and many of the horses had been moved back to the mainland for their long winter's nap. She hadn't noticed the absence of the smell then, but now it filled her nose, triggering a flood of memories, both happy and sad. She pushed the sad ones aside for now. No sense in dwelling.

The next thing Emily noticed was Dmitri Krushnic in his beekeeper's hat talking to a man on a horse. This in and of itself was not that unusual because she'd known Dmitri Krushnic since she was a little girl and he always wore his beekeeping hat, even when he was nowhere near his bees. Seeing a man on a horse wasn't that odd either. Cars had been banned on Wenniway Island since 1891, so horses, bikes, and good old-fashioned walking were the general modes of transportation. What was slightly askew about this scene, however, was that the man on the horse appeared to be wearing nothing but a very tiny loincloth and a very large Native American headdress.

"What the what?" Emily muttered, reaching out to cover the unsuspecting eyes of her too-young-for-this daughter. "Chloe, don't look."

"It's too late," Chloe said mildly. "The vision is already seared into my retinas. That's the whitest skin I've ever seen."

"Yes, it is." Emily nodded, dropping her hands to stare alongside her daughter.

"It's authentic, you idiot. We're reenacting, and this is just how Chief Eagle Feather did it." The exhibitionist on the horse shook his fist in Dmitri's general direction.

Dmitri jabbed a pointed finger back at him, accidentally poking the horse. She didn't seem to notice. She just looked around, bored as an old gray mare who'd seen it all and just wanted to go back to her barn and eat some oats.

"Listen, Clancy," said Dmitri, "I'm as devoted to the history of this island as you are, and yes, those of us on the historical committee recognize and appreciate your passion for authenticity. And while we also concur that Chief Eagle Feather rode naked through the streets warning the townspeople that the British were invading, that doesn't mean you can ride down Main Street today wearing nothing but a smile and SPF 75. There are children present." His arms swung to the side, indicating the presence of passersby, many of whom were now scurrying away. Dmitri turned his head and spotted Emily and Chloe standing just a few feet away. Standing and staring. "Look! See? There's a child. She's traumatized."

"Oh heck no. Leave me out of this." Chloe ducked behind her mother, and Emily bit back a smile. Good to know she was still needed for something, if only to serve as a human shield.

"She's fine, fellas," Emily called out, turning and nudging Chloe toward the opposite sidewalk. "We'll be moving along now."

"Peach?" Dmitri pulled off the beekeeper's hat, exposing long, dark hair liberally streaked with gray. "Peachy-keen, is that you?"

So much for making a quiet entrance back into town. She'd hoped to get to Gigi's place and get settled in before the locals knew she was there. Her sisters knew she was arriving today, but not an exact time, and she'd only hinted to her father that she might be dropping by sometime this summer. So much for stealth.

"No, it's not me. I'm someone else entirely." She nudged Chloe a little harder with the knuckle of her index finger.

"Ohmygosh," Chloe whispered, "I forgot they all call you Peach."

"Of course it's you, Peach. I heard you were coming, and I'd know those blue eyes and freckles anywhere." He rushed toward them, smiling broadly and apparently forgetting, for the moment, the naked guy on the horse.

"Speaking of freckles"—Chloe's whisper turned to an amused murmur—"I don't think SPF 75 is going to be strong enough for that marshmallow on the horse. I can smell him burning from here. Is he starting to puff up?"

Dmitri reached them, his grin revealing a significant gap between his two front teeth. "And is this little niblet your daughter? It can't be. She's too grown up!"

"Oh no way. Do not let them nickname me niblet!" Chloe's amused murmur became a hostile mutter into Emily's ear. Preteen mood swing, but Emily could hardly blame her. Niblet was probably going to stick.

Emily smiled. "Hello, Dmitri. How are you? Good to see you. Yes, this is Chloe, my daughter."

"Of course, of course. So are you back for good this time? Or just here for the Lilac Festival?" He pushed a lock of sweat-dampened hair away from his forehead. Apparently things got a little hot under that beekeeper's hat.

"I'm not *back* back. I mean, I'm staying for a few months. I'm here to do some work for Gigi."

He put the hat back on but kept the netting pushed to the top. "Oh yes. Working on Gigi's rental cottage. I heard something about that from the Mahoney sisters. They're in quite a tizzy about the whole thing. All up in arms about who's doing what to which properties. Those women buzz, buzz, buzz more than my bees do." He turned his head. "Don't think I can't see you trying to ride away, Clancy," he shouted over his shoulder. "Chief Callaghan is going to hear about this, and now his own daughter is a material witness."

"No, oh no." Emily shook her head and took hold of Dmitri's forearm. "My dad doesn't know I'm here yet. I want to surprise him, okay? Can you help me do that?"

He pulled the veil back down with a dramatic twirl of his wrist. "But of course. Do you want to borrow my hat? No one will suspect a thing."

"You're sweet, but no, that won't be necessary. If you'd just let Chloe and me be on our way and not mention to anyone that you saw us, that would be great. Give me at least a couple of hours."

"No one can keep a secret like I can, Peach. You have no idea. Be on your way then, and remind Gigi she owes me three dollars from the last time we played euchre."

"Absolutely."

"Excellent. I shall now create a diversion." He turned his back on them and started shouting again at naked Clancy on the horse.

Emily turned Chloe by the shoulders. "Quick, go that way!"

"Don't we have to get our luggage?"

"I already tagged them to go to Gigi's house. We're all set. Now scoot before someone else sees us."

On the list of people Emily was hoping to avoid, which included basically everyone on the island, she and Chloe ran into six of them as they made their way from the center of Main Street to the corner of Huron and Marquette. What should have been a five-minute excursion took them two hours. First they saw Mr. O'Doul, who informed Chloe that he owned the oldest grocery store in Michigan. His ancestors had, according to his genealogist uncle, accompanied the first Jesuit missionary to the island in 1670. As a kid, Emily had always thought that old Mrs. O'Doul was so very, very ancient, she just might have been that first priest's housekeeper.

Then they saw Vera VonMeisterburger, the librarian, who told them all about her recent efforts to reintroduce bats to the island after the recent plague of white nose syndrome. There was going to be a town meeting that very evening. She certainly hoped they would attend. There would be cookies.

They also saw Edgar White, the man in charge of painting the front porch of the Imperial Hotel, which might not seem like such an important job, but he assured them that it was because that porch was six hundred and sixty feet long and took him all summer to paint.

Next they ran into, or rather were *run into by*, Gloria Persimmons. She was admiring her reflection in the tiny mirror of her purple bicycle when she crashed into them. The white wicker basket on the front of her handlebars went flying in one direction, and Gloria's rhinestone-studded sunglasses flew in the other.

"Peachy-keen, oh my goodness gracious! As I live and breathe, I just heard from Mr. O'Doul that you were back. And I said to myself, I said, 'Gloria, if Peach is back in town, then you better go put on your party dress because that girl loves to party!' And now look, here you are! Bejeebers, how long has it been?"

Gloria reached down and picked up her sunglasses from the ground, exposing the green-and-white polka-dot panties she had on under her lemon-yellow sundress. Emily heard Chloe gasp and then giggle as she handed Gloria her basket. It was covered with pink plastic flowers, surely the envy of every six-year-old girl on the island.

Emily should have known she wouldn't get far without news leaking out of her arrival, and now that Gloria had spotted them? Well, the naked man on the horse would be the second thing everyone talked about that day because when a wayward daughter returns, it makes the headlines.

"Gloria, my goodness. You look just the same as you did in high school!" Emily gave her a hug and mentally noted that her comment was entirely true. Unfortunately, in high school Gloria did not look that great. Uncharitable? Maybe. But poor Gloria Persimmons had the face of a walrus, right down to the long teeth and the fuzzy cheeks.

"Oh, why, Peach, you always were such a good liar!" Gloria threw her head back and laughed way too loud at her own joke, but she sobered quickly and squeezed Emily's arm. "Oh, but as much as I want to catch up with you and hear all about your glamorous life, we'd better do that later. Right now you need to skadoosh because Reed's mother was just in the post office and she could be coming out any minute. She's as icy as ever. I got frostbite the last time I sat next to her at church."

Emily looked down Main toward the post office, and sure enough, here came Olivia Bostwick. Her stomach went splat, like an ice-cream cone onto hot pavement. On that list of people she was hoping to avoid? Olivia Bostwick was at the very top.

"Thanks, Gloria. We'll definitely have to grab a cup of coffee soon. Come on, Chloe. We need to roll." She grabbed ahold of her daughter's sleeve and started walking. Too late, though.

"Emily? Emily Callaghan, don't think I can't see you there. I heard you were coming to the island."

"Sorry, girlfriend. I'm outta here." Gloria hopped on her bike and pedaled away.

"Shit," Emily muttered under her breath, then screwed her face into some semblance of a smile before turning back around to face her foe. She wouldn't bother reminding Mrs. Bostwick that her last name was now Chambers, not Callaghan.

"Mrs. Bostwick, how lovely to see you." *Did you bring your flying monkeys?*

Chloe squeaked a little and tugged the material of her red cotton shirt from her mother's clenched hand. Emily hadn't realized she'd wadded the fabric in her fist quite so tightly.

"Well, it's certainly something to see you here, too, Emily. What's the special occasion? Don't tell me you're getting married again?"

Shields up, phasers on stun. "Nope. Not getting married again."

Mrs. Bostwick was wearing a big floppy sun hat and oversized sunglasses tinted a nearly opaque black. Still, Emily could feel the woman's beady little eyes boring into her through the lenses. Her kelly-green capri pants were covered with little pink flamingos to match the pink sweater draped around her narrow shoulders. Emily was glad she'd put on another one of her *I'm a successful businesswoman* dresses. Today's was a sedate but attractive royal-blue shift with a narrow white belt, and her hair was clipped back in a no-nonsense ponytail. Olivia Bostwick could not fault her for what she was wearing.

She could fault her for a whole bunch of other stuff, though. Including breaking her son's heart when she'd run away with Chloe's father. Reed Bostwick had been Emily's high school sweetheart—on an island where pretty much everybody married their high school sweetheart. Emily had done him some serious wrong by running away with Nick. She'd left Reed a note saying goodbye, of course. It was a heartfelt note, too, but that was no way to break up with someone she'd known her entire life. She'd realized that soon after leaving, but by then the damage was done, and Mrs. Bostwick was not one to let bygones be bygones.

"Just here for a short visit then? Your family should be pleased."

The woman held a black belt in passive-aggressive comments. So many meanings in those few little words. Your family is pleased the visit will be *short*. Your *family* should be pleased, but no one else is. And last but not least, your family *should* be pleased, but are they?

Are they *really*? *Are you sure?* Mrs. Bostwick should travel with a complimentary cryptologist for all her skill at weaving hidden messages into what she said. Emily had spent many an afternoon trying to decipher just what was meant by all the words Mrs. Bostwick *didn't* say, because Reed's mother had disliked her looooong before Nick showed up. No one on the island would have been good enough for her son, but without a doubt, Emily was the least-appealing candidate.

"I'm here for the summer, actually. I'm helping Gigi renovate one of her rental cottages. And this is my daughter, Chloe." Surely even Mrs. Bostwick could not hold such a grudge that she'd be rude to a little girl. Okay, again, Chloe wasn't technically little. But she was young, and fortunately Mrs. Bostwick's maternal instincts, although never sensitive to Emily, did extend to Chloe. No doubt because Mrs. Bostwick felt sorry for Chloe for having such a lousy mother.

"Hello, Chloe. It's a pleasure." Meaning it was Mrs. Bostwick's pleasure? Or it should be Chloe's pleasure? Damn, the woman was clever with the double entendre! But Chloe, bless her heart, read all the signals and kicked into her Gracious Manners Barbie routine.

"Hello, Mrs. Bostwick. It certainly is a pleasure to meet you, and what a lovely hat that is. You remind me of Audrey Hepburn."

Score one for the kid, and thank goodness Emily had made her watch all those old movies. Any woman of Mrs. Bostwick's generation would consider that the highest of compliments, and it seemed to work. She fairly preened. If she were a peacock, Emily would have just been slapped in the face with tail feathers.

"Why, aren't you sweet?" Mrs. Bostwick said. *And how did that happen when your mother isn't?*

Emily smiled stiffly. "Well, we don't want to keep you from your errands any longer, Mrs. Bostwick. I do hope we see you again." Meaning *I hope we see you first so we can run in the other direction.*

"Reed's back for a few weeks, too, you know."

Emily had started to turn but halted her movement, her gaze returning to the bug-eyed sunglasses. "Is he now?"

"Yes, with his wife and their family. He's terribly successful, you know. And terribly important. He works for the governor, you know, and he's terribly happy."

"That sounds terrible," murmured Chloe, and Emily resisted the urge to elbow her precious daughter in the ribs.

"Well, that's just wonderful news, Mrs. Bostwick. Please give Reed my best regards."

"I don't imagine I'll mention seeing you, Emily, but if your name comes up in conversation, I'll be sure to tell him."

Oh, as if her name was not coming up in conversation all over the damn island. The place was only eight miles in circumference with a population small enough to fit inside any given Olive Garden. Reed probably already knew she was there and was undoubtedly *terribly* unconcerned about it.

"Have a pleasant visit, Chloe." Mrs. Bostwick turned, her floppy hat swaying in the wind, and Emily was summarily dismissed.

Finally, they were on their way again. Running into Mrs. Bostwick had been inevitable, and at least now Emily had gotten it out of the way. She couldn't very well spend the summer avoiding her. There wasn't much chance she'd be able to avoid seeing Reed, either, and she didn't quite know how she felt about that. She'd wondered about him over the years. Moments like at 3:00 a.m. when she couldn't sleep, she'd try to imagine what her life might have been like had she stayed and married Reed like she was supposed to. Sometimes she sincerely wished she had, but then she'd think of Chloe, and without Nick, she wouldn't have her daughter, so no matter what mistakes she'd made in the past, she wouldn't wish to change anything because Chloe made it all worthwhile.

Still, she wondered what Reed looked like now. Paunchy and bald? Still trim with a nice headful of wavy light brown hair? Did he still laugh at stupid jokes, or was he serious and intense now that he was so *terribly* important working for the governor? She had heard from her sister Brooke that he'd gotten married to someone he met in grad school. She'd felt a momentary tug on her heart at that news, but it passed, just like their chance at a future together had passed.

"You good, Mom?" Chloe asked, slipping her hand into Emily's as they walked. Emily squeezed her fingers and smiled.

"I am good. Are you good?"

Chloe nodded. "I'm okay, but I'm kind of nervous. What if my cousins are mean? Who am I supposed to hang out with all summer?"

"I'm sure they won't be mean, honey. They'll probably think you're pretty fascinating because you live in San Antonio."

"What's so great about San Antonio?"

"It's just different from what they're used to, so they'll probably be curious, just like you must be curious about them, right? And anyway, I won't be busy all the time. I'll be working at the cottage a lot, but I'll have some free time so we can go see all the touristy stuff, like the fort and all the fudge shops. We can go to the beach at Trillium Bay to watch the boats. We can go camping and make s'mores."

"Camping? Like, in a tent?" They continued on along the sidewalk, and Emily breathed in the lilacs and let the sound of the waves and the clip-clop of hooves soothe her. She was nervous, too, although she tried her best to hide that from Chloe. Seven years was a long time to have gone between visits. There were the phone calls and emails between her and her sisters, of course, and even the obligatory calls she made to her father every few months just to put in the appearance of trying to have a relationship with him, but she still didn't quite know what to expect this time around. It wasn't as if she'd *tried* to avoid visiting.

Well, okay. Yes, she had avoided it, but her reasons for that were perfectly . . . reasonable. The trip from San Antonio was expensive and time-consuming. And emotionally draining. Emily's relationship with her father had always been complicated, full of misunderstandings and unmet expectations, but since her rather spontaneous—some might call it impetuous—marriage thirteen years ago, she and Harlan had settled into a sort of Callaghan Cold War policy. Neither attacking nor retreating. Both equally stubborn. Gigi once said that Emily and Harlan were like two peas in a pod, but two peas who each thought the other was wrong all the time and needed to apologize.

Well, Emily had tried to apologize for her past misdeeds, such as that running away and getting married thing, but on an island full of professional grudge holders, Chief Callaghan was the champ. People around Trillium Bay always said he'd never been the same after his wife died, but Emily had been just ten years old when that happened, so all she knew was that he'd spent most of *her* life treating her like an inconvenient nuisance. So she'd figured out quite a while ago that the best way to maintain a quasi-functional relationship with her father was to do it from a distance.

"Sure, camping in a tent," she said to Chloe, swinging their arms together. "Why do you sound so surprised?"

Chloe giggled. "I just can't picture you sleeping outside or peeing next to a tree."

"You forget I lived here. I used to be quite outdoorsy."

Chloe puckered up her lips and glanced to the sky as if deep in thought. Then she shook her head. "Nope, can't picture it."

Another few minutes of walking and at last they rounded the final corner. There was Gigi standing on the white front porch of her pale blue Victorian cottage, wearing a shimmery teal running suit and holding a martini glass, which was pretty much what she was doing the last time Emily had seen her, except that last time she'd been indoors and standing next to a Christmas wreath. Gigi loved her martinis. Dry, three olives, *why bother with vermouth* martinis. She said the pickling kept her young, and she must be right because she looked as fit and as spry as ever, as if she could kick up her heels any moment and dance a little jig. Her short gray hair was tightly curled and didn't budge in the breeze, thanks to weekly visits to the Trillium Bay Beauty Salon and several sweeping sprays of Aqua Net. Emily's heart swelled unexpectedly as she blinked fast to whisk away equally unexpected tears. Happy tears. In spite of the reasons for this visit, she was suddenly excited to be back home. She breathed in deeply and let herself enjoy the moment—because it was sure to pass.

"Gigi O'Reilly-Callaghan-Harper-Smith," Emily called from the sidewalk. "It's only eleven thirty in the morning and you already have a cocktail in your hand?"

Gigi's smile spread wide, nearly hitting her ears. "I'm celebrating."

"What are you celebrating?"

"I'm celebrating the fact that I have a cocktail in my hand." Then she laughed and trotted down the wooden front steps, not spilling a drop. "Come here, you! I've been waiting all morning. Let me get a good, long look at you and my great-granddaughter!"

Within minutes the three of them were giggling like teenagers, and an hour later, they were sitting at the kitchen table, drinking lemonade, and still giggling like teenagers. This was the house Emily's father had grown up in. The red-and-white checked tablecloth added to the nostalgic coziness of it all, and Emily couldn't help but think that being here was nothing short of stepping into a life-size time capsule. Like most islanders, Gigi was frugal and made do with what she had, which meant every appliance in the kitchen predated VHS tapes, and every piece of furniture had been repainted, reupholstered, and repurposed a dozen times. Mason jars full of pickles, peaches, and tomatoes lined up like toy soldiers along the pine shelves off to the left, and an assortment of mismatched dishes filled the cupboards. A faint whirring sound came from the decades-old avocado-hued Frigidaire, and one of Gigi's three cats lay on the hardwood floor in a beam of sunlight, purring right along with it.

"How about if you go upstairs and unpack your stuff, hon," Emily finally said to Chloe. "Our luggage is here now, and Gigi and I need to talk about some of the renovating stuff."

"But I'm having fun," Chloe answered. "And unpacking is not fun."

"Neither is having to iron your clothes because you left them stuffed in a suitcase for too long. Go unpack."

Chloe slowly dragged herself up and away from the table. "Can I take this lemonade with me? I've never drunk from a jelly jar before. Mom, can we get some jelly jars for back home?"

Emily chuckled. "I'm sure we can."

"We're supposed to be at Brooke's house by five o'clock today. She's cooking dinner for us and Harlan," Gigi added. "Your room is the one on the right, Chloe. I hope you like it. You can see the bay from your window and watch all the sailboats go by. Freighters, too. It never gets old, watching those huge ships go by."

Chloe leaned over and hugged Gigi around the shoulders with one arm. "I can't wait to see one, and I'm sure I'll like my room. Thanks a bunch."

"That is one smart, charming young lady you have there," Gigi said to Emily once Chloe had trotted upstairs with all of her suitcases.

"Thanks. I hope you still feel that way at the end of the summer when all her good first impression manners have worn away and you've tripped over her shoes a thousand times."

"I'm certain I'll still feel that way. You're doing a good job with her, and I know it hasn't been easy."

Emily leaned forward over the kitchen table, toward her grandmother. "Thanks for saying that, Gigi. It means a lot to me. And thanks times infinity for loaning me the ten grand I needed to make repairs on that flip house in San Antonio. I don't know what I would've done without you."

"Don't mention it," Gigi said, patting her hand.

Emily cast a glance at the doorway to be certain Chloe was gone before turning back to her grandmother. "Speaking of not mentioning it, please don't forget Chloe doesn't know anything about any of this. She has no idea we're in so deep. You haven't told anyone on the island, right?"

Gigi straightened her spine, looking slightly miffed. "Of course I haven't told anyone. I've kept all the details of our arrangement to myself, just as you asked me to."

Emily's gratitude was tempered by a hefty dose of realism. She knew the score. Gigi was keeping her secret simply because it gave her leverage. The old bird was not above a little emotional extortion. Apparently she wasn't above taking hostages, either, because the only way she'd agreed to the $10,000 loan was if Emily and Chloe spent the summer with her on Trillium Bay. If Emily's instincts were correct, and she was certain they were, her grandmother had thrown in the cottage renovation just to make their deal more palatable, a little less like charity. Either way, Emily was deeply grateful and intended to pay Gigi back every single dime just as soon as that disastrous flip house in San Antonio sold.

Gigi patted her helmet of gray curls. "You know I'm not one to judge, but how exactly did you find yourself in this spot, anyway?"

Not one to judge? Emily nearly chuckled at that. Gigi was very much one to judge, but then again, so was everyone on this island. It was a favorite pastime, ranking right in between gossiping and eavesdropping. Nonetheless, this time the question was valid. For ten thousand bucks, Gigi deserved an honest answer.

"I trusted Jewel instead of trusting my own gut, I guess."

Jewel was Emily's friend, housemate, and more recently, her house-flipping business partner. "About four months ago, she found a house listed way under market value. I was suspicious, but Jewel said she'd had the place inspected. What she failed to tell me was that she used a new guy instead of the one we normally work with, and this new guy was a bottom-feeding crook. I'm not sure he even looked in the attic or the basement, but by the time we figured out just how much work the place really needed, we were stuck with it. I know Jewel feels terrible, and there's not much point in being angry. She didn't do it on purpose—plus now she's as broke as I am." Emily picked up the pitcher sitting on the table and poured herself more lemonade.

"Jewel always sounded a little flaky to me. How long are you planning to live with her? I thought that was going to be a temporary thing." Gigi helped herself to some lemonade, too, then pulled a pint of gin from one of the cupboards and added a liberal splash to her jelly jar. Emily pushed her jar forward to let Gigi put a little shot in hers, too. She was going to see her father in a few hours. This gin was medicinal.

"She's not flaky. Just a little, well, sometimes she gets too excited and doesn't think things through." That was true enough, but Emily could hardly call her out on that since she had a propensity to do the same thing. "Living together was going to be temporary, just a place to stay until I got back on my feet after the divorce, but Jewel has a nice house in a good school district for Chloe. It's a good deal for us both because with me paying her rent, she's been able to fix it up. It takes some of the pressure off from being a single parent, too." That was definitely true. Jewel had been Emily's only support throughout her divorce, and she was wonderful to Chloe, too. "I do realize now, though, we shouldn't have both sunk all of our savings into that one flip. It was a mistake."

Gigi crossed her skinny legs, the nylon of her track pants giving a little swish. "What about that deadbeat, Nick? Has he gotten any better? Does he help out at all?" A frown had formed on Gigi's face. She never had liked Nick. No one had, except for Emily. Speaking of getting too excited and not thinking things through.

"Nick is currently back living with his parents in Dallas, which is, of course, all my fault."

"How is that your fault?" The ice clinked in Gigi's glass as she took a drink.

Emily smoothed a wrinkle out of the tablecloth beneath her hands. "Because, according to his mother, I ruined his life by agreeing to marry him when he was too young to understand the consequences. Then I ruined it even more by letting him father a child before he was mature enough to handle it. Apparently I also ruined his ability to pass the bar exam, because in spite of my supporting him all through law school, he has failed it repeatedly. He hasn't called Chloe in months."

Gigi's frown deepened into a scowl. "Well, shame on him. How does Chloe feel about that?"

This was one of those topics that filled Emily with guilt and agitation and no place to direct it because she'd tried and tried and tried to fix this for Chloe, and she just couldn't. She couldn't *make* Nick be interested in his daughter any more than she'd been able to *make* his parents be interested.

"She handles it well enough, I guess. She doesn't know any different because even though we got divorced when she was four, Nick wasn't around much before that either. And her comparison is me and Dad. You know I don't have that great of a track record with him. Sorry. I know he's your son and all, but he hasn't exactly begged me to come home, and the two times I've come back since Chloe was born, he's been pretty aloof."

"I think you remind him of Mary." Gigi peered over at her, as if to gauge a reaction.

"My mother? You think I remind him of her?" Of all the things Emily expected Gigi to say, that was last on the list.

"You look like her. God knows you have the same rebellious streak. I could be talking out of my ass here, of course. It's not as if Harlan ever confides anything to me. I'm his mother, but not one day of his life did he ever seem to need me. Even so, you do favor her, and I think that rattles him."

Emily's chest felt simultaneously hollow and full. If what Gigi said was true, it was both a compliment and a curse.

"Yeah, I'm pretty sure you're talking out of your ass, Gigi, but whatever. I've tried to make amends for my side of things. Every time we're on the phone and I try to bring up the past, he starts talking about the weather. Maybe one of these days he'll come around. In the meantime, I am excited for Chloe to get to know all of her cousins. I want her to have a really wonderful summer."

"Me too," Gigi said, smiling again. "I think that can be arranged. We'll make sure of it."

Chapter 4

Ryan Taggert had overslept this morning. He never overslept, but this morning he had, and he knew why. Because the hotel mattress was rock-hard, the room was stuffy and smelled slightly of bleach and old tobacco, and let's face it, he could not stop thinking about the secret lacy stuff hiding underneath Emily Chambers's blouse. What. The. Hell? Sure, she was attractive, and they'd had some nice conversation during the taxi ride from the airport. Her daughter had fallen asleep, so Emily had whispered, making everything she said seem slightly naughty, especially when she told him about a few of her youthful escapades, but that didn't explain why his subconscious had done the horizontal mambo with her all night long. He wasn't some pimply, hormonal teenager staring at a poster over his bed. He was grown-ass man. Too old to let some harmless flirting turn into a distraction and ruin his night's sleep.

Now he was grouchy and pissed because not only had he overslept, but he'd missed the early ferry, which meant he'd also missed seeing her in person. And the fact that he was frustrated by not seeing her in person only aggravated him further. Seriously. What the actual hell?

Thankfully, the boat ride to Wenniway Island was uneventful and blissfully short, the breeze off the lake was refreshing and served to wake him up more efficiently than the twenty-ounce coffee he had in his hand, and now he was walking down Main Street on Trillium

Bay looking for the restaurant where his father wanted to meet. Emily Chambers and her lacy secrets were tucked into the back of his mind so he could instead focus on the Victorian architectural details of each storefront and restaurant. His tastes ran more toward the sleek and contemporary. He liked clean, uncluttered lines, but he could see why people found this place charming. Every detail seemed accounted for, right down to the wrought iron streetlamps and the constant echo of horses' hooves. Of course, he would be bored inside of an hour, but if you were interested in just enjoying the quaint view of the lake and wandering aimlessly through artsy boutiques and antique shops, then this would be just the place.

The pervasive aroma of fudge was overwhelming, and Ryan stopped in front of a candy store to peer through the huge window, taking a minute to watch a man in a tall chef's hat and a white apron use a long-handled wooden spatula to shape a pool of chocolate decadence into slabs. His mouth watered even though he didn't particularly like fudge. People pedaled by on bikes, cruising around the horse-drawn carriages filled with smiling tourists. Yep. He nodded to himself. The place was cute. He wasn't a huge fan of cute, but again, for a weekend getaway, Trillium Bay wasn't half bad.

He started walking again, at last spotting the sign his father had described over the phone. It was shaped like a pig, just like his dad had said, and it read *Link & Patty's Breakfast Buffet* in thick block letters. And wow. Just like his dad had said, the place was pink. Ryan had never been to a pink restaurant before, but his dad had assured him the food was good. He sure as hell hoped so. It was the only thing that could make up for the color. Plus, Ryan was ravenous. He'd never made it down to the hotel bar last night, so the last thing he'd eaten was pretzels at the Wawatam airport. No wonder he was grouchy. He was running on fumes, and seeing all that fudge had kicked his appetite into overdrive.

He maneuvered across the busy street, dodging families with strollers, around a row of parked bicycles, and opened an unadorned screen door that led into the tiny waiting area of the restaurant. The place was crowded and too warm, but the smell of bacon and waffles nearly doubled him over.

A plump woman well into her fifties with purple-hued hair and thick eyeglasses greeted him from behind a pink podium.

"Well, hiya, cutie pie. I've never seen you before. Welcome to Link and Patty's. I'm Patty."

He hadn't been called *cutie pie* since he was a little kid, and how the woman could even get a good enough look at him through those Coke-bottle lenses was a mystery, but he smiled at her nonetheless. "Thanks. I'm supposed to meet someone here."

The wattage of her cheeky smile doubled. "Your father? Are you meeting your father? Are you little Tag Junior?"

Ryan was taken aback by her familiarity—and her correct assumption. "Um, yes. Sort of. Not the junior part, but the . . . the little Tag part. I guess."

Everyone called his father Tag. Sometimes even Ryan and his brothers called him Tag, but Ryan was surprised that this random hostess at an equally random restaurant would know any of that. He looked back at her, and his empty gut twisted with a terrifying thought. Oh please do not let this woman be the bimbo after his father. If they ever got married, he couldn't possibly handle Thanksgiving dinner staring into her magnified eyes. It would be like staring at her through a fishbowl.

She moved from behind the pink-lacquered podium, patted his arm with a sticky hand, and grabbed a couple of plastic-coated menus with her other hand. "Well, it sure is good to meet you, Little Tag. Why, you could have just slapped Jack with a flapjack when my husband, Link, told me Tag's son was coming to visit. We just think the world of your father. What a wonderful man."

Relief. Okay, so she wasn't the bimbo. That was good, but how the hell did she know his dad so well? And wait a minute . . . her husband, Link? Link and Patty were actual people? Go figure.

"Your father isn't here yet," Patty said, bustling toward the back corner of the room, hitting a chair with each swing of her bulky backside. "But you just come on over to his favorite booth and I'll get you some coffee. You do want coffee, don't you?"

His father had a favorite booth? "What? Oh, coffee? Yes, please." Clearly he needed some. That twenty ounces from the ferry was not going to get him through this morning. She'd better bring the pot.

He sat down and looked around, summing up the place with just two words. Pink pigs. They were everywhere. Painted on the walls, in picture frames, covering the menu. Some looked like real pigs, and others were more cartoon in nature. A few had wings. The door handles on the restroom were pink pig noses. Even the salt and pepper shakers on his table were two little pigs, one wearing an apron, the other wearing a chef's hat. Clearly the theme here . . . was pigs. Link and Patty's. It made sense. Sort of.

His father walked in just seconds later, standing tall and looking fit and tan. He smiled when his gaze landed on Ryan.

"Hey, Dad!" He stood up and they embraced, thumping each other on the back.

"Good to see you, son. Glad you finally made it!"

"Me too. It was quite the adventure trying to get here."

"Sounds like it. I wish you'd called me last night. I could have had one of the guys fly over and pick you up."

"One of the guys?" They sat back down in the booth, and Patty waved at Tag from the counter.

Tag waved back. "Yeah, there's a nice little airport on the island. I've actually been taking flight lessons, but I'm not certified to fly alone yet."

Ryan had picked up a menu but set it back down. "You're learning to fly a plane? Isn't that a little risky for a guy your age?" It seemed risky to Ryan. Tag wasn't old, per se. He was only fifty-nine, but that still seemed to be a little too old to be learning new things. Especially things that could crash.

His dad didn't seem to appreciate his concern. "Uh, I'm pretty sure a guy my age can do just about anything a guy your age can do, other than read small print, and yes, I'm taking flight lessons. I wholeheartedly recommend them. The truth is, I might even buy my own plane since . . . well, since I plan to spend more time here."

A fast glance across the pig-colored table told Ryan his dad was serious. "Spend more time here? Bryce told me you had another project you were looking into. Can this tiny island really support two jobs for the company?"

Taggert Property Management was hailed as a premier corporation in the hospitality industry, handling everything from initial construction and design of multi-unit condominiums and hotels, to remodeling, rebranding, streamlining reservation systems, and even market studies to analyze if a location was a wise investment. They didn't typically take on projects with less than fifty units, but for some reason, his father had contracted with the owner of a modest twelve-room hotel on the shore of Trillium Bay who wanted a simple upgrade to the interiors. The job wouldn't turn much of a profit, and neither Ryan nor his two brothers understood their father's attachment to this particular project. They hadn't argued with him, though. He'd been pretty glum since their mother died last year, and this job was the first one he'd seemed enthusiastic about in a very long time.

"Tell you what, son. Let's eat first," said his dad. "We've got all day to talk about business."

And that was another thing. It wasn't like his father to talk about anything *but* business. Nonetheless, Ryan found himself nodding like a bobblehead. "Yes. Food. I'm legit starving."

"What?" Tag crooked an eyebrow.

"What?" Ryan looked up from the menu lying on the table. "Oh, nothing. That's just teen-speak for seriously hungry. Never mind. I take it you've been here a few times. What's good?"

Tag pushed the menu to the edge of the table without even reading it and picked up his coffee. "You have to try the pancake buckets. Best pancakes you've ever had. And they're circles. Smartest trick ever."

Ryan gave him the side eye. "Aren't all pancakes circles?"

Tag laughed, and Ryan couldn't help but think he looked ten years younger. Maybe it was the tan? Or maybe it was just that he hadn't heard him laugh in a while.

"I mean rings, I guess. Like doughnuts. It's a stack of pancakes with a hole in the center for you to fill up with syrup. Like a bucket. Funny, right? And brilliant?" Now his father was nodding with a *what will they think of next* kind of smile.

"Hmm, clever."

They ordered pancake buckets, eggs, bacon, and hash browns because Ryan's hunger was, as he'd said, legit. Patty kept their coffee cups full as he told his dad about the old, not remotely helpful dude at the Wawatam airport. They talked about a few random friends and family members back home in California. The food came, and as they ate, Tag seemed to dance around Ryan's questions whenever the topic of the island projects came up, but he was determined to get to the bottom of things.

"So tell me, Dad," Ryan said one more time, "why exactly did you need me to come out here for two months? I've looked at the portfolio for this job, and you could have handled it yourself while riding a unicycle blindfolded. Now you're being evasive about this other job. I'm getting all kinds of mixed signals from Bryce, and quite frankly, we're all feeling a little confused."

Tag wiped his mouth with a napkin, then wadded it up to toss on his plate. "I'm not trying to be evasive, son. It's just I have some things going on that I haven't been ready to talk about."

"Well, I'm here now to work, so eventually you're going to have to give me some details, and this seems like as good of a time as any, doesn't it? What's this other project Bryce mentioned?"

Tag shifted in his seat and glanced around the restaurant. "There is another project I was interested in, but this isn't the best place to discuss it. I can give you the specifics later, when we're alone, but the bottom line is, if you like it, and I think you will, I think you should take the lead."

"Why wouldn't you take the lead? You're the one who's been here for a month already and gotten to know your way around. Shoot, according to walleye-vision Patty over there, you even have a favorite booth at this restaurant."

Tag shifted again, and Ryan could swear his dad's cheeks flushed red under that tan, and that made Ryan start to heat up, too. Something was off.

"I told you I'm working on some future plans of my own. Ryan, I guess there's just no easy way to say this. I'm thinking about retiring."

Ryan felt his jaw go slack. "Retiring? You can't retire."

Tag's sudden smile was sympathetic. "Actually, I can. And I'm thinking of buying a house here, maybe moving to the island permanently."

This time Ryan's jaw nearly hit the pink laminate tabletop. "Move here? You can't move here. Is this all because of the woman you met? Bryce said there was some woman." It sounded more like an accusation than he had intended, but his dad was talking crazy, and the Taggert family didn't waste time on hidden agendas. It was part of what made them so successful in the industry. Everyone always knew the plan and knew where they fit in, but obviously his father had been keeping some big-time secrets.

Tag glanced around again and then ran a hand over his close-cropped hair. This time the blush was obvious. He looked like a teenage boy coming home after curfew instead of the CEO of a multi-million-dollar company. He chuckled self-consciously. "Bryce is right. There is a woman. I like her. She likes me. Birds and the bees kind of stuff."

Those pancakes stirred in Ryan's gut, and he wasn't sure if it was from the notion of his father having romantic feelings for some woman or the fact that he wanted to explain it with a birds and bees analogy.

"Okay. That's okay. You're entitled to that, I guess. I understand you wanting some female companionship, but why would you retire and move just because of some woman?" There was that tone again, but he couldn't seem to help it.

"She's not just some woman, Ryan. She's very special. And very beautiful. You'll think so too when you meet her. Trust me."

Ryan had nothing against older women, but he doubted he and his father used the same scale. Plus, there was the whole *potentially a gold-digging bimbo* aspect to all of this. "I'm sure she is, Dad, but the pieces still don't fit. Why retire? Let's start with that."

"I want to retire because, first of all, I just want to. I've earned the break. And second, she's lived here all her life and wants to travel, but I can't travel and still be an active CEO of the company. You and your brothers are more than capable of running the company without me."

Without him? "Dad, if she wants to travel, then take her on a vacation. Shoot, take the rest of the summer off if you want to, but don't retire. You're not thinking this through. It's all very sudden."

"I'm sure it seems that way to you because I haven't talked to you boys about things much lately, but it's been hard, you know? I didn't want to burden anyone, but I've been having a tough time adjusting to your mother being gone."

Ryan's chest tightened. "That's no secret, Dad. We knew that, and we know it now, so what do you need from us support-wise? Because you know we'll give it."

"Then support me in this. I'm going to retire and buy a place on this island." Tag sat up a little straighter in his seat, almost defiantly, as if he, too, was just coming to grips with the reality of what he wanted.

Where did support end and enabling begin? The line here seemed razor-thin. "Yeah, okay, anything but that, Dad. It's too extreme. Like I said, take a vacation. Buy a little place here and come back anytime you want. Go buy yourself a damn airplane if that will make you happy, but you're too young to retire. The company does need you, plus you'll go stir-crazy inside of a month. I know you will." Ryan was already getting twitchy, and he'd only been here an hour. Maybe it was all the pink. Or the fact that his father had completely lost his marbles.

His father's smile was somehow both patient and patronizing. "I won't go stir-crazy. I've been here for a full month, and I'm not the least bit bored. When I'm not working, I'm busy all the time. Do you know what I do? I hike. I swim. I kayak. I watch birds. Not sissy birds like chickadees and shit like that. The big ones, like hawks and eagles. The majestic ones."

Bird-watching? His father was bird-watching? "You can't watch birds full time, Dad. That's something you do for an afternoon when there is literally nothing else to do and someone is holding a gun to your head. It's not an occupation."

His father chuckled, as if he enjoyed the process of convincing Ryan of all the reasons he should throw away his career for some island floozy. "Of course it's not an occupation. That's sort of the point. It's a hobby, and they are beautiful creatures. What I'm trying to say is that I've been getting regular exercise since I came here, and I feel better physically than I have in years. I sleep great. Up with the sun. I'm regular." Tag patted his chest with pride, as if predictable bowel movements were a real victory.

The more his dad smiled, the more frustrated Ryan became. Was this a joke? Was Bryce behind it? Because that's the kind of thing his brother would do. *Let's send Ryan on some wild-goose chase to some Podunk island and tell him crazy shit until he figures out it's a hoax.* Being the youngest of three brothers, Ryan was a constant target of their pranks, but as near as he could tell, his dad's story was . . . legit.

"I'm glad you're feeling good, Dad. Really, and I'm sure there are some great bird sanctuaries in California for you to check out and some awesome places to do that other stuff, too. You don't need to move here for that."

His dad went on blithely as if Ryan hadn't even spoken.

"Did I mention I even go biking? Can you picture it? Me on a bike?"

"No, I cannot."

"Me neither, until I tried it. Turns out it really is just like riding a bike." He chuckled at his own joke. Ryan did not.

"Guess what else I do."

Those pancakes were flipping themselves in Ryan's stomach as he recognized the dare in his father's voice. His father was challenging him to ask. Ryan gave in with one big sigh. "What else do you do, Dad?"

Tag leaned back in his seat and stretched one long arm across the back of it. His chin lifted defiantly. "I square-dance."

Ryan sat motionless, waiting for the punch line. Surely there was a punch line. None arrived. "Square-dance?" he finally choked out.

"Yep. That's where I met her. Every Wednesday evening down at Saint Bartholomew's Catholic Church they have square dancing. She was there the first night when I arrived on the island, and we've gone back a couple of times since." He leaned forward and put his elbow on the table, as if to fully capture Ryan's attention. As if he hadn't already. "The truth is, son . . . I like to do-si-do. I like to promenade. Sometimes I allemande left. Sometimes I allemande right. What are you gonna do about that? Huh?"

Ryan fell back in his seat. "What the fuck has happened to you?"

Tag burst out laughing. "Call me crazy if you want to, but it's true. I'm having fun. I'm relaxed. I'm pretty sure I've fallen in love, and I'm not interested in apologizing for it, or trying to analyze it, or even worrying if people think I'm a silly old man."

His father was in love? After a month? That stirred up a ruckus in Ryan's gut for sure, but he wasn't certain if it was due to the speed at which this relationship seemed to be traveling, or because it felt like a betrayal of his mother. He'd have to figure that out later. "No one wants you to apologize, Dad. We're not going to judge you." None of that was actually true. He and his brothers would totally judge him because he was talking like a lunatic, but it wouldn't be prudent for Ryan to pick a fight with his dad in the middle of this little pink, pig-filled diner. His best bet was to handle this like he would handle a dense client. Slow and steady breaths. Voice calm. "But put yourself in my shoes, Dad, and tell me how you think it looks. I've never known you to take a vacation or even a sick day, and all of a sudden you're ready to give up your job as president and CEO of the company you founded for some woman you just met. Just so you can travel and . . . and square-dance? Don't you see how that's a little drastic?"

Tag knew the ploy and responded in kind, with the same calm, slow manner. It was irritating. "You're answering your own question, Ryan, and you're exactly right. I never took a vacation. I never took a sick day. I worked my ass off and pulled you boys in to work with me just so I'd have time to see you. God bless your mother for putting up with my schedule. I wish I'd figured this out when she was still alive. I would have taken her on that trip to Europe that she always wanted."

"She went without you."

"I know, and she spent a shitload of money to show me just how mad she was about that, too." Tag chuckled softly, then sobered a bit. "Life is short, Ryan, and I'm starting to realize that I wasn't that great of a husband. I guess I wasn't that great of a father, either."

More crazy talk. Crazy, crazy talk. "Of course you were a great father. Do you think we'd all be working with you now if we felt otherwise? Would I be sitting here arguing with you about retiring if I wanted to stop working together?" Seriously, what the hell was his dad talking about?

"I'm glad to hear you say that, son, but I sort of dragged you into the business. I don't remember ever really asking any of you boys what you wanted. I just assumed if I was having fun, you must be having fun."

"We were having fun. We're still having fun. I love my job."

"But if you gave it up tomorrow, what would you have?" Tag's face was earnest, and his question stumped Ryan into a momentary silence.

After a pause, Ryan said, "Give it up? Why would I do that?"

"Just try to imagine it. What else have you got in your life besides your job? When's the last time you had a really good, meaningful conversation with someone that didn't revolve around the job? Or more importantly, when's the last time you had a truly healthy, satisfying relationship with a woman?"

More gut churning. "Are we back on that birds and the bees stuff, Dad? Because I think that bell's been rung."

Tag shook his head. "I'm not talking about great sex. Although great sex is, well, you know. Great sex."

Ryan took a moment to wonder what those bucket cakes were going to look like when he upchucked them back onto the table. Meanwhile, his dad kept on talking.

"I'm talking about something meaningful to your soul. Something . . . spiritual."

"Spiritual? Dad, what the hell did they do to you down at that Catholic church?"

Tag laughed again. "Not that kind of spiritual. I just mean, you know, deep. I don't know how to explain it if you haven't felt it yourself. I did have that with your mother for nearly all of our marriage. There were a few times when it got rough, but we always worked through it, mostly thanks to her. We understood each other. We were a team. Have you ever had that with a woman, where you look at something and you see exactly the same thing?"

"I don't know, Dad. You're talking in circles here. I think all that hiking has given you altitude sickness. You didn't ever fall down on one of those nature walks, did you? Maybe lose consciousness for a few minutes?"

His father smiled broadly. "You think I had a stroke out there in the woods?"

"Maybe. All I know is you've gone completely off the reservation here, and I don't know what to do about it."

"Nothing. Just enjoy your breakfast. Enjoy your time here. Let yourself relax, and you'll start to see why I like it here so much. Trust me."

Nothing good ever happened after someone said *trust me.* Ryan took a deep breath and wondered if this place served alcohol because he could use a shot of Jack Daniel's right about now. "Dad, Bryce and Jack expect me to talk some sense into you and to convince you to finish up your project on this island and come back home to Sacramento. What the hell am I supposed to tell them?"

Tag took a slow sip of coffee, staring at Ryan for a moment. "Tell you what, son. You brought some vacation clothes, right? Some shorts and some T-shirts? Some comfortable shoes?"

Ryan had brought a couple pairs of basketball shorts to wear in case he found time to go for a run and a handful of white T-shirts to go under his dress shirts. He'd been planning on working for most of his stay. "Technically, sort of. I have running shoes."

"Okay, we're going to go to the store right now and get you some good hiking boots. Then we'll head out and hike to the top of Bent Rock. It's a good workout, and it's the best view of Petoskey Bridge on the entire island. You're going to enjoy it, I promise. The Lilac Festival starts this weekend. They tell me that's a big deal around here, so we'll go to that, and the next day, we'll go for a bike ride around the entire island. It only takes a couple of hours. Or we could go see Fort Beaumont. We'll do all the stuff I should have done with you when you were a kid, and I'm confident that if you let yourself relax, you'll come to understand what I like about this place."

"You're not going to make me square-dance, are you? I think I really have to draw the line here someplace." If his dad tried to make him wear a cowboy hat or cowboy boots, well, that just wasn't going to happen. No amount of concern over his father's welfare was going to prompt Ryan to promenade.

"I will not force you to square-dance, but I might strongly encourage you to give it a try."

Holy shit. His dad really had cracked under the pressure if square dancing and something called a *Lilac Festival* could get him so excited. Ryan needed to think. He needed to strategize, but his only hope for the moment was to go through the motions. If necessary, he'd go hiking and biking and humor Tag until he came to his senses of his own accord. It couldn't take that much longer. Maybe his father hadn't gotten bored in the month he'd been here, but eventually he'd miss the thrill and the satisfaction of work. He'd miss negotiating the deal and the sense of accomplishment that accompanies a job well done. He'd miss the corner office looking out over his city.

And hopefully that shiny new woman would lose her luster, too, because she seemed to be the thing that really had him confused. But what could they possibly have in common? She'd grown up on this tiny island. Realistically, how long could you talk about how majestic a bird was? This was all just a phase, some sort of grief-triggered existential crisis. His dad would get over it, and life would go back to normal. Ryan needed to make sure of it.

Chapter 5

Like nearly every house on Ojibwa Boulevard, Brooke Callaghan's was surrounded by a white picket fence. Purple lilac bushes bloomed nearby, and the front stone path was lined with pink and white petunias. The whole place had a sweet, welcoming quality. Emily's older sister? Slightly less so.

It's not that Brooke was unfriendly. She was just frugal with her displays of affection. At thirty-five, she was only four years older than Emily, but somehow the age gap had always felt wider. Probably because it was Brooke who stepped up and took care of the house after their mother died. No one had asked her to or expected her to. She just did it because it needed to be done. She'd often been the cushion between Emily and Harlan, too. She still was. In fact, if it weren't for Brooke, they probably wouldn't be speaking at all.

It was a mixed blessing, really.

Chloe trailed her fingers along the tips of the fence as Emily and Gigi walked behind her on their way to dinner. The screen door of the homey little house opened onto the front porch as they got closer, and Brooke stepped out. "Take your time, people. I've only been waiting all day to see my niece."

Chloe giggled and skipped forward, on up the steps to hug her. "Hey, Aunt Brooke. Thanks for the book you sent me on my birthday. I really liked it."

Brooke hugged her tightly, then leaned back from their embrace. "Who are you? You can't be Chloe. You're much too tall."

"It's the vegetables. Mom always makes sure I eat the vegetables."

Emily tried to think of a time she'd had to tell Chloe to eat her vegetables, but none came to mind. Still, she was glad to know Chloe thought that was the rule.

Emily climbed the steps next, feeling a flood of sweet emotions. Brooke had done a lot for her, and she'd never really said thanks. Not that Brooke would even let her. They didn't have a mushy-gushy, *let's braid each other's hair* kind of relationship, but maybe this summer Emily could display a little subtle gratitude. She definitely owed her sister that.

"Brooke! I'm so glad to see you." She flung her arms wide with enthusiasm, deciding there was no time like the present to start being a kinder, gentler version of herself.

Brooke, pragmatic as ever, offered back a tight but perfunctory hug that left Emily wishing for a little more. Just a little bit more. Her sister quickly took a step back to observe her, head to toe, just as she had done with Chloe. Then nodded. "Yep, I figured. You look as great as always."

Though Trillium Bay attire in the summer was almost exclusively sundresses and shorts, Emily was wearing a pair of pale gray dress pants and a white shirt with a floaty chiffon ruffle on the front. It wouldn't have been considered dressy in San Antonio, but Emily suddenly wondered if it was a little much for a family reunion dinner. She'd wanted to look nice. And professional. And not broke. She most especially wanted to look *not broke*, but her sister was wearing denim shorts and a red T-shirt that said *Geology Rocks* on the front, so Emily probably could have toned it down a bit.

"You look great, too. I love that haircut."

Brooke's dark hair was full of natural waves and fell just past her jawline with a cute, bouncy bob that fit her efficient, no-nonsense personality.

"Thanks." Her laugh said she didn't quite believe Emily, but she didn't seem bothered by that either.

"Is Lilly here yet?" Emily asked.

Brooke shook her head, making the waves bounce. "She was around last night because we thought you were arriving yesterday, but tonight she had a thing she couldn't cancel. She said to tell you she's sorry and she'll call you first thing tomorrow."

That was disappointing. Lilly was good at keeping a running commentary on topics she found fascinating and could help lighten the mood in case things with Emily and her dad got too dour. She was the bouncy, outgoing counterpart to Brooke's more serious nature. At twenty-six, Lilly was the youngest Callaghan sister. The baby of the family. She'd been just five years old when their mother died, and after that, she kind of became everyone's baby sister. And everyone's favorite. Of course, with Brooke as the smart, responsible one and Lilly as the bubbly, pretty one, that left Emily stuck in the middle, and whether by nature or nurture, she ultimately became the sassy one. The loudmouth. The troublemaker.

The thorn in Harlan Callaghan's side.

"But Dad's inside," Brooke added, speaking of the devil.

Dad was inside? No avoiding him now.

Gigi breezed past them and opened the door. "I'll just let myself in if you don't mind. There must be some thirsty olives in there just waiting to be dunked into my glass. Chloe, come on with me and I'll show you how to make the perfect martini."

"She's twelve, Gigi. Too young to make a martini," Emily said.

"Too young to drink one, but not too young to make one." Gigi pulled a giggling Chloe inside as Emily looked to Brooke.

"So, Dad's inside, huh? Has he tenderized at all since the last time I saw him?"

Brooke's shrug was noncommittal, as shrugs are apt to be. "Hard to say, Peach. I mean, it's not like we sit around watching *Oprah* and discussing our feelings. You know how Dad is."

She did know how Dad was. She was just hoping he'd changed. "*Oprah*'s not on television anymore. At least, not the talk show."

"She isn't? Oh, well see? That tells you how out of touch I am. I'm pretty much out of touch with Dad's feelings, too, so if you want to know anything, I guess you'll have to ask him yourself, but I will say that he got a haircut and bought a new shirt when he found out you were coming to visit." Brooke arched an eyebrow to emphasize the significance of this. And it *was* significant.

"He bought a new shirt?"

Harlan Callaghan never met a threadbare T-shirt that he didn't think he could wring just a little more life out of. Some of them predated the first settlers on the island. So if he went out and bought a new shirt just because Emily was coming to visit? Well, that was something.

Brooke stepped through the door and motioned for Emily to follow. "Come on. Let's get this over with. Hey, Dad. Look who I found on the front porch."

Chloe was only a few steps in front of them, and she took the lead, stepping toward her grandfather and extending a hand.

"I'm so pleased to see you, sir. I'm really looking forward to getting to know you better this summer."

Emily blinked. Chloe must have learned that from watching television, or maybe Jewel had been coaching her on the sly because she hadn't learned that from Emily. Either way, Emily offered up a silent prayer of thanks to the patron saint of wayward daughters because Harlan looked almost, maybe slightly misty-eyed as he accepted Chloe's hand. "I look forward to that, too."

"And look who else I found," Brooke said, nudging Emily forward.

She stepped up as Chloe moved to the side, and leaned in for a hug that ultimately became more of a leaning forward of two people, looking over the other person's shoulder, and tapping them ever-so-lightly on the back with their fingertips. Still, it was progress. Last time they'd seen each other, he'd pretended to be blowing his nose so his hands were too busy for a hug. "Hi, Dad. Good to see you." Pat, pat, pat with her fingertips.

He stood upright and nodded with the kind of smile one usually reserves for the person handing you a subpoena. "Likewise. Glad the weather held for you gals. It's supposed to be a sunny one all week."

Annnnd he went straight for the weather. That was okay. She could work with that.

"Yes, it's lovely weather. Chloe and I have really been enjoying the scent of the lilacs."

"And the fudge," Chloe added. "Oh my gosh. The smell of the fudge makes me so hungry."

"Well, you have Harvey Murdock to thank for that," Harlan said. "It was his idea to vent all the candy shops toward Main Street so the tourists would be lured in by the smell. That's why we call them fudgies."

"You call the tourists fudgies? That's funny," Chloe said.

"Yep. Nothing sells it faster than the smell."

Emily's father slipped his hands into the pockets of his well-worn jeans, assuming his storytelling posture, and she felt a swell of relief. If he could spend the evening talking to Chloe, sharing tales about his beloved Trillium Bay, then the conversation would flow from there. Even without Lilly's help. Nothing too personal, of course, but enjoyable, and maybe even entertaining, especially if Gigi added her two cents, which she was sure to do. Between the two of them, Gigi and Harlan had so many stories that, with any luck, Emily wouldn't have to say anything for the rest of her visit.

~

"Being a caddie at Trillium Heights golf club was always a good job," Harlan said, regaling Chloe with yet another tale of his childhood on the island as Brooke served homemade apple pie for dessert. "But even before I was old enough for that, my pal Brian Murphy and I used to scour the woods to find golf balls that players had accidentally hit into the brush. We'd polish them up and then go hang out by the water traps, sell them for a quarter apiece, and make an easy buck."

"That's pretty clever," Chloe said, digging her spoon into the whipped cream.

"You learn to be resourceful on the island. We recycled around here long before it was trendy, and we knew how to turn just about anything into a toy. Laundry baskets, trash can lids, tree branches, rocks. We didn't have to rely on electronic gadgets to have fun. I see all these kids today, walking down beautiful Main Street but never looking up from their phones. In my day, we knew how to appreciate our surroundings."

Chloe reached back and tucked her phone deeper into her back pocket. "That's a shame, Grandpa. They should be paying attention to how pretty it is here."

"That's right."

Emily hid a smile behind her fork. Chloe was working him like potter's clay, reshaping him into a fairly pleasant dinner companion. So far her father hadn't directed any questions or comments her way, and she wasn't even sure he'd really looked at her, but that was fine. As long as he was nice to Chloe, she'd consider this evening a win.

"Sure, that's right about turning everything into a toy," said Gigi. "Don't let him dazzle you, though, Chloe. Every time he stole our garbage can lids to use them as shields, we had raccoons digging around in our trash, and I can't tell you how many times my laundry basket came home smelling like the fish he'd caught."

Everyone chuckled, even Harlan, and Emily wondered if maybe, just maybe, Chloe could soften that old man up enough for Emily to find a way back in. It was a long shot, but she was known to take a risk or two.

The rest of dinner was a mostly relaxing affair, and all the taboo subjects were conveniently avoided. Emily was careful not to bring up anything too controversial that might turn her father's mood sour, such as what she'd been doing since she left the island. If she didn't bring up her life in San Antonio, he could pretend she'd never run off. That left her with not much to say, but Chloe artfully filled in any gaps in conversation. They ate on the back patio where the breeze ruffled the tree branches and the sound of waves could be heard until the crickets got too loud. The sun was setting when Harlan's chair scraped against the brick as he pushed back from the table.

"Thanks for dinner, Brooke. I should check in on things downtown. Lilac Festival starts tomorrow, and they'll need help setting up some of the barricades for the parade. I'll see you gals later." He stood up and gave Chloe's shoulder a little squeeze. It was subtle but felt to Emily like a significant sign of affection. Her father might not ever approve of her marriage to Nick, or basically any decision she'd made before or since, but at least he was willing to accept Chloe, and that was a huge leap forward from their last two visits. He nodded at the rest of them, and he maaaaay have been smiling. Or he may have been burping. With Harlan there was just no telling.

Gigi motioned to Chloe as they both stood up. "Come on inside with me, sweetheart. I'll show you some old picture albums and fill you in on all the island gossip. Nothing gets by me. I know all the dirt. Especially all the stuff about your relatives."

"Mom, should I help clean up first?" Chloe batted her lashes and smiled innocently. Now she was working the *I'm adorable so please don't make me help with cleanup* angle. Emily waved her away with a laugh.

"You go ahead with Gigi. I'll help Aunt Brooke clean up."

Skepticism slanted Brooke's eyebrows. "You sure? You don't want to get barbeque sauce on that white shirt." There was a tone there. Nothing too overt, but loud in sister-speak. Brooke thought Emily was overdressed. So did Emily, but it was too late to fix that now.

"That's what bleach is for," Emily answered, picking up a tall stack of dirty plates and carrying them into the kitchen. She wanted the family to think she was successful, not arrogant. Brooke came in behind her carrying half a dozen water glasses.

"So you're remodeling a place for Gigi, huh?" Brooke asked as Emily set the plates next to the stainless steel sink.

"Yep, her second husband's place. I haven't seen it yet, but we're going tomorrow after church. I vaguely remember it from when we were kids, and it has a lot of potential."

"You haven't seen it yet?" Brooke snickered. "That explains why you're still speaking to her."

"What do you mean?"

"I mean the place is falling apart. She's been renting it to college kids for the past few summers, and they were pretty rough on it. I'm honestly surprised she decided to renovate. I thought she was going to sell it."

"Sell it?"

Brooke's expression was impassive. "I thought so, but I guess she changed her mind."

"I guess so."

Emily busied herself with the dirty plates. Gigi hadn't said anything to her about selling it, but even if that was a consideration, it wasn't something Emily wanted to discuss with her sister at the moment. Too many questions could lead to her having to admit she'd borrowed a serious chunk of money from Gigi. She needed to steer this conversation in another direction. "So, are you dating anyone?"

Brooke halted with a drinking glass poised over the sink, staring at Emily as if to gauge the legitimacy of the question. "Sure," she said dryly. "I'm dating twins. Their names are Slim and None. How about you?" She opened the dishwasher and started loading the glasses in.

"Nope. I'm too busy working and taking care of Chloe." And she was, so the fact that Ryan Taggert popped into her mind just then meant nothing. Even though she could very clearly picture the red tie hanging around his neck, and the day's worth of stubble that covered his face as they'd stood in the hall of that hotel last night. But so what? He hadn't come down to the bar to have dinner with her and Chloe, and he hadn't been on the ferry this morning either. If he was interested, he wasn't making much of an effort. So, yeah. It meant absolutely nothing at all.

She scraped away the thought of him along with the leftovers on the plate she was holding over the trash bin.

"I'm pretty busy working, too," Brooke said. "And . . . I'm thinking about running for mayor." The comment was tossed out with nonchalance, as if she'd just mentioned how she'd bought a dozen eggs from O'Doul's grocery store.

Emily looked up from the plate in her hand. "You are? Isn't Harry Blackwell still the mayor?"

"Yes, and he's about a hundred and forty years old. Just because this island is historic doesn't mean the mayor has to be, too." That was said with a little more passion, like maybe that dozen eggs had cost twice as much as she'd expected.

"That is an excellent point. What about your job at the school? Wouldn't you miss teaching?"

Brooke was the one and only science teacher at the one and only school on the island. Grades one through twelve all fit inside the same building with about 150 kids attending each year. Academics had come naturally to Brooke, so it was a surprise to no one when she went into teaching. In fact, it was often said of her that the only time she'd ever been sent out into the hall, it was for extra credit.

Brooke turned on the faucet to rinse the knives and forks. "Sure, I'd miss academics, but I think being the mayor might be a nice change of pace. I could use a little of that, you know? I've got lots of ideas, and I think I could have a positive impact."

That was Brooke. It wasn't enough that she'd taken care of her family or even her students. Now she wanted to take care of the whole island. And if anyone could, it was her. "I think you'd be great at it. You're great at everything."

Brooke chuckled, brushing away the comment with a wave of her hand. "I know a thing or two about a thing or two, but I seem to be good at herding cats, so if I can handle a classroom full of noisy kids, I think I could manage this island's government. But I don't know. I haven't decided for sure yet."

It wasn't like Brooke to be indecisive, and there weren't that many times in their lives when Emily was the one to offer reassurance. Here was a chance. "I think it's a really good idea, Brooke, and I'm not just saying that to be nice. You know I never say stuff just to be nice. I think if you want to be mayor, you'd be a fantastic one."

Brooke fussed with the faucet handle and blushed. Accepting compliments was nowhere on her résumé.

"And besides," Emily teased, "Mayor Blackwell used to pinch my cheek every time he'd see me and I hated it. For that reason alone, you have my vote."

That got a laugh from her sister. "Good to know you're willing to stand up for your convictions. I promise to never pinch your cheek."

Chapter 6

The sun was low in the sky, casting pink and purple shadows as Ryan climbed aboard a horse-drawn taxi to head to the cottage his father had rented. They'd spent the afternoon shopping for all the stuff Tag had insisted he'd need in order to fully experience the island. He now had new hiking boots, thick socks, waterproof pants that zipped off at the knees to turn into shorts, a hat with a wide brim, and several T-shirts depicting the various and supposedly appealing aspects of Trillium Bay. One shirt simply said *Up North*. Apparently that was a place. At any rate, he'd bought so much damn stuff he could stay the entire summer and never have to find a Laundromat. In fact, they'd shopped so long that they ran out of time to go hiking.

"See?" Tag had said as he'd left Ryan at the Rosebush Hotel with his arms full of new merchandise. "I told you that you'd be busy here. We've already had to postpone something."

Shopping was not Ryan's idea of being busy. Being busy involved work, and as of yet he hadn't seen the hotel project his father was currently involved with, nor had they discussed the hush-hush project that Tag wanted Ryan to consider, and it was hard to consider anything when he had literally no details. That was something he fully intended to address tonight. Tag was cooking him dinner. Because apparently that was a new thing for him, too. Cooking.

Cooking?

What the hell had happened to him?

A woman. That's what had happened to him.

As the horse-drawn taxi meandered down Main Street, they passed a few more fudge shops, a tiny grocery store called O'Doul's, and a library painted a bright aquamarine blue. Ryan breathed in and tried to calm his mind. He had a million and twelve things he should be working on right now. A million and twelve reasons why he wanted to be back in California, but his task here was important. Taggert Property Management needed its president back, and obviously his dad needed his help. Not with the job, but with the bimbo. Bryce and Jack would never let Ryan hear the end of it if he couldn't make this right.

Competition among the Taggert brothers came as easily as breathing, and as the youngest of the three, Ryan often felt the need to catch up and prove he was just as good as they were. At everything. Just by virtue of being the last one born, Ryan was at a disadvantage, but he made up for that in tenacity and drive.

"That's the fort, up that way," the taxi driver said. He was a young guy, probably just shy of twenty, with a mangy head of light brown hair and a day's worth of scruff.

"The fort?"

"Yeah, you know. Fort Beaumont. Built in 1780 by the British. Wenniway was considered a strategic military location on account of the straits."

The kid rattled on with a dozen more historical details about the fort and the island, but Ryan blanked on most of it. "And then Chief Eagle Feather rode through the town in his altogether, warning the Americans that the British were coming. Or so the story goes."

The kid looked back at him, so Ryan smiled and nodded. He'd learned a long time ago how to at least appear to be listening. Especially because he didn't choose to not listen. It was just that his brain was busy doing other things. "How much farther is it to Beech Tree Point?" he asked.

"Not much," the kid answered.

The paved road curved and transitioned into a dirt two-track as the horses continued on for another few minutes, until it was nothing but woods all around them. Begrudgingly, Ryan had to admit that the pine trees did smell good. A squirrel ran across the road, and birds were chirping all around him. He could hear the waves rolling over the shore, and just off to his left, in the small spaces between the branches, he could see Lake Huron. This island was pretty. Definitely pretty. Not *I want to quit my job and move here* kind of pretty. But certainly *I could probably hang out here for about a week* kind of pretty.

"Whoa, girls. Ease up," the driver said, and the taxi came to a lurching halt. Ryan slid forward and bumped his knees on the seat in front of him. The kid could use some parking lessons. Ryan adjusted his tip accordingly. He handed the driver some bills and climbed down from the carriage. "Keep the change."

"Hey, thanks, mister. Enjoy your stay here. Git'up, girls. Let's go." The driver slapped the reins against the horses' round backsides, and off they went. As the sound of the taxi faded away into the noises of the forest, Ryan found himself standing in front of a little gingerbread-colored cottage that Hansel and Gretel would have found very enticing. There were window boxes full of flowers, and yellow-trimmed eaves. If his father answered the door wearing lederhosen, he would not be that surprised. Although that was German, not Victorian. He was getting his cottages and eras and fairy tales mixed up, but he could hardly be blamed for that. This place had an otherworldly, time-warpy quality that had him all turned around.

Ryan crossed the small expanse of grass to knock on the door, but his dad opened it before his knuckles hit the wood.

"Hi there. I heard the taxi." Tag seemed a little breathless, a little overly animated.

"Hi, Dad," Ryan said cautiously and curiously.

"Listen, before you come in, I want to let you know I've invited my friend to join us. I was going to wait a few days and let you settle into the idea, but then I figured the best way for you to understand things is just for you to meet her."

"Meet her? Tonight? Dad, I was hoping we could talk a little shop tonight. I'm here to work, not socialize."

His father patted Ryan's chest. "Shh, keep your voice down. We can talk shop tomorrow. These projects aren't going anywhere."

Sure, they weren't going anywhere because his father didn't seem interested in pushing them. This was not the Tag he knew. The Tag he knew would have dragged him to the worksite before Ryan had even had time to set down his luggage. The Tag he knew would've shoved blueprints under his nose and asked for a market analysis before Ryan could have even said hello. This one-hundred-eighty-degree change in his father's personality just confirmed to Ryan that something was very, very wrong. He quickly sorted through his options. They were few, and none seemed particularly helpful.

"Yeah, okay, Dad. Whatever you say."

Tag's grin was more disturbing than encouraging. "You're going to like her. I promise."

Someone saying *I promise* was a lot like someone saying *trust me.* If they had to make a point of saying it, then it probably wasn't true.

His dad turned and led the way through the doorway and into a narrow foyer full of tiny framed paintings of kittens. No lie. Kittens.

His father pointed at them, and his grin remained. "It's a rental. These aren't mine."

That was a mild relief. They turned the corner into the family room area. There were more dime-store-quality paintings and an odd assortment of mismatched furniture. A blue-and-green plaid couch. A burgundy leather recliner. Tiny end tables with spindly legs. All the kind of dated stuff you might expect to find in a summer rental place, but what Ryan hadn't expected to find was the woman. He felt his mouth fall open stupidly. Because this must be *the* woman. The Gold-Digging Bimbo.

He'd thought Tag's new girlfriend would be modestly attractive, a mature woman with a few extra pounds on her frame. Maybe some glasses, probably wearing a Trillium Bay T-shirt with a lighthouse or something on it. Someone who looked like she might have been a retired high school English teacher, or maybe the cashier at the grocery store. That was not this woman.

"Ryan, I'm so glad you're finally here. I've been looking forward to meeting you." Her smile was warm as she extended a tan, toned arm to shake his hand. "Tag has told me so much about you and your brothers, I feel like I already know you."

It took all of his mental capacity to reply with anything coherent. "Um, well you have me at a slight disadvantage then. Dad's been a little secretive about you." It came out sounding rude, and he hadn't intended to. It was just that she was so not at all what he was expecting. She had long brown hair, dark soulful eyes, a beautifully bright smile.

And she looked to be about twenty-five years old.

Now, Ryan knew he was a terrible judge of such things. She might be older than she looked, but even being generous with his margin of error, there was no way she was older than him. What the hell was his father thinking? Ryan would have chuckled at his own question if it wasn't so glaringly obvious what his father was thinking. But still! What the hell was he thinking?

"I haven't been secretive, Ryan," his father said. "I've just been too busy enjoying myself to fill you boys in on all the details."

What a bullshit comment. His dad had most certainly been withholding details. He may have hinted to Bryce that his new romantic interest was younger, but not that she was younger than Ryan! And his dad could have warned him at lunch that she was fresh out of college. This wasn't love. It was straight-up scandalous lust. It was practically criminal. His father must be having one massive midlife crisis, and any question of *her* motives was obvious. She must absolutely be after his dad's money. Why else would a woman like her fall for a guy so much older than she was? Ryan had no idea how to handle this, but since he couldn't very well turn and leave, his best option now was to gather as much intel about the situation as possible.

He made a point to smile, although it felt stiff and unnatural. "Well, I'm certainly interested in the details now. Tell me everything. Dad said you grew up here?"

She nodded. "Born and raised. I've lived here all my life."

Yeah, all twenty-some years of it. Ryan hoped his thoughts weren't mirrored by his expression.

"Let's say I get everyone a drink," said Tag, clearing his throat. "Honey, would you like some wine?" His hand trailed along her arm as he turned to walk into the kitchen. Their fingers caught, just for a brief second, clinging, as if the contact was essential, and Ryan's breath went shallow in his chest. It was a subtle move but spoke volumes about the intimacy between them. It felt significant, even if it really wasn't. It left him feeling as if he'd seen something raw and private. Like walking in on your parents watching porn. Only she wasn't one of his parents. She wasn't even old enough to have ever been one of Ryan's babysitters. This girl was just that. A girl.

Do-si-do, indeed.

Chapter 7

"Yeah, her name is Daisy, and she looked too young for *me* to go out with," Ryan told Bryce over the phone as he gulped his morning coffee. They'd already discussed the insanity of their dad wanting to retire and had since moved on to the surreal topic of Tag and his teenage girlfriend.

Last night, Ryan had stayed just long enough to force down the chicken marsala his dad had made, which he refused to admit had been delicious, and then he'd hightailed it out of there. On foot. He hadn't even called for one of the horse-drawn taxis, instead choosing to stomp all the way back into town, which had seemed like a good idea until it started to thunderstorm. He was soaked by the time he got back to his hotel, and he'd nearly been struck by lightning, but it was worth it. He couldn't sit there a minute longer in that kitten-picture-infested cottage trying to make chitchat with the prom queen while his father gazed at her adoringly and touched her hair. He touched her hair! It was just wrong on so many levels. The age difference was the obvious issue, but the speed at which this relationship appeared to be moving was another significant fact to consider. Ryan's mother had only been gone for eight months, adding to his unease. Wasn't there some sort of obligatory grieving period? His father was moving on much too fast, and it was just . . . wrong.

He paced back and forth on the tiny balcony of his hotel room overlooking Main Street as he spoke to his brother and watched a steady stream of tourists disembarking from the various ferries. A marching band could be heard practicing in the distance because apparently this Lilac Festival thing included a parade. A parade. His father wanted him to sit and watch a parade. Ryan shook his head and peered over the railing. People were scurrying around all over the place, setting up banners and outdoor food stands. And then, of course, the smell of fudge, always the smell of fudge. Ryan could feel a cavity forming just from the aroma.

"Exactly how young are we talking here?" Bryce asked. Ryan could picture his brother driving his Porsche down Interstate 5 toward Sacramento where the Taggert Property Management headquarters were located. It would be about six thirty in the morning in California, but his brother always liked to be the first one in the office.

"I'm guessing twenty-five, maybe? She's a preschool teacher, and get this—apparently the preschool is right next to a retirement center. The old people help take care of the little kids."

Bryce chuckled. "Well, maybe that's her angle. Maybe what she's really interested in is putting Dad in a home. That would make more sense."

Ryan didn't chuckle back. "No kidding, and maybe we should let her because he's clearly lost his ability to reason."

"Twenty-five. Damn. I don't think I could land a twenty-five-year-old anymore. So how did they seem? I mean, how serious are they? Not very, right? She might be after his money, but Dad can't be very serious about her, right?"

Ryan practically shuddered. "It was . . . revolting. Dad was all goofy and smiley, and he kept calling her honey and sweetheart and my darling. Seriously? My darling? Who even says that anymore?" He took another hit of scalding coffee, because that's just what his mood needed. More stimulants. "What if he marries this girl? Honest to God,

Bryce, I don't believe in ghosts, but if I'm wrong and ghosts are real, then Mom is sure as shit going to come back and haunt the hell out of him for this."

Bryce laughed again, but Ryan still didn't. He'd seen it up close and personal. Too up close, and too personal. He understood better than Bryce what they were up against. This Daisy person had their father wrapped so tight around her finger that a chainsaw couldn't separate them.

"Mom would make a menacing ghost, but are you sure he's not, just, you know, having a little recreational fun? Just taking this hottie out for a test drive?" Ryan heard a car honking over his brother's phone. No surprise. He'd seen Bryce drive, and honking was inevitable.

"Oh, he's having all kinds of fun all right. Do you know what they like to do?" Ryan replied.

"Do I dare ask?"

"Well, aside from the obvious, they go biking."

"Biking? You mean, like . . . on bikes? Bicycles? Please don't tell me they ride a tandem."

This time Ryan did smile. His father on a tandem would be something to see. "I don't know about that. Probably. And they bird-watch. And it gets even better. Guess what else they do?" It was worth building this up because it was just so damned absurd.

"What else do they do?"

"They . . . square-dance. Dad now square-dances." Ryan held the phone away from his ear until his brother's very expected laughter quieted down. "You think it's funny, I know. It is funny. But what's not funny is the way this girl has her claws into him. What the hell is her story? I mean, this is Dad we're talking about. Not some handsome, jet-setting, aging movie star or something."

"It's got to be the money," Bryce answered, honking again. "If she's as young as you say, then that's got to be it. You said she wants to travel, right? He's probably her ticket off that island."

"Maybe."

"Hey, what if she convinces him to go to some foreign country and then he gets kidnapped and held for ransom? Maybe she has some real boyfriend pulling all the strings and this is just some kind of con." Bryce loved a good conspiracy or caper, apparently even if it included their father.

Ryan shook his head, even though his brother couldn't see it. "This isn't an episode of *Dateline*, Bryce. Plus, I don't think she's that clever, unless she's a really good actress. If she hadn't been draped all over Dad, I would have thought she was just a really nice, sweet girl."

"What about her family? Did she mention any ailing relative in need of an expensive, life-saving surgery? Or a brother who needs to get bailed out of jail? If she has some financial hardship story, then she could be totally playing him."

"No ailing relatives that she mentioned, at least not to me, but apparently they're trying to keep things very low-profile when it comes to this *relationship*." Ryan's air quotes were implied in his tone. "Her family supposedly doesn't know anything about him yet."

"Okay, now see? That seems suspicious to me right there. Why not share this joyful moment with her family?"

"Oh, I don't know, Bryce. Maybe because he's probably as old as her dad? I don't think that's the kind of news a woman shares until she's pretty darn sure the relationship is going somewhere."

"I guess, but something is very shady here. It's all fun and games until somebody signs over all the stock options to our company. You need to find out more about this gold-digging bimbo before Dad does something unfixable, like marrying her. Ask around the island. I'll see if I can dig up anything from here. What did you say her name was again?"

"Daisy. Daisy Calhoun. Or Carpenter. Or Calamity. Damn it, you know I can't remember names. Anyway, I do have someone I can ask. I met this woman at the airport and—"

"Whoa, whoa, whoa," Bryce interrupted. "Not you, too? You met a woman? That's all we need is you distracted by some bimbo, too. Am I going to have to send Jack out there to rescue you both? That place is turning into the Hotel California. You know, you check in but you can never leave?"

"Relax, you jackass. She's not a bimbo. She's a mom."

"Uh, hate to break it to you, bro. Moms can be bimbos, too. Have you not met my first wife? Or my second?"

Bryce was on marriage number three. Because he did marry bimbos.

"Listen to me. She's not like that. I mean, she's attractive and everything but—"

"What's *and everything*? Dude, stay focused."

"Yes, Bryce. I've got it." Geez, his brother could be a dick sometimes, and Ryan didn't like him referring to Emily as a bimbo. She wasn't at all. "Anyway, I met this woman at the airport who grew up on the island. She's here for the summer, so I'm thinking I should call and invite her out for coffee or drinks or something. She's got to know this girl, right? They're close enough in age that if they both grew up here, they have to know each other, and then she can give me the scoop."

"Make it coffee. I know you, and if you have cocktails with this chick, you'll end up in the sack with her, and I'll have to send Jack out there for sure. Hey, come to think of it, what if meeting that woman at the airport was no coincidence? What if they're in cahoots?" Bryce loved his word-of-the-day calendar. That must've been a recent one.

"There's no cahooting, Bryce. No grand scheme other than a too-young girl after Dad's money. Unless your secretary was in on it, too, because she's the one who booked my flights on Outer Effing Mongolian Airlines, remember?"

"Yeah, okay. Listen, I'm about to pull into the parking ramp and I'll probably drop the call, but do whatever you need to do. Call your airport friend today and find out everything you can about this Daisy person, and remind Dad he has family obligations. Tell him if he wants some young chickie-poo for a distraction, I'm sure we can find somebody in Sacramento. And tell him he doesn't have time for square dancing. What the fu—" And the call dropped.

"Coffee sounds nice, Ryan. Thanks for the invite, but one of my sisters has coerced me into helping out at the Buy-Buy Miss American Pie tent during the Lilac Festival today. Can we do it another time?"

Seeing Ryan's name pop up on her phone this morning as she sat in Gigi's kitchen had started Emily's day with a tingle and a smile. He hadn't completely forgotten about her.

Gigi cast a speculative glance her way, adjusting her bifocals and leaning in closer over the table like the big, bad wolf. *All the better to hear you with, my dear.* Emily pretended to ignore her, as if that were possible given their close proximity.

"Tell him I said hi," Chloe said, taking another waffle from the stack in front of her. Gigi had cooked enough food for six people, but they were doing their best to eat it all. Fortunately, her daughter must be heading into a growth spurt. Lately it seemed as if all that girl did was eat, sleep, and text.

"Sure, we can go another time, I guess." Ryan sounded more distracted than disappointed. Then he added, "Say, remember talking about the woman my dad had supposedly met? The Gold-Digging Bimbo?"

"Um, yes."

"Well, I met her. Her name is Daisy something, and guess what?"

"What?"

"She's about twenty-five years old. Maybe a little older but not by much. Do you know her?"

"Your father is dating a twenty-five-year-old? How old is he?" That was gross.

"Fifty-nine." Ryan's tone indicated he was not thrilled about this matchup either, and she could understand why. That just wasn't right.

"Well, that's . . . that's quite an age difference. Is she . . . nice?"

Gigi picked up Emily's nearly empty coffee cup and moved toward the silver percolator to refill it. Emily smiled and nodded in thanks. Nosy or not, her grandmother was taking good care of her this morning, and it felt nice to be waited on.

"Nice? I guess, but since she's obviously way too young for my dad, she must have some hidden agenda. She's definitely after something. So do you know her?" His voice was muffled for a moment, like he'd tucked the phone between his ear and shoulder. She could hear him rustling around some papers, and a mild annoyance flickered. He'd called *her*. The least he could do was pay attention.

"I can't think of anyone by that name."

"But she said she lives here, and you said you grew up here. You must know each other."

"I haven't lived here in a long time, Ryan. Maybe she moved to the island after I left."

Gigi set the cup back down, and Emily breathed in the scent. She hoped there was coffee in heaven, because if there wasn't, she wasn't going. Then again . . . she might not be invited in anyway.

"No, I'm sure she said she was born on the island." Ryan was now sounding pretty insistent, as if Emily was the one making a mistake. Her glow over his invitation waned.

"Um, speaking of hidden agendas, did you really call to invite me for coffee, or did you just want to interrogate me about some floozy that your father is . . . keeping company with?" She would have said *banging*, but since Chloe was sitting right there, Emily went PG-13.

His pause was about a millionth of a second, but just long enough for Emily to realize he had to think about his answer. Which was all the answer she needed.

"What? Yes. I mean, no. Yes, I called to see if you wanted to have coffee, but I admit I was hoping you could help me figure out this girl's angle. She must be after his money or running some kind of con. My dad told me yesterday that he wants to retire and move here, and they plan to travel all over the world. He's only known her for four weeks, and she's less than half his age, so yeah, I'm worried."

He sounded more annoyed than worried.

"I don't have any idea who she is, but this isn't exactly the kind of place someone comes to scam somebody."

"Maybe it wasn't something premeditated, but I think this girl met him, saw her chance, and pounced. I think he's her meal ticket off this island. And if he brings her back to Sacramento and marries her? Well, California is a fifty-fifty state."

"Meaning that if he marries her, she gets half of his stuff in the inevitable divorce?"

Emily had met enough wealthy people in her life to know that most of them were worried that other people were after their money. Nick's parents had been those kinds of people, convinced she was just some country mouse after their son's good name and inheritance. She wasn't, of course. She was only after his great body. What a mistake that had been.

"Right. And potentially half of our family company. My father is just not himself these days. He's not thinking clearly. If she *is* a gold-digging bimbo, I'm afraid he'll do something he can't easily undo, like sign over his shares and promise her everything."

This definitely sounded like Nick's family. Ryan's worries might be well-founded, but it still struck a little close to home. Emily had no idea who this woman was or what her intentions were, but Ryan probably needed to cut her some slack until he had more information.

Emily turned away from her grandmother, but Gigi scooched her chair closer. She wasn't even trying to be subtle about eavesdropping now.

"You know, it's quite possible that she just likes him because she likes him. Does there have to be some big ulterior motive behind it?"

"She's half his age."

"True, which is probably something to worry about, but if she's just interested in his money, she wouldn't want him to retire, would she?"

"Like I said, she wants to travel. I think it's his whole lifestyle she's after."

Emily stirred a little cream into her coffee. "I don't know what to tell you, Ryan. I don't know this Daisy you're talking about."

Emily really had enough of her own drama to deal with, both personal and professional. She didn't need his, and if he'd wanted information, he should have been straight with her instead of inviting her out for a pseudo-date. He needed to take care of his own problems. "I'll ask around, okay? I'll see if anyone knows who she is, but in the meantime, I'd say just let him have his fun."

"Emily? Are you here?" The screen door slammed, and a millisecond later her sister's sandals squeaked across the linoleum as she halted in the kitchen doorway, looking windblown and rosy-cheeked. Her dark hair was in a high ponytail, and she wore white denim shorts that made her tanned legs look a mile long.

"Hey, I have to run," Emily said into the phone. "My sister just got here. If you come to the Lilac Festival, I'll be in the pie tent. Bye." She disconnected the call and dropped her phone on the kitchen table while simultaneously being enveloped into Lilly's enthusiastic embrace. Her sister's arms wrapped around Emily and squeezed her tight before she could even stand up.

"Oh my gosh, I'm so glad you're here."

She turned to Chloe. "Oh. My. Gosh. Will you look at you? You're gorgeous!" She hugged her niece until Chloe squeaked.

"Hi, Aunt Lilly. How are you?" Chloe asked breathlessly.

"I'm famished." She plopped down into the chair next to Emily and grabbed a waffle, taking a bite from one corner. "So sorry about missing dinner last night on your first day back. I had a thing."

Lilly's hair was the same dark shade as Brooke's but without the curl, and her smile was nearly constant.

Gigi got up from her chair to pull another coffee mug from the cabinet. "You had a *thing*? Does that thing have a name? And a tallywacker?"

Lilly blushed. "It's not what you think, Gigi. There's no guy. I know everyone thinks there's a guy, but there's no guy."

"Uh-huh." Gigi's tone echoed her disbelief. "Myrna Delroy said you were late to work twice this week and acting very strangely. And Dmitri Krushnic said he was out checking his bees a few evenings ago and could have sworn he saw you walking toward the old lighthouse with some fella."

Lilly rolled her eyes as she accepted the cup of coffee from Gigi's outstretched hand. "Yes, you nosy old coot. I was walking to the lighthouse a few nights ago. With Percy O'Keefe. Only we weren't walking together on purpose. He saw me and insisted on tagging along. You know how he is."

"You think Dmitri wouldn't have recognized Percy O'Keefe?" Gigi was a pit bull on the prowl.

"What I think is that it was dusk and Dmitri can't see shit through that stupid beekeeping hat he always wears. I could have been walking with a yeti and he wouldn't have been able to tell. Everyone on this island just needs to chill and stop trying to create a romance for me."

"Good to know that the gossip mill is still going strong," Emily said, squeezing her sister's arm in solidarity. She'd been on the receiving end of that often enough.

"The gossip mill is alive and well, and no thanks to this one." Lilly nodded at Gigi, but her smile was sweet and her tone teasing. "Why don't you get married again, Gigi? Then you won't have so much time on your hands to make up stories about me."

"Oh, you know I'm always looking. I've still got room for one more on that mantel."

"Mantel?" Chloe asked.

Emily and her sister turned in unison to gaze at the mantel above Gigi's green-tiled fireplace where three distinctive urns sat. Each one held a husband. And while three dead husbands all for one woman might have aroused some suspicion, the manner in which each man met his untimely death clearly exonerated Gigi of anything except exceedingly bad luck. Not as bad as the luck of those dead husbands, but bad nonetheless.

Gigi put a hand over her heart. "Yes, that's where I keep them, the dears."

Chloe's eyes went round as she stared. "There's a dead guy in each of those vases? How did they die?"

"Well, your great-grandfather died when he insisted on proving that lightning *can* strike twice. Turns out he was right."

It was wrong to chuckle at the misfortune of others, but Emily had heard these stories enough times to find them funny.

"Husband number two, Conroy Harper, was just in the wrong place at the wrong time, flying his kite on the beach when a Porta-John blew off the bluffs at Hawkeye Point. Landed right on him. He never saw it coming." She shook her head.

"A shitty way to die," Lilly murmured into her coffee cup.

"And the third?" Chloe asked, as if not certain any of this was true.

"Ah, that was my Bert. He never could resist a dare, but even he should have known better than to eat a taco from Cinco de Mayo on ocho de Mayo. His sombrero is still on the wall down at the Adobe Tavern, but I'm pretty sure they don't serve tacos anymore."

"Please tell me you are making this up," Chloe said, waffle in hand.

"Hand on the Bible. It's all true."

Emily nodded, and Chloe set the waffle down.

"Maybe you should get a very large life insurance policy on the next husband," Lilly suggested, slurping her coffee loudly. "You know, before he makes an ash of himself."

"Very funny, but don't think I haven't thought of it. It's an unpredictable way to score more rental properties, but I do seem to be good at burying men. Plus, I haven't had a husband in a while. At my age, pickings are getting a little slim. I've got my eye on a few gents, though. Just waiting for their wives to move along." She flicked her hands over the table as if shooing away a fly. The sisters giggled while Chloe looked at them as if they were quite, quite inappropriate.

Emily knew Gigi had loved each of her husbands for their own unique attributes, but the Callaghan pragmatism wouldn't let her dwell on losing them or feel sorry for herself. Irish, you know. Self-pity was about the biggest sin you could commit. It was a lesson Emily had clung to during the roughest days of her marriage and the even rougher days of her divorce. Feeling sorry for oneself didn't get the bills paid. It didn't feed your kids, and it didn't improve your situation. Action and movement was the only thing that did that, and so, like any good Callaghan, Emily had just kept moving forward. Maybe without much direction or without much strategy, but still . . . forward.

That's sort of what she was doing now, too. Taking it one day at a time. Once she was finished with renovating Gigi's cottage on the island, and once Jewel had sold the disaster house back in Texas, Emily would have some decisions to make. Assuming they got their asking price on that money pit, Emily could pay off her current debts and hopefully have some left over to buy another flip. If not, well, she'd have to find a regular job. Maybe go back to being a secretary at the construction company. That's where she'd met Jewel in the first place. But she'd figure that out later. She could only handle one catastrophe at a time, and her catastrophe du jour was Gigi's cottage.

"Oh goodness, look at the time," Gigi said, glancing down at a thirty-year-old Timex wristwatch. "Chloe, we should hurry up and get dressed if we want to go watch the parade. We can't go in our pajamas. You do want to see the parade, don't you?"

"Of course I do," Chloe answered, hopping up from her seat, the dismay of dead husbands disappearing. Emily smiled, thinking that just yesterday Chloe might have scoffed at the idea of a parade, but it appeared she was already starting to sink into the charming atmosphere of Trillium Bay.

"Mom, you're coming to the parade, aren't you?"

"Absolutely. That's why I'm already dressed for the day, so you guys had better hurry up and change."

"So catch me up on everything," Lilly said to Emily after Gigi and Chloe had left.

"Catch you up? Let's see." Emily started counting off with her fingers. "I'm still living with Jewel, we're still flipping houses, I spend all my extra time driving Chloe around to all her after-school activities, I'm not dating anyone, and . . . yeah, that's it. You're all caught up."

"Oh, there must be more going on than that?"

Emily shook her head. "No, not really." She wished she could confide in Lilly about all the sleepless nights she'd spent worrying about finances and bankruptcy and the disaster house in San Antonio, but this wasn't the time. Lilly might not be able to keep it a secret. It was bad enough depending on Gigi to keep her lips buttoned up. "So catch me up on you. What's new with you?"

Lilly shrugged and stood up, moving toward the coffeepot. "Oh, you know. Same old, same old. Nothing much ever changes on this island. Did you know Reed is here?"

"So I've heard."

"Mm. Did Brooke tell you she's thinking about running for mayor?"

Watching her, Emily got the distinct impression her sister was trying to divert the topic of conversation off of herself. Normally Lilly was full of stories about her latest adventures, and even if they were not particularly adventuresome, the way she described everything made it sound fun. Now she seemed a little evasive. There must be a guy.

"Yes, she told me about running for mayor. Why does Gigi think you're hiding a man?"

"Because this island is full of nosy old busybodies with nothing better to do than to speculate about who's doing it with who."

"Yeah, so . . . who are you doing it with?"

Lilly's eyes skirted to the doorway that Gigi and Chloe had just exited through. "No one. There's no guy."

"Liar. She's gone now. You can tell me. You know I can keep a secret."

Lilly plucked a nonexistent piece of lint from the front of her shirt, stalling for time, no doubt, and avoiding eye contact. Although Emily's relationship with Brooke was often cautious and a little complicated, Emily's connection to Lilly had always been comfortable and easy, but something was different. Something had changed. Maybe Lilly had learned to keep some secrets after all.

"Look, there might be a guy," she whispered. "But he's not from around here, and it's all really new, so I don't want to jinx it by saying too much. You know how things go around here. I don't want Dad catching wind of it until I've had a chance to tell him myself. You know how he is."

Emily gave a little snort. "Yes, I know how he is, but if Gigi and Dmitri are already suspicious, you can be pretty certain that a whole bunch of other people are, too. You don't think Dad already knows?"

"Oh, I'm sure of it. Dad definitely doesn't know yet."

"What makes you so sure?"

"Because he's still speaking to me."

"Mom," Chloe shouted out from the top of the stairs. "I can't find any of my underwear. Please tell me you packed my underwear!"

Emily very much wanted to continue this conversation with her sister, but it would have to wait. She couldn't have Chloe going to the parade commando.

"You and I are going to talk about this later," she said, wagging a finger in front of Lilly's nose.

"Sure. Sure." Lilly giggled and pushed away Emily's hand. "In the meantime, go find that poor kid some underwear."

Chapter 8

The sky was robin's-egg blue with just a few wispy clouds playing a slow game of tag as Emily, Chloe, Gigi, and Lilly made their trek down Anishinaabe Trail toward Main Street. Squirrels chattered from the branches of the mammoth old oak trees lining the path, and ragtime music floated up from the outdoor stage at Trillium Park. It was a perfect day for the Lilac Festival, but then again, it always was. It was in the bylaws of the island board of tourism that the second weekend in June must always be sunny, dry, and pleasant. Today was no exception.

Chloe kept a running commentary, snapping selfies every few seconds and telling Lilly all about her life back in San Antonio and how the mean girls at school often teased her, calling her giraffe because of her height and long legs. Emily knew about these girls, and they were mean. She'd made more than one phone call to a mean girl's mom, but unfortunately, mean girls often get that way because they learn it at home. Emily had alienated an entire posse of mothers from her own neighborhood just for trying to stand up for her own kid. That kind of thing would never have flown on Wenniway Island. If one mom called another mom around here, somebody's kid was going to get punished.

"Don't let them get to you, sweetie," Lilly said. "They're just jealous because you're so pretty. I was in the pageant world, you know, and nothing brings out the worst in a person like jealousy."

Chloe skipped ahead a few steps and turned around to face them while walking backward, her red flip-flops slapping against the pavement. "Mom told me you were in a beauty pageant once. That sounds amazing. Was it fun?"

Lilly's smile was momentarily wistful. "A few parts of it were fun, but overall, I wasn't really cut out for it, plus the costumes and stuff were expensive. A bunch of people on the island chipped in so I could complete in the Miss Michigan Teen Starcatcher Pageant down in Lansing. That was pretty much a disaster."

"Why was it a disaster?" Chloe spun once more and fell back into step between Emily and Lilly.

"Wardrobe malfunction."

"What?"

Emily bit back a smile and turned her face so Lilly wouldn't notice.

"That's a bit of an understatement," Gigi said.

Emily knew this story, and Gigi was right. Wardrobe malfunction? It really was more of an epic wardrobe clusterfuck so grand in scale it was probably the sort of horror story pageant mothers told their little girls around the campfire just to scare them into compliance.

Chloe had been a baby at the time, and in spite of Nick's complaints, Emily splurged on an airline ticket from San Antonio to Lansing, taking back-to-back red-eyes so she wouldn't have to pay for a motel, and so she wouldn't be away a moment longer than necessary, but it was worth it just to be there.

Lilly had held up just fine during the swimsuit portion, managing to walk across a slippery stage in four-inch heels while keeping her face frozen in a Joker-esque smile, but during the evening gown segment, she'd accidentally stepped on the hem of her sparkly dress. Her sparkly *strapless* dress. She tripped gloriously and fell with a flourish, sliding toward the front of the stage like she was making a play for home plate. And when she sat up . . . her sparkly strapless dress didn't. She popped right out of it. And there were her two big boobs, right up in the judges' faces.

She didn't realize at first and just sat there giggling, but when she tried to stand up, she just got more and more tangled in the damn chiffon skirt, effectively pulling her dress down even farther. The more she struggled, the worse it got. Finally, the judge from Ypsilanti took off his tuxedo jacket and tossed it to her while trying to avert his eyes. The only saving grace was that the pageant wasn't televised, and it happened just before every person on the planet had a smartphone with a camera in it. If that happened today, the video would go viral faster than you could say, "Here she comes, Miss America."

"I tripped and fell," Lilly said. "I got up, and my dress didn't." Her voice was matter-of-fact, and Emily was incredibly proud of her sister's handling of the situation. Then and now. Emily would have been so mortified that no hole on earth would have been deep enough to hide in.

"Your dress fell off?" Chloe's gasp was appropriate to the occasion. "Seriously?"

"Well, not all the way off. Just the top part. So I guess it could have been worse, right? That's something to be glad about. I guess being voted Miss Lilac Festival during my senior year of high school was pretty much the pinnacle of my beauty queen career."

"Wow." Chloe shook her head and stared down at her toes as they continued walking in silence.

"So, after the parade, how long am I stuck in the pie tent?" Emily asked a moment later, hoping to lighten the mood once more. Public humiliation was never a fun topic. Familiar, but not fun.

"Only an hour or two," Lilly answered, swinging her pink sun hat by her side. "It's actually a pretty good gig. You'll be in the shade, you can hear the music, and everybody stops by to see you."

Oh, awesome. That was great. Word was certainly out by now that Emily was back on the island, and no doubt everyone *would* stop by and ask her the same three questions. When are you moving back to the island? Whatever happened to that guy you ran away with? And finally, did you know Reed was in town?

There was really no way to avoid any of it. At least this way she'd get it all over with in one day. Everyone could come and look at her and make their assessment, form their opinions, and then go whisper about her and her questionable life choices while stuffing their pieholes with actual pie. But hey, if Lilly could laugh off wiping out on a stage and ending up topless in front of a panel of judges, Emily could handle an afternoon full of pseudo-friendly interrogations. Maybe Mrs. Bostwick would stop by, and under the guise of handing her a pie, Emily could trip and nail her in the face. Now there was the silver lining.

"Lilacs aren't really my thing, Dad."

They really weren't, but so far Ryan had been entirely unsuccessful at dissuading his father from dragging him to this quaint, down-homey festival. Only the promise of there being a beer tent had finally convinced him to go along. That and the fact that Emily had said she'd be in the pie tent, which gave him a convenient excuse to find her and ask if she'd found out anything about the Bimbo. Even if she hadn't, well, again. Pie. And Emily.

He'd dreamed about her again last night, and try as he might, there was just no denying— something about Emily Chambers had sunk under his skin. Maybe it was her peaches-and-cream complexion or the way she playfully interacted with her daughter. Maybe it was the way she'd laughed and blushed when telling a story about herself in the cab. Or maybe it was something even less mysterious. Maybe it was simply that Emily Chambers had a great body, and he hadn't been on a date in a while. He'd been so busy working lately that the only women he encountered were coworkers, and he had a very strict no-fraternizing-with-the-employees rule. So that was probably it. He just had an itch that needed scratching. If that was the case, Emily wasn't a good choice. One did not mess around with the daughter of the chief of police, nor did one toy with the emotions of somebody's mother. She was both. Not to mention the fact that they were on a pretty small island, a place where, he gathered, nothing stayed secret for long.

Ryan and his dad rounded the corner at Beaumont and Main and headed into the thick crowd of tourist traffic, which today was human only. The road had been blocked off to wheeled and hoofed transportation. Tables draped with purple fabric were set up in front of many of the stores, displaying their crafts, and lavender banners flew overhead reminding everyone that it was the day of the Lilac Festival, as if anyone could forget that given that the blooms were everywhere and the scent, for once, overwhelmed the aroma of the fudge.

"Where's that beer tent?" Ryan asked, hoping to park himself there while his dad strolled around looking at homemade glass beads, vases made from gourds, homespun scarves, and a seemingly endless assortment of stuff shaped like an oven mitt. It took him a few minutes to make the connection. Ah, Michigan. He'd never really thought about the fact that the lower half of the state was shaped that way, but there was just no missing it now. He'd never take something hot out of the microwave again without remembering this trip.

"It's not even noon yet, Ry. Too early for beer, but there's lemonade over this way." Tag had that goofy, happy grin on his face again. Maybe the Bimbo was slipping antidepressants into his dad's coffee. Or . . . maybe it was the sex. Visions of Emily blazed into his mind again. Where was that pie tent? Maybe he should go see her right now. "Lemonade sounds good, Dad, but do you know what sounds even better? Pie."

Tag smiled in agreement, nodding his silver-haired head. "Now you're getting into the spirit of it. Let's go find you some pie."

A few minutes later they were standing under a bright yellow canopy filled with a couple dozen people, including some guy in a beekeeping hat. Down the center stretched three long tables covered with pies of every sort. Apple, blueberry, banana cream. The temptation was distracting, but then he spotted her. She was standing off to the side, laughing with Chloe and wearing a pale blue sundress covered with big, bold sunflowers, a completely different look than the white business suit he'd seen her in before. Her hair was loose and fell around her bare shoulders in waves, and the sweet, feminine simplicity of her appearance kicked him right in the gut and rolled lower.

Chloe saw him first and waved, and when Emily looked in his direction and her eyes lit up, his knees nearly buckled. What. The. Hell. What was wrong with him? He stood there, paralyzed like a fainting goat just because she smiled at him? The clerk at his hotel had told him that the ancient Ojibwa believed this island had magical properties. Looking at her and the way she glowed, he wondered if they weren't that far off base.

He cleared his throat and walked over to her, trying to act all nonchalant-ish, as if, you know, he was just there for the flaky crusts and the gooey filling. Tag was on his own. Ryan had some flirting to do.

"Hi, ladies," he said. "How goes the bake sale?"

"Good so far," Emily answered. "Do you see anything you like?"

He couldn't contain the smirk, and his eyes went immediately to Emily, who then offered up a *Mona Lisa* smile in response. His throat went dry even as his mouth started to water, and it wasn't from the pastries. He bit back the reply he wanted to give and said instead, "Um, what do you recommend?"

Chloe leaned toward him over the table as if to confide a secret. "Well, I can tell you that I don't recommend the mincemeat. Apparently it's really got meat in it, and fruit. Disgusting! Other than that, though, the rest look pretty good. And don't tell Gigi I said this, but rumor has it the Mahoney sisters make the best strawberry-rhubarb pie."

He looked to Emily. "How about you? Which one do you recommend?"

She was on the same side of the table as he was, standing a mere two feet away. Close enough that he could see a hint of cleavage above the neckline of that dress and smell her perfume. It smelled even better than pie, and he recognized it from that evening in the cab. It was also quite possible he'd dreamed about it, if dreams could have fragrance.

"I'm a bit of a traditionalist, I guess. I like apple," she answered.

He pointed at one with some crumbly topping and cocked an eyebrow. "You mean like this one? How about them apples?" Chloe groaned loudly, while Emily's smile was indulgent, as if she appreciated the gesture but found his skill at humor a bit lacking. He could hardly blame her. He cringed a bit inside at his own lame-assity. It was the sundress. The sundress had made him stupid.

"Just for that, you have to buy an entire pie," Chloe said, still shaking her head. "But we can have it delivered to your hotel. That way you don't have to carry it around."

He didn't know what he was going to do with an entire pie, but now he'd seem cheap if he didn't buy something. "That's a pretty good deal, I guess. I'll take a whole apple pie, then." He reached back with one arm to grab his wallet and turned slightly as he did so, catching sight of Tag on the other side of the tent . . . talking to the Bimbo.

"Holy shit, that's her!" His voice came out in a strangled whisper as he leaned toward Emily and tried to point discreetly.

"What?"

"That's her. That's the Gold-Digging Bimbo over there talking to my dad." His discreet pointing became a little more frenzied as Emily gazed in the direction he was indicating.

"Which one is your dad?" she asked, her whisper matching his, and her neck craning to see around the crowd.

"Right there, in the green golf shirt, talking to the Bimbo in the pink shorts."

There was a slight hesitation, and then Emily's gasp was loud in his ear.

"Hey! Wait a minute! That's not a bimbo! That's my sister!" Her voice carried like a Tibetan gong, bouncing and reverberating around the space, and everyone from the tent all the way up to the International Space Station froze in place to stare at her. Including Tag and the Bimbo.

Heat cascaded over Ryan as his eyes darted from his father, to the girl in the pink shorts, to Emily, and then back around again. "Your sister?" He had the good sense to keep his voice at a whisper. "You said you didn't know anyone named Daisy!"

"I don't, you moron. Her name is Lilly. And she is not a bimbo!" Her eyes flashed, but she managed to lower her voice again. Unfortunately for him, she also crossed her arms defensively, effectively pushing her breasts higher and deepening that cleavage, but he didn't have time to fully appreciate that right now because he sensed a bit of a shitstorm coming. The Bimbo's name was Lilly? Shit. Ryan was always lousy with names. He must have gotten his flowers mixed up, and when Tag had made introductions last night, Ryan was so damned distracted by her age he'd only been half listening.

"Well, whatever her name is, she was with my father last night. Did you know that?" The whisper burned in his throat.

Her forehead creased in a frown as she pulled him by the arm into the corner of the tent. "No, of course I didn't. I also didn't realize your father was a dirty old man, but I guess I should have figured that out this morning when you said he was involved with a twenty-five-year-old. She's twenty-six, by the way, but still, what the hell is he doing toying with my little baby sister?"

Ryan felt his surprise turn toward irritation. "My father is not a dirty old man. If anyone is toying with anyone, it's your sister toying with him. My father is a good man."

"Yeah, right. I'm sure his intentions are very *honorable*." She said honorable like the word was too big for her mouth.

Ryan tore his gaze from Emily and looked back over at the other two. Whatever the hell that girl's name was, her face had turned as hot pink as those incredibly short shorts, and a burgundy flush had crept over Tag's tan face, too. They both looked guilty as sin. Bystanders in the tent continued to observe, clearly wondering just what was happening in the Buy-Buy Miss American Pie tent. The guy in the beekeeping hat even raised the veil to get a better look.

"You have to be making a mistake. There's just no way," Emily whispered.

"I'm not making a mistake. I know that's her. The three of us had dinner together last night."

"Well, then your father is totally taking advantage of her. He should be ashamed of himself."

"Uh, excuse me. I think it's the other way around. She's taking him for a ride."

"Oh really? He's the president of some big company in California, and she's a girl who's never lived off the island. Who has the upper hand here? Your father is a dirty old lecher."

Ryan tried to keep his voice down, but what he really wanted to do was shout. Not his style, but given the circumstances it was understandable. "He's not a lecher! And if anyone is taking advantage here, it's her. She thinks he's her ticket off this island. She's using him."

As they bickered under their breath, the cluster of speculating tourists parted like the Red Sea and Ryan's dad crossed the small expanse of the tent to reach his side. Another millisecond later Emily's sister, oh my God, Emily's sister? She crossed over, too, until the four of them squared off, with Chloe having snuck in behind her mother.

"Lilly? Seriously?" Emily hissed, quiet but insistent. "This is the guy? Do you realize he's fifty-nine years old?"

"How do *you* know how old I am?" Tag asked, as if that was remotely important at the moment.

"I told her," Ryan said, trying to draw in a breath but feeling like his lungs were full of sludge. It was really hot under this tent all of a sudden.

The crowd started to murmur and move again, but the bystanders were doing a collectively piss-poor job of trying to act as if they weren't listening. The beekeeper had sidestepped a few feet closer, lowering his veil again as if it made him just a little stealthier.

"You told her how old I was? When?" Tag asked.

"At the airport. Or on the phone. I don't remember exactly, but this is the woman I shared a taxi with, and apparently she's your . . . *girlfriend's* sister." It was as awkward to say as it was to hear.

"Could we talk about this someplace else? Please?" The Bimbo looked over her shoulder at the interested crowd of bystanders. "Or better yet, talk about it later?"

"So this really is the guy?" Emily asked again.

"He's the guy," Ryan said tersely, "and she's the Bimbo."

"I'm not a bimbo!" That one was loud, too. For a couple of women trying to keep a secret, Emily and her sister sure weren't very discreet with their exclamations. People were starting to pull out their phones to snap pictures. If Trillium Bay had a gazette, this would surely be front page, above the fold. Meanwhile, his dad had the stones to look at him with a stern, fatherly expression. "Ryan, Lilly is not a bimbo, and I didn't raise you to insult women that way. You need to apologize."

He tried to wrap his head around the irony of that. "Really, Dad? You're going to lecture me about respecting women right now? I'm not the one who jumped into bed with a twenty-five-year-old."

"I'm twenty-six," the girl said, as if that made all the difference.

"Eww, Aunt Lilly!" Chloe gasped. "You were in a bed with him? He's like a grandpa."

Shit, Ryan had forgotten Chloe was there. Now he did feel like an asshole, and maybe he felt a little bit bad about calling Emily's sister a bimbo, too. It hadn't felt like such an insult back when he didn't know anything about her. Now he did.

"I'm sorry, Chloe. I forgot you were there. And . . . Lilly, I didn't mean to call you a gold-digging bimbo."

"A what?" she gasped. "A *gold-digging* bimbo?"

Shit. He'd let that one slip out. This was not his day.

"Yes, Lilly, Ryan and his brothers think you're after Tag's money." Emily arched an eyebrow and crossed her arms more tightly, adding to that cleavage. He wished she'd stop doing that. He could hardly claim the moral high ground about respecting women if he was staring at her breasts.

"After my money? What?" Tag glared at him. "She's not after my money, Ryan. That's ridiculous. Now you owe her two apologies. And you owe me one, too."

What? How the hell was he ending up as the bad guy in this scenario? He was only trying to help. Only trying to protect his dad and the company. Ryan could usually think pretty fast on his feet, but this situation had him at a complete loss. What was the protocol here? The beekeeper sidestepped closer still, holding a pie in front of his chest like a cartoon character trying to hide behind a too-small decoy.

"Chloe," Emily said, staring at said beekeeper. "How about if you take Mr. Krushnic to that cash register over on the other side of the tent and let him pay for that pie he's manhandling."

"But this is more interesting," Chloe said, earning her a hard stare from her mother.

"Oh okay, fine. Come on, Mr. Krushnic. We've been shunned."

Emily pointed at her daughter's retreating form, and the beekeeper's shoulders drooped as he turned to follow.

"You guys need to leave," Lilly said quietly, staring over at Tag. "Please. We'll talk later, but we can't stand here. Everyone is trying to eavesdrop."

Tag started to reach toward her but dropped his hand before actually touching her. "Are you sure? I don't want to toss you to the wolves. I don't need to keep this a secret if you don't."

"I do need to keep this a secret. I mean, at least until I've had a chance to talk to my dad."

"Oh my gosh," Emily said. "Dad is going to have a coronary, Lilly. Holy shit. Do you realize this guy is the same age as him?"

"Shhhhh! Keep your voice down and listen to me. Tag and I have a right to some privacy, so please respect that. And you two"—she tossed a glance at the men—"you both need to get out of this tent."

Ryan could not agree more. He needed to get out of this tent and find the damn beer tent. Maybe there was even a whiskey tent someplace? That would be even better.

What. The. Hell.

"That was completely uncalled for, Ryan," his father said as they strode from the tent. "Lilly doesn't deserve that, and if you think she's just after my money, well, then you've insulted me as well."

Ryan stopped walking and turned to face his father. "I'm not trying to insult anyone here, Dad, but that girl is half your age. Less than that, even, and I'm worried that you're not thinking straight."

"Why? Because I'm enjoying the company of a beautiful young woman?"

"Because you're talking about quitting your job and moving across the country for some woman you hardly know. A woman who is younger than I am. How do you think this . . . this *relationship* is going to play out?" He called it a relationship for his father's sake, but it still seemed like too substantial a word to assign to this midlife crisis masquerading as a love affair.

His dad was flushed, his face stern. "I don't know, Ryan. I don't know if it's going to last a month, or a year, or a decade. I'm not really thinking that far out. What I do know is that I feel alive again. Lilly is sweet and funny, and she makes me feel happy. We're having fun. I've earned that. If I learned anything from losing your mother it's that fun, just for the sake of fun, is a worthwhile thing. Work is important, too, but it shouldn't come at the expense of enjoying life. Fifty-nine is not that early to retire, you know. And it's not as if I'm letting the company fold. I'm leaving it to you boys. You three are more than capable of running the show, so how about you get off my back, huh? How about you mind your business and leave me alone."

Tag turned on his heel and stomped off toward Market Street, and Ryan watched him go, his mouth opening to say . . . something. But what? What could he say that his father didn't already know?

He stood there a moment, letting tourists flow around him like water encountering a rock in the center of a stream. He needed to think, because what this situation called for was some good old-fashioned mulling, and nothing helped with mulling like a cold beverage. Time to go find that beer tent. He had definitely earned himself a drink.

Chapter 9

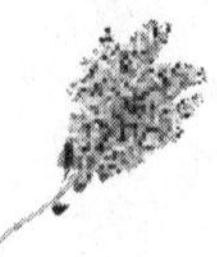

Sunday morning church services on Wenniway Island were roughly one part spiritual rejuvenation and five parts catching up with the neighbors. Not that they all didn't keep pretty close tabs during the week, but during the summer months everyone was busy dealing with the tourists and their normal socializing time was reduced. Still, they weren't so out of touch that everyone didn't know who would be late, who would be a little hungover, who would sit in front and sing the loudest, and who would make a big show of putting money into the donation basket.

"Oh, you see those diabolical Mahoney sisters, sitting there and thinking they are all that and a bag of chips," Gigi muttered as she, Chloe, and Emily made their way into Saint Bartholomew's and took their place in the fifth row back, on the right. It was the same place Gigi had sat for the past seventy-five years. It was the same place her father had sat when he was little, and the same place her grandparents had sat. Gigi was willing enough to move from house to house when she got married, but no matter what her life circumstances were, that was her spot in church. Fifth row back, on the right. Woe be it to the poor, unsuspecting island visitor who accidentally sat there. She was not above shooing away a total stranger with her black patent-leather handbag.

"That June Mahoney," Gigi added, "she says they have plans for those rental cottages of theirs over on Crooked Tree Trail and that I'll be downright flabbergasted when I see what they're up to. As if anything those old hags could do would knock my stockings off. I don't care what they do. I'm not going to let them lure away my renters, and I told her as much. I told her, I said, 'June, you mind your own business, and don't you know I have my granddaughter working on the place my second husband left me? And it's going to be fabulous.' She thinks she can scare me, but she can't."

Emily was only half listening to Gigi's monologue. On an island full of Irish, holding a grudge was an Olympic sport, and the feud between the Mahoneys and the Callaghans was intricately woven through the tapestry of Trillium Bay history dating all the way back to the eighteen hundreds. There were arguments, of course, about who started it and how and why, and every now and then it would flare up, then eventually fade into the background again. The last significant event occurred nearly thirty years ago when old Dewey Mahoney chopped down a one-hundred-year-old fifty-foot pine tree because it obstructed his view of Lake Huron. He didn't seem to notice, or care, that the tree was smack-dab in the center of the Callaghan family's front yard. He apologized later, when he sobered up, but some questioned his sincerity when he paid off the $1,000 court-ordered restitution entirely with Canadian pennies.

Emily glanced over at the Mahoney sisters. They were staring back and whispering behind their hands. She couldn't be sure if they were gossiping about her, about what had happened in the pie tent yesterday, or spreading tales about some other poor, unsuspecting victim. Still, they never had seemed all that diabolical to her. They looked like harmless little old biddies. April, May, and June. Those were their names. They had a brother, too. August. He'd run off and joined the marines when his sweetheart left him for another. Then he'd come back home covered in so many explicit tattoos that June forbade him to ever go shirtless in public again. And Gus obeyed. Marine or not, he wasn't about to make his sisters angry. So, now that she thought about it, maybe looking harmless was just part of their diabolical disguise?

Three rows in front of them was old Bridget O'Malley. She'd been old for Emily's entire life and was currently closing in on 103. The old spinster had never been married. Maybe that's why she'd lasted so long. Gloria Persimmons sat down next to her, wearing a traffic-cone-orange dress. She helped Mrs. O'Malley take the songbook from the rack attached to the pew in front of them, and then she waved at Emily.

Emily waved back just as Brooke joined them. She had on a white dress covered in cherries, and red sandals to match. She even had on mascara, and Emily wondered what the special occasion was. This was church, sure, but Brooke never dressed up.

"Hi," Emily whispered. "You look cute."

Brooke blushed. "Thanks. So do you. Of course you do."

Harlan sat down on the other side of Gigi, his face so stoic this might have been a funeral. Then again, any face on Mount Rushmore was more apt to display emotion than Chief Callaghan, so when Lilly sat down next to him and he patted her arm, Emily knew for certain that the scandal had yet to break. Or at least he had yet to hear of it.

Yesterday, after Tag and Ryan had left the pie tent, Lilly excused herself. She'd come back twenty minutes later, looking moderately relieved. When Emily asked where she'd been, she said, "Damage control. I just gave Dmitri Krushnic twenty bucks for his silence. Let's hope I shouldn't have offered him fifty."

The sisters hadn't talked much after that, and the rest of the day had been full of Lilac Festival festivities. Emily was kept busy fielding questions about her own life, and love life, but no one said anything to her about Lilly's, and that was a relief. Still, there did seem to be a number of people in the congregation with their heads bent toward the person next to them, murmuring something into their ear. For once she found herself hoping they were talking about *her* instead of Lilly.

After Mass, everyone slowly ambled out to the front yard of the church where the Saint Bart's Ladies' Auxiliary always had sugar cookies and lemonade waiting. Harlan was usually accosted during this time by people with very important issues to discuss, such as when the new No Trespassing signs might be going up near the golf course because teenagers loved to drink on the greens after dark and then pee into the sand traps, and what to do about the trash that tourists left behind on the walking trails, and whether or not he'd need extra deputies on hand when Independence Day rolled around. Today was no exception, and he was quickly surrounded.

"So what are your plans for today?" Brooke asked Emily as they sipped lemonade while standing next to the statue of Antoine St. Antoine, a French fur trader who had established the first outpost on the island. He'd married an Ojibwa woman, and together they had sixteen children. That being the case, it really was Mrs. St. Antoine who deserved the commemorative statue.

"Gigi is taking me to see the cottage I'm renovating. What is Lilly doing over there?"

Lilly was off to the side, whispering to Chloe, who nodded slowly. Emily followed her daughter's gaze, and there was Ryan. Her heart gave a traitorous little skip. Sure, he'd called her sister a gold-digging bimbo, but damn, he did look good in a dress shirt. Had his shoulders been that broad yesterday? Probably, but they seemed even more broad today. Too bad he was officially the enemy. And too bad he was standing next to Tag. That was not good, but there they were, not looking the least bit sheepish or guilty. Not looking at all as if Tag was the type of man to get handsy with the chief's daughter. What was wrong with them, showing up here like this? Were they not in the pie tent yesterday? Did they not think keeping a low profile today might be a wise decision? Certainly a better decision than showing up at church. Then again, maybe Tag was here for confession and absolution. He'd better hurry, because the churchyard just wasn't that big, and Harlan was about fifteen feet away.

Dmitri strolled past, nodding at Emily with a knowing smile and a conspiratorial wink. Add that to the column of *not good.*

"Good morning, Peach. Brooke. Lovely day today, isn't it?" He carried his hat in his hand. If he had actually kept his mouth shut, it would be twenty bucks well spent, but Emily had her doubts.

"Good morning, Dmitri," the sisters said in unison. He kept on going, and Emily breathed a tiny sigh of relief, which was cut short as Chloe left Lilly's side, skipped right past the beekeeper, and walked right on up to Tag and Ryan. No, no, no. This could only end badly, but Lilly's face was calm. Mostly calm, although a muscle around her jaw seemed a little tense, and Emily realized that was what the whispering was about. Lilly had probably been reminding Chloe not to tell Harlan about Tag, which reminded Emily she needed to talk to Chloe about how it was never okay to keep secrets or tell lies . . . unless, of course, your twenty-six-year-old auntie was dating a man as old as your grandpa. In that case, lying wasn't just okay. It was essential. If Harlan Callaghan found out his baby daughter's boyfriend was a card-carrying AARP member, shit would fly, and wasn't nobody ready for that, especially not in the front yard of Saint Bartholomew's. A church was no place for full-frontal honesty.

Uncertain of what her role in this little drama was supposed to be, Emily just stayed to the side until Harlan approached the Taggerts, and then she quickly crossed the grassy expanse of lawn to join them, pulling Brooke with her.

"That's the guy I met at the airport. Let's go say hi."

They reached Tag and Ryan at the same moment their father did. Lilly came too, and so did Gigi. It wasn't very subtle, the entire Callaghan family descending on the two Taggert men all at once. Dmitri changed direction, sensing a showdown, and came to stand off to the side. Emily wanted to shoo him away like one of his bees, but that would just draw more attention.

Mrs. Bostwick turned toward April Mahoney and said something—something unflattering, no doubt—and Delores Crenshaw adjusted her glasses as she leaned forward and nodded. There was a good chance Emily was imagining this, but there seemed to be clusters of onlookers . . . looking on. Either because they were still fascinated by her long-overdue visit . . . or because twenty bucks did not buy silence like it used to. Dmitri put on his beekeeping hat and pulled down the veil.

"Gentlemen, I don't believe we've met. I'm Chief Callaghan. It looks as if you know my granddaughter." Everything Harlan said sounded like an accusation, but the men appeared unruffled.

Chloe smiled up at Harlan and batted her lashes. "Yes, Grandpa. This is Ryan. He's the one we rode in the taxi with because the plane was broken."

"Ah yes, Emily mentioned something about that. Not sure why you wouldn't have flown through Pellston, but I guess you'll know better for next time."

Ryan nodded and shook his hand. "Yes, sir. Thank you for that advice. This is my father, John Taggert."

Tag didn't flinch at all as he reached forward to shake Harlan's hand. Very smooth. "Good to meet you, Chief Callaghan."

"Good to meet you as well, Mr. Taggert."

"Please call me Tag."

Emily glanced toward Lilly, but her sister was wearing sunglasses and showed little expression.

Harlan clasped his hands behind his back and assumed a stance that Emily was all too familiar with. It was his *I'm going to size you up* stance, but both of the Mr. Taggerts seemed relaxed and unperturbed. Ryan reached up and ran a finger around the inside of his collar, though, and Emily saw his chest rise and fall with a deep breath. Tag flicked a tiny droplet of perspiration away from his temple. Hmm, maybe not so unperturbed after all.

"This is Aunt Brooke," Chloe said, moving on with introductions, just as casual as any hostess introducing dinner guests to each other. "And this is my mom, and Aunt Lilly, and Gigi. There. That's everybody."

There were so many ways this could go wrong, but everyone just smiled politely at one another, nodding. There were a few innocuous comments about the amazing pleasantness of the weather and how delightful the island was. Brooke seemed to pick up on a bit of the tension and crooked an eyebrow at Emily, but Harlan didn't appear to notice any of it. He didn't seem to notice all the parishioners giving them sideways glances, either. So much for crack police work, if he couldn't pick up on some fairly obvious body language.

Lilly's jaw clenched and unclenched, and then she gave a weak little smile to Emily once she realized Emily was not about to spill her beans. As if Emily would. Their father was not above killing the messenger, and Emily had no intention of telling him anything about anything. Lilly was on her own here.

"Harlan!" A big, booming voice came from the left side of the churchyard, and Emily recognized it immediately as Judge Murphy. He was a short, stocky man who, rumor had it, once ate an entire raw fish, bones and all, just because someone said he couldn't. "Harlan, I didn't see you in church this morning. Where were you?"

The chief stared down at him for a minute. "Brian, I've sat in the same spot in that church my entire life, and you're saying you didn't see me?"

"No, I looked right in that spot, and I couldn't see you. In fact, you're a mite blurry now, come to think of it."

"Do you think it's possible that you're wearing your wife's glasses again instead of your own?"

"Don't be ridiculous. Why, I never . . . wait a minute." He took off his glasses and looked at them. "Well, I'll be damned. No wonder Mary said she felt dizzy this morning. Poor woman probably can't see a thing. Anyway, we need to change our poker game from my house to your house on Thursday. The missus went and scheduled a book club that night, as if she didn't know it was my turn to host. As if my poker night hasn't been the third Thursday of the month for fifteen years. Anyway, can we play at your house?"

Harlan nodded. "I don't see why not."

"Excellent. Thanks." The judge squinted over at Tag and Ryan. "Forgive me. I don't seem to have my glasses. Do I know you?"

Dmitri sidled closer. He lifted his glass of lemonade to take a drink and fumbled with his veil. Emily might have laughed at him, but at the moment, he held their fate in his hands.

"John Taggert. This is my son Ryan."

"Brian Murphy." They all shook hands, and the judge squinted. "You fellas staying on the island for long?"

Tag nodded. "For the summer. Maybe longer."

Emily heard a little squeak come out of Lilly's throat and saw a smile tilting at the corners of her mouth before her sister quickly looked down at the ground.

"Longer, huh?" Judge Murphy's voice rang out louder than the church bell. "Well, in that case, do you play poker?"

"Yes, I do." Tag nodded.

Emily was fairly certain she heard Dmitri chuckle. That dude needed to mind his own . . . beeswax. Her breath went shallow, and Lilly leaned against her just the least little bit, still staring at the ground, her smile fading.

"Good," the judge said. "Never trust a man who doesn't gamble. That's what my daddy used to say. Anyhow, we play every Thursday, and you're welcome to join us. You don't mind if we add another old man to geezer-night poker, do you, Harlan?"

Another tiny noise from Lilly's throat, this one more of an *oh shit* kind of gasp.

"Not at all." Even if Harlan did mind, his face was as impassive as Stonehenge. Emily hoped hers was, too. She didn't even dare look at Ryan or Tag. Lilly's boyfriend playing poker with their father? Not good. Not good. Not good.

Chapter 10

"Oh, Gigi, this place is in much worse shape than I thought."

Sunday afternoon, Emily stood in the center of a Victorian cottage that had not been updated since before women had the right to vote. She'd remembered it as being much nicer. The exterior footprint was large enough, and at least the place had a wonderful, if somewhat dilapidated wraparound front porch, but inside the rooms were tiny and dark with tarnished brass light fixtures that would never pass today's inspection standards. The plumbing was questionably noisy, the kitchen seemed to have a slant that made all the cabinets hang open, and that moss growing on the roof was neither decorative nor harmless. She could practically hear it munching on the cedar shingles.

"I think this place has old-world charm. Like me," Gigi answered.

Emily sighed with resignation. "Sure, if by old world you mean cave-like dwelling. This place is primitive."

"Well, so was my second husband, and this place belonged to him. I've had college kids staying here for the past few summers, and they've done some damage, but I'm sure you can work a little magic and make it far better than any of those dumps the Mahoney sisters rent out. I want top-of-the-line everything, but don't go over budget," Gigi added. "And everything needs to be reliable. No cutting corners."

"That's pretty much what every person doing a remodel wants. I'll do my best, but keep in mind we'll need electricians and plumbers and general carpenters. Back home I had a crew I trusted, but here I'm going to have get quotes and references. Everything we order will have to be shipped from the mainland, and that won't be cheap. Plus, once we start taking down walls, there's just no telling what we'll find. This is going to be a huge project, Gigi."

Her grandmother patted her shoulder lightly. "I have complete and total faith in you, Peach. And the good news is, I've lined up a great crew of available men."

"You've hired a crew already?"

"Just some local fellas, but they're all strong and they work cheap."

"What's that smell?" Chloe asked, coming into the room from the kitchen. Her two thick braids bounced on her shoulders as she walked.

"Which smell?" said Gigi. "The sour smell or the dank, musky smell?"

"Um, the musky smell, I guess?" Chloe looked at Emily as if she'd know which odor was currently assaulting her daughter's nostrils.

"I think the musky smell may be a dead squirrel in the attic, but I'm not certain."

Chloe covered her head with her hands as if that dead squirrel might drop down on it at any second. "That's nasty, Gigi."

"Oh, if you want nasty, you should smell a dead possum. Of course, those things are nasty even when they're alive. Beadiest little eyes you ever did see. And long, spiky claws." Gigi squinted and curled her hands into her own version of spiky claws, pawing playfully at Chloe's head and making her giggle.

"Maybe one of the workmen you found for me is an exterminator?" Emily asked hopefully. "That would be handy. And how about a foreman? Is there a foreman in the bunch? Because I'd like to talk to him first."

Gigi took off her glasses and breathed on the lenses before wiping them with the edge of her striped shirt. "Tiny Kloosterman would be the best one for that job. He's the most responsible."

"Tiny Kloosterman?" That sounded familiar, but she couldn't quite place him.

"Don't let the name fool you. He's strong as an ox and nearly as big, plus his tether allows him to go anywhere on the island."

Emily had to let that one sink in for a second before she could respond. "His tether? Did you get me a chain gang to remodel this house?"

The glasses went back on as Gigi shrugged. "Of course not, but like I said, I have a tight budget to stick to. Tiny might have a little issue with authority figures. He didn't do so well in the military, but he loves to punch his fist through drywall, so he's sure to come in handy for tearing stuff down."

The military. Now she remembered him. He was from one of the newer families. Newer meaning his ancestors had moved to the island sometime after 1910. He'd gone off to enlist in the navy the moment he turned eighteen, so he'd been gone for most of Emily's childhood. Apparently he was back and in need of something to keep him out of trouble.

Emily began to perspire. The cottage was warm to begin with in spite of the breeze, but the enormity of what she was about to undertake was what really heated her up. This was the first remodel she'd ever done without Jewel. Without any crew that she had a relationship with. It was ten times more of a job than she was expecting, and her foreman was on a tether. The odds were stacked against her, but she was going to make this happen. No matter what.

"Gigi, I think I need to meet with Tiny before we officially hire him. I need somebody I can totally trust. Does he have any references?"

Gigi pursed her lips for a moment, thinking. She tapped an index finger against her chin, thinking some more. "I suppose his parole officer would be a good source of information. Or better yet, Judge Murphy. He's the one who tried Tiny's case, so he's got all the goods on him. Of course, I could also ask your second cousin, Father O'Reilly, but I think he has some confidentiality issues."

"Why is the carpet squishy?" Chloe picked up her foot and looked at the bottom of her sandal.

Gigi turned around. "No idea, but it's up to your mother to fix that now. Come on, let's go take a look on the second floor. You can see the Petoskey Bridge from the window. Wonderful view."

Each step creaked as they went up the wide stairs, and Emily mentally added that to the list of things she'd need to address. Her face got a little hotter, her breath a little more labored. All she was doing was standing there, but on the inside it felt as if she was running at top speed. Through an obstacle course full of rattlesnakes and scary clowns. She needed some air.

She pushed open the screen door and stepped onto the porch, half expecting her foot to go right through the wood. It didn't, thank goodness. She tentatively stomped her foot, then boldly jumped up and down a few times just to see what cracked or creaked or splintered. Her highly scientific testing strategy suggested the porch was sturdy enough, in spite of its appearance. With any luck, it just needed some powerwashing and a fresh coat of paint.

She stepped over to the railing and knew one thing was for certain—the view from here could simply not be beat. The cottage sat on a low hillside near Anishinaabe Trail, and from this spot, Emily could see an abundance of gorgeous old trees on the property just down the slope. Through a small clearing she could just barely see the rooftop of old Bridget O'Malley's little pink house, but past that was an unparalleled view of Lake Huron and the Petoskey Bridge. With the sun high in the sky, the water glittered gold and the breeze smelled like fresh heaven. This was what this cottage was all about. This was its best feature, the view, and that's what Emily needed to play up.

Her mind started processing. Bringing the place into the twenty-first century was her number one priority, but keeping the historic

Victorian charm was essential, too. Nearly all the summer homes and cottages of Trillium Bay were Victorian, with lots of lacy woodwork, gables with high-pitched roofs, and intricate color palettes. The town library should have some old photographs so she could see what color this place used to be, because right now it was sort of moldy green with mildew accents. Not very appealing. No wonder Gigi was losing her renters.

Now she wanted Emily to turn this place into an upscale one-family unit instead of the summer-worker flophouse it had become. That was a tall order, but Emily owed her. Not just because of the loan, but because Gigi had confidence in her. Gigi believed she could do it, and quite frankly, Emily needed this victory, because doing a spectacular job on this renovation would show her family she was reliable and responsible. She *could* do great work, and she *was* a successful businesswoman, in spite of her recent turn of fortune. A lot was riding on this flip. It wasn't just about the house. It was about her reputation and her pride. No, not her pride. Her *worth.*

"So, let me get this straight," Bryce said to Ryan over the phone. "Our dad is supposed to play poker with her dad? Our dad. And her dad. That's . . . I don't even know what that is. What the hell is he even supposed to say?"

"I have no idea." Ryan shook his head and stared out from the balcony of his hotel room at the setting sun. "All I know for sure is that her father is the damn chief of police for the entire island, with access to weapons and jail cells. He could probably make our dad disappear. You know, maybe toss him off the Petoskey Bridge in the middle of the night? And then be in charge of the damn investigation! That's what I would do if I were him and she were my daughter."

"Nice loyalty, bro." Sounds of chaos echoed over the phone. Someone was yelling, and someone was crying. A typical Sunday evening for Bryce, wife number three, and their two children.

"I'm loyal, Bryce. I didn't say I was going to throw Dad off the bridge. I only said that if I was Harlan, I'd throw him off the bridge. Totally different."

The crime rate for Trillium Bay had to be so low as to be nonexistent, but Harlan Callaghan did not look like a friendly, easygoing kind of guy. It seemed entirely plausible that tossing a man off of Petoskey Bridge would seem to him like an entirely plausible solution.

"You have to go, too," his brother said. "To the poker game. You can't let Dad go alone. You know how ethical and honest he is. Can't you just hear it now? 'Hey, Tag, I raise you twenty.' 'Oh okay, Chief, I'll call you, and oh, by the way, I'd like to call your daughter, too.' What the fuck?"

"I know. I know. Listen, I'll see if I can go, but it's only for the old guys." Ryan rubbed his forehead, hard, as if wishing he could push some good ideas into his mind. It kind of worked. "You know, maybe this isn't a bad thing. I mean, if Tag comes clean to her dad, that could be the end of things right there."

"Uh . . . because he throws Dad off the bridge?"

"No, because Harlan is sure to be entirely against it. Tag won't keep seeing her without her father's approval. Would he?"

"Her father's approval? I understand the entire island is historical, but you do realize you have not actually traveled back in time, right? I don't think he needs her father's permission for what he's doing."

Ryan couldn't help but chuckle at that. "I'm just grasping at straws here."

"Do you need reinforcements? Do I need to send Jack out there?" More yelling and crying in the background. Ryan loved Bryce's kids, but they were chronically loud.

"No, not yet. I think the bimbo's sister may be my wingman on this. She's every bit as against this thing as we are."

"How do you know that?"

"Because she's the woman I met at the airport. I don't think she currently likes me very much since I called her sister a gold-digging bimbo, but like me or not, she and I are now on the same team."

"What team is that?"

"Whatever team that can get Dad to come to his senses and come home."

Chapter 11

Joe's Cuppa Joe Coffee Shop was buzzing with people trying to get their Monday morning caffeine fix as Emily made her way toward the counter, past hipsters with their laptops and earbuds, a gaggle of moms with chubby babies stuffed into ergonomic front-carriers, and even April, May, and June, the diabolical Mahoney sisters. They were sitting in a booth with Olivia Bostwick, casting spells, no doubt. Sunlight poured in through an abundance of oversized windows and bounced off of the polished brass fixtures, while outside on the patio several other customers sat at the collection of wooden tables, enjoying the view of the water while sipping five-dollar lattes.

"Just a regular coffee, please," Emily said to the freckled, bespectacled cashier behind the register. The girl blinked at her slowly and pushed her dark-framed glasses against the bridge of her nose with one thumb. "What kind of regular coffee?"

"Um, just . . . black coffee."

"We have fudge frenzy, milli-vanilla, fofana-banana, or blueberry bonanza. Those all come in regular."

This made Emily's head hurt. It was simply unfair to offer so many options of coffee to a woman who had not yet had her coffee, especially when she'd barely slept at all last night. Her mind had been a pinball machine with ideas for the cottage bouncing off one obstacle after another. So many details and so many things that could go wrong. It was overwhelming, but she was meeting her crew tomorrow, and she'd need a decent plan for them to follow. Currently, her best plan was to get herself some damn plain coffee.

"Do you have any that's just, oh I don't know, coffee flavored? Like, French roast or medium blend or something?"

The girl turned around to look at the list of coffees written on the blackboard behind her. Sort of like she had no idea. Which seemed quite likely.

"See?" Emily said, pointing over the cashier's shoulder. "There on the bottom left it says regular coffee."

"Huh. I've never had anyone order that before." She shrugged and turned back to the register. "That'll be a dollar fifty."

"I've got it." Ryan's voice breezed past Emily's ear, and she turned to see him standing right behind her. His nose was a little sunburned, which was cute. Which was therefore aggravating. She didn't want to think Ryan Taggert was cute. She'd made a point of not speaking to him at church yesterday, just so he'd know she didn't think he was cute. But he was. And she did. His sunglasses hung from the neckline of his light blue T-shirt, which was also cute, and kind of stupidly sexy for no logical reason whatsoever. Twinges and ripples and flutters filled her body, also for no logical reason, other than the fact that he was just . . . sexy. But he'd called her sister a gold-digging bimbo, and in spite of all the nicey-nice chatter the rest of them had fumbled through during that charade at church yesterday, he was not someone she wanted to be . . . rippling and fluttering over.

"I can pay for my own coffee. I know how precious your money is to you Taggerts."

He grimaced. "I got this, Emily." He handed the girl a ten-dollar bill. "Make that two regular coffees, please."

The cashier shrugged again and shook her head, as if wondering what was to become of the world if everyone started getting unflavored, un-chemically enhanced coffee with no milk, foam, or sprinkles. "Suit yourselves."

"Do you have a few minutes? I was hoping we could talk," Ryan asked as they walked to the other end of the counter to collect their drinks.

She tapped her foot on the floor. He was doing the soulful eye thing, the bastard. "Sure. I have a little bit of time."

He smiled, and she fluttered inside. Damn it.

They walked outside and sat in some white plastic chairs at a table in the shade of an enormous oak tree. It was another gorgeous day on the island, compliments of the chamber of commerce mandate.

"So how did you happen to find me here? Just lucky?" Emily took the top off of her coffee and blew on it.

"I texted my dad who texted Lilly who texted Chloe, and Chloe said that you were here."

"Sounds like you were determined." That felt sort of nice, but she wasn't going to let him off that easy. "I hope you plan to apologize for insulting my sister."

"Now you've gone and spoiled the surprise." Wistful smile. Damn him. "Yes, I do want to apologize. I should not have called your sister a gold-digging bimbo. At least . . . not to her face." Ryan chuckled, and Emily felt herself doing the same, in spite of herself.

"That's a terrible apology."

"Well, I've never given one before, so I haven't had much practice," he teased. "And now maybe you'd like a chance to take back what you said about my father?"

Emily straightened in her chair. "Why would I take that back? He's got no business hitting on my sister."

Ryan cleared his throat. "Your sister is a grown woman, Emily. Barely, I'll admit that, but old enough to make her own decisions. It's not like he lured her into some kind of trap. He didn't get her drunk or offer her candy. She asked him to dance."

Emily swallowed a mouthful of too-hot coffee, and it burned all the way down her esophagus. "She asked him to dance?"

"Yes, at some square dancing thing at the church. She told you that's where they met, right?"

"No, she hasn't been very forthcoming with the details, and we've been surrounded by family ever since the whole pie tent debacle. What was that at church, by the way? Was that planned?"

"Apparently, but I was as much a pawn in that as you were. My dad didn't tell me until we were walking back to his place that Lilly wants her dad to get to know him before she tells him the truth."

"That's a terrible plan. My dad's going to be livid."

Ryan nodded. "Everything about this smacks of *terrible plan*, but that's how your sister wants to play it. My dad is willing to try it her way, although he did tell me he'd much rather just face Harlan, man to man."

"I'm not sure that would be much better." There really was no good way to break that kind of news to Harlan. "So, they met at a square dance? I guess maybe your dad misunderstood the meaning of the term *hoedown*."

She earned a chuckle from Ryan for that one. "Very funny. You just called your sister a ho. See how easy it is?" He gazed at her from over the rim of his cup.

"Oh, you're very funny. So, my sister asked your father to dance, but that doesn't mean he had any right to, you know, practice all his suave and debonair moves on her."

Ryan burst out laughing, leaning back in his chair. His T-shirt rode up a little around the waistband of his shorts and she caught a glimpse of flat, tan abdomen, and suddenly she didn't need coffee. She needed smelling salts. Girlfriend was about to swoon. Good heavens, Emily needed to go on a few dates. Obviously it had been far too long if a tiny glimpse of happy trail had her so hot and bothered. She'd add that to her list of things to do when she got home. *Get laid.*

"Why is that so funny?" she said to Ryan, sounding a little more irritable than she'd intended.

He kept laughing. "Because you make it sound like he's got some great game, Emily, but trust me. My dad has no game. Zero gameage. He was married to my mother for forty years, and I've never seen him so much as flirt with a secretary or a waitress. So this whole image you have of him being some kind of dirty-dog playboy is absurd. Why do you think my brothers and I were so convinced that some woman must be conning him? It's because he's so clueless."

"He may be clueless by California standards, but this is Trillium Bay, and other than four years of college in Northern Michigan, my sister has not had much life experience. Seriously, Ryan. Just by virtue of being from someplace outside of this state makes him like a celebrity to her."

He observed her for a moment. "Well, that sort of supports my theory that she thinks he's her ticket out of here, doesn't it?"

Emily pressed her lips together. Ryan might be onto something, but she wasn't ready to admit to it. "Okay, look, there might be a hint of possibility to that, but it's not because my sister is some kind of gold digger. She would never hook up with some guy just so he'd take her on a few nice vacations. She must genuinely like him, for whatever reason, although I'm sure I can't imagine what that is." She could not resist adding that last dig.

He took a slow sip of coffee, still staring at her in a rather unnerving fashion.

"I'll concede that after having met your sister, I don't think she seems like the type of person to take advantage of someone else. She doesn't seem conniving," Ryan said.

Emily leaned forward and folded her arms on the table. "She's not remotely conniving. If anything, she's gullible. That's why I'm so worried about her. I feel like your dad is going to break her heart."

"Or she'll break his. When she decides she doesn't want someone his age, she'll dump him, and I don't think I can stand to see him grieving again. My mother died about eight months ago, and he had a hard time coping after that. Now he's done a complete one-eighty, and at some point, he's going to realize she isn't what he really needs. No offense to your sister, but either way, they both get hurt."

"So what do we do about it? Just . . . let them have at it and pick up the pieces later?"

"Probably. I guess. I think the harder we push them to break up, the more united they're going to be in staying together, but maybe we can, you know, nudge that inevitable breakup to happen sooner rather than later. Before they get even more emotionally involved?"

She sipped her own perfectly plain black coffee. "How do we do that?"

"That is the big question, isn't it?" He stared out at the bay for a moment. "I guess we need to just keep steering them toward their obvious incompatibilities until they come to the conclusion on their own. And maybe we should try to create some negative associations."

"Negative associations?"

"Yeah. They have all these positive associations with each other because they're having fun, but if they do some stuff and don't enjoy it, maybe it'll help them start to be a little more objective about each other."

"I'm not sure I follow."

He leaned forward, putting his arms on the table just as she had. Those were some nice arms he had. Flutter, flutter, flutter. Damn it.

"Okay," he said. "Let's say you go to a movie and eat all your favorite candy. That will make you like the movie more because your brain links it to pleasure you get from the candy. But if you ate brussels sprouts, you'd enjoy the movie less. And if you ate brussels sprouts every time you saw a movie, eventually you'd be convinced that you don't like movies. It's a positive association versus a negative association. We need to create negative associations between my dad and your sister."

"You sound like a psychologist. Is that your background?"

"Nope." He smiled. "But I watched a TED Talk once, so now I'm an expert. 'Train Your Brain in Three Easy Steps,' or something like that. It makes sense, though, right?"

"Sort of. So you're suggesting we try to stop them from having fun? How do we do that?"

Ryan tapped his fingers together, as if it helped him concentrate. "Does your sister golf? My dad is horrible to golf with. It's the only thing that makes him lose his temper."

"My sister loves to golf."

"Hmm. It might be worth a shot, but they might have fun. I know"—he snapped his fingers—"maybe we could get them to go horseback riding. My dad hates horses. He got kicked once when he was little, and he's just sure it's going to happen again. He'd be miserable for sure. If we could arrange for the four of us to go together, you and I could help each other out in making sure they, you know, didn't have fun."

"You would make your dad go horseback riding knowing he won't like it?"

Ryan nodded sadly. "Tough love time."

Emily pondered this for a moment. She didn't like the idea of manipulating her sister, but she also didn't like the idea of Lilly falling deeper into a doomed relationship. She knew from firsthand experience how much that sucked. She had been in Lilly's spot, falling for a guy who wanted to whisk her away from the only home she'd ever known. Promising her a life of fun and excitement, when the reality was anything but. She knew how it felt to be rejected by someone else's family, and the pain of dealing with the consequences of Harlan's disappointment.

"Create negative associations," she said, almost to herself. "It sounds pretty far-fetched, but I guess it's worth a try. Of course, the other option is for me to tell my dad the truth, and then he'll get his police rifle and shoot Tag right in the groin. Problem solved."

Ryan's eyebrows rose in surprise. "Um, let's leave that as plan B for now, shall we?"

Emily smiled. "I guess. If you say so."

~

She was wearing a snug, faded gray T-shirt with a cartoonlike picture of a hammer about to strike a nail. Stretched right across her breasts were the words *Nailed It!* Quite frankly, Ryan didn't think it was fair that faded jeans and an old T-shirt could be so sexy on a woman. It didn't seem fair that her hair was every bit as shiny in the sunlight as he'd expected it to be, either. She had it pulled up in a ponytail that swung back and forth every time she moved. It was adorable, and the very fact that she seemed to be utterly unaware of her God-given adorableness made her twice as adorable. So how was he supposed to concentrate on the problem with his father and her sister when Emily was sitting there looking so . . . you know. Adorable? And the real kicker was, he couldn't do anything about it. Emily Chambers was off-limits. She was obviously not a hit-and-run kind of woman, and since that was all he'd really have time for, it just wasn't going to happen.

This made him irritable. It made him twitchy. It made him want to empty his pockets of any electronic devices and take a walk right into the cold water of Lake Huron. He'd just have to settle for a cold shower back in his hotel room.

"Well, hello, Peach." Ryan heard a voice that sounded as if it came from deep within a rusty tin can—nasal and hollow, and not very pleasant. "I missed you at the lecture the other night. Remember? The one about the island's bat population? Hmm?"

Ryan looked up at a rather severe-faced woman with straight gray hair that hung nearly to her waist. Her skin was red and splotchy with pores large enough to sink a golf ball into, and she wore a navy cardigan sweater even though it had to be eighty degrees outside.

She squinted in the sunlight, giving her a very vicious expression, although Ryan suspected that was the expression she went around with most of the time anyway. He was so distracted by her appearance that it took him a second to register the fact that the woman had called Emily *Peach*.

Emily turned in her chair and offered up a tight smile. “Good morning, Mrs. VonMeisterburger. I’m sorry Chloe and I couldn’t make the meeting. We were still getting settled in at Gigi’s.”

“Well, be that as it may, white-nose syndrome is no laughing matter, and it’s up to each of us to do our part to reintroduce our nocturnal winged friends back to Wenniway. You know we need our bat population to take care of the flying insects. If your sister is serious about running for mayor, she needs to make sure this crisis is at the top of her political platform. We librarians are not a force to be ignored.”

Emily nodded somberly. “Yes, Mrs. VonMeisterburger, I’m sure of that. I’ll definitely pass your concerns on to Brooke.”

“If we wait too long, the mosquitoes will be so voracious they’ll drive away the tourists, and she’ll end up being mayor to a ghost town. You tell her I said so. And you tell her if she’s interested in my vote, she should come over to my house to see my bat cave.”

Ryan felt himself squinting just as squintily as Mrs. VonMeister-whatever.

“Your . . . your bat cave?” Emily responded.

“Yes, I’m quite proud of it. I put those visiting Boy Scouts to good use building bat houses, and now I’ve got dozens and dozens of them lining the walls of my tool shed.” She ran a hand down her long, witchy hair. “Bat houses, I mean. Not Boy Scouts. I don’t have any Boy Scouts in my shed.” She looked around, and Ryan couldn’t help but wonder if anyone might indeed be missing a Boy Scout. “I’ve applied for a grant to reimburse me for my efforts, of course, but since those Lansing bureaucrats in the Department of Fish and Wildlife can’t seem to get their guano together, I guess I’m on my own. But you’re not on your own right now, are you? Hmm?”

Her head practically swiveled, and her laser-beam stare honed in on Ryan, thoroughly scrutinizing him. He'd felt less violated after a TSA strip search.

"Hello," she said, and her voice went from nails-on-the-chalkboard to 1-800-SEXPOT. "Who might you be?"

Emily filled in the answer. "Mrs. VonMeisterburger, this is Ryan. He's just visiting for a few weeks. We're, um, discussing some business."

Ryan nodded but kept silent.

"Business, huh? Monkey business, I'd say. Hmm?" She threw back her head and laughed, and it was quite possibly the eeriest thing Ryan had ever seen.

"No, ma'am," Emily answered, quelling the woman's cackle. "Actual business. Ryan is a consultant." She looked at him and nodded, clearly hoping he'd pick it up from there.

"Ah, a *consultant.*" The librarian made air quotes around the word. He wasn't sure why. She stuffed a hand deep into the purple canvas tote bag that dangled from her arm and pulled out a pink leaflet. "Well, anyway, we're having another meeting next Thursday. I expect to see you there, Peach. Bring your sister, and bring this fine fellow, too." She fluttered her short, pale lashes at him. He would have thought she just had something in her eye were it not for the waggling of her eyebrows.

"I'll certainly try, Mrs. VonMeisterburger."

"Excellent. Carry on your business, now, and if you see any mosquitoes you know it isn't because I haven't done my part."

The woman turned and ambled away, and Ryan let out a breath he hadn't realized he was holding. "Nice lady," he said, his tone implying just the opposite.

"She's a pest, but don't get on her bad side. Our family dog ate a library book once, and she banned my sister from the library for three months. It was wintertime, and Brooke cried and cried, but that old coot wouldn't give in."

"Brooke? That's the sister running for mayor, right?"

Emily nodded and took a sip of coffee. "She's thinking about it, and once she latches on to an idea there is really no stopping her, so she'll probably win."

"So you'd be sister of the mayor. Does that come with any perks?"

She shook her head, and the ponytail went sway, sway, sway. "None whatsoever. It would probably lead to more encounters like the one we just had with the bat-shit crazy librarian. You know, people coming to me to get favors from Brooke? Although, I won't be here, so I guess it wouldn't matter."

"Heading back to San Antonio, I take it? More house flipping?"

"That's the plan."

Something about the way she said that made her sound *indefinite*, and he wanted to ask her more about that, but something about the *way* she said it also made her sound like she didn't want to talk about it, so instead he said, "Why did she call you Peach?"

Emily covered her face with both hands and groaned. "Please don't ask me that. It's not a story I like to tell."

"Tell me anyway." Now he simply had to know.

Her sigh was a great big huff, but a smile played at the corner of her lips. "Fine, but only because you bought me coffee. When I was a baby, I had a really round head and kind of short, fuzzy, orangey hair . . . and everyone always said my head looked like a peach, and it stuck."

She rolled her eyes, but her smile was full now, and he couldn't help laughing.

"Even my family calls me Peach half the time. I don't even notice it anymore."

More adorableness. So much so he couldn't resist saying, "That is totally adorable." And so was the blush that suddenly rushed across her cheeks.

"If you say so."

Chapter 12

"I'm telling you, wearing a white suit to a work site is just asking for disaster," Gigi said as they walked down the hill toward the cottage. It was 7:00 a.m. Tuesday morning, and Emily was about to meet her crew. She was practically nauseous about it. Back in San Antonio, she and Jewel had established a rapport with several dependable subcontractors. Most of them Emily knew from her time as a secretary at a construction company. So she knew who they could trust, who was going to underbid a job and then overbill, and who was going to show up when they promised, but Emily had none of that to fall back on here. She was flying solo. The pressure to succeed was mounting, and she hadn't even started yet!

"I have to establish myself as the boss, Gigi," Emily said, "or they'll never take me seriously. Trust me. Jewel and I have worked with enough men in this business to know that you have to set the ground rules right up front. I won't have them talking down to me like I'm some dumb girl who doesn't know a monkey wrench from an Allen wrench."

"*Do* you know the difference between a monkey wrench and an Allen wrench?" Gigi asked.

"Yes. I do. I also know what a cotter pin is, and how to use a drill, and in a pinch, I can use a table saw except they scare the hell out of me. The point is, Gigi, these guys need to believe in me, otherwise they'll take advantage, so don't talk to me in front of them like I'm your sweet little granddaughter. Let's make them think I'm a real ballbuster."

Gigi shook her head slowly. "If you want them to take you seriously, you should wear some jeans and a T-shirt. Show them you're not afraid to roll up those sleeves and do some of the work, too."

"I'll do that tomorrow. Today, I'm the boss. I'm wearing this suit like a boss, too." She smoothed down the front of her jacket. Gigi *tsk, tsk, tsked,* but Emily ignored her. She was nervous enough without her grandmother making it worse.

They approached the cottage from the left, and Emily nearly stumbled on the rocky driveway. Even if her suit was a good idea, maybe the heels were not. It wasn't so much the uneven pathway that caused her wobbling footsteps, though. It was the cluster of miscreants standing on the front porch. That was her crew? Good Lord, Gigi must have found them on the Island of Misfit Toys.

"There they are!" Gigi exclaimed, waving excitedly. Then she cupped her hands to holler, "Hiya, Tiny. Looking good!"

"Feeling good, Miss O'Reilly," bellowed back the multi-tattooed, talking mountain leaning against the front post. He raised one beefy hand in salute, revealing that some of those tattoos went all the way around his arm.

"Miss O'Reilly?" Emily whispered, trying to plaster a smile on her face when what she really wanted to do was turn around and run in the other direction.

"Yes, Miss O'Reilly. You know I like to go back to my maiden name in between husbands. It makes me more marketable. That's Tiny there, in the red shirt."

That's certainly what Emily would have guessed. Tiny was six and a half feet tall, minimum, and wore a tattered Red Wings T-shirt with the sleeves cut off. Calling him Tiny put the *ox* in *oxymoron*. Next to him was a reed-thin wisp of a man with dirty-blond hair. Wide, rainbow-striped suspenders held up his pants, and Emily was glad for that because if those trousers of his fell down, well, she did not want to get a look at anything going on under there. Sitting on the step was a stocky man with jet-black hair woven into a braid who Emily recognized from childhood. That was Wyatt Greenwell, and next to him was a . . . wow. A young man, probably twenty-five or so, with shoulder-length wavy brown hair who would look right at home on the cover of a historical romance novel. She could feel the pheromones just pouring out of him. Shoulders and muscles and dimples, oh my! Sexual harassment was never, ever okay . . . but if she were to ever consider hitting on an employee, it would be him. She couldn't, though, of course. Maybe she could steer him toward Lilly, though. He was age-appropriate, and really, someone needed to get a piece of that.

As Emily and Gigi reached the steps, Wyatt and the Adonis stood up, and another man, who'd apparently been lying down on the porch, lifted one hand to shield his eyes from the sun.

"What's going on?" he asked, his voice rough and scratchy.

"Get up, Georgie. Boss lady is here," Tiny said.

The prone figure rose and shuffled to the edge of the porch. Wearing baggy overalls and a white tank top, Georgie was slender, with blondish hair nearly shaved on the sides but long on the top and pulled into a ponytail. "Goddamn cramps are frickin' killin' me."

Oh? Well, okay. Georgie was not so much one of the guys as she was completely and totally a woman. Emily was glad to see a female on the team. If the men accepted her to work with them, then they'd have an easier time accepting Emily, too. This was good news.

Suspender guy rubbed the back of his grimy hand under his narrow nose. "You know, Geo, if you got knocked up and stayed in the kitchen where you belonged, you could lie down on a nice soft sofa when Aunt Flo came to visit."

"Go screw yourself, Garth," the woman responded as the men chuckled, and Emily added *create non-hostile work environment* to her list of things to do.

"Boys and girl," Gigi said, "play nicely. Not a one of you is so old that I won't go tell your mother if you're being rude."

Each of them stood up a little straighter. "Yes, ma'am. I'm sorry, ma'am," Garth answered.

Gigi nodded. "All right, then. If you don't already know, this is my granddaughter, Emily Chambers. She's a real ballbuster, so don't go giving her any sass. We can find someone to replace you if you don't work out on this team."

Emily's smile stiffened. She knew Gigi was not one for subtlety but had hoped for a bit more finesse with that ball-busting thing. Oh well. It was out there now.

"Good morning, everyone. I'm really excited about this project and want to thank you all for being a part of it. We're going to take this poor old house and turn it back into a wonderful rental cottage. Let's start with some introductions, shall we?" She walked up onto the porch, careful to not let her heel plunge into some crevice in the wood. Falling out of her shoe was no way to make a good impression.

"I'll leave you to it then," Gigi said. "I'm off to take my great-granddaughter to Fort Beaumont, and then we're going shopping. You kids have fun."

They all called out their goodbyes, and Emily was on her own with getting to know her new crew. She extended her hand to Tiny, and his paw nearly swallowed hers.

"Pleased to meet you, Tiny. I'm Emily."

His eyes were pale blue with a nice twinkle in them, and she allowed herself to hope that he might not be such a menace after all. Maybe he'd be like the kind of grizzly bear that wanted to rummage through your camping cooler looking for snacks and not the kind of grizzly bear that was planning to kill you.

He took over with introductions, stepping into his role as foreman already. That was a good sign. "This here is Garth Reynolds, and that's his sister, Georgiana," Tiny said, gesturing toward Suspender Guy and

Cramps Girl. Emily shook hands with Garth and resisted the urge to wipe her own afterward, what with his nose rubbing and all.

"Nice to meet you again, Emily," Garth said. "You probably don't remember me, but my family lives on Big Pine Lane. I was about nine when you hightailed it out of here with that visiting college fella. Big news that summer. Whatever happened to him?"

Excellent. That's exactly what she wanted to talk about right now. "I married him, and then I divorced him."

Garth's sister stepped in front of him, pushing him aside with her hip. "Ignore my brother. I'm Georgie. Or Geo. Whatever. Do you have any ibuprofen? These cramps are a bitch."

What Georgie lacked in charm, she made up for in . . . lack of charm.

"Um, I don't think I have any ibuprofen, but you've reminded me I'd better make sure we have a first aid kit on site. Thanks."

Georgie turned away and slumped down against the wall, and Emily smiled at Wyatt, reaching out to shake his hand.

"That's Wyatt," Tiny said.

"Hi, Wyatt. I remember you. How are you?" It was nice to see at least one familiar face on this crew. She'd been friends with his sister, and that made him an ally of sorts. Hopefully.

"Can't complain, Peach. Uh, I mean, Ms. Callaghan. Or, uh . . ."

"You can call me Emily," she said to the group in general.

Wyatt smiled. "Welcome home, Emily. I'm glad for the work. My sister told me to tell you hello."

"Tell her I said hello back. What's she doing now?"

"She's a teacher. Moved to Manitou a few years ago, but she visits the island all the time."

"Good. I hope I get a chance to see her this summer."

Wyatt nodded as Emily turned to Hottie McSix-Pack. Damn. He really was distractingly cute. She felt like a snowman melting under his deep-blue gaze.

"I'm Matt," he said, as he clasped her hand in both of his and gave a tiny little bow of his head. "Namaste."

What? "Um, thanks?"

"The energy in this house is very sad, but I'm sure we can bring it joy. You were very wise to wear white."

"I was?"

He nodded. "It calls forth the light. My spirit guides tell me you are just what this place needs."

Hm. Interesting. Perhaps Matt could share some of his meds with Georgie to make her cramps go away.

She extricated her hand from his. "Thank you, Matt. I certainly hope your spirit guides are correct." She looked around. "Is this everyone then?"

The sound of a bike tire pealing out on gravel hit her ear, and she turned to see a disheveled man hopping off a rusty Schwinn and running up the steps, two at a time. One of his plaid shirttails was tucked in while the other flapped in the wind, and he appeared to be wearing two different shoes.

"Hi! Hello! Hey there! What'd I miss? Sorry I'm late, Peach!" He jabbed his hand forward, grabbing Emily's and pumping it up and down.

Horsey Davidson. They'd gone to school together, and like her nickname, his had stuck. He'd had some big yellow teeth as a teenager, and when he smiled, she saw they were still big and still yellow, and now they seemed to protrude forward even more than she remembered.

Garth leaned toward Matt. "He thinks we call him Horsey on account of his teeth, but my cousin Alma says otherwise."

The men chuckled, Georgie made a retching sound, but Horsey shushed them all with a glare. "Behave yourselves, you hogs."

"That's everyone now," Tiny said, and Emily didn't know whether to laugh or cry or just crawl under this front porch to hide. This was a team of mutants, to be sure. Hopefully they had some hidden superpowers that would help them band together and get this cottage renovated in record time, but either way, it was going to be One. Long. Summer.

DUDE, ANY PROGRESS?????

Ryan read the text from his brother and responded, WORKING ON IT. CALL U LTR.

"For goodness' sake, Ry. You're just like a teenager. I can't keep you off that damn phone long enough to enjoy the view," Tag said, walking five feet ahead of him on a rocky ascending path. They were on their way to something called Bent Rock. Ryan had at least convinced his father that they didn't need to do it before sunrise, so it was midday, sunny, but windy as hell high up on these bluffs.

"Some of us work for a living and have emails to check, but I guess you wouldn't know anything about that, now, would you."

"You're hilarious, son. I got up at six this morning and worked for two hours before you even called me. You're the one who didn't want to drag his ass out of bed. We can head over to the Clairmont Hotel this afternoon and I'll show you what I've done so far." The Clairmont was the twelve-guestroom hotel that Tag was working on. As of yet, Ryan hadn't gotten him to say much about the other project.

"I read the portfolio and saw the status updates. Sounds like you're making good progress with the new interior designs."

His father nodded and pulled his baseball hat down, adjusting the brim. "I have some ideas to show the owners, but I was hoping you'd look them over and see what you think. It's my opinion that we should go for a boutique hotel feel, but they're worried that if they spend too much on the upgrades, they'll have to raise their rates and will lose customers."

"Time for a little rebranding lesson, I take it?"

"Exactly. That's where you come in, since you're so good at convincing people to spend money to make money. I've done the market analysis and the island can support the business, but so far their marketing plan has been a static website with a phone number to call to check on reservations. I wonder how many customers they've lost just because of that antiquated method?"

"I guess that goes with the horse-and-buggy mentality. Nothing too modern." This was just about the time he wanted to ask his father, again, why he'd taken on that project in the first place, but he didn't want to start another fight. Arguing with Tag about Lilly was the only battle he could handle at the moment.

"The Clairmont definitely needs to move into this century with their systems, even if we decide to keep the décor timeless. And speaking of timeless, this sure never gets old. Come on up here and check out this view."

Ryan made his way forward and reached the plateau where his dad was now standing, and looked around.

"Well, shit, Dad. You're right. This is an amazing view." The fresh blue water went on all the way to the horizon, and off to the left was the Petoskey Bridge, a suspended structure that connected Michigan's upper and lower peninsulas. From both an esthetic and an engineering standpoint, the thing was impressive.

Tag pointed. "That's Petoskey Bridge, of course. According to the locals, it's five miles long and weighs over a million tons. Impressive, right?"

Ryan chuckled because the very same word had been in his head. He and his father shared a similar appreciation for design and functionality. "Very."

"Link, down at Link & Patty's, told me there were four thousand engineering drawings and eighty-five thousand blueprints. Can you imagine? With that many drawings, they could have built the damn thing out of the paper they used."

"Makes me pretty damn glad we build hotels and condos instead of bridges."

"No kidding, but speaking of building, turn and look that way." Tag pointed off to the east. "See that area over there? The hilly spot with the pink cottage?"

Ryan shielded his eyes from the sun. It was far from where they stood, but he could just barely make it out. "I think I see where you're talking about."

"That's the spot I talked to Bryce about. It has amazing potential. There are a few hoops to jump through for this one, but I think it would be worth it."

"What kind of hoops?"

"Well, for one thing, the investors don't actually own the land."

"Is it for sale?"

"Not exactly." Tag hesitated, smiling and looking off toward the little pink cottage.

Ryan was feeling his patience thin. "Dad, I can't do whatever it is you want me to do unless you tell me what you want. What's the story here? Who are the investors?"

His father actually chuckled, and Ryan wasn't sure if that made him feel more annoyed or slightly less annoyed.

"April, May, and June Mahoney. Three sisters, well into their seventies, who have apparently been saving their pennies for a very long time. They want Taggert Property Management to buy that place for them and design a three-story bed-and-breakfast, but there are two issues. First, no one on the island can know that it's them trying to buy it."

"Why?"

"Apparently there is some bad blood between the Mahoneys and some of the other local families, and our investors are worried that if anyone finds out it's them trying to secure the place, they'll lose it to another buyer."

"Okay. We should be able to work around that. What's the other problem?"

"They're waiting for the owner of that pink cottage to die."

"What?" The rocks shifted a little under Ryan's feet, causing him to wobble.

"It's not quite as bad as it sounds," Tag replied. "The woman who lives there is a hundred and two years old. She has no family left because she's outlived them all, except for some derelict nephew down in Tampa who never comes to visit. The Mahoneys are sure she's going to kick the bucket any day now, and when she goes, they want to be ready. They want the surveys done and the plans drawn up and everything."

Ryan crossed his arms and stared at his father. "So, if I'm hearing you right, we are waiting for some poor little old lady to die so that three other little old ladies can swoop in and snatch up her property before some nephew shows up and lays claim to it? Classy, Dad. Real classy. No wonder you've been avoiding the details."

Tag did not seem at all chagrined about this deal. "What? It's a good deal, and I wanted to discuss it with you in person so you could see what a great spot it is. It's a perfect place for a bed-and-breakfast. It's even got access to the water, but obviously I can't head up the project. I'm retiring, you know, and I can't wait around for this poor woman's imminent demise."

"Oh, but I can?"

Tag stepped forward. "All I'm asking you to do is look into the basics. Figure out if the current electrical and water systems are in place to support a six- or eight-room bed-and-breakfast. See if there are any liens or if that house has a historical designation and can't be torn down. Maybe draw up some rough sketches for them to see. I already did a few for the Mahoneys, but I made copies, so I'll give those to you."

"So have you committed to these Mulligan sisters? Have they signed a contract?"

"Mahoney, and no, but they want to as soon as possible. One of them told me that apparently the pink house's owner, Bridget O'Malley, was looking none too lively at church last week."

Ryan couldn't help but laugh at that. "Geez, Dad. That's cold."

Tag shrugged. "It's just business, and trust me, these Mahoneys are not sweet little old ladies. They are barracudas. Somebody is going to buy that place pretty soon, and it's a win-win for the company either way. The Mahoneys are willing to pay us for all the plans and research even if we ultimately can't get the property. That's how determined they are to be ready. They also have a handful of cottages, four or five, I think, and they'd like those remodeled, and they also want us to computerize their reservation system. They're worse off than the Clairmont. They don't even have a website. They just count on word-of-mouth recommendations. How's that for antiquated?"

"Very antiquated, but Dad, I'm still not feeling great about this. It seems like there is a lot of potential for this to be a dead end."

Tag laughed, and Ryan joined him once he realized his poor choice of words.

"Tell you what. The truth is, I've already set you up for a meeting. Just talk to them, see what you think, maybe take a walk over to the property to see it up close. What can it hurt? You're already here, right?"

"You know, for a guy who's retiring, you seem awfully interested in the company taking on a new project."

"It's more like a favor. My flight instructor is April Mahoney's son, and I promised him I could help them out. I got six free flying lessons out of the deal."

"If I meet with them, shouldn't I be the one getting the free lessons?"

"Sure, if you want them, but I'm not letting you fly my plane. You'll have to get your own."

Chapter 13

"I'm not sure I can do it, Jewel," Emily murmured into the phone from her bedroom at Gigi's house. "You should see this place I have to renovate, and you should see my crew. One of them is so skinny I'm not sure he can lift a hammer."

"You'll be fine, hon. You're like a cat. You always land on your feet."

Jewel had the most positive outlook of any person Emily had ever met, and although she sure did need the pep talk at the moment, she couldn't help but remember how it was Jewel's delusional sense that *everything would always work out* that had prompted them to buy the disaster place in San Antonio.

"I need this flip to go flawlessly, though," Emily said. "The last thing my family saw me do was run away and get married to a loser. And then get divorced. If they find out I borrowed money from Gigi, I'll never live it down, so this is my chance to show them that I've grown up, that I'm a responsible adult now and not still the wild, obnoxious kid I used to be."

"They're going to see that, Em. Just be yourself. I've seen you succeed time and again, under the toughest of circumstances. You've got this." If Jewel had pom-poms, she was certainly waving them wildly on her side of the phone. Still, her vote of confidence was encouraging. They had handled some pretty intense remodels over the past few years. This was not Emily's first rodeo.

"Okay. I hear you. I can do this." *Put me in, Coach. I'm ready for the big game.*

"Yes, you can. Write that on your bathroom mirror with lipstick to remind you every day. Hey, by the way, how's our Chloe holding up? Is there Wi-Fi?" She asked about Wi-Fi with the same gravity as asking, *Is there a cure?*

Emily laughed. "Yes, there's Wi-Fi, thank goodness. She's taken about a thousand selfies since we got here, which is down from her usual two thousand per day."

"She's slipping. Tell her to send me some. I miss seeing her face. I miss seeing your face, too, but Kevin has been keeping me company."

"Kevin the electrician?"

"Yeah, we've been spending some time together since he's working at the disaster house. The other night he offered to come to our house and fix that broken light fixture in the hallway. You know, the one that only turns on half the time? Anyway, he offered to fix it, but he wouldn't let me pay him with cash, so I made him dinner instead. It was fun."

"Fun, huh? Just fun? Or something more?"

Jewel's pause was telling. "I think it's just fun, but I'll keep you posted. I'm cooking for him again tonight. It's sort of like playing house with a Ken doll instead of a place full of Barbies. He loves our pink bathroom, by the way. He says it's bringing out his more sensitive side."

Jewel sounded cautiously hopeful. Her boyfriend status was even more barren than Emily's, so this was a nice change. "That sounds like it could lead to more than fun. You'd better keep me posted on those details, but speaking of bathrooms, how's it going getting the plumbing fixed in the master bedroom at the disaster house?"

"They're just about finished, and I have the drywall guys coming back to fix all the walls damaged by the leaks. We're on track to have everything done next week so I can get it on the market. I cannot wait to sell that place."

"You and me both. Don't forget to keep me posted, okay?"

"I will, and you keep me posted on your cottage. And tell Chloe to call me. I'd like to hear what she thinks of Exile Island."

Emily smiled. "I think she's pleasantly surprised. She met some kids the other day at the Lilac Festival, and she's got about ten distant cousins here who are roughly the same age. I think she'll be spending some time with them. And she thinks my dad's jokes are funny, so she's becoming his favorite, which is a huge relief. Last time I came here, he barely looked at either one of us."

That last visit had been rough for Emily in so many ways. She'd known a divorce from Nick was imminent, and she was testing the waters to see if maybe, just maybe, it was time to come home. But it wasn't. Harlan wasn't done being angry, and Emily returned to Texas without even telling anyone her marriage was over. She told them about a year later, when everything was finalized. But so far, this visit was going much better, and it seemed she had Chloe's Lilly-esque charm to thank for it.

~

"You've got Tiny Kloosterman on your work crew?" Harlan chuckled as Emily took a bite of pot roast. He was sitting at one end of the rectangular table in Gigi's kitchen, and she sat at the other. Emily and Chloe sat on one side with Lilly and Brooke across from them. Emily looked around at the group and wondered how many dinners such as this she'd missed over the years, and it made her chest ache. She hadn't realized how she'd stuffed away that appreciation for being surrounded by family. It wasn't always good, of course, being with family, but it was . . . familiar, and that made it nice.

"Tiny is eager to repay his debt to society, Harlan," Gigi said. "Give him a chance."

Nostalgic feelings notwithstanding, Emily hesitated to ask her dad for anything, most especially his opinion, but she had to know how dependable her ragtag collection of workpeople was going to be, and if anyone could supply her with the worst-case-scenario situation, it would be her dad.

"You have a guy working for you named Tiny?" Chloe picked up the gravy boat and all but drowned her mashed potatoes.

"Tiny isn't actually tiny," Emily said. "He's huge, and so is that tower of potatoes. Do you really think you can eat all that? You'll get a tummy-ache."

"Yes, I'm legit starving, and I'm sure I'll burn off every single calorie since I have to walk everyplace. I wish I had a Fitbit. I'd crush those ten thousand steps in this place."

"What's a Fitbit?" Harlan asked. His eyebrows seemed especially bushy this evening, like he'd messed them all up when washing his face that morning and had forgotten to tame them again afterward. Lilly usually kept on him about things like that, but she'd been a little distracted, and now Emily found herself distracted, too, by those bushy eyebrows.

"It's a wristband that counts how many steps you take in a day," Chloe answered.

"Why on earth would you want to know how many steps you take in a day?" Brooke asked. She was wearing another cute outfit, a kelly-green sundress, and Emily wondered if her sister had stepped up her game because Emily had been overdressed that very first night. It wasn't like Brooke to concern herself over something like that, though. Maybe she was just trying to professionalize her image for that mayoral bid.

"You measure your steps for exercise. All the girls at my school have them so they can work on their thigh gap," Chloe answered.

Emily gasped. "Oh my goodness, Chloe. Please tell me you are not concerned about something like that. You know those girls at school are basing that on pictures in magazines that are not realistic."

"They're not realistic," Lilly said, gesturing with her fork. "I'm in fantastic shape, and even I don't have a thigh gap."

"What the hell is a thigh gap?" Gigi said. "It sounds very naughty."

"It's the space you're supposed to have between the top of your legs to prove you're not fat," Chloe said.

"Oh my gosh. That's ridiculous," Brooke said.

"It's totally ridiculous, and Chloe, we've talked about this, remember? The important thing is to make healthy food choices and exercise to keep your body strong. It's not about being skinny."

Chloe rolled her eyes. "I know, Mom. I know. But Anastasia Whitcomb has one, and everyone thinks she's the prettiest girl in school."

"Including Anastasia Whitcomb," Emily responded. She knew she shouldn't criticize a twelve-year-old classmate of her daughter's, but she'd met that kid. She and her mother were country-club snobs, and Chloe had been reduced to tears on more than one occasion by something Anastasia had said to her. "She's not a very nice little girl, and being nice is way more important than being skinny. And besides, you're perfect just the way you are."

"Yes, you are," Lilly said. "And don't ever let anyone make you think otherwise."

"A thigh gap," Brooke murmured, shaking her head.

"So, it's not naughty, then?" Gigi asked. She sounded disappointed.

Harlan cleared his throat. "Ladies, please. Could we talk about something other than women's thighs?"

"Yes, Grandpa. Sorry about that. Want to hear a joke?" Chloe asked, grinning.

"Sure."

She looked around the table to make sure she had everyone's attention. "What do you call this? Clip-clop, clip-clop, clip-clop. Bang. Clip-clop. Clip-clop."

The ever-present creases in Harlan's face deepened for a moment until he said, "I don't know. What is it?"

"It's a Trillium Bay drive-by shooting."

The ensuing laughter was modest, but Chloe appeared to be pretty proud of herself, and it warmed Emily's heart to see her daughter so relaxed and happy.

"That's a good one," Harlan said, taking a bite of dinner roll.

"Thanks. I heard it from a new friend. Hey, by the way, Mom, after dinner can I go hang out with some kids I met at the festival? They invited me."

"Which kids?" Harlan immediately transitioned into his overprotective police officer voice, but now that she was a parent and not the recipient, Emily understood better where it came from.

"Carrie Crenshaw, Susie Mahoney, Mike Somebody, and some guy named something like John or Jack or Joe. Or Leo. I can't remember. But they seemed nice."

"Mahoney? Uh-oh." Emily looked over at Gigi, but her grandmother just shook her head.

"They don't get nasty until they're adults. The little ones are fine," Gigi said. "And those kids are all right. If it's the Mahoney and the Crenshaw girls, then it's most likely Mike Tupper and Joe Leonard."

Chloe snapped her fingers and pointed at her grandmother. "That's them. His name was Joe, but they called him Leo. So, Mom, can I go hang with them later?"

Emily looked at her dad. Again, it was killing her to ask his opinion, even if she wasn't asking out loud, but she wasn't going to send Chloe off with kids he didn't approve of. History was not going to repeat itself. He gave her a quick, single nod.

Emily turned to Chloe. "I guess that would be okay, but keep your phone turned on so I can get ahold of you if I need to."

Chloe arched an eyebrow. "Thanks, Mom. And when do I ever, ever turn off my phone?"

"Good point."

Chloe immediately pulled said phone from her pocket and started texting, and Emily looked back at her father. "So, Dad, about Tiny and the others. What do you think? Are they reliable?"

"I'd say so. Tiny has a lot of construction experience, and he's done work all over the island. Haven't heard any complaints. Garth is mostly useless but not dangerously stupid. Wyatt's an excellent electrician. Horsey and Georgie are fine, as far as I know, but I can damn near guarantee Horsey will be late more often than not. Who'd you say was the other guy?"

"Matt. He just moved here a few months ago from New York."

Harlan picked up his fork and stabbed a piece of roast. "Is that the yoga guy? Yoga Matt?"

Emily chuckled. "I've not heard him called that, but yes, he teaches yoga."

"I've seen that guy," Lilly said. "He teaches a class at the Episcopal church, and all the single girls have got their eye on him."

"All the single girls, you say? Does that include you?" Gigi directed her question to Lilly, whose face proceeded to turn bright pink.

"I told you, Gigi. There's no guy."

"What's this?" Harlan asked, looking confused, as if the conversation had veered into uncomfortable territory for him again.

"Well, all I really care about is if he can use a hammer." Emily jumped back in, anxious to pull attention away from Lilly. "And I'm sure he'll do just fine. What time did you say your friends wanted to meet you, Chloe?"

Talk turned to other topics after that. When the community hall would get a new paint job. Brooke's potential run for mayor. The cartful of crazy that was Vera VonMeisterburger. Chloe left to meet her friends, and Emily felt confident that they'd be doing something fun instead of sitting around and worrying about their thigh gaps. Life on the island was insulated from crap like that.

"Thanks for not telling anyone about Tag," Lilly said quietly later that evening as the two sisters sat together on the front porch swing. Brooke and their father had both gone home, Chloe was still off with her new posse of friends, and Gigi was banging around in the kitchen making muffins for the morning.

"You're welcome, I guess. I want to be supportive, but Lilly, you can't possibly be serious about him. He's all wrong for you."

"That doesn't sound very supportive, and no offense, Em, but you don't have the best track record when it comes to men."

Ouch. That was hurtful.

Accurate. But hurtful.

"No, I don't have a very good track record when it comes to men, so maybe you should learn from my stupid mistakes. This is going to end badly, and you're going to get your heart broken."

"Don't worry about me. Tag is wonderful, and we are being very cautious about the whole thing. That's why we've been keeping it a secret. Not because we're ashamed, but because we just want to figure out if what we have is really real before we go telling people."

In spite of having agreed with Ryan that a direct assault wouldn't work, Emily felt her frustration bubbling over. "How real could it be? He's more than twice your age. What could you two possibly have in common?"

"Lots of things. The things that matter, anyway, and he's funny and smart and—"

"And old. Lilly, he has three sons who are all older than you are. Doesn't that make you uncomfortable?" Geez, it made Emily uncomfortable just thinking about it.

"No, his age doesn't faze me."

"Well, it should. It makes it hard for Ryan and his brothers to believe you're not just after Tag for his money or because he's willing to take you places."

"*Willing*? That's a nice word. That makes me sound pretty pathetic." Lilly frowned and crossed her arms.

"I don't mean it that way. Not at all. It's just that everyone you meet is going to make assumptions about you. They won't care what the truth is. All they'll see is some very young woman hanging onto the arm of a rich old man."

"Stop calling him old. He's not some doddering old grandpa with a walker and a hearing aid. Geez! You make it sound like he's one step away from a nursing home, and that's just not accurate. A couple days ago we went hiking up near Bent Rock, and I had to keep up with *him*."

Emily did not seem to be making any progress, but still she persisted. "I get that, Lilly. I do. Tag is a nice-looking man and he's fit and in great shape, but that doesn't change the fact that he's significantly older, and it doesn't change the fact that he's a wealthy guy who travels in much different circles than you're used to."

"You're flattering me again," Lilly said dryly. "Now you're saying that not only am I too young for him, but I'm also not good enough for him."

"I'm not saying that. What I'm saying is that not everybody is as nice as you, and they might not welcome you. Nick's family never accepted me. It was one of the things that ruined our marriage."

"They didn't accept you? You never told me that."

"You were a teenager. Plus, I was embarrassed. His parents were horrified when Nick and I showed up on their doorstep already married, and his mother spent the better part of five years trying to make sure I knew that I did not belong there. The only nice thing she ever did for me was to pay for my divorce lawyer. She was that determined to see me gone, even if it meant taking her granddaughter with me."

"And that's what you think Tag's family would do?"

Emily paused. "I've only met Ryan, and he seems to be nice enough, but I do know that he and his brothers are determined to make sure Tag doesn't retire. And . . . honestly, they're worried that if you guys ever got married, you'd eventually leave Tag and take a lot of money with you."

Lilly reached out and pressed a hand to Emily's arm. "Oh my gosh, I would never do that! You know I would never do that."

"I know, but it's going to be hard to convince them."

The swing creaked slowly back and forth as Emily wondered if she was helping the situation or making it worse.

"It wasn't very easy after you left, you know," Lilly said quietly a moment later.

"What?"

"After you left, things got harder. I was fifteen when you ran away with Nick, and Dad was so worried I'd do the same thing, he put me under house arrest."

"He did?"

"Well, not literally, but for all practical purposes. Every adult on this island was watching out for me. I couldn't go anyplace without Dad knowing. Do you know how hard it is to get kissed by a boy under those circumstances? I finally had to drag poor Percy O'Keefe out behind Colette's Riding Stable and plant one on him just to get that first one out of the way."

Emily chuckled at the mental picture of her sister, or anyone for that matter, locking lips with Percy O'Keefe, but her thoughts turned quickly. She'd never really thought about how anyone else's life had changed after she left. She'd been so absorbed in her own drama and just assumed life on the island would remain business as usual. Because who would have really missed her anyway? But in hindsight, maybe that was kind of selfish.

"I'm sorry, Lil. Sorry you had to deal with that, and with Dad."

Lilly's slender shoulders rose and fell. "It's okay. I guess I didn't even realize that's what Dad was doing until years later. I thought everybody's father was overprotective like him, but once I got to college, I realized that all the other girls had managed to gather up a lot more experience than I had. I'm pretty sure I was the only virgin in my entire dorm, and I'm also pretty sure there was a betting pool on when I'd finally lose it. Rumor has it that if I'd waited one more week, my roommate would have made two hundred dollars." There was a chuckle lacing Lilly's voice.

Emily smiled, glad her sister was seeing some humor in it now that it was behind her.

"That's what I mean, though, Lil. I didn't rack up much experience while I lived here, either. The few times with Reed were . . . unsatisfying because neither one of us had a clue what we were doing. Nick came along, and it was so easy for me to get swept away because apparently he had gotten lots of practice. Maybe that's what's happening to you. Maybe you think what you have with Tag is awesome just because you have so little to compare it to, and no offense against him, but somebody your own age might be more . . . exciting."

Ryan would probably be pretty exciting in bed, but Emily shoved that thought from her mind with the force of a charging rhinoceros.

Lilly's cheeks went pink. "Tag and I manage quite nicely, thanks."

Emily's mind went from picturing herself with Ryan to picturing her sister with Tag. It was not a good comparison. Tag was definitely handsome for an old guy, but no matter how Lilly wanted to spin this, he was too old for her.

"Um, that's great. Really. But again, a younger guy could manage nicely, too, without having to take a Viagra first. Yoga Matt probably doesn't have to take a Viagra." Yoga Matt was the poster child for masculine virility.

Lilly's tiny smile evaporated. "I told you, Tag's very fit. He does a lot of cardio. Plus, he thinks I'm clever and beautiful."

"You are clever and beautiful. I understand his attraction to you, and I also understand why you're flattered by his attention, but I think you'd be happier in the long run if you focused on someone your own age."

"Like Yoga Matt?" Lilly crossed her arms again and arched a brow, daring Emily to answer that one. She rose to the challenge. Yoga Matt might ultimately be just a little too head-in-the-clouds to make a good long-term boyfriend, but he certainly was hot enough to distract Lilly from Tag. "Sure. I could introduce you. Or we could take his class together. Just meet him and see if any sparks fly. If you're so certain about Tag, what could it hurt?"

Lilly looked at her as if weighing her options. "Here's my counteroffer. I'll take the yoga class with you if you agree to have dinner with Tag and me. I want you to get to know him better so you can understand where I'm coming from."

Dinner? Together? She didn't want to spend an evening with Tag and Lilly. According to Ryan, it was hard to watch. She wasn't about to face that alone.

"Um, could we invite Ryan, too? That way he can get to know you better, and see that you're not a gold-digging bimbo."

Lilly's gaze turned from contemplative to coy. "I see what you're doing here. You like him, don't you?"

"Who? Tag?"

"No. Ryan. That's why you want him to come to dinner with us."

Now this was an interesting hiccup. She did kind of like Ryan, even though she wasn't going to do anything about it, and she certainly didn't want anyone to know because, well, because the last time she'd been attracted to someone on this island, everyone had seen her make a fool of herself, and she was not going through that again. However, if Lilly thought she had her eye on Ryan, it would sure make the four of them spending time together easier to arrange. Oh, what tangled webs.

"He's okay. I guess. And dinner is okay, too, but do you know what would be even better? Horseback riding."

Chapter 14

"We understand this is a risk, Mr. Taggert, but it's one we are willing to take." June Mahoney adjusted her black-framed glasses and stared at Ryan like a bull about to charge. She was a formidable woman wearing a navy-blue dress and big, chunky jewelry made of red plastic beads. Ryan didn't typically notice jewelry, but this stuff was so big that it was loud. Every time she leaned forward, her necklace went *thunk* against the table, and her bracelet did the same every time she set her arm down. It was distracting.

So was the fact that one of her sisters sat next to her and continued knitting throughout the entire meeting. The needles went *plink-plink-plink* and kept catching rays of sunshine and blinding him in the eye. He couldn't remember the name of that other sister, but it didn't seem to matter. June was clearly the boss here, and her sister just repeated what was already said.

"Willing to take that risk," she muttered, twirling soft pink yarn around the needle. *Plink-plink-plink.*

"My sisters and I have had our eye on that property for some time," June continued, "and when my cousin Herb, who owns the Clairmont Hotel, told me about your company, well, I considered it divine providence. Then I discovered my nephew knew your father, too. It was just too much of a coincidence to be ignored. Tag has been kind enough to sketch out some ideas for the bed-and-breakfast, and I cannot tell you how impressed we are."

"Impressed," the other sister said.

It really was a slam-dunk win for Taggert Property Management. The Mahoney sisters wanted to hire them to renovate their current properties. Easy as shit and then ka-ching. Computerize their reservation system. Even easier and then ka-ching. And the company could do everything they needed for the bed-and-breakfast. Draw up plans, do a market analysis, check with the township to ensure the property was properly zoned. Constructing a three-story building was nothing compared to the places they usually worked on. The real kicker was that these old broads were willing to pay for all the prep work without even owning the damn land.

"Have you spoken with Mrs. O'Malley about her designated plans for the property? She may have a stipulation in her will deeding it to someone, which would stall your project. We can't just move the bed-and-breakfast to another location because the geography will be different."

He could not, in good conscience, let them pay for all these plans without informing them of the realities. Easy money was one thing, but reputation and integrity was another. He didn't want to get sued if this deal fell through.

June glanced at her sister and then back at him. "The truth is, Mr. Taggert, that Bridget O'Malley is not in her right mind. As you can imagine. She's almost a hundred and three years old. We've offered to buy it from her and let her live there until she decides to move, or until the Good Lord moves her for us, but the old ninny won't listen to reason. She won't sell it to us."

"Did she say why?"

"I already told you she's not in her right mind, so her logic doesn't make any sense, but I'm sure if you went and talked to her and left our names out of it, she'd be happy to sell. We've never mentioned to her anything about building on the land, so perhaps if you show her the drawings of the new bed-and-breakfast, she'll see how lovely it could be."

"So lovely." *Plink-plink-plink.*

"I'm not sure how seeing what will happen *after* she's gone will inspire her," Ryan said.

"Rely on her pride, Mr. Taggert. Tell her you'll be calling it the O'Malley House. She'd like that," June replied.

The sister tugged on June's sleeve and shook her head vehemently. June brushed her hand away. "Don't worry, April, we won't call it that. It's just an idea to get that old bitch to agree. Pardon my French, Mr. Taggert. As you can imagine, we're not fond of Mrs. O'Malley, but we are very fond of her property. We are determined to get that piece of land no matter what it takes. If your company isn't up to the challenge, then we'll just have to find another developer."

Ryan saw the ultimatum in her eyes. If these old broads were so bound and determined to pursue this project, well, then better it be handled by his company than some other builder. It wasn't as if Ryan hadn't specifically outlined all the obstacles, so he could now go forth with a clear conscience. He could do all the prep work and get paid for it. If the deal fell through, he could just move on without losing the company any money. Bryce would agree on this deal for certain, even though he'd wanted Tag and Ryan back in Sacramento. This was a good solution. Ryan had to stick around Trillium Bay to keep an eye on his father anyway. At least this way he'd be making the company some money at the same time.

"Mrs. Mahoney, I would certainly hate to see you take your business to any other developer. We at Taggert Property Management would be very happy to work with you. I'll get the contracts drawn up, and we can meet again in a few days to fine-tune things before you sign. How does that sound?"

June Mahoney reached out to shake his hand, and her bracelet clunk-clunk-clunked on the tabletop. "Mr. Taggert, I believe we have a deal."

Chapter 15

Friday afternoon was dull, gray, and muggy as Tag, Lilly, Chloe, Ryan, and Emily walked down Blueberry Lane toward Colette's Riding Stable. Off to their right was Lake Huron and the Petoskey Bridge, and to the left was a cluster of stores and restaurants including Eden's Garden of Eatin' Salad Buffet, Judge's Fudge, and the Go Fly a Kite Shop, which sold, not surprisingly, kites.

"Hey, Mom." Chloe pointed at the sign. "Can we go in the kite store?"

"Sure. You guys go on in. I need to run to the ladies' room first, but I'll be right there."

Hanging back, she gave a discreet tug to the sleeve of Ryan's green T-shirt. He turned toward her as the others walked inside the shop.

"Hey, I have an idea," she whispered, even though the others were far out of earshot. "You said we needed to create negative associations, right?"

"Um, I saw one TED Talk, so don't quote me on anything I told you."

"I won't, but listen. If we want to make sure your dad has a lousy time today, I could help make that happen. Are you with me?"

"How lousy? Not like dangerous lousy, right?"

"No, of course not. Just *not* fun."

"Yeah, okay. Do what you have to do." Ryan heaved a big sigh. "It's hard raising parents."

Ryan moved on toward the kite store as Emily quickly made her way across the street and down one short block to find Colette's Riding Stable. The place looked exactly as it had for her entire childhood. It was a long, low stable painted dark green on the outside. On the inside was a row of stalls, along with all the accoutrements needed for non-horse riders to have an experience. Saddle, tack, helmets. There was a high counter on the right-hand side, next to a bathroom door labeled "Cowgirls." The smell of hay and horses took Emily back twenty years. She'd worked at this barn once. Not for very long because it turned out that no matter how much she enjoyed riding, she did not enjoy the scooping of the poo, and if you worked in a stable, you really had to be okay with the scooping of the poo. She didn't mind the smell for the most part, but manure was heavy. She'd lasted about a week, if memory served, before her boss suggested that maybe this was not the place for her. She'd gone to work at the Mustang Saloon instead.

Still, looking around she recognized a few familiar faces that had been there nearly as long as the barn itself, and as luck would have it, there was Percy O'Keefe. Emily used to babysit him back in the day, and she always let him have as many popsicles as he wanted. There was also that one incident when he was about twelve when she'd caught him sneaking a Victoria's Secret catalogue into his bedroom. She'd never told a soul. He owed her for that, and it was time to collect. His long-standing crush on Lilly might work to her advantage, too.

"Hey, Percy!" she called out.

He turned, his wild black hair going in every direction. Percy never was much for personal grooming. Even scrubbed up for Sunday morning church, he always seemed to have a smudge of dirt on his face.

"Hiya, Peach. I heard you were back on the rock. How are you?"

Emily reached his side and leaned in for a friendly hug. Percy leaned as well, but stopped just short of actually touching her. "You don't want to get too close to this. Colette's had me mucking all day. You know how that goes."

He was pretty ripe with soil and exertion, so Emily just squeezed his shoulder instead. "I'm great, Percy. How are you?"

"Oh, you know. Same old, same old. You here to ride?"

Emily took a quick glance back over her shoulder to make sure she hadn't been followed into the barn. The coast was clear.

"I am here to ride, Percy, but I was wondering if you could help me out with a bit of a, oh, let's call it a prank."

His eyebrows rose slowly, creating lines of dirt on his forehead. "A prank, you say? Oh, you know I'm always game for something like that. What are you thinking? Setting some manure on fire and leaving it on Judge Murphy's front step? We sure haven't done that in a while."

Emily chuckled. "No, nothing quite like that. Here's what I'm thinking . . ."

~

Half an hour later, the five riders stood in the paddock, each wearing a riding helmet. Everyone's was navy, except for Tag's. His was a bright neon orange.

"Are you sure this is the only helmet that will fit me?" Tag asked Percy as a stocky teenage girl with pink braces on her teeth led two horses from the stable. One was black with white socks, and the other was a dappled gray covered in spots.

Percy grinned over at Tag, looking a little crazy-eyed. "Yes, sir. Sorry about the color of your helmet, but that's the only one we have in an extra-extra-large, and I don't mean to insinuate any sort of insult on your part, sir, but you do seem to have an abnormally large head."

"Percy, he does not," Lilly said, frowning at him.

"You don't think so? Oh, maybe it's just his forehead then," Percy muttered just loud enough to be heard. Emily coughed into her hand to smother her chuckle, and Ryan arched an eyebrow in her direction. Percy took the reins of the white-and-gray horse from the girl.

"Thanks, Lydia. After this could you please go get Spirit and Duke? And then bring out Periwinkle."

Her blue eyes widened. "Periwinkle?"

"Yes, ma'am. That's what I said."

The girl looked confused for a moment but then nodded. "Okay, if you say so."

Percy nodded and motioned to Chloe. "Okay now, princess, let's get you saddled up first. This here is Lulubelle, and she's about the sweetest girl we have. You two are going to get along just fine." Chloe beamed as he gave her a leg up, and Emily smiled, too. That was one of the true joys of having kids, getting to experience something through their eyes. Emily had been around horses all her life and didn't really care about riding one way or the other, but seeing Chloe's broad smile and feeling the enthusiasm emanating from her typically hard to impress teen was a refreshing change.

Chloe patted the horse's thick, speckled neck. "Well, Lulubelle, you are certainly one magnificent mare, aren't you?" Lulubelle looked around in a decidedly mundane and not-at-all-magnificent way, but Chloe didn't seem to notice.

"You're next, Peach. Tilly's the girl for you." He grabbed the reins of the other horse as the stable girl went back into the barn. He linked his fingers for her to put her knee into, and seconds later she was settled into the saddle. "You remember how to do this?"

Emily nodded. "I think so. I just put the key in the ignition and press the gas pedal, right?"

Percy chuckled. "Right." He adjusted her stirrup and winked as he grinned up at her. "I'll be looking forward to hearing all about your ride when you get back."

"I'm sure I will enjoy telling you all about it. Thanks, Percy."

"Oh, you know you're welcome."

Lydia brought out two more horses, two dark bays that looked virtually identical. "Percy, did you say I should bring out Periwinkle next?"

Percy nodded. "Yep."

"Periwinkle."

He stared at the girl like an owl about to swoop in on a mouse. "Periwinkle," he said.

"Okay," she said slowly, and went back into the barn.

"Lilly, how's about you saddle up on Spirit? I know you know your way around a horse, and if memory serves, you know your way around behind a barn, too." He did the double-barreled wink-wink complete with sound effects, and Emily pretended to adjust her helmet just so she could shield her smile behind her hands.

Lilly snatched the reins from his hand. "I got this, Percy. Thanks."

"All right, you there, with the movie-star veneers, you can ride Duke." Percy motioned to Ryan. "He'll suit you fine. He's good with totally inexperienced riders such as yourself. If you can walk a dog, you can manage him, but if he does give you any trouble, just let the reins go real slack and he'll know just what to do."

"I have been on horses before," Ryan said. "I'm not totally inexperienced."

Percy's slow nod was condescending. "Oh, well that's real good news then, but there's no shame in being a little bit scared. Horses are pretty big."

Ryan glared at him. "I'm not afraid of horses. I never said I was."

Percy nodded, his lips pressed in a line. He leaned in toward Ryan's ear as if to whisper but didn't lower his voice. At all. "I understand. You don't want to be shown up by the young ladies here, but a little natural fear is a good thing. If you weren't a mite nervous, then I'd be worried you did not fully appreciate the magnitude of the danger you are about to partake in."

Ryan's mouth opened, then shut, and Emily struggled not to laugh out loud. She'd told Percy to pick on Tag but seemed to be getting two pranks for the price of one.

Chloe glanced her way. "It's not actually dangerous, is it, Mom?"

Emily shook her head. "No, honey. We'll be fine." There was always an element of risk when one was near any animal that weighed north of a thousand pounds, but riding these mild-mannered, mostly resigned saddle ponies was about as dangerous as feeding ducks in a pond. Sure, you might drown, but the ducks were certainly no threat.

Meanwhile, Tag stood and waited in his carrot-orange helmet. His eyes darted around, and he looked a little pale. Emily almost felt sorry for him.

At last Lydia brought Periwinkle out from the stable. She was a beautiful horse, a piebald covered in black-and-white splotches. Her tail swished and she had a bit of a prance to her step, and Emily felt a little disappointed. She'd been hoping for some mopey old nag that would spend the entire ride just trying to get back to the barn, but this horse looked fresh and strong.

"Here you go, mister." Percy helped Tag mount, grunting a bit as if Tag were too heavy. "Let me adjust those stirrups a bit. They don't look quite right." Percy fiddled with a few straps, and Emily's disappointment waned as she watched him shorten the straps to an awkward position. Wily. That Percy was wily, and Tag looked none too comfortable on the back of that horse.

"So, Lilly, where shall we ride to?" Emily asked, nudging Tilly forward so her sister wouldn't notice those too-short stirrups.

"If you don't mind me making a recommendation," Percy said, "I think the ride along Gilbert Trail is a good bet. That'll take you right through some real pretty sections of woods. Then when you reach Lakeshore Avenue, you can give the horses a little break. Maybe let them get a drink from the lake since it's awful warm today. They don't mind getting their feet wet."

"That sounds good to me. How's that sound to you, Lilly?" Emily asked. She wasn't sure why Percy suggested that path, but since he had, there must be some good reason judging from the conspiratorial smile he sent her way.

"Sounds fine to me. Let's go."

"This so awesome!" Chloe's giggle made Emily giggle, too. Hopefully this would be awesome. At least for some of them.

Ryan didn't know what to expect, but today he was just along for the ride, literally. If he saw an opportunity to get in a subtle dig, he'd take it. So far, that wild-haired, overgrown stable boy had done his part. Ryan tamped down a chuckle at the sight of his father in the big orange hat. He looked like a pumpkin. No matter how infatuated Lilly might be, that hat would not work in his father's favor. Wearing an orange helmet was definitely *not fun*.

They left the paddock with Emily in the lead, followed by Chloe, Lilly, Tag, and then himself bringing up the rear. Not the best view, staring at a long line of horse rumps, but from back here at least he could keep an eye on things. Lilly was much quieter today, a noticeable shift from the bubbly, gregarious person she'd been that first night when they'd all had dinner at Tag's. Getting called a gold-digging bimbo probably still stung. Remorse buzzed past him like a menacing horsefly.

The sounds from Main Street faded away as they made their way down a wide path toward the trees, and other sounds took over. A dozen different chirping, clicking, and chattering noises, along with waves and the wind in the trees. People always said the woods were so quiet and peaceful, but if you really stopped to listen, it was actually noisy as hell. A branch smacked him in the face as his horse veered too close to a pine tree, and Ryan tightened his grip on the reins. He tried to maneuver his horse, but Duke seemed to have his own ideas.

Ryan got smacked by a second branch. He pulled at his shirt. The air was thick and sticky, and he was wearing jeans because the only thing worse than being too hot would be getting rubbed raw from a saddle. Hard to explain that kind of injury to the guys at the gym. "Oh, this road rash on my inner thighs? Just something involving leather. I won't bore you with the details." Yeah. That was not a conversation he wanted to have. Ever.

"Hey, Ryan! Smile." Chloe turned in her saddle and held up her phone to snap some photos. Because, you know, nothing says *back to nature* like a kid on a cellular device. Still, he smiled big and hoped he didn't look like too much of a moron. At least his helmet was blue.

"Okay now, you guys," Chloe called out to Tag and Lilly. They were riding next to each other, and instantly and comfortably leaned in together. Awesome. They could use that for their engagement photo. Chloe giggled and turned back around, clucking at her horse until she'd moved forward enough to ride by her mom. Now both their ponytails went sway, sway, sway. From this vantage point Ryan could just barely see Emily's legs stretching out on either side of her black horse. The straddle triggered a mental picture for him that made his saddle suddenly more uncomfortable and yet the ride somehow more pleasurable. Probably not a thought he should indulge in, but he was going to anyway.

"Selfie time, Mom!" Up ahead, Chloe stretched her arm as far as she could reach and took more photos of herself and Emily. He heard their laughter floating over the breeze, and it made him smile. They were cute together, and Chloe seemed like a sweet kid.

"Everybody doing okay?" Emily called out a few minutes later as the trail got narrower and the woods thicker. She looked back over her shoulder at him. He offered up a brief salute.

"Doing great," he answered as another pine branch whacked him in the shoulder. Seemed like old Duke here might be a little near-sighted. Or he was doing that on purpose. His horse also seemed to be inordinately interested in the backside of his father's horse. Every time he got too close to her big, round rump, she'd whip him with her tail and give a little hop and a skip.

"Sorry to tailgate you, Dad. I'm not doing it on purpose."

"Yeah, back it up. I think you're making my horse jumpy." Periwinkle gave another little hop in response. "Whoa, whoa there, girl." Tag patted her neck, and she gave her head a rigorous shake.

"I don't think that's what's bothering her," Lilly said. "She seems a little skittish. Do you want to trade? This horse I have is mellow as a hound dog."

"No, of course not," Tag responded tersely. "I can handle her. I'm certainly not going to have you ride the more dangerous horse."

Lilly chuckled. "No offense, honey, but I've been riding since the first grade."

"So, about ten years then?" Ryan said loudly.

She tossed a dirty glance his way. If she wasn't annoyed with him before, she was now.

"I can handle a jumpy horse better than you can," she said, turning back to Tag. Ryan leaned forward in his saddle. This should be interesting. He'd never heard anyone tell Tag that they could do something better than he could. He saw his father sit up straighter, his tangerine helmet tilting at an angle.

"I've got this, Lil. I'm good. If Ryan would just back up." Now his father's voice sounded downright testy. Ryan tugged back on Duke's reins, for all the good it did. Then he pulled his phone from his back pocket to see if he was talented enough to text and drive. His thumbs moved over the screen to send a message to Bryce.

GUESS WHAT? I'M ON A HORSE.

Bryce's response was almost instantaneous. WHY ARE YOU ON A HORSE?

RIDING WITH DAD AND BIMBO. BTW HER NAME IS LILLY, NOT DAISY.

WHATEVER. A ROSE BY ANY OTHER NAME . . .

VERY FUNNY.

I THOUGHT DAD HATED HORSES?

HE DOES. I WILL EXPLAIN LATER.

Duke stretched his nose forward for another nuzzle with Periwinkle's ass, and much to Ryan's dismay, the horse chose that exact moment to blow the biggest, loudest, horsiest fart imaginable. A colonic breeze reeking of hot, musty grass hit him in the face like exhaust fumes. Nonplussed and undeterred, his own horse walked right into it. And then it happened about eight more times. Loud, squeaky, anus-flapping farts, until at last Periwinkle unloaded a dozen road apples directly in front of them. Ryan's eyes watered as much from the heat as from the velocity. How did horses even do that? Walk and poop at the same time? It was efficient, really. If dudes could do that, he could totally picture Bryce trying to multitask in just such a fashion. He texted his brother again.

DAD'S HORSE IS A GAS BAG AND KEEPS FARTING AT ME.

GOT ANY MATCHES?

IF I LIT A MATCH RIGHT NOW, THIS ENTIRE FOREST WOULD BLOW UP LIKE ONE GIANT FIREBALL. EACH FART LASTS TEN FULL SECONDS. YOU COULD FLY A HOT AIR BALLOON WITH THIS MUCH GAS.

THAT IS NOT A BALLOON I WOULD EVER RIDE IN.

GOT TO GO. HAVE TO CLEAN MY SUNGLASSES BECAUSE I'M PRETTY SURE THERE IS HORSE SHIT ON THEM. YOU'RE AN ASSHOLE.

WHY AM I AN ASSHOLE BECAUSE YOU GOT HORSE SHIT ON YOUR SUNGLASSES?

NO CONNECTION. YOU WERE AN ASSHOLE WAY BEFORE I GOT HORSE SHIT ON MY GLASSES. I'LL CALL YOU LATER.

He tucked his phone back in his pocket and pulled off his glasses to wipe them on his shirt, telling himself it was just a smudge and not equine organic matter from Periwinkle's ass.

"She's really not very cooperative," Tag said as his horse stepped from the path and just suddenly stopped. Duke bumped into her, his face pressed against her butt, and Ryan dropped his glasses.

"Shit. Oh, I mean, shoot."

Chloe rolled her eyes. "Oh, like I haven't heard worse."

"Sit tight, Ryan. I'll get them." Lilly was off her horse and handing him his glasses before he could even comment.

"Thanks," he said, taking them from her hand.

"You're welcome."

Periwinkle sidestepped, bumping Duke in the nose, which was the horse's own damn fault because he was being quite persistent. Clearly Duke was an ass man.

"Seriously, Ryan," Tag said. "Could you please back up?"

"Emily, let's change up the order here, okay? I'll take the lead with Tag, Chloe can go in the middle, and you and Ryan bring up the rear," Lilly said.

"I think that's what my horse has been trying to do," Ryan said.

Minutes later Lilly and Tag were in the front, Chloe was in the middle, and Emily rode beside him. That was a nice turn of events. She looked completely at ease on that horse, holding the reins in one hand while the other rested casually on her thigh. Today she wore jeans and a red tank top, and Ryan couldn't help but wonder just how many versions of her there were. The white business suit Emily, carefree sundress Emily, and now cowgirl Emily. Was there a seductress Emily in there somewhere? If so, he'd very much like to meet her. The idea of her in some slinky nightie, or better yet, wearing nothing at all, hit him hard. His attraction to her was just not helpful. Yet it seemed unavoidable.

"A word of warning," he said, clearing his throat. "Periwinkle seems to be having some gastrointestinal distress, so I'm not sure you want to be downwind of her." Periwinkle responded to his comment with another robust fart. "See what I mean?"

Emily smiled. "Yeah, horses will do that. You get used to it."

"I don't particularly want to get used to it. In Sacramento we have these newfangled inventions called automobiles. You know, horseless carriages? They're all the rage."

A tiny dimple appeared near the corner of her mouth. "Just a fad, I'm sure. I've heard the smog and pollution on the freeways is so not pleasant."

"True, but then again, I don't usually have my face a mere two feet behind a tailpipe." He smiled at her, hoping to look clever, then grabbed onto the pommel of his saddle as Duke veered from the path again, letting a thick branch wallop him in the arm. "And call me crazy, but it seems like this horse is doing that on purpose."

Emily nodded, her smile staying right in place. "You're not crazy. He's totally doing it on purpose."

"Why? Why would he do that?"

"If you had somebody straddling you, wouldn't you be trying to get them off?"

He let that sink in for a second before responding. "I guess I'd sure give it my best shot, depending on who she was and how much fun we were having."

The blush started at the neckline of that little tank top and floated its way upward until her cheeks were bright crimson, but her smile was discreet. She gave her head a little shake. "Ryan Taggert, the things you say."

"Sorry, I couldn't resist," he said, then for the sake of his own sanity, he quickly changed the subject. "So, how goes the renovation at your grandmother's cottage?"

She rolled her eyes and looked skyward at his question in a move that reminded him of Chloe. "It's going to be like running a marathon at a sprinter's pace. Everything needs updating, I have about eight weeks to make it happen, and my foreman is on a tether."

"A tether? For what?"

"Drunk *riding*."

Ryan couldn't contain his chuckle. "Drunk riding? How is that even possible? Is it even possible?"

"It's totally possible. Apparently he and one of the other guys on my crew got drunk and broke into his neighbor's barn, stole a horse, and tried to ride it. They were allegedly going to the store for more beer but, you know, thought biking it would be irresponsible."

"Drunk riding. So I guess that's . . . an RUI?"

She dipped her head as she laughed, making that ponytail sway. "An RUI and grand theft equine, I suppose. Fortunately for Tiny—that's his name, Tiny, even though he's not remotely tiny. Fortunately for him, the horse's owner did not press charges for the borrowing of the pony, but my dad still arrested him for drunk and disorderly."

Ryan thought about this for a moment. "So, wait a minute. He's got the tether, but if it allows him to move around the island, how does that stop him from drinking and stealing horses again?"

Emily's smiled widened. "Well, turns out it's not really so much a tether as it is an electric dog collar. If he gets too close to the barn that was the scene of the crime, he gets shocked in the leg."

"You are making that up." She must be making that up.

"No, I'm not. We have our own brand of justice here on the island." She winked at him, and he squeezed the pommel again, wishing he could have a few minutes alone. It was going to be another cold shower for him when this day was over.

"You're making that up. How would your father even enforce such a thing?"

"I'm not lying. Ask around. And anyway, Tiny felt so bad about nearly crushing that poor horse, he's willing to do whatever he's told. Lucky for me, because for the moment, I'm his boss and I'm the one telling him what to do."

Ryan was beginning to realize life on this island did not run quite the same as life back in Sacramento. "What's the rest of your crew like?"

"Unique. Unruly. But sincere. I think they're all intent on doing their best work. You'd kind of have to meet them to really get the true flavor."

"Maybe that can be arranged? I'd like to see the place. I do know a thing or two about building and remodeling. I'd be happy to throw in a few suggestions." He hadn't meant to make such an offer, but now that it was out there, he didn't regret it.

Emily's nod was slow and deliberate. "Hmm. I'm on a pretty tight budget if you're asking me to hire you as a consultant. I know how you Taggerts are about money, and I wouldn't want you to think I was taking advantage of your expertise." Her words could have been an insult, but her smile said otherwise. She was teasing him, and he liked it.

"No charge for my expert services," he said. "Strictly pro boner."

What? Shit.

He slapped a hand over his mouth and glanced at Chloe. Fortunately, she had her earbuds in, not that she would have been able to hear him over her mother's laughter. He smiled wide.

"I meant pro *bono*. The boner just slipped out. I mean . . . um . . . shit."

Heat, like another massive horse fart, radiated over his skin. What the hell had he just said?

"That's some real selfless charity work there, Ryan," she sputtered out between giggles, and suddenly he was laughing right along with her. Pro boner? Really?

"Well, what can I say? I'm a real giver."

Chapter 16

Fifteen minutes later they reached the shoreline near Potter's Pointe. The woods receded to reveal a grassy area with a few picnic tables, a public restroom, and a drinking fountain. The gray clouds had given way to glorious afternoon sunshine, and the breeze over the water was a nice break from the muggy stillness of the woods.

"This is Potter's Pointe," Emily said. "The spot where the British landed, causing Chief Eagle Feather to ride naked through the town warning the Americans, or so the story goes. I'm not sure there's much truth to it, but if you ask our historical committee, they will quite emphatically defend it."

"I'm thirsty, Mom. Can I get a drink?" Chloe asked, pointing at the fountain.

"Whoa! What the . . . Whoa!" Tag's exclamation rang out, and Emily turned just in time to watch Periwinkle lie down right in the middle of the grass and roll to her side. Tag landed with a grunt and a thud, his feet slipping from the too-short stirrups. He lay on the ground as his horse, just as easy as she pleased, popped right back up.

"What the hell?" Ryan said breathlessly. "Dad, are you okay?"

"Tag?" Lilly slid off her horse and reached his side before Emily could even comprehend what had just happened. "Are you okay?" Lilly echoed Ryan's question.

He sat up and started to pull off his helmet. "Um, I'm fine. I'm just not sure what happened. She just laid down all of a sudden."

"You sure you're not hurt?" Lilly asked.

"Um, guys?" Chloe said. "Where is she going?"

Emily's gaze traveled from Tag to where Chloe was pointing, and there was Periwinkle, wading straight into the water. In seconds she was belly deep in Lake Huron and getting herself a drink. Emily coughed over a chuckle. That's why Percy told them to head to this spot. He must have assumed the horse would pull this kind of prank. Although it was a little risky since that horse could have rolled right over Tag's leg. Lilly would never forgive her if Emily broke her boyfriend.

"That's legit messed up," said Chloe, pulling out her phone to photo-document the event with various apps.

"You didn't hurt your leg, did you?" Lilly said. "She didn't land on you, right?"

Tag finally unfastened his helmet, tossing it on the grass beside him. "No, I'm fine. The only thing bruised is my ego." He chuckled. "I did not know horses ever did that."

"Well, they're sure not supposed to! I'm going to have a word with that Percy O'Keefe when we get back. Are you sure you're okay?" Lilly asked again.

"Yes, I'm fine. Stop fussing." He stood and rubbed his hip, tilting to the left a bit before straightening up.

"Um, should somebody go get that horse out of the lake?" Chloe asked. "She's going kind of deep."

Ryan clambered down from Duke's back and handed the reins to Emily. "I'll go get her."

"Do you have your phone?" she asked.

"We don't need to call anyone. I can go get her," Ryan responded.

"No, I mean you don't want to go in the water with your phone."

"What? Oh, yeah. Right. Not waterproof. Thanks." He pulled his phone from his pocket and handed it her. She resisted the urge to see if there was a passcode. Because it might be kind of fun to peek into Ryan Taggert's virtual black book. Maybe see a few photos of girlfriends, or just to see what stuff he found important enough to photograph. So maybe she just oh-so-accidentally bumped that button with her thumb . . . yeah, there was a passcode.

"I can get her, Ryan. She's my horse," Tag said, taking a step and listing again. Lilly took his arm, and he let her.

"I got her, Dad." Ryan hurried toward the shoreline.

"Shoes!" Emily shouted, and Ryan kicked them off just before hitting the water. She watched as he waded in chest deep until he finally reached the horse, but Periwinkle seemed none too interested in coming back. Ryan tugged and cajoled and even slipped once and went all the way underwater, only to come up sputtering and shaking the water from his short hair. "Come on, you rotten horse," he muttered.

This day was supposed to be rough on Tag, but so far Ryan seemed to have gotten the worst of it. Emily and Chloe had dismounted by the time he finally made it back to shore with a drenched and seemingly reluctant mare behind him. Ryan was, of course, soaking wet, too, his gray T-shirt now molding to all those muscles Emily had suspected were under there. She was right. There they were. This was not a man who spent his time on the sofa, and Emily found herself mentally tabulating how long it had been since she'd last had sex.

A long time. These days she was just too busy with work and taking care of Chloe to cultivate a relationship. Even the *casual but with benefits* kind, so sex just wasn't readily accessible. But here was Ryan Taggert rising up out of the water like Poseidon. Okay, probably not Poseidon, but maybe rising up like a really good-looking man pretending to be Poseidon. He could totally pull that off. And speaking of pulling it off, he handed the reins to Emily and proceeded to pull off that wet shirt.

Emily heard a soft, faint little sound, like the coo of a baby dove, and realized in an instant that it had come from her own throat. She coughed and turned around to hand the reins to Chloe as Ryan twisted up his shirt to wring it out.

"Well, that was refreshing. That water is not warm," he said, using the knotted shirt to try to wipe droplets of water from his skin. The air was balmy enough, but the breeze was strong, and Emily could see goose bumps cover his skin, and that gave her goose bumps of her own.

That damn horse had nearly rolled over his father, and then she'd nearly drowned him. Ryan did not like that horse. Now he was standing on the grass in wet clothes praying that the frigid water hadn't reduced him to prepubescent sizing, because he couldn't exactly pull at his jeans. He couldn't take them off to wring them out. He just had to stand there, dripping, trying to pretend that he didn't feel stupid for having slipped in that water. He hadn't expected it to be so rocky, and his bare feet had given him zero traction.

"Thanks for getting her, Ryan. I could have done it, you know," his dad said. "Do you want my dry shirt?"

Oh. Yeah. That wouldn't make this worse, him taking the shirt off his father's back. "No, I'm good. This will dry. Eventually." He flapped the shirt in the wind a few times. "See, practically dry." It wasn't. Not even a little.

Periwinkle had the audacity then to bump her nose against his shoulder and offer up a friendly little nicker as if they were pals. Stupid horse. "You know," Ryan said, "if she'd farted in that water, she could have jet-propelled us to shore in a heartbeat." She bumped him again, and he waited for some laughter at his joke. It was sort of lame, sure, and maybe a little off-color, but he'd expected at least a bit of a chuckle. At least from Chloe. Didn't all teenagers love fart jokes? But he looked over her way as Periwinkle's nose bumped him even harder this time.

"Oh. My. Gosh." Chloe's big blue eyes went round, her voice squeaky as she looked past Ryan.

"Oh good Lord!" Emily exclaimed, looking in the same direction just as Lilly started shouting, "No! No! No!" and waving her arms. Periwinkle made another noise, this one not so much a friendly nicker as an insistent whinny, and Ryan turned around to see what everyone seemed to be staring at. And there they were, in all their horsey glory. Periwinkle, fresh from the lake, being thoroughly romanced by Duke. If Ryan had felt insufficient from the cold water, he felt doubly so after seeing what Duke had to offer, and Periwinkle seemed a pleased and willing participant.

"Holy shit," he heard his father say, but Ryan couldn't say anything at all. He just watched, fascinated and oddly intrigued. Was that weird? And gross? It seemed weird and gross, so he tucked those thoughts away and tried to adult for the moment. But nonetheless, it was pretty fascinating, and there was certainly no stopping it now. The whole thing only lasted for a few minutes anyway, and at least in that area Ryan felt superior. He had far more stamina than Duke did, and he left his partners with a little more to smile about. So . . . there was that.

Duke hopped off Periwinkle, his long, horsey face looking neither smug nor abashed. In fact, all the horses looked chill and relaxed. Nothing to see here. Just move along.

Not so much the humans. They were all standing there looking as if they were waiting for a bomb to be defused.

"What the hell do we do now?" Lilly finally said.

"Light them cigarettes?" Tag said.

Ryan chuckled, but the women didn't.

"That was legit crazy. Did I just see what I think I just saw, Mom?" Chloe asked.

Emily's voice was hesitant. "Um, what do you think you saw?"

"I think I just saw Duke hittin' that with Periwinkle."

Ryan chuckled again, but he probably wasn't supposed to.

"Okay," Emily said calmly. "Okay, well, then, yes. You did see what you thought you saw, and we are very much going to discuss all the aspects of that very soon, but now is not really the best time."

Chloe nodded, still staring at the horses as if one of them might sprout wings. "I'm good with that."

"I think maybe I should call Percy," Emily said.

Chapter 17

"So, that was your big plan? To have my horse violate my dad's horse?"

It was Saturday morning, and Emily and Ryan were back at Joe's Cuppa Joe to debrief about yesterday's horse-riding/orgy debacle. "No, of course that wasn't the plan! Percy swears he didn't know that mare was in season."

"How could he not know?"

"I guess she didn't tell him? I don't know. Percy's not that bright. Anyway, he said she was notorious for walking into the lake, but she hardly ever rolls anyone off, and he had no idea that Duke would . . . take advantage. Percy seemed genuinely surprised."

"I think we were all genuinely surprised, including Periwinkle. Talk about associations. I'm not sure if that one was negative, positive, or just . . . educational."

"It ended up being pretty educational for Chloe. We had quite the conversation last night when we got back to Gigi's."

Ryan chuckled. "I'll bet. I think the thing that surprised me even more, though, was how good of a sport my dad was about the whole thing. Actually, what he said to me last night was, 'Now that's what I call horsing around.' He seemed to think it was all pretty funny, so as far as negative associations go? Yeah, we failed."

Emily sighed and moved her chair slightly so the sun wasn't shining right in her face, and then she pushed her sunglasses up to the top of her head. “Lilly didn’t seem that upset, either. She was annoyed with Percy, and I’m pretty sure she thinks I put him up to it, which, of course, I did, but she sure wasn’t angry. I think in spite of everything, Tag and Lilly still had a great day. So I agree with you. We failed at that whole negative association thing.”

Ryan shook his head sadly. “My brother says it’s the chemicals in their brains and they can’t help it.”

Speaking of brains, her own was turning to mush because Ryan had on a white golf shirt that made his tanned skin look downright sinful, and she now found herself staring at the fingers he had wrapped around his coffee cup. She’d hardly slept a wink last night because every time she closed her eyes, she could see him standing near the lake with rivulets of water trailing all over him. If men had wet T-shirt contests, Ryan Taggert would surely win.

“Chemicals in their brains,” she repeated back. “Is he a doctor?”

“No. But he watched a TED Talk once,” Ryan teased.

“Ah.” She nodded. “So now he’s an expert, right?” She tore her eyes away from his hands, only to lock her gaze with his, and that didn’t help either. She pulled her sunglasses back down.

“Exactly. I talked to Bryce last night, and according his extensive research—meaning twenty minutes on the Internet—when people fall in love it releases all sorts of chemicals, like dopamine, and it makes them do crazy, irresponsible shit because they can’t anticipate the consequences. And Bryce should know about this. He’s been married three times so far, and he’s also the biggest dope I’ve ever met.”

Ryan grinned again. She needed him to stop doing that because whatever was going on in *her* brain was not helpful. All the tingling and rippling and fluttering that was going on in the rest of her body wasn’t helpful either.

“Dopamine, huh? Is there an antidote?” she asked hopefully. She could use a shot if there was.

"Just time and distraction, but my dad should already be distracted. He should be solidly preoccupied with that hotel project, but obviously it hasn't been enough to keep his mind off her."

"Or his hands." Tag was very touchy-feely with her sister. Even Chloe noticed.

"No kidding. I saw them say goodbye yesterday. Romeo and Juliet had an easier time parting ways. If my dad had to fall for someone, why couldn't it have been someone in Sacramento?"

"I know, right? Why couldn't Lilly fall for someone here? I'm trying to hook her up with one of the guys from my work crew. If we're lucky, maybe she'll transfer all that chemically induced haze onto someone else. Someone her age."

"Her age? You mean sixteen?"

"You're hilarious," Emily said blandly. "You know she's twenty-six. I think Matt is twenty-five, and I heard him telling the rest of my crew that he was an underwear model for a while but all the focus on his external body left him *spiritually empty*, so he started doing yoga and traveling, and he wound up here."

"You have a traveling yogi on your work crew who used to be an underwear model?" Ryan did not sound happy about that, which for some reason made Emily feel *more* happy. Sure, his seemingly jealous reaction could be nothing more than pride and male ego, but the fact that he cared that there was at least one other attractive male in her life? Well. Yeah. It made her *more happy*.

"Yes, and he's very charming and, oh my gosh, handsome as hell." She said that just to poke at him a little more. That was for *her* pride and her ego.

He rolled his eyes and fanned his face with one hand. "Charming and handsome. Oh, stop. You're getting me all dewy over here. He sounds dreamy."

~

Awesome. She had a guy on her work crew who used to be a model. An *underwear* model? A charming, handsome underwear model? He did not like that at all. But what business was that of his? She could have fifteen underwear models waiting at her beck and call back in San Antonio for all he knew. But somehow, he didn't think she did.

Ryan had his doubts about some of the stuff his brother said. In fact, he had his doubts about virtually everything Bryce said, but his brother might be onto something with this brain chemical nonsense. In fact, what he'd said over the phone last evening had made alarmingly good sense because whatever Ryan had going on his own brain these days, there had to be a reason for it. His attraction to Emily was a little overwhelming and a lot out of character for him. So to learn there was some scientific, biological reason for his state of mind was a bit of a relief. Now that he knew that, he could face it head-on and tackle it. He was smart enough to understand that as soon as he left this island, he'd forget all about her. In the meantime, he just had to stay on the alert and not listen to the dope inside of his brain. Which was always a good policy.

Unfortunately, she had on a little pair of denim shorts, and damn he loved a little pair of denim shorts.

"You can meet him if you want," she said. "You said you wanted to come see the cottage I'm working on. Want to stop over on Monday? Do some of that pro *bonnnno* work you mentioned?" She drew out the word, teasing him into thinking she might say *boner*. Not that he was thirteen and the kind of guy who got a funky kick out of hearing a girl say quasi-naughty words, but the reality was, at that very moment, he and Emily Chambers were both thinking about erections. Which, naturally, made him think about his own. And so he blushed, just as if she'd shouted the word to the table next to them.

"I would enjoy that very much," he said, as neutrally as possible, but she laughed anyway. "But it can't be Monday. Tag is insisting I take a flight lesson with him on Monday."

"A flight lesson? Is he a pilot? Oh, wait. Let me guess. He watched a TED Talk on it once." She wrapped her lips around the straw of her iced tea and took a drink.

Was she flirting with him? It seemed like she was flirting with him. He usually had pretty good radar for stuff like this, but maybe on this remote island, like the spotty Wi-Fi in his hotel, his radar just wasn't working. Stupid brain chemicals.

"Fortunately, there have been actual lessons involved this time," Ryan answered. "And we'll be going with an instructor. I'll just be observing, but I should probably get my affairs in order before I go, just in case. If I show up on Tuesday with two broken legs, you can guess how it went."

"Well, hey, Peach. Fancy seeing you here." A swirl of colors appeared in Ryan's peripheral vision before he turned and saw a woman in a tie-dyed jumper and lime-green high-top tennis shoes.

"Hi, Gloria," Emily said, a look of concern coming to her face. "How are you?"

The woman gave a sigh that included a frowny face, a flop of her hands, and even a little stomp of one foot.

"I'll tell you, Peach. Do you ever have one of those days when you're in a bad mood but you're not sure why so you just keep looking around for someone to argue with? That's the kind of day I'm having."

"Oh, I'm sorry to hear that, Gloria. Have you met my friend Ryan?"

The woman extended a white-gloved hand. "Pleased to meet you. Do you have any issues you feel strongly about that you might want to pick a fight with me over?"

"Um, no?" This coffee shop attracted the strangest patrons.

She sighed again. "Oh, fine. I'll keep looking. By the way, Peach, Bethany Markum is hosting drunk puzzle night tonight if you want to come. Seven o'clock. Sorry, mister. No dudes allowed."

The tie-dye slowly faded from his view. He looked back at Emily. "Drunk puzzle night?

She smiled. "I didn't realize they were still doing them."

"What the hell is drunk puzzle night?" he asked.

"Pretty much like it sounds. You sit around a table working on a puzzle, and if you find a piece that fits, you make somebody drink a shot. In all the times I've done it, we've yet to finish a puzzle."

"Sounds pretty fun. Sounds like something I would have done in college. What else did you used to do for fun around here?"

She pushed her sunglasses back up on her head, and he was glad. He liked to see her eyes, even though they left him feeling a little breathless and not quite in charge of himself.

"We did lots of stuff, most of which my dad was not happy about. There are reasons I'm his least favorite daughter."

"Oh, I'm sure that's not true." She seemed earnest and yet oddly matter-of-fact about this statement. He couldn't imagine how he'd feel if he thought he was Tag's least favorite. Clearly that was Bryce.

"No, it's true. I was a pain in the ass. My friends and I were always drinking out in the woods and stealing candy from the fudge shops."

"That doesn't sound so bad. I've done worse."

"Yes, but he was the chief of police, so it was always extra embarrassing for him when I got busted for something." She looked at him for a moment, as if weighing her words. "And once he caught me skinny-dipping with a boy in the pool at the Imperial Hotel."

Not that shocking. He'd like to skinny-dip with her. "Hmm. How old were you?"

"Nineteen."

"Technically a legal adult."

"Sure, but it still wasn't legal to be naked in a hotel pool at midnight. Dad was pretty pissed."

Ryan picked up his own iced tea. "I guess I can understand that, him being your father and all. Although in the scheme of things, it's not *that* bad."

She paused for another moment before adding, "He told me I couldn't date that boy anymore. So I ran away and married him. If Dad wasn't my biggest fan before, that pretty much sealed the deal. I can count the number of decent conversations we've had since then on one finger. We are an Irish people on Wenniway Island. Slights are not easily forgotten." She said this conversationally, too. Like she was reporting the weather instead of telling him something that would seem momentous in his family.

Ryan and his brothers had gotten into their own share of trouble, but no matter what it was or how bad they'd been, Ryan never doubted that his parents always loved them.

"That's . . . I can't imagine that. I'm sorry."

She brushed a strand of hair away from her face. "It's all right. Chloe and I are here now, and we're having a pretty nice visit. I actually think my dad might be starting to thaw, so as long as I don't screw anything up while I'm here, maybe we'll start to get along better. And speaking of not screwing things up, I'd better get to Gigi's cottage. When I left yesterday, there were light fixtures dangling from wires, and we're still trying to figure out where a particularly odoriferous aroma is coming from. Even the fudge can't cover it up."

Ryan nodded and stood up when she did. "I suppose I should get over to the Clairmont, too. Dad's got some blueprints he wants me to look over."

"The Clairmont? Is that who you're consulting for?"

Technically? No. But he couldn't tell her anything about those Mahoney women because there was a very strict confidentiality clause in the contract they'd signed yesterday morning. He was doing a few things at the Clairmont for his father, but as soon as possible, he planned to head over to old Bridget O'Malley's place to try to woo her into selling him her property.

"Um, yes. The Clairmont."

"Oh, you're working for the enemy then." Emily tucked the chair in under the table, and her smile was easygoing.

"The enemy?"

"Oh yeah. Big feud. Herb Mahoney owns the Clairmont, and the Callaghans and Mahoneys haven't seen eye-to-eye since, well, since forever. Not sure why." She chuckled and started walking. "It's silly, really, but Gigi and June Mahoney are determined to keep it going. Right now we're having rental wars. It's partly why I'm here."

He fell into step beside her. "Because of a feud?"

She nodded. "Gigi is convinced the Mahoney sisters are trying to lure away her summer tenants, and they probably are. That's why this renovation I'm working on is so important. Gigi wants her cottages to be nicer than the Mahoneys' cottages."

Ryan's step faltered. Because. Shit. If what Emily said was true, then he really was working for the enemy. "I'm sure there are enough tourists and visitors to keep all the cottages rented."

"I'm sure there are. It's really just the principle of it. Like I said, it's a silly feud."

It was. Certainly it was, and yet Ryan couldn't help but feel a little bit awkward knowing he was about to go buy more property for June Mahoney. That wasn't going to sit very well with Gigi, and possibly not with Emily, but the contract was signed. Nothing he could do about that now. Business was business, after all.

Chapter 18

Sunday morning, back at Saint Bart's, and Emily had a headache. Not a terrible headache. Just the dull kind that made her feel sleepy and kind of stupid. Drunk puzzle night had been a little too much fun. Seeing a cluster of her old friends, reminiscing about good times and past antics was just what Emily needed. Somewhere in Texas, she'd forgotten who she was. Being back at Trillium Bay, being with friends and family, was helping her to remember. That girl she'd been in the past? She wasn't so bad. Unruly? Very much so, but other than her friction with Harlan, life on Wenniway had been pretty good.

It didn't feel quite so good this morning, though. She had a teensy hangover, and Gigi was muttering something about the Mahoney sisters. She was on a roll, though, and didn't require much response, so Emily just nodded at regular intervals and made sympathetic sounds when it seemed appropriate.

"There's Grandpa," Chloe said. She waved at him as he approached, and he almost, very nearly smiled as he sat down next to her.

"Good morning, ladies. How is everyone?"

"I'm fine, Grandpa. Happy Father's Day."

Shit. It was Father's Day? No wonder Harlan didn't like her. She didn't even know what day it was! Some of the other guys had rosebuds pinned to the lapel of their jackets, but Harlan wasn't wearing a jacket. In fact, he was wearing his uniform. Probably because he figured no one had planned a party for him. Someone should have reminded her. Where the hell was Brooke? She was usually in charge of this kind of thing, wasn't she?

"Guess what I saw the other day," Chloe said to her grandfather.

"Turtles?"

"Nope."

"A freighter?"

"Nope. I saw a couple of horses doing it."

Emily gasped. "Chloe! We're in church!"

Harlan quickly pulled out a handkerchief and proceeded to blow his nose, but if Emily didn't know better, she might think he was chuckling behind that little square of fabric. Hope he'd still be chuckling later when he found out she'd forgotten it was Father's Day!

Lilly slid into the pew with only seconds to spare, looking flushed and radiant. She grinned at Emily, and Emily rolled her eyes in response. Geeeeez. She may as well be wearing a sign around her neck that said, *I just had delicious Sunday morning intercourse.* Good Lord, it was so obvious that Father O'Reilly was sure to call her out for her wanton, lascivious ways. The very notion of it stirred up a collection of emotions for Emily. Dismay. Disapproval. Jealousy.

Wait a minute. Jealousy? What did she have to be jealous of?

Oh. The sex. She was jealous about the sex. Because while her sister had been rolling around in the sheets an hour ago with a man who by all appearances seemed to adore her, Emily had been taking ibuprofen and B vitamins in the kitchen of Gigi's house while bitching at Chloe to get her heathen butt out of bed. Then she'd gotten into a fight with her grandmother over how many scoops of coffee to put into the percolator just because Emily needed it to be extra strong today.

Plus, with a little bit of mental math and a review of her electronic calendar, Emily had figured out it had been exactly one year and seven months since she'd had sex. And that last time, it had been thoroughly un-memorable. The only way she could even recall that it was that particular night was because the name of the restaurant was still listed under the date, and she remembered the morel linguine. Delicious linguine that had brought her much closer to an orgasm than her date had.

Her mind wandered, as it was apt to do in church, as she thought about linguine. And sex. And the wanting of the sex. There was something especially naughty about thinking of it in church. Like God was just that much closer, and therefore it was just that much more risqué. Her thoughts wandered even further . . . and there was Ryan Taggert, first in the red tie, then in his soaking wet T-shirt. God bless him. And then Ryan without his soaking wet T-shirt. Shit. Shit. She did not need him in her mind, especially in church, and double-especially when she was already thinking about sex. But the image of him coming up out of the lake, all of the droplets dripping off all the muscles. Whoever that last guy had been, linguine guy whose name she could hardly recall, he had not been muscular. Ryan was. Oh, was he ever, and now, damn it, she was going straight to hell, because her mind flooded with all sorts of wonderfully unholy thoughts. Thoughts of Ryan, who was muscular and handsome and who had nice hands.

And who was standing in the aisle next to her.

That was not her imagination. He was actually standing there, and Emily prayed to God, ironically, that her wicked thoughts were not written all over her face. Ryan smiled over at her and stepped forward, moving down the aisle behind his father. They sat down just a few pews in front of Emily and her family. It was pretty bold of Tag, all things considered, sitting so close to the pulpit, knowing how he'd spent his morning. Then again, who was she to judge?

Lilly took a big breath and let it out slowly. Then she leaned closer to whisper into Emily's ear. "We're going to tell Dad today."

"What?" Emily's voice went an octave too high, and she quickly looked around to see who had noticed. It all made her head hurt. Fortunately, the acoustics in that old church were terrible, and so no one could tell exactly where that yelp had come from. "You can't tell him today," she whispered urgently. "It's Father's Day."

Lilly's eyes went round. "It is? Why didn't Brooke tell us?"

"Shhhh," Gigi hissed, and their conversation was over for the time being.

"Hey, look," Chloe whispered loudly and pointed blatantly. "There's Tag and Ryan."

"Who?" Harlan asked, arching his neck a bit to see them.

Emily pushed Chloe's hand down and leaned in toward Harlan. "You met them last Sunday. John Taggert and his son Ryan."

You know. John Taggert, who is having sex with Lilly, and Ryan, the guy I wish was having sex with me.

The thought was so not appropriate, but she was in church, and there was no lying in church . . . so she had to tell the truth.

The truth was . . . she did want to have sex with Ryan Taggert. She didn't want to just go back to San Antonio and start looking for some other guy. She liked Ryan. But that just couldn't happen. Because . . . um . . . Why, exactly? She was a grown woman, after all. She was in charge of her own body and responsible. She knew how to be safe while still enjoying herself. He was nice and sexy and made her laugh, and he made her . . . well, he made her want to have sex, apparently. Not that it was much of a shock. Guys like him pretty much made every woman want to have sex.

That didn't mean it was going to happen. It couldn't happen. At least, it shouldn't happen because if Lilly actually married Tag, Emily and Ryan would be . . . how would that work? Gosh, this was not the time to have a hangover. She was trying to figure something out. Let's see . . . Ryan would be Lilly's stepson. And Tag would be Emily's brother-in-law. So that would make Ryan . . . her stepnephew? Seriously? Her head started to ache again, and the organ music added a nice dramatic backdrop to her thoughts as Delores Crenshaw banged on the keys. Dun-dun-dunnnnnn.

There was no way Tag and Lilly would get married, of course. Just no way. Somehow she and Ryan would make sure, but . . . what if they failed and his father really did marry her sister? She and Ryan would be stuck together as relatives of a sort. She didn't need that. She needed some random sex buddy that she could get away from when she was through. Not one who might show up on her sister's Christmas card every year. Nope, she could not have sex with Ryan. It was a bad idea all the way around.

Nothing wrong with just imagining it, though. Right? So for the next hour, as the church choir sang and Father O'Reilly pontificated about doing unto others, Emily fantasized about doing unto Ryan.

After Mass was the usual rigmarole, with everyone milling around. Lilly quickly disappeared, but Brooke arrived. She was wearing a short blue dress and a wide white headband.

"Don't you look nice," Gigi said.

"Where have you been?" Emily asked.

"Getting the Father's Day brunch buffet ready in the community hall. You didn't forget, did you?" She arched an eyebrow, already knowing the answer.

"Of course I didn't." So much for honesty in church. They were outside, so it didn't really count.

"Chief. Chief Callaghan, a word please."

"I'll give her a word. How about *yikes*," Brooke murmured into Emily's ear just as Gigi snorted into the other.

Emily turned to see Vera VonMeisterburger bearing down on them.

"Chief Callaghan, someone has been tampering with the locks on my shed. They're going after my bat houses. I'd like a security detail stationed there until the culprits are apprehended."

Harlan looked down at her, as dour as ever. "You want one of my officers to stand outside your shed all night long just to protect your bat houses?"

"Yes, that's what I said. White-nose syndrome is nothing to be taken lightly. Imagine the police force you'll need when mosquitoes start carrying away young children."

"Vera, mosquitoes don't do that."

"Well, of course, they don't now because of my efforts to keep them at bay, but mark my words. If we do not address this bat problem, well, children may not be carried away, but they could certainly be drained dry of all their precious blood. The island will be littered with little empty shells of bloodless children everywhere. Think of that now, would you?"

"I am quite certain I'll think of little else for the rest of the day, Vera," he said, patting her arm.

"You think about it, too, young lady." Mrs. VonMeisterburger turned and pointed a finger at Brooke's face. "This will be the first scandal of your new administration if you don't do something about it."

"I'm not the mayor yet, Mrs. VonMeisterburger, but if I run, and if I win, you can be sure I'll look into this. I'll even put you on the task force."

Mrs. VonMeisterburger suddenly smiled. "A task force. Does that position come with a uniform?"

"Um, do you want it to come with a uniform?"

"Yes."

"Then I'll look into that as well." Brooke exhaled as the bat-shit crazy bat lady walked away. "How does that woman still scare the crap out of me?"

Emily smiled. "She scares everybody, but you're going to make an excellent politician someday because you just said all that shit to her with a totally straight face."

"It's good practice, I guess."

"Oh, don't let that woman scare you, Brooke," Gigi said. "She thinks she's so special because she knows about bats. Well, she's got 'em in her belfry, if you ask me. And everybody knows she makes the soggiest pie crusts on the entire island."

Harsh words spoken in a place where a woman's baked goods established her rank in society. One undercooked Bundt cake could ruin your standing for life.

"Harlan, take me over to the community hall," Gigi added, putting her arm through his. "Girls, we'll see you there."

"I think Gigi is giving me time to go buy him a card," Emily said as her father and grandmother walked away.

"Hmm, maybe that's where Lilly was off to in such a hurry."

"Lilly? Where did you see her?"

Brooke's smirk could have melted butter. "Heading down Marquette Street with that sexy old Taggert guy. You know. The one she's been sleeping with."

Emily gasped. Would her sisters please stop dropping bombshells on her today? Did no one care that she had a hangover and a very dull headache? "What? Who told you that?"

The smirk turned into a full-on smile. "Oh, come on, Emily. Have you really been gone so long that you've forgotten what this place is like? Did Lilly really think twenty bucks was going to keep Dmitri Krushnic quiet?"

"Holy shit, Brooke. How many people know?"

"Um, let's see." Brooke started counting off on her fingers. "One, two, three . . . Oh yeah. Everybody. Everybody knows. Except Dad, of course."

"No one has told him?"

"Oh hell no. Nobody wants to be that messenger. Those honors are all on Lilly."

"Does Gigi know?"

Brooke snorted. "Who do you think told me?"

"What did she say, exactly?"

Brooke pulled a tinted ChapStick from her pocket and applied some before answering. "Basically she said, 'How's an old gal like me supposed to compete if the fellas can have Lilly instead?'"

"That was her main concern? Her shrinking dating pool?"

"Gigi has her own set of priorities. Plus, she has a new urn and no one to put in it." She slipped the ChapStick back into her pocket. "You know, this situation with Lilly and the old dude is all kinds of messed up, but all things considered, I guess I can kind of understand why you took off with Nick without telling anyone."

"It seemed easiest at the time, but as you know, it caused a lot more problems than it solved. Did you know Lilly wants to tell Dad today?"

That got a startled reaction from Brooke. "Today? She can't tell him today. It's Father's Day. Is she crazy? Well, I guess we all know the answer to that. They are good-looking men, though . . ." Brooke's voice trailed off, and her gaze floated past Emily.

Emily turned, and there was Ryan, looking very sharp in dress pants and a white button-down shirt.

"Hi," she said breathlessly.

"Hi. How was drunk puzzle night?"

"Fun, but they ganged up on me. We did not finish the puzzle. Have you seen your dad lately? And my sister?"

"My dad took off right after the service. Why?" He nodded at Brooke, who gave a circular wave in response.

"Hi there," she said. "I'll leave you two to it, then. Seems like you have some talking to do. I'll see you at the community hall, Em. Don't forget it's Father's Day."

"Oh shit. It's Father's Day?" Ryan said.

Chapter 19

It was eight o'clock Tuesday morning as Emily walked up the path to Gigi's rental cottage hoping to find her crew hard at work. They normally started around seven o'clock, except for Horsey who, just as Harlan had forewarned, always seemed to be late for one reason or another. One day it was because his bike chain had come loose. Another day it was because his barn cat was having kittens and he felt he should be there since, even though he wasn't technically the father, emotionally he felt as if he were. And then there was the morning he was late because he'd fallen back asleep next to his cereal bowl. The cornflakes in his hair confirmed his story.

This morning his bike was near the front gate, which was a good sign. Tiny sitting on the front porch steps was *not* a good sign. Georgie was next to him, her arm slung around his big, drooping shoulders. He glanced up at the sound of Emily's approach, but the ever-present twinkle in his eye was definitely missing.

Garth was sitting on the porch railing looking like the slacker he was. "Mornin', boss lady. How are you on this fine day?"

"Pretty good. I'd be better if you were all inside working. What's the story? Tiny, is something wrong?"

Garth wiped his hand under his nose, and Emily wished he'd get himself some allergy meds. If she had an insurance plan for her employees, that's the first thing she'd get him.

"I'm fine. Just a little blue. Nothing some good hard work won't fix," Tiny said.

Emily clapped her hands together. "Excellent. Wonderful to hear. Let's get to it." She took a step closer, but Georgie patted Tiny's back and gazed up at Emily with concern.

"We'll be inside in just a second," she said.

This is where *real* Emily needed to pretend to be *ball-busting* Emily, but Tiny really did look sad. Even *ball-busting* Emily wasn't *heartless* Emily.

"Is there something I can help with?"

Garth filled in the blanks. "Tiny's got a big old case of puppy love, just like a big old slobbery Saint Bernard."

"Shut up, Garth. You don't know anything about anything," Georgie said.

Tiny's head dropped back down. "Naw, he's right. It's just puppy love. It'll pass."

"It doesn't have to pass, T. You just have to tell her how you feel. Maybe she feels the same way about you." Who would have guessed Georgie was so sentimental? Along with all those tattoos and piercings and chronic PMS.

The sunlight bounced off Tiny's bald head as he shook it. "An exotic beauty like her? She'd never go for a jughead like me."

"I don't know about that. Let's give her a little credit. If she's smart enough, she'll realize she'd be lucky to have you."

Georgie's soft side was endearing, but whoever this woman was, and however earnest Tiny's affection might be, Emily couldn't imagine a woman jumping at the chance to be his girl. He was three hundred pounds of tattooed bad judgment. He had a dog collar on his ankle, for God's sake. And as if the collar alone wasn't insult enough, Garth had gotten him a little pink bone-shaped dog tag that said *Tiny* on it, so now when he walked, he jingled, like Bad Biker Santa.

"Um, I don't mean to pry, but since we're technically talking about this during business hours, might I ask who is the object of your affection?" Emily asked.

"More like the object of his affliction." Garth snickered at his own pun.

"Shut up, Garth," Emily and Georgie said in unison.

The screen door slammed as Horsey wandered out onto the porch eating an apple with his enormous teeth. "What's up, pussycats? Oh, pardon me, boss lady. I didn't mean you. Didn't see you down there." His skin flushed, but Emily smiled back.

"No problem. We were just having a discussion about the state of Tiny's love life."

"Oh, so he told you about Gloria, huh?"

"Gloria?" Emily responded. "Not . . . Gloria Persimmons."

Tiny's jack-o'-lantern-like head popped up and his cheeks went scarlet, confirming her guess. "Do you know her?"

"Of course I know her. I grew up here, remember? Gloria and I are friends."

"You are?" His tone was reverent, and Emily had to wonder if they could possibly be talking about the same Gloria Persimmons. Walrus-faced, too-loud, bubble-gum-popping Gloria Persimmons. But there could not possibly be two of them. She was a true original.

The screen door slammed again as Matt and Wyatt joined the rest of them, and Emily resigned herself to the fact that she'd get no work out of them until this topic had been thoroughly discussed. Over the past few days, remodeling progress had been delayed by discussions about why *deer* was plural for the animals but *dear* wasn't plural for people, if the moon landing had actually happened, followed by a lively discussion about Area 51, and why anyone thought that a tree falling in the woods wouldn't make noise if there was no one there to hear it. And of course there were the yoga breaks that Matt said he needed, which meant Georgie stopped whatever *she* was doing just so she could discreetly watch him. It really didn't take much to get this group off track, but it took an enormous amount of effort to get them back *on* track.

"What's going on?" Matt asked, looking around at the group.

"Nothing you'd understand, dude," Horsey answered. "Not with your chick-magnet man bun and all your caramel sultra sexy yoga moves." Horsey swayed and moved his arms around slowly in what was probably supposed to look like a . . . yoga pose? Please be a yoga pose and not his idea of a sex position.

Matt smiled, and all the angels smiled back. "*Kama Sutra*."

"Huh?" A little piece of apple fell from Horsey's mouth.

"It's *Kama Sutra*. Not caramel sultra."

"Well, now see?" Horsey tossed his hands up in the air. "That's why you get the babes and the rest of us don't."

That was not the reason. Well, it might be why Matt *did* get the babes, but it was not the reason why the rest of them didn't. There was a long, exhaustive list of all the reasons why these other derelict guys did not get the babes. Starting with their lack of attention to personal hygiene and ending with . . . more lack of attention to personal hygiene.

"Tiny is certain that Gloria Persimmons would never go out with him, and I'm trying to convince him that he should at least ask her," Georgie said. "No guts, no glory. And no Gloria, right?"

Matt nodded and sat down on the other side of Tiny. "You haven't even asked her out, bro? Why not?"

"Because she's . . . enchanting, like a princess. Have you seen her hair? It's like spun gold."

Spun gold growing out of brown dirt. Emily had just seen Gloria, and her dark roots were as wide as Tiny's beefy thumb. Any woman could have that gold hair if they bought it from a box like she did.

"Have you at least talked to her?" Emily asked. "I don't think she's dating anyone." Actually, she knew for a fact that Gloria was not currently dating anyone because they'd discussed it endlessly at drunk puzzle night.

"Of course she's not. Who on this island is worthy of her?" Tiny said.

Perspective was an amazing thing. Maybe the dopamine in Tiny's brain had somehow been kicked into overdrive, blinding him to some of Gloria's more unique attributes.

"You are worthy of her," Georgie answered. "I totally think she'd say yes if you asked her."

"You know she comes to my yoga class every Monday, T. Maybe you should join, and then you can have a chance to talk to her," Matt said.

"Oh, I think that's not the best idea," Emily blurted out. "I mean, yes, I think you should definitely talk to her, but I'm not sure yoga class is the best place."

"Why?" Horsey asked, taking another big bite of apple.

"Why?" Garth said, laughing. "You think seeing Tiny's big lard-ass pointing up at the mountain dog or whatever they call it, you think if she's behind him and sees that she's gonna think, 'Oh yeah. Get me some of that.'"

Georgie scowled at her brother. "Shut up, Garth! Gosh, you're so mean. Don't listen to him, Tiny. He's just jealous because he knows Gloria will probably say yes to you and she'd never say yes to him."

Actually, Emily had been thinking exactly what Garth had said, but she just might have phrased it a little more gently. In fact, she might have turned it around completely. Like this.

"Tiny, what I meant was that Gloria likes to keep herself very put together, and if she sees you in yoga class, she may feel a little shy or awkward. But I think if you approached her in some other way or at some other time, you'd have better luck."

"You think? You're her friend. Do you think I have a shot?"

Knowing Gloria . . . yes. Tiny had a pretty good shot. "Yes, I do."

That sparkle lit his bright blue eyes.

"In fact, I happen to know that she does, upon occasion, go to the Wednesday night square dancing at Saint Bart's. I could find out if she'll be there this week." She'd promise anything if it would help get them back to work.

Tiny's face fell again. "Square dancing? Oh, that's no good. I'd just end up watching her have fun with all the other guys because I don't know how to square-dance."

"I can teach you," said Wyatt, finally joining the conversation. "I'm a decent caller."

"How you gonna teach him all by himself?" Horsey asked. "Square dancing has to happen in pairs. And you need at least . . ." He counted on his fingers. "Four pairs. And four pairs of people would be . . ." He counted on his fingers again. "That would be eight people."

"Well, we've got seven people right here," said Georgie.

"Six dancers. I'm the caller," Wyatt said.

Emily really needed her people to be working today. Not square dancing. But Tiny looked so sad, and the truth was, he and Gloria would make a damn fine couple. And maybe if she got those two together it would make up for all the bad karma she was creating by trying to break up the romance between Tag and Lilly. If there was some sort of karmic score sheet, maybe this would balance things out.

"I can get Chloe and Gigi," she said.

Ryan had seen a collection of interesting things while on this island. A pink restaurant, people in colonial military garb during a tour of the fort with Tag, and slabs of fudge being made. He'd watched his father fly an airplane and ride a bike, and he'd even seen two horses getting it on. In short, Ryan had learned to expect the unexpected around here, but what he never would have anticipated on this mild Tuesday afternoon was seeing a group of wild and mangy guys in work boots dancing around in the front yard of a Victorian cottage while some sort of twangy, hillbilly hoedown music played from a tiny set of speakers. There was a huge guy with a bald head and tattoos, a Mohawk-ed girl with even more tattoos, and a couple of guys so skinny they could blow away in a strong breeze. The last guy did not fit in with all the others and must certainly be the infamous Yoga Matt. Chloe and Gigi were there, and right in the thick of it all was Emily, a big smile on her face and the sound of her laughter louder than any of the rest of them.

"No, I said promenade, Garth. Not spin your partner." A dark-haired man with a long braid sat on the railing next to the speakers.

"That's your left hand, Horsey. Use your right," Chloe called out over the general mayhem.

"Do I lead with my right foot, then?" someone asked.

"No, your left foot," someone answered.

Whatever was going on here, clearly no one was really in charge. Ryan observed from the side of the house for a minute, until he found his head bobbing in time with the music. Oh hell no. He was not going to start liking square dancing. It was bad enough that Tag was so fascinated. He stepped out from his spot in the shade and walked up to the group.

"Hello?" The music stopped, and everyone turned to look his way.

"Hey, Ryan," Emily gasped, pushing an errant strand of hair away from her face. She was flushed and disheveled, and it hit him in the gut like a sucker punch. That's probably just what she'd look like after a good roll in the hay, and suddenly all his determination to keep everything between them strictly business evaporated. Stupid dopamine. No wonder his father enjoyed square dancing.

"Hey, yourself. You told me to stop by, but I didn't realize you were having a hoedown."

"Not so much a hoedown as a dance lesson. Let me introduce you to everyone. Chloe you know, of course."

"Hi, Ryan." She waved as if he was not just feet away from her.

"And of course you met my grandmother, Gigi O'Reilly-Callaghan-Harper-Smith. She owns this place."

She made the rounds, saying names like Tiny and Horsey, and he shook everyone's hand. They were polite enough, but with the exception of the infamous Yoga Matt, every single one of them, even the young woman, eyed him with some suspicion. He'd run into this kind of reaction from construction crews before. If you didn't have calluses on your hands, they didn't trust you.

"Well, I guess we've had enough dancing for today, gang," Emily said. "How about if you all take a lunch break while I show Ryan around."

"Sure thing, Miss Chambers." Tiny nodded. The group turned and headed toward a little shady spot where a beat-up picnic table sat.

Emily, Chloe, and the grandmother who continued to undress him with her eyes stood at the bottom of the steps, and Ryan turned to get his first good look at the place.

"So, what do you think of the outside of the cottage?" Emily asked.

Ryan had to smile. "I think calling it a cottage is misleading. It looks huge. A house this size in Sacramento would not be considered a cottage."

"Most of the houses on the island are called cottages because they were built as summer homes for rich lumber barons and such back in the eighteen hundreds. It's got about three thousand square feet, but unfortunately about five square feet of that is kitchen, so I'm trying to figure out how to upgrade everything while keeping the charm."

"Well, let's go inside and have a look."

Two hours later, Chloe and the grandmother had left, the crew was downstairs making a ruckus, and it was just him and Emily standing in an upstairs bedroom. Listening to her describe all the plans she had for the cottage had made the time fly by. Her enthusiasm was engaging, and he was more than a little impressed by her knowledge. Not that he hadn't expected it.

"If I can figure out a way to replace these windows with something more energy efficient without losing the historical charm, that would be ideal. Haven't figured that one out yet. I'd also really love to make them bigger since the view from this room is one of the best in the house. See that lilac tree? It's about one hundred years old."

Ryan turned and looked out the window she was standing next to. There was a small front yard, and then the hill sloped downward toward a gnarled tree that looked like something from a fairy tale. His eyes traveled past it, on down the hill. There was a cottage, and beyond that was the lake, but it was the cottage that caught his attention. It was pink. And he was very nearly certain it was the place the Mahoney sisters were so determined to buy. Ryan had come from the other direction to get to Gigi's place earlier today and hadn't noticed until just now. But there it was. Right down there. The pink cottage.

"Isn't that a great view?" Emily prompted as he stood there trying to think of what to say. Because what he wanted to say was, *"My company has been hired by the Mahoney sisters to buy that land and build a three-story bed-and-breakfast right there that will almost certainly ruin this awesome view of yours."*

"That is a great view. You don't often see a pink house," was the best he could come up with.

Emily moved closer, and he could feel the heat of her body. Or maybe that was just heat from the sunshine coming through poorly insulated window frames? No, it was Emily. She smelled really nice again today. It was hot, and he hoped his antiperspirant was doing its job, yet there she stood next to him, warm as sunshine, smelling like flowers, with just a hint of moisture giving her face a glow. So even though Emily Chambers was technically off-limits, and even though his company was poised to ruin her view, he really wanted to give in to his baser desires and make her glow all over. What would happen if he just leaned over and kissed her?

"That pink house belongs to Bridget O'Malley," Emily said, wiping a smudge off the window glass, clearly not reading his mind. "She is closing in on a hundred and three years old. Last I knew she was still baking all her own bread, but Gigi said she's starting to get forgetful. The fire department would really like her to stop cooking because they get called out here every time she forgets to take something out of the oven."

Bridget O'Malley, huh? He tamped down a sigh. It was definitely the place the Mahoney sisters were interested in. He wished he could mention that to Emily, but all he said was, "One hundred and three? That's amazing. If my dad lives to that age, he'd still have another forty-five years to go."

"Sure, and Lilly would have seventy-seven. By the way, did you tell him that their clandestine rendezvous are the worst-kept secret on the island?"

He shook his head. "Did you tell your sister?"

"No, not yet, but at least my dad is still in the dark. Father's Day was not the day to tell him, and I convinced Lilly to keep it to herself for a while longer. I'm having such a nice visit, and quite frankly, I don't want her making Harlan all grumpy and spoiling that. Let's go sit on the porch. It's stifling up here."

He followed her down the stairs, and they went outside to literally sit *on* the porch, because there were no chairs. Even so, the breeze was nice, and he sure could use some cooling off.

"What do you think I should do with the teeny-tiny kitchen in this place?" she asked, pulling her knees up in front of her.

Ah, at last. A problem Ryan could solve. "I have a couple of ideas. Do you have any drawing paper?"

"I think so." She hopped up and went inside, returning a minute later with a notebook and pen.

He talked as he sketched. "If you take out that powder room to the left of the kitchen, you can expand this way and add an island in the center, and then you can add another section of cabinets right here."

"I love that idea," she said. "I never would have thought of that. You're pretty good at this construction stuff, I guess."

Ryan knew he was pretty good at this construction stuff, but hearing her say it and having her gaze at him with that light in her eyes, he felt like he was the best in the world.

"I have lots of ideas." He did, too. He kept silent on the ones involving her and a mattress and focused instead on suggestions for the cottage renovation. An hour later, they were surrounded by sheets of paper, torn from the notebook and covered with sketches.

"Wow, I'm not joking. You really *are* good at this stuff," she said, holding up a drawing of two tiny bedrooms transformed into a luxurious suite. "You're practically a superhero. Like . . . Remodel-Man. Or Construct-Thor."

"You're funny." He flipped the page and started another drawing.

She leaned over to see it, and her hair tickled his nose. He laughed and reached up to push the strands away, and damned if her hair wasn't every bit as soft as he'd imagined. His fingers curled around it, catching, twisting. She looked up at him in surprise, and the urge to kiss her nearly overwhelmed him. Gazes locked, the moment hung suspended. Her lips were only inches away, looking so soft and so tempting. He leaned forward, nearly closing the distance, and something went *crash*! Followed by more *crash, crash, crash* inside the house, and Ryan and Emily jerked backward like they'd been zapped by a live wire.

"Nothing!" Georgie called out, almost immediately. "That was nothing. Just dropped a big frickin' jar of about five hundred frickin' nails down the stairs."

"Butterfingers!"

"Shut up, Garth!"

Ryan looked back at Emily, who was now staring at her shoes and not at him, and he knew the moment had passed.

Chapter 20

"I've decided I want to try every flavor of fudge and every flavor of ice cream on the island," Chloe said as she licked a dribble of triple-caramel swirl from the side of her waffle cone.

It was a beautiful evening near the bay, and after a tough day of dealing with cabinets being delivered that were the wrong finish, Horsey being late because the shoelace of his work boot had broken so he'd had to run to O'Doul's to get some new ones, the Trillium Bay building inspector stopping by to let Emily know she had more forms to fill out, and smashing her thumb with a hammer just when she was trying to show off to her crew her hammering prowess, Emily had decided that this was a good night to have dessert for dinner. She'd gotten no argument from her daughter, and so they were now sitting on a bench near Trillium Park, having ice cream and watching the ducks paddle around in the water.

"Every flavor of ice cream? That's a lot of flavors," Emily said. She'd gotten a strawberry sundae, just as she had as a kid whenever Gigi would take her for ice cream. She never got these in San Antonio and had no idea why. Surely they'd taste just as good there, but then again, maybe they wouldn't because Texas just wasn't Trillium Bay.

"Yep," Chloe said with another swipe at her cone. "But you've always told me it's important to have goals. I think tomorrow morning I should have coffee ice cream. Because, you know, coffee in the morning?"

"Not sure about that, but I'm glad to know you consider goals important. So, what did you do earlier today?"

"I went up to Holmes Point with Susie Mahoney. I know we're not supposed to like them because of, you know, that feud stuff, but I really like her. I like all the kids here. Everybody is so nice."

"Don't worry about the feud, honey. No one pays any attention to that except for the old folks, and most of them think it's silly, too. I'm just glad to hear you've found some nice kids. Seems like you're having a pretty good summer so far."

Chloe nodded, moving her ice-cream cone along with her head. "I am. I'm having the best summer I've ever had. Can we come back here next year?"

Next summer? Heaven only knew what would be going on for them next summer. "Um, probably. If you want to."

"I do want to. Can I take riding lessons? I saw that guy Percy, and he said he gives group lessons on Tuesday and Friday mornings."

"Riding lessons?" That might cost some money, but if Chloe was interested, Emily would find a way to make it work. "Yes, you can take riding lessons. That sounds fun. Just stay away from Duke and Periwinkle."

Chloe giggled. "That's a deal. Can I ask you something else? You're probably going to say no, but I really, really, really hope you say yes."

That was quite a windup. It must be something big. "You can ask me."

"Can I go camping overnight this Tuesday with a bunch of the girls? There won't be any boys, and Carrie Crenshaw's mom and aunt are going, too, so there will be grown-ups with us."

"Camping overnight. Like outside? Are you sure you can handle sleeping outside and peeing next to a tree?"

Chloe's expression was indignant. "I think if you could do it, then I can do it."

Emily wasn't sure if her daughter was trying to insult her or just demonstrate her own confidence. She chose to give her the benefit of the doubt and go with the latter.

"Let me talk to Carrie's mom tomorrow. If she says it's okay with her, then it's okay with me."

"Ohmygosh, thank you!" Chloe's arms closed around her, and the hug was very much appreciated. Less so was the ice cream that Chloe got in Emily's hair. They were in the process of trying to wipe it out when Ryan showed up. He'd made a habit of that the last couple of days. Showing up. He'd come back to the cottage three days in a row since they'd first made those drawings on the front porch. He'd brought her a few more sketches and told her all about the stuff he and his father were doing for the Clairmont Hotel. She had him assist her with cutting some trim wood just so she could show off how well she could manage a table saw, and she told him that Gigi used a regular old spiral-bound notebook to keep track of her reservations—which made him cringe in a distinctly comical fashion. They'd talked about all sorts of other things, too, like how the remote location of the island created unique challenges for getting things like new carpet and appliances delivered, and she'd explained to him that the best way to receive any goods in a timely fashion from the boat docks was to bribe the dray drivers with a case of beer or a nice bottle of whiskey. It wasn't corrupt, exactly. Just effective enough to move your cargo to the front of the line.

The chats had been friendly, flirtatious, but not overtly so, yet the butterflies in her stomach seemed to be growing exponentially. He'd nearly kissed her the other day, right on the front porch. And she'd nearly let him, which would have been a terrible idea, but oh so appealing, and tonight just the sight of him sent her body into quiver, sizzle, throb territory. It was getting tougher and tougher to remember why a fling with Ryan was such a bad idea. But it was. It really was. There was the Tag/Lilly connection, for starters, but Emily was also starting to realize that her other hesitation revolved around liking Ryan *too much*. The truth was, she liked him too much to have sex with him. Or, at least, too much to have sex with him and then forget about him. She knew this was the kind of feminine logic that made men think women were crazy, but it was the truth.

"Hi, Ryan," Chloe said, waving that ice-cream cone around again.

"Oh my goodness, Chloe. You are a hazard with that thing. Move farther away before you hit me in the nose," Emily said, laughing.

Chloe slid her bottom down to the other end of the bench.

"Ah, perfect," Ryan said, settling comfortably between them. "So, what are you two up to?"

"Mom says I can take riding lessons and go camping," Chloe answered.

"Sweet," he answered, earning him a high five from Chloe's non-ice-cream-covered hand. "That sounds very fun. I think my horse-riding days may be over, but I love camping."

"I've never camped before."

"You haven't? Why not?" He looked at Emily as if this was a gaping hole in her parenting résumé.

"There just hasn't been an opportunity, I guess."

He turned back to Chloe. "Well, I'm glad you'll finally get to try it. Watch out for grizzly bears because they can unzip tent flaps and they'll come in when you're sleeping."

Emily chuckled under her breath, and Chloe had the good sense to not believe him.

"First of all, no. They can't unzip zippers. No thumbs, but nice try. Second of all, there are no bears on the island."

"Really? Are you sure? Because I was hiking with my dad, and I'm sure I saw one. Either that or it was a humongous man-eating badger. With fangs. It might have been frothing at the mouth."

"Man-eating, huh? No problem then. I'm a girl." Chloe gave a sassy little toss of her head, making him laugh and give up.

"All right. Fine. But don't come crying to me when that badger shows up at your campsite." He turned back to Emily. "Are you going camping?"

She shook her head and wished she'd taken a little time to change into something nicer before heading out with Chloe. She had on a striped T-shirt dress that should have been retired from her closet ages ago. He had on tan shorts and a Trillium Bay T-shirt that was obviously brand-new.

"Nope. No camping for me this time. I'll be working at the cottage, no doubt. There is fifty-year-old wallpaper that someone must have shellacked to the wall. I've been scraping it off for days. Of course, I had to take a break yesterday to help Tiny with his dance steps, and he's insisting I go to the square dance on Wednesday night to lend moral support because he's finally ready to make his move on Gloria Persimmons. He chickened out last week."

Ryan chuckled. "He's got his eye on a woman? Well, I hope she's . . . sturdy."

Chloe stood up and tossed the little bit left of her waffle cone out into the water and the ducks pounced. "I think Tiny and Gloria would make a perfect couple. I think it's sweet and romantic." She turned back around. "Ryan, you should go to the square dance, too. That's where Aunt Lilly met your dad, you know. She told me they put up twinkle lights and it's all magical and stuff."

Her kid was about as subtle as a foghorn, but Emily didn't want Ryan to think she and Chloe had been plotting ways to lure him in. One Taggert/Callaghan combination was more than enough.

"I probably won't be there very long. As soon as Tiny asks Gloria to dance, I'll be scooting on out," Emily added.

Chloe pulled her phone from her pocket and looked at the screen for a second. "Speaking of scooting on out, can I go meet Susie and Carrie and those guys? They just texted to say they're swimming over at Leo's house. He has a pool."

"We're on an island surrounded by water and the kid has a pool?" Ryan said.

"The lake water is cold most of the time. You've been in it. You should know. Anyway, Mom, can I go?"

Emily wanted to say no because, quite frankly, being alone with Ryan made her nervous. At the cottage, there were always other people around, but if Chloe left, it would be just Emily and Ryan, and there was no telling what might happen. She didn't exactly trust herself, but she couldn't very well explain that to her daughter.

"We were supposed to take a walk, though. I was going to show you the old lighthouse and the place where Brooke and Lilly and I had a tree fort."

The level of disinterest in those things was apparent in Chloe's expression. She'd been excited about the prospect earlier, but it seemed Emily's plan had been trumped by a kid with a pool. "But, okay. We can do that another time. Be home by eight o'clock, though."

"Nine o'clock?"

"Seven fifty-five. Want to keep going?"

Chloe giggled and turned to sprint away. "Okay, got it. See you at eight o'clock." She got about ten feet away, then sprinted back for a hug, and Emily knew she hadn't really been trumped by the kid with the pool. Not permanently anyhow.

"See ya, Ryan. Go for a walk with my mom, will ya? She doesn't have anything to do."

Damn that kid.

~

Ryan sure liked that kid. She knew how to make him laugh, and then she knew just when to scram. The perfect combination of charm and intelligence. She must take after her mother. He smiled over at Emily, looking at her expectantly.

A smile played around the corners of her mouth. "Um, well, this is a little embarrassing because it appears my date for the evening just stood me up."

"Kids these days. So . . . want to show me the lighthouse?"

"Would you like to see the lighthouse?"

"I believe I would." He definitely would.

They left the park and headed away from the bay and all the shops and restaurants of Main Street. They passed the bright blue library and the riding stable and the kite store. The conversation was easy and not about anything in particular.

"Did you know my father played geezer night poker with your father last Thursday?" Ryan asked.

"Heaven help us. Did anything interesting happen?"

"Not that I heard of, so I guess that means everyone is still keeping a lid on it. Maybe the old dudes are the last demographic on the island to not hear about Tag's May/December romance."

She gave a rather unladylike snort, which he somehow found endearing. "More like February/December. How are things at the Clairmont?"

He hadn't really done much for the Clairmont project. He'd been too busy researching Bridget O'Malley's place. Of course, he couldn't tell her that. "Not bad."

Talk turned to more personal things, like good movies they'd seen, least favorite subjects in school, and beloved pets.

"I had a dog when I was fifteen," he found himself telling her as they discussed childhood pets. "The thing was ninety-five pounds of pure, drooling moron. He ate everything he could get in his mouth, including the certificate from his obedience training."

Emily laughed, and every time she did that, he found himself feeling more uncertain about the future in general, but very certain about at least one thing. He was not leaving this island without kissing her at least once. Where that might lead was anybody's guess, but Ryan was tired of fighting against it. The pull was inevitable, and he was an opportunities kind of guy. He just couldn't let this night pass by without creating one.

"Your dog ate his obedience certificate?" Emily laughed as he told her that story. "That's a bad dog. Of course, our dog ate that library book I told you about, remember?"

Now it was his turn to laugh. "Oh, that's right, and the scary librarian banned you from the library."

Emily shook her head. "No, not me. It was Brooke. I wasn't in the library often enough to get banned. I was too busy getting into trouble doing other stuff. Want to see the scene of some of those crimes?" Her smile was playful, and the chance of him saying no was zero point zero percent.

"Absolutely. Lead the way."

They walked another few yards and then turned, taking a well-established path into the woods. This looked promising if he was hoping for that kiss. She led him to the mouth of a small cave.

"Hello?" she called into it. No response. "Do you have a flashlight on your cell phone?"

He pulled it from his pocket and lit it up before handing it over.

She looked mischievous, and it was damn near killing him.

"We are way above the age limit for going in here, but I'm alumni so I think it's okay." She walked into the cave, and he followed close behind. The interior wasn't very big, maybe twenty feet long and about ten feet wide, but the entire thing was littered with tool chests and duffel bags and boxes of various sorts, each with a padlock, and each with a word or two scrawled across the surface.

She looked back over her shoulder, smiling. "Good to know some things never change. Welcome to the booze bank."

"The booze bank?"

Emily was chuckling. "I can't believe they still keep stuff here, but it looks like they do. I guess you could say this is like the vault, and these are safety deposit boxes. See the labels? Everybody has a code name, and these bins are full of illicit contraband. Liquor, weed, whatever.

The cardinal rule is that you never, ever mess with someone else's stash, and you never, ever reveal anyone's code name, especially to an adult."

Ryan laughed and fully appreciated the moral flexibility of these law-breaking teens, since he'd been one himself back in the day. "Honor among thieves, huh? I love it."

"Every once in a while, when I was a teenager, a couple of deputies would come thrashing around in the woods near here, making a shitload of noise so we all had plenty of time to run, and then they'd pretend like they couldn't find the cave." Emily's laughter made her breathless, which somehow seemed to leave him a little short on the breath factor, too. She had a great laugh. That's not something he'd ever noticed in a woman before, and he wondered if he liked her because he liked her laugh, or if he liked her laugh because he liked her. Either way . . . he liked her and he liked her laugh.

"Of course, I realize now my dad totally knew where this place was. It's probably the same place he and Judge Murphy and Father O'Reilly hid their booze back when they were hell-raisers."

"The chief of police, the judge, and the priest were hell-raisers? That's sounds like the beginning of a joke."

Emily nodded, still snickering. "My father likes to act all holier-than-thou, but Gigi admitted to me the other day that Harlan was no angel. Somehow that makes me like him a little better."

She was still smiling, yet Ryan was struck again by the fact that she and her father didn't get along. As much as Tag might aggravate Ryan or his brothers, they genuinely were one big, happy family. Nothing would ever change that. Not even his father having a fling with someone far too young.

He and Emily left the cave and the woods and strolled along the road again. Every now and again their shoulders would graze each other or her hand would oh-so-accidently brush against his, and like a kid, he had the unquenchable urge to hold her hand. He didn't. But he wanted to.

Ten minutes later a red lighthouse came into view. It was short, as lighthouses went, maybe three stories tall, and it looked as if it had been out of commission for a very long time. A rusted ladder ran along one side, leading up to a small catwalk.

"Ready to see another glimpse into my checkered past?"

"Of course."

"This is not the tour I was going to take Chloe on, by the way. I would have told her about all the times I rescued injured animals and how I collected wildflowers to press between the pages of my diary."

"I get the impression that your diary might be a very entertaining read."

"Count on it. Go on up that ladder." She pointed at the rusty rungs.

"Me first?"

She pointed at her hips. "Dress."

"Damn. There goes my chance to get a little peek."

She might talk a big, wild game, but Emily Chambers still blushed every time he said anything the least bit suggestive. She just wasn't as bad and bold as she seemed to think. He'd dated a few barracudas in his day, and Emily was nothing like them. She was nothing like any of the women he'd ever dated, come to think of it. What that meant he had yet to determine, but he wasn't analyzing or second-guessing. He was just taking a walk with a girl and climbing up to the top of a lighthouse to see whatever he could see.

He got to the top and had to climb under the railing, and then he reached behind him to help Emily do the same, not that she seemed to need it. She popped up next to him and immediately looked into the center of the lighthouse where he imagined a big light used to be. Most of the surrounding windows were now broken, and inside the little room were hundreds of rocks scattered across the floor.

"Wow," she gasped. "Looks like the kids have been busy."

"Meaning what?"

She laughed and the wind caught her hair, whipping it around her head. She lifted her arms to catch it in both of her hands, which made the hemline of that dress lift several more inches up her thigh. A gentleman might not notice such a thing, but it was hard to miss. Those legs of hers went all the way up.

She kept her hair captured in one hand and lowered her other arm. "I'm not sure when the tradition started, but for my generation, if you lost your virginity, you were supposed to throw a rock in the center. Some kids even put their initials on there. Usually the boys. Girls like to be a little more discreet."

Ryan looked down at all the stones again and saw that many of them did indeed have initials. Some even had two sets, indicating the couple, no doubt.

"Wow," he said, nodding with respect and awe. "That is quite the shrine to premarital fornication. Is one of those stones yours?"

"Of course not," she said, but her laughter indicated otherwise, and his urge to kiss her quadrupled. She moved around to the other side where the wind wasn't quite so strong, and the setting sun was nearing the horizon. The sky was full of pinks and blues and even purple. If he'd seen those colors in a painting, he would have thought the artist overdid it, but it seemed to be an almost nightly occurrence here.

They leaned back against the one window that wasn't broken, and a little bit of ledge provided a place to sit. Emily tugged the hemline of her dress down, proving her bad-girl persona was mostly exaggerated. Too bad. Too bad she wasn't the type for a meaningless fling, but then again, the fact that she wasn't the type made her that much more appealing. This was a bit of a problem, but he'd figure that out later. He was at the top of a lighthouse under a magical sky and next to a beautiful woman with a smile that was starting to make his heart ache. Shit. This really was a problem.

He turned his head to look at her, trying to think of ways to plead his case. Some way to dazzle and beguile her and make her glad that it was him she was here with. Something witty and persuasive, but she turned at precisely the same moment he did, with invitation in her eyes, and all he could come up with was, "God damn, I really want to kiss you."

Her hesitation was a mere fraction of a second. "Me too," she whispered.

It was all he needed to hear, and in an instant she was in his arms. He kissed her, hard, with no prelude, no artful negotiations or seductive machinations. Just hungry kisses that sent his mind spinning and his body following. She kissed him back with equal enthusiasm, with one hand on his chest and the other wrapped tightly around the back of his neck, pulling him closer. Her mouth was sweet, as sweet as he'd imagined, with lips so soft he could have fallen over the edge of that lighthouse and thought the sensation was just from her touch.

But then the hand against his chest pushed instead of pulled, the hand behind his head let go, and she leaned away with a breathless gasp.

"Um . . ." She pressed her lips together, as if to capture the kiss. "Um, yeah, I wanted to kiss you, too. Obviously." Her short laugh was self-conscious now. "But you live in Sacramento."

"What's wrong with Sacramento?" Why was she talking about Sacramento?

"Nothing, it's just that I live in San Antonio, and they're really far apart. And your father is screwing my sister." Her eyes met his, big and uncertain. "Sorry. That sounded really crass, but it's also the truth. It just seems to make everything else a little more complicated, you know?"

Yes, he knew. He just didn't care. No enough to stop kissing her. "Those are just details. We can talk about that stuff later."

That hand on his chest stayed put. "I like you, Ryan. I really do, but the last time I got kissed at the top of this stupid lighthouse, I totally lost my head and made some really bad decisions. I shouldn't have brought you up here."

He didn't like the sound of regret in her voice. "I'm glad you brought me up here, and I'm not trying to sway you to do anything you don't want to do. I just really want to kiss you."

"Oh, swaying me would not be much of a challenge at the moment. I would very much like to continue on with this little escapade, but the timing is bad, and the obstacles are big, and I have a lot going on in my life right now that needs . . . fixing. I can't get distracted from that. As much as I would like to be distracted."

Now, see? This was where men and women differed. If he wanted to be distracted from his troubles, Emily Chambers would be the first person on this island he'd call. In fact, she'd be the only person he'd call. She might even be the person he called when he *wasn't* on this island. But women liked to have everything organized and labeled *before* the enjoyable and entertaining distractions began. That never did make sense to him, but it wasn't the first time he'd heard it.

He leaned back against the ledge and window again, keeping one arm around her waist. "What needs fixing? Stuff with Chloe's dad? Or your dad?"

"No, nothing like that. It's not personal stuff so much as it is professional stuff. I need this island renovation to go well. Like I really need it go to well, and . . ." She hesitated, as if weighing her words and deciding if she could trust him or not. "Can you keep a secret?"

"I can say without reservation that I keep secrets better than any person on this island."

That scored him a weak smile from Emily. "I have a flip house back in San Antonio that my business partner is trying to sell, and the place has been a nightmare since the moment we got the keys. Because of all the problems we had with it, well, I ended up a little overextended. Financially speaking. I borrowed some money from Gigi, and that's why I'm renovating her cottage for her. Sort of my down payment on the money I owe her." She looked relieved to have told him, but added, "But no one knows. Just me and Gigi, so please don't tell anyone. Don't tell your dad because he might tell my sister, and then she'll tell everyone else. And see? That's why we can't kiss each other. Because if I keep kissing you, I'll keep telling you secrets and then you'll tell me secrets and then we'll both be keeping secrets from our families and it will all get too confusing."

"We don't have to tell secrets. We don't have to talk at all. We could just, you know, kiss . . . and stuff."

That earned him a roll of her eyes. He thought his solution was pretty practical, but she wasn't going for it. He stood up and pulled her with him, his hands resting loosely on her hips as she faced him. "Emily, is it possible you might be overthinking this just a little bit?"

It took a moment for her to meet his eyes, and the faintest tilt of a smile crossed over her lips.

"Maybe. Probably. But until I know for sure, there should be no more kissing." She sounded very prim, like a teacher telling him to shush. He felt duly reprimanded but not at all as if he'd learned his lesson.

"Just one more?" he said, holding up his thumb and index finger to indicate *tiny*. Oh so small. "Just one more little one? I don't think that was my best work, and what if this is the only time we ever kiss? Then you'll go on for the rest of your life thinking that's the best I can do. I don't think my ego can take that."

He sure as hell hoped this wouldn't be the only time they ever kissed. In fact, he was going to make damn sure of it, and then some. But for the moment, this angle was going to work for him. He could see her indecision. He leaned closer, his lips nearly touching hers. Her eyes fluttered shut as he whispered against her mouth, "Just one more."

Chapter 21

"I will take the damn yoga class, Emily, because a deal is a deal, and yes, I think Yoga Matt is cover model material, but don't think I'm going to forget all about Tag just because of some sexy yoga instructor. Besides, even if I did like him, I'd be waiting behind about fifteen other women. He's like the pied piper around here. Haven't you seen all the future Mrs. Yoga Matts lining up?"

Emily and Lilly were walking down Anishinaabe Trail on their way to Monday evening yoga at the Episcopal church, and according to Emily's friends from drunk puzzle night, Matt was very hands-on with his instructions. So much so that several of them did positions wrong on purpose just so that he'd come and adjust their pelvis.

But Emily didn't want Yoga Matt adjusting her pelvis. The only person she wanted anywhere near her pelvis was Ryan. Holy hell. What was she going to do about that? They'd kissed for half an hour at the top of that lighthouse Saturday night, and if it weren't for a group of unruly teenage boys riding by on bikes, hooting and hollering and cheering them on, they might be there still. That's just what she needed. Local kids seeing her fooling around in public and word getting back to her dad. At least they weren't spotted by Dmitri Krushnic.

After that, Ryan had walked her back to Main Street and offered to go with her all the way to Gigi's house, but she'd told him no. She needed to get her bearings before facing her grandmother because Gigi would take one look at her face and know she'd been up to something. The woman couldn't see well enough to pick out matching shoes, but she'd spot those invisible kisses from a mile away.

Sunday at church had been particularly painful. Father O'Reilly droned on about . . . something. Emily hadn't been listening. She was too busy fantasizing about Ryan showing up at her cottage with a picnic basket full of grapes and cheese and wine and seducing her on the front porch, which was a ridiculous and impractical fantasy because whenever she was at the cottage, she was grimy and sweaty and wearing her rattiest clothes, and she'd never have sex on the front porch where anyone could see them. So she'd start the fantasy over where somehow she was at the cottage but freshly showered and wearing a sundress and Ryan wouldn't bring cheese because that kind of stuck to her teeth and would ruin the kissing part of the fantasy. But then Tiny or Horsey or Georgie would show up and spoil everything. Seriously? What was the matter with her? Even in her own fantasies she could not overcome the roadblocks. It was as if God had put a mental firewall up in her brain because she wasn't supposed to be thinking about sex in church.

It didn't help her any that Ryan and his dad had been sitting three rows in front of them, and Ryan's hair was still just a little bit damp from his morning shower. She'd really wanted to touch it and run her fingers through it. She knew how soft it was because she'd had a fistful of it at the top of the lighthouse, and her palms longed to feel it again. So she'd clasped her hands together in church instead, hoping to appear pious and prayerful instead of horny and desperate, and when Ryan and his father left right after the service, she wasn't sure if she was annoyed or glad.

He'd texted her later that day, saying he and Tag were flying over to Seneca Falls in Northern Michigan to spend a couple of days fly-fishing, which left her feeling equal parts relieved and flustered. Relieved that she wouldn't have to decide if she could, should, would kiss him again, and flustered by the fact that she wanted to so very badly.

Now it was Monday evening, and Emily was hoping some mountain pose would bring her peace of mind. Maybe she'd let Matt adjust her pelvis after all. So what if he was her employee? So what if it was really Lilly she was hoping he'd be interested in? That had been her goal for this evening, after all. One *last*, last-ditch effort to redirect her sister's affection toward someone her own age, but after tonight she was pretty much giving up on that. Since everyone in town knew, and no one seemed in a rush to tell Harlan, Emily didn't think that any of her superficial efforts were going to make an impression on her sister.

They turned the corner on Marquette. "Okay, okay," Emily said to Lilly. "I'm not trying to force you, but like you said, a deal is a deal. I went horseback riding and spent time with Tag, just like you asked."

Lilly scoffed. "Sure you did, and you told Percy to give us the worst horses ever. I figured that out before we even left the barn."

"I didn't tell him that, exactly, and anyway, I was just trying to create some negative associations and redirect the dopamine in your brain," Emily said, sounding terse and slightly ridiculous.

"The what now?"

"Nothing. Just some stupid TED Talk. Never mind. Anyway, I'm not trying to talk you out of this anymore. I've told you what I think, and now it's up to you to make those decisions. Just keep in mind that Dad will have a very hard time with this, and it's important for you to think about five to ten years from now."

"What happens in five to ten years?"

"In ten years, Tag will be almost seventy, and you'll be thirty-six."

"I can do math, Emily. I know how old we'll be, but what else will happen?"

"Well, I don't know exactly. That's the whole point. You need to think about what you want your life to look like in the future, and decide if Tag fits what you'll want then."

A frown creased Lilly's smooth forehead. "Does your life look the way you thought it would look ten years ago?"

Emily sighed. "Not even a little bit. That's why I'm trying to warn you now. I didn't set a good example, but at least I can be your cautionary tale. Tag's talking about retiring and moving. Those are huge steps, and you've only known each other for such a short time."

"It's not the amount of time you spend with someone that matters, though. It's how that time makes you feel."

Emily didn't even try to hide her disdain over that Hallmark card comment. "That's cute, Lilly, but it's just not true. I'm worried you'll have regrets later."

"But who's to say I wouldn't have regrets if Tag leaves my life, I never see him again, and I never, ever meet anyone else who makes me feel the way he does?"

Well, shit. That was a very valid question, and one for which Emily had no answer. The truth was, Ryan had made her feel pretty damn good on top of that lighthouse. He pretty much made her feel good every time he was around. What if *she* never met anyone else who made *her* feel that way ever again? Maybe she was sacrificing a chance at something good just because there was a chance it might go bad. Now she was even more confused.

"You do realize that pretty much everyone knows, right?" Emily said a moment later. Lilly stopped short, right in the middle of the sidewalk.

"Everyone knows? About me and Tag? Has anyone told Dad?"

"Is Dad still speaking to you?"

"Yes."

"Then no one has told him."

They started walking again. "Everyone?" asked Lilly.

"According to Brooke, who heard it from Gigi, who heard it from Maggie Schofield, and so on, and so on. I have to imagine that Dmitri Krushnic is patient zero, but he wasn't the only witness in that pie tent."

"What are people saying about us?"

"That I don't know. I don't imagine I'd be the one they'd come to."

They walked in silence for another few minutes, before Lilly said, "Well, it's nobody's business but mine and Tag's, and if people know, then maybe we can stop being sneaky. I didn't tell Dad on Father's Day because you told me not to, but maybe it's time to go public."

"Mmmmm . . . I don't know about that. Denial is a beautiful thing, and as long as you and Tag are keeping things on the down-low, it maintains a balance in the Force, you know? I still think you should give this whole situation a little more time before throwing it in Dad's face."

"Throwing it in Dad's face? That's not a very nice way to put it."

"I know, but that's how he'll take it. He's going to be embarrassed, Lilly. This will be awkward for him. Don't you remember how he was when he caught me skinny-dipping with Nick?"

"But my situation with Tag is different."

Sure it was. It was worse. There was just no way Harlan was not going to be upset, but Lilly suddenly seemed so sad that Emily slung an arm around her shoulder.

"I'm sorry. I don't mean to drag you down. I know what it feels like to disappoint Dad, but who knows? Maybe he'll be fine with it?" *Sure he would.* "And anyway, word at drunk puzzle night is that Matt has magic hands. You'll feel better after yoga."

Saint Augustine Episcopal Church's hall was full of women and a smattering of men when they arrived minutes later. Emily dragged Lilly right up to the front and wiggled them in between Gloria Persimmons and Jenny Mahoney. Jenny gave them a dirty look, and Emily wasn't sure if it was because they'd nudged her to the side or simply because they were Callaghans. Either way, Emily and Lilly were now front and center.

"Hey, boss lady!" Matt waved, earning her a few more hard stares. She waved back as he came over to them.

"Hey, Matt. Have you met my sister Lilly? Lilly, this is Matt."

He turned up his dazzling smile, placed his palms together, and bent slightly.

"Namaste, Lilly."

Lilly looked back at him. "Uh-huh," she said, and Emily noted that her sister was not as immune as she'd expected to be. Yoga Matt was just that hot.

"I'm so glad you're both here. May this bring you peace and fulfillment."

"Okay," Lilly answered, and Emily smiled. Matt was so pretty he did take a little getting used to.

"Okay, dear friends," he called out, turning around and heading to the front of the room, "we are gathered here to celebrate. Celebrate our bodies and all the wonderful things they can do. Who would like to join me?"

A chorus of "Me. Me," echoed through the church hall.

Lilly leaned toward Emily's ear. "I volunteer as tribute."

Emily smiled. "I told you."

"Yes, you did, and you were right, but I'm still not giving up Tag."

Chapter 22

"I am impressed!" Brooke said as she stood inside the cottage, admiring the progress Emily and her crew had made.

It was Wednesday morning, and Emily hadn't heard from Ryan since that brief text Sunday, which shouldn't bother her, because, you know, they'd agreed to not do the kissing thing again. Nonetheless, she missed him. She didn't want to miss him, but she did.

Fortunately, the praise from her sister lightened her mood considerably, and Emily had to admit, the place was starting to shape up. The outside had been scraped, power-washed, and repainted with a pale green and lavender palette that would have looked garish anyplace else, but it fit in on the island quite nicely. All the floors had been stripped and refinished to a nice glossy sheen, and modern wallpaper with a vintage design was up in most of the rooms. Even some of the new furniture had arrived, including several wrought iron beds and mattresses, charmingly distressed bureaus that Emily had found at the antique shops in town, a red velvet sofa, and even an old pianoforte.

"Thank you. It has come a long way," Emily agreed, looking around.

"No kidding. The last time I was here, a family of raccoons was living in one of the upstairs bedrooms. They're gone, right?"

"They must have moved on to nicer accommodations before I got here. Come sit outside. Tiny just added a porch swing. You may christen it with your butt because no one has sat there yet."

"My butt is honored."

Emily grabbed two bottles of water from the newly installed refrigerator and joined her sister on the porch.

Brooke sank down on the swing with a relaxed sigh and accepted the bottle of water. "It's really nice here, Em. You have done an amazing job. Gigi needs you to remodel all of her places. What do you think of that?"

"I think it would be hard to do from San Antonio." She sat down next to her sister.

"Mmm, I suppose." Brooke opened her bottle and took a sip as she gazed off toward the lake. "How are you and Dad getting along? It seems like some of the tension is gone."

"Some of it is. He likes Chloe. That helps. They've even gone hiking together, so apparently he can be nice to her without actually forgiving me, which is good enough."

"I think he forgave you a long time ago. I'm certain he's glad you're here, not that he'd ever say so."

"Certain?" Emily crooked an eyebrow. "That's a pretty strong word."

Brooke smiled back. "Okay, ninety-nine point nine percent certain that he's glad you're here. I know I'm glad you're here. It's been nice to have you around again."

Brooke was as effusive with her feelings and compliments as their father was, so this was a big statement from her, and whether it was from the soothing motion of the swing, the nostalgia of sitting next to her sister, or Brooke's nice words, Emily realized she felt the same way.

"I'm glad I'm here, too. This summer has gone better than I'd expected, in spite of all the hard work at this place." She motioned with her thumb, pointing at the door. "Chloe and I have managed to have a little fun, too. Hey, speaking of fun, Gloria told me she's hosting drunk puzzle night next week. You should come."

Brooke shook her head. "Sorry. Can't. I'm fun-repellant."

Emily laughed. "You are not. Don't be silly."

"I'm not silly. That's my whole point, and drunk puzzle night is all about being silly. Hey, isn't that Ryan?" Brooke leaned forward from her spot on the swing to look down the hill.

Ryan? The long-lost Ryan who had kissed her senseless on Saturday but hadn't called her since? Emily stood up, and sure enough, there he was coming up the hill. She leaned against the railing and waved. He waved back and she nearly giggled, forgetting for the moment that her sister was there, until Brooke uttered, "Oh shit. Not you too? Don't we have enough to worry about with Tag and Lilly?"

So much for discretion. Emily turned and shrugged. "I don't know what to do about it. I like him."

"Well, stop it."

"I'm not sure if I can."

Brooke was right. Emily knew that. She should stop liking Ryan, but she knew she wouldn't. Getting his advice and sharing her ideas about this cottage with him had been fun. Riding horses and taking walks and having coffee with him—all fun. And heaven knew kissing him had been fun. More than fun. It had been thrilling, and she hadn't been thrilled about anything in a very long time.

Her sister sighed and pushed her feet against the porch with a squeak, making the swing sway back and forth. "I'm just going to mind my own business from now on. No one listens to me anyway."

Ryan reached the bottom of steps in another minute, and Emily's body hummed with anticipation, which she tried very hard to contain. It wasn't as if she could, would, should fling herself into his arms, even if Brooke wasn't there.

"Hi," she said. "You're back."

"I'm back," he answered, and then they stood there staring stupidly at each other and smiling.

"Oh good Lord," Brooke muttered.

Ryan's head turned in surprise. "Oh, hi, Brooke. I didn't see you there."

"Gosh, I wonder why?" She stood up. "Did you just come through Bridget O'Malley's yard?"

He looked over his shoulder and down the hill. "What? No. I mean, I don't know. I just came up this way because, um, I got lost."

"Lost."

"Yeah, I was heading here and I guess I took a wrong turn somewhere."

"That's generally how people get lost," Brooke said mildly.

"Yeah. Hey, listen, Emily. I can't stay because Tag's waiting for me at the Clairmont, but, um, we're back from Seneca Falls, obviously, and he's dragging me to that square dance tonight. I'm a little terrified. Are you still going? To help out Tiny?"

"Of course she is," Brooke said, stepping up to the railing and resting on her forearms. "She wouldn't miss it for the world, would you, Em?"

"So, you'll be there?" He looked up at Emily, his expression so optimistic and mischievous she knew there was just no way she wasn't kissing him again.

"I am. I guess I'll see you there."

"I guess you will. Okay, see you later then." His smile was lopsided, his gait a little jaunty as he turned and walked back down the hill. The sisters watched him until Brooke rested her chin on one hand. "I wonder if he knows where he's going?"

Chapter 23

"Oh, Mom, it does look magical, don't you think?" Chloe said, twirling around slowly.

Emily was inclined to agree. The churchyard of Saint Bartholomew's Catholic Church was transformed by a few cheap white twinkle lights surrounding the patio. Old wine barrels cut in half served as seating, and Father O'Reilly had tied a red bandana around his black-and-white priest's collar and put on his straw cowboy hat. Clancy, also known as *He Who Rides Naked*, had thankfully put his clothes back on and was playing the banjo. Jimmy the mailman and Tom the veterinarian were strumming guitars, and Gladys the bank teller was on the keyboards. Gigi was holding court on one side of the patio with several of her stiff-haired geriatric friends, while Mrs. Bostwick and the Mahoney sisters sat at a table near the punch bowl. Eye-darts were flying back and forth. You could practically hear them zinging by.

"Now circle to the left," Father O'Reilly called out over the music and the laughter. "And shoot the star."

Emily's gaze scanned the crowd, looking for Ryan.

"Hi."

She spun around and there he was, standing there looking just as fine as always. Her heart did a slow twirl of its own.

"Hey, Ryan." Chloe hopped over and gave him a fist bump. "Good to see you. Got to run, though. I see some friends."

"Hey, wait a minute," Emily said, laughing. "What about me?"

Chloe gave an exaggerated shrug, along with an expression that said *uh, what about you?* "You wanted me to make friends, didn't you? Mission accomplished. See you later." And with that she was gone.

Emily turned toward Ryan, feeling awkward and exhilarated at the same time. "That's the second time that kid has stood me up."

"I like that about her."

Emily felt a blush stealing over her skin even as she smiled. "So, what do we do now?" she asked.

"Pretty much anything except dance."

"Now acey-deucey to the right," Father O'Reilly shouted as Ryan stepped a little closer.

"I have some suggestions," he said quietly in her ear, not that anyone would be able to hear them over the clamor.

She had some ideas, too, but at the moment, her brain was too distracted by the width of his shoulders to respond. She'd had her arms around those shoulders, so now she knew they were all muscle.

Before she could come up with any sort of clever response, Emily felt a hand touch her elbow.

"Peach? Finally! People kept telling me you were in town, but I didn't believe it."

She turned again to find Reed Bostwick garbed in full colonial costume, and her breath came out in one big huff of surprise. Thirteen years. Thirteen years since she'd seen him last, and other than the outfit and the British wig perched on his head, he looked exactly the same as she remembered. Maybe a little bit thicker, with a man's face instead of a teenager's, but mostly the same. A bored-looking stick figure of a woman with big eyes and small glasses, also in colonial costume, stood by his side.

"Reed, oh my goodness! How are you?" she said, leaning toward him. The hug was only mildly awkward, made slightly more so because when he leaned forward, his white wig fell right off his head. The stick figure automatically bent to pick it up and handed it back to him. This must be Mrs. Reed Bostwick, and she did not appear to be a fan of square dancing, judging from her *terribly* bored expression. Or maybe she didn't like wearing a costume. Or the most likely reason? She may have heard Emily's name before, and not in a flattering way. *Thanks for that, Olivia Bostwick.*

"I'm very well, thanks. Doing great, in fact. I work for the governor, you know. I'm terribly important, according to my mother." He laughed, proving he thought his mother was just as pretentious as everyone else did, and the sound of it was also just as Emily had remembered. Big and genuine. She'd probably been dumb to leave him. She'd often thought that, and yet seeing him now? Nothing stirred inside her other than mild interest in an old friend and a wave of sweet nostalgia. No flutters or ripples or twinges. No regrets. Not really.

"Yes, your mother told me as much, but I was very glad to hear you're doing well. And is this your wife?"

He seemed startled by the question, as if he'd forgotten she was there. "What? Oh, yes. Emily, this is Marissa. Marissa, this is Emily. You've heard me mention Emily."

The stick figure smiled tightly. "Only about a thousand times. Nice to meet you, Emily."

Somehow Emily did not think Marissa found it nice at all. "Likewise."

Ryan cleared his throat beside her.

"Oh, Reed, this is . . . my friend Ryan. Ryan, Reed Bostwick. He works for the governor and he's terribly important." She and Reed laughed. Marissa and Ryan did not.

Reed reached out to shake Ryan's hand, forgetting he was holding the wig. He tossed it to his other hand at the last second, leading to a fumble of motions, some nervous laughter, and a roll of the eyes from Marissa.

"Good to meet you." They did the he-man single shake.

"So, what's with the outfit, Reed?" Emily asked. "You look quite convincing, by the way."

He bent at the waist like a proper colonial might do, then righted himself. "I am currently wearing a British uniform of the King's Eighth Regiment as earlier this evening I had the dubious honor of representing Captain John MacGillicuddy of His Majesty's service during a reenactment at the old fort. Of course, I'm sure you recall MacGillicuddy is the guy who lost the fort to the Americans."

"Well, I guess it could have been worse. You could have been representing Chief Eagle Feather."

Reed laughed and nodded. He turned to Marissa. "Chief Eagle Feather was the one—"

"Yes. Yes, I know. He was the guy who rode naked through the town. I've been here before, Reed. I've heard the story a thousand times."

He turned back to Emily, not seeming very insulted by Marissa's manner. Something told Emily he was used to it.

"So, rumor has it you're renovating one of your grandmother's rental cottages. Which dead husband did that one belong to?"

Emily laughed again. "The second one."

Reed asked another question, and another. Locals were observing but quickly grew bored when they saw that this was nothing much to gossip about. Reed mentioned something about a particularly wild party they'd had in the woods near Croton Hill back when they were about sixteen, and soon the two of them were laughing at old memories, but still, nothing stirred inside her other than a sense of thirteen years of guilt floating away. She'd always wondered how it would feel to see him again. Would he be angry or wounded? Insulting or dismissive? Nope. He was just Reed. Smiling, affable Reed. The same one she'd left before.

Marissa tapped her colonial fan against her wrist, not even trying to look interested. After a few minutes, Ryan moved a little closer, his shoulder coming into contact with hers in a not-so-subtle statement of possession, and he put his arm around her waist. It caught Emily off guard, but she didn't react, as if she didn't even notice it at all.

Reed did seem to notice, though. "Well, I'll let you two get back to your evening. Emily, let's grab a coffee soon and catch up some more, shall we?"

"Definitely. Let's. It was nice to meet you, Marissa."

Marissa blinked pale eyes behind her tiny glasses. "Uh-huh. You too."

Reed and his wife moved on to chat with a group of other friends, and Emily turned toward Ryan, crooking an eyebrow. "Very subtle."

He dropped his arm from her waist. "Just trying to protect you. Obviously you didn't notice his wife giving you the stink-eye."

"Was that Reed?" Lilly said, showing up next to them, her voice breathless. "How did that go?"

"Fine," Emily answered. "Just two old pals catching up."

Lilly chuckled. "Glad to hear it. You guys are going to dance, right?"

"No," they said in unison.

"Excuse me, Ms. Chambers?" Another voice from another side. Emily suddenly understood how her father felt after church services with so many people coming up to talk to him. She turned again to find Tiny standing next to her wearing the biggest plaid shirt she'd ever seen in her life.

"Hi, Tiny. How are you doing?"

"I'm very well, thank you. And yourself?"

Matt had been coaching Tiny on his people skills, and it was definitely helping. "I'm very well also. Thanks. Tiny, you know my sister, don't you? And you remember Ryan?"

Tiny nodded. "Nice to see you, Ms. Callaghan. Mr. Taggert. May I say both of you ladies look very fetching this evening."

"Why thank you, Tiny. You look very handsome in that shirt." She patted his meaty arm.

"Thank you. Matt suggested that perhaps I should ask one of you ladies to dance so I could get a little practice. He says if I dance with you, Gloria will notice me."

There was very little chance of Gloria not noticing him. He was about as unobtrusive as a hippo in a tutu.

"Hey, speaking of Matt," Lilly said as she leaned toward them and lowered her voice. "Did you guys hear he was asked to do a porno film?"

"He was?" Emily gasped.

"Yep. He turned it down, though. Rumor has it that's when he had his *spiritual awakening* and decided to leave New York. Guess what the title was? *Scrotal Recall.*"

"Eww." Emily grimaced, but Tiny and Ryan chortled like a couple of frat boys.

"I know, right?" Lilly said to Emily, ignoring the other two. "But at least he turned it down."

"That shows some good judgment, if you ask me. And he's cute, don't you think?" Emily prompted, from habit.

"Yep. He's cute. Doesn't matter."

"So, about dancing?" Tiny said again.

"Oh, yes. Dancing. Okay, Tiny. I have a slightly better suggestion. Will you trust me on this?" Emily wanted to get this ball rolling, get Tiny taken care of so that she could talk to Ryan.

"Um, sure. I guess." He looked doubtful but willing.

"Excellent. Okay. Wait here. Don't move."

Emily looked around, and it didn't take long to spot Gloria in her lime-green and white polka-dotted sundress and her rhinestone-studded sandals. She had her *spun gold* hair twisted into an updo decorated with silk clip-on daisies, and she was drinking a can of orange soda from a straw. She was a vision of garish colors and questionable choices. Tiny gasped as Emily strode directly over to his dream girl.

"Hey, Gloria."

Gloria had her back to them, and Emily maneuvered around her to keep it that way. "Why, Peach! How are you, girl? Recovered from drunk puzzle night?" Gloria leaned forward and did the air kiss-kiss near Emily's ear. "How are things going at your granny's cottage?"

"The cottage is an adventure, but it's coming along nicely. I have a great crew." That was stretching it, but there was no point in giving Gloria the actual rundown on the caliber of her workers. "And I'm really fortunate to have an impressive foreman, Tiny Kloosterman. Do you know him?"

"Oh yeah, sure. Everyone knows Tiny. He's kind of hard to miss!" Gloria threw her head back and laughed, making her equally hard to miss. Then again, that lime-green dress didn't exactly cause her to blend in, either. Emily leaned forward and felt like they were twelve again, passing notes back and forth. "What do you think of him?"

"Who?" Gloria wrapped her glossy, frosty, plum-colored lips around the straw and slurped loudly as she sucked up the last of her drink.

"Tiny. I'm not sure, but I suspect he may have a bit of a crush on you." *Bit of a crush* was an understatement, but she didn't want to oversell things.

"A crush on me? Really?" She set her pop can down and patted at her hair, securing a loose daisy and peering around at the crowd as if to find him. Tiny took a step backward, hiding behind Lilly, which was entirely pointless because he was three times her width.

"I think he might. Would you like me to see if he'd like to dance with you?"

Gloria's smile was wide. "Why, you know I love to dance. In fact, I said to myself tonight, I said, 'Gloria, tonight would be a fine night to kick up these heels,' so if he'd like to dance, why I sure as hell would say yes."

"Perfect. Stay here. Don't move." Emily strode back over to Tiny. If only breaking up Tag and Lilly was half as easy as getting Tiny and Gloria together, Emily's life would be a lot simpler. "All right, Tiny. I've primed the pump, as it were, so now the rest is up to you. If you go ask her to dance, she's going to say yes."

He pulled out a handkerchief and wrung it in his hands. "Are you sure? What did you say to her? Are you sure she didn't think you were talking about someone else?"

"How many Tiny Kloostermans are there on this island?"

He thought about that a moment, as if tabulating. "One."

"Right, and that's you." She patted his broad chest. "I told her I thought you might like to dance with her, and she said that was great and she'd like to dance with you, too. So, you'll have to take the rest from here. But Tiny, I think you have a real shot, so just be yourself and be bold."

He nodded. "Be bold. Be bold," he muttered as he took baby steps in Gloria's direction. She'd turned around by the time he got there, and she practically lunged toward him and dragged him to the center of the patio.

"Did you just play matchmaker, Emily Callaghan Chambers?" Lilly asked.

"I sure hope so."

~

It was nearly eleven o'clock by the time Ryan and Emily finally left Saint Bart's. Chloe had left with Gigi an hour ago, and now the moon was high and the sky sparkled with stars. Off in the distance Ryan could hear music coming from the park, but that would be ending soon. He had learned that things on the island quieted down well before midnight, with only a few pubs staying open into the wee hours. Now they were walking down a flower-lined avenue without another person in sight. Emily was wearing a white dress that seemed to shimmer under the few streetlights, and fireflies were everywhere.

"They're pretty, aren't they? The fireflies?" she asked.

"Mm-hm." In truth, he wasn't really thinking about the fireflies. He was thinking about her skin. And her hair, and her mouth. Pretty much all of her.

"I used to love seeing them. When we were little, my mom would turn off all the outside lights and we'd sit on the back porch and try to count them. She told us that the ones that glowed bluish weren't actually fireflies at all. They were angels waiting to go on up to heaven."

Her tone was wistful, and no wonder. Her mother had died when Emily was just a kid. Far too young. His mother had died last year when he was thirty-three, and even as a grown man, it was hard to take.

"That's sweet," he said softly.

"Yeah. Sort of. But I remember the day of her funeral. No one would really talk to me. The adults just kept trying to give me something to eat. I'm sure they had no idea what to say, and I'm not sure I really grasped the situation anyway. She died so unexpectedly."

Ryan felt a sudden pressure in his chest that had nothing to do with wanting to kiss her and everything to do with wanting to hold her tight and squeeze her sadness out, if only that would help, but of course, grief didn't work that way. You couldn't squash it out or get *over* it. You just had to get *through* it, but it was like a spider's web. It clung to your skin. Sometimes you could barely feel it, but you knew it was there. He slipped his hand in hers and gave it a squeeze anyway, and she went on, speaking slowly, as if she was just dusting off an old memory she'd found in an attic chest.

"As soon as it got dark that day, I came outside with a jar and tried to catch as many fireflies as I could because I thought for sure one of them was her."

"I'm sorry," he said, because he didn't know what else to say.

"Yeah, I tried really hard, then my dad came outside and yelled at me for chasing fireflies on such a sad, terrible day. I wanted to explain, but he just yelled louder and then sent me to my room. For the longest time I thought he'd ruined my chance to say goodbye to her." Her sigh was soft and shallow, her tone contemplative. "I was mad at him for so long after that, and he had no idea why. Then I got older and realized they were just bugs, so I got mad at her for telling me a lie."

Emily gave another short, abrupt sigh, as if blowing the thoughts away. "Anyway, it's no one's fault. Dad didn't understand about the fireflies, and she was just trying to be fanciful."

"Did you ever tell him that story?"

She looked up at Ryan, her eyes luminous under the glow of the moonlight. "No. Actually, I've never told anyone that story. I never think of it anymore, but I guess seeing the fireflies reminded me."

"Maybe you should tell him."

Her laugh was soft but full of dismissal. "I don't see much point in that. Effective communication is not really in our DNA, and it doesn't really matter anyway. But look—here we are." Her smile brightened considerably as she pointed to a pale blue house just up the lane.

"That's where I'm staying. Gigi's house."

He turned the corner with her, still holding her hand. He had *no* intention of going home without a few more of those kisses, especially after she'd shared such a sad story. He had *every* intention of cheering her up.

"I can probably make it from here," she said, stopping and turning toward him.

He pulled their clasped hands up between them. "I'm sure you can, but since this is such an old-fashioned place, I've decided to act like an old-fashioned gentleman. I'm going to walk you all the way to the front steps. Then I'm going to hope you invite me up to sit on the porch swing for a spell."

His lame attempt at charm seemed to do the trick. "For a spell?"

"Isn't that what they used to say in the old days? I think I saw that in a movie once."

"Uh, sure. I guess I can't argue with that. So, Mr. Taggert, would you care to join me on the front porch swing and sit for a spell?"

"I would like that very much, Miss Chambers."

"Delightful." They walked the short distance up the street and climbed the porch steps. A sconce light near the front door glowed amber, but the inside of the house was dark. Ryan spotted a swing off to one side, covered with flowered cushions. It looked very inviting and just the sort of place where a guy like him could steal a kiss. Even better than at the top of a lighthouse, although in truth, he was not that picky. He'd kiss her just about anywhere.

"I think we are fresh out of mint juleps, but I do believe there's some cold beer in the fridge. Or a glass of wine?" she asked.

"Why, Miss Chambers, do you intend to get me intoxicated and take advantage?"

Emily smiled. "You sound very optimistic, Mr. Taggert. So, beer or wine?"

Well, now he was feeling optimistic. "Either. Whatever you're having. As long as it's beer."

The porch swing gave a charming, predictable creak as he sat down, and a few minutes later the porch light turned off and Emily returned with two bottles of beer. She sat down next to him, turning sideways and bringing her bent leg up to rest on the cushion between them. She handed him a bottle.

"Thank you, miss."

"You're welcome, sir."

They clinked bottles and drank, and Ryan couldn't help but think of how things were so different here. Slow and quiet and peaceful. If Xanax were a village you could visit, then this was it. Damn it all. Tag was right. He liked this place. It pulled on him like a magnet, subtle but steady.

Ryan stretched his arm along the back of the swing and rested his hand against Emily's shoulder.

"Why did you turn the light off?" He hoped it was because she had illicit intentions.

"To keep the moths away."

So not what he was hoping to hear. He took a drink.

"So who was the guy in the military getup? Tell me about him."

"Oh, that was just Reed."

He didn't believe that guy had been *just* anything. "And? Let's hear that story."

"You don't want to hear that story." She shook her head, making her hair slide over her shoulders.

"Sure I do."

"Why?" She looked at him with curiosity but not suspicion.

"Because I'm sitting next to a pretty girl in the moonlight, and I have a nice cold beer in my hand, and I'd like to hear a story." *And you need to keep talking because if you stop, I'm going to start kissing you.*

She smiled. "Wow. The lack of Internet on this island is really getting to you, isn't it?"

"Quit being evasive. Tell me about the guy with the wig and the scrawny, disappointed wife."

She laughed, and every time she did that it felt like winning a blue ribbon. "Fine. Reed was my high school sweetheart. Everyone thought we'd get married, even me, right up until the time Nick showed up."

"Nick, Chloe's father?"

"One and the same. As you can imagine, the dating pool here is pretty limited, but the unspoken rule on the island is that local girls do not fraternize with the out-of-state college boys. It's a good rule, and one that I broke."

"So he was the skinny-dipper?"

She nodded and took an extra-large gulp from her bottle. "Yep. Maybe if I'd known about dopamine then, I could have saved myself a lot of trouble, but instead, I fell into what I thought was the forever kind of love. When he left at the end of the season, I went with him, back to Texas, but we swung through Vegas first and got married."

Ryan took a long pull from his own beer. "It sounds kind of romantic, in a doomed sort of way."

"Exactly. I think Nick was rebelling just as much as I was. His parents had some pretty specific expectations for him. He was supposed to become a lawyer and then a judge, just like his daddy."

"And that's not what he wanted?"

"I'm not sure he knew what he wanted, but for a while he convinced himself it was me. By the time we figured out we'd made a huge mistake, I was already pregnant with Chloe. Harlan shut me out completely for about a year after that. Brooke finally negotiated a peace treaty, but it's not ideal. Now that I have a daughter, I have a slightly better understanding of how my dad felt, but the good news is, I see signs of a thaw. Maybe. Now you know all about my family. Tell me about yours. You have two brothers, right?"

Ryan nodded. "Jack and Bryce."

"And one of them has been married three times?" She sounded a little incredulous, with good reason.

"Yep. That would be Bryce. We like to say he never met a woman he wouldn't like to divorce someday."

~

Emily couldn't help but laugh, partly because it was funny, and partly because she was happy to be sitting here on Gigi's porch with Ryan Taggert. "How about your other brother? Is Jack married?"

Ryan chuckled and looked down at his beer. "No, Jack has never been married."

"Why is that funny?"

"Well, he asked a girl once, but she said no."

Ryan sounded awfully lighthearted about this.

"Hmm, still not getting why that's funny. It seems kind of rotten."

His chuckle became more of a hearty chortle. "It's totally awful. Especially since he proposed to her during the first ten minutes of a hot-air balloon ride." Full-on laughter overtook him.

"No, he didn't!" Emily covered her mouth with one hand, trying to comprehend the humiliation, in spite of Ryan's indication of the opposite.

"He did. It was awkward. I was there videotaping the whole thing."

"No." Certain moments in life should not be captured on film, and this had to fall under that category. Yet, Ryan's gleeful laughter made her giggle. Obviously it wasn't a painful memory for him, even if it might be for his brother.

"That is the saddest story I've ever heard. She said no, and then they had to hang around in that wicker basket until the balloon landed? How long was that?"

"A full hour. The pilot couldn't land sooner than that because the pickup crew wasn't ready. Plus, Jack had told some friends he was going to propose, so there was a group of people waiting for us to come down. I think the only thing that stopped him from jumping out of that basket was thinking he'd only break his legs and not be put out of his misery."

"That is so awful." And it was, but now she was laughing, too.

"Yep. People were cheering as the balloon came down, but as soon as they saw our faces, they quieted down pretty fast. At least Jack got his three hundred dollars back. The balloon pilot felt so sorry for him that he refunded the money. Jack and I went out and spent it on tequila. The rest of the night is a little hazy after that, but I sure wish I could forget the next morning."

"A little hungover?"

"A little."

They laughed again, and each took a drink, and Emily couldn't resist asking. "So, how about you? Have you ever been married?"

They were both turned now, facing each other. His arm was still stretched across the back of the seat, his hand sending lovely tremors through her with every casual caress.

"No, I've never been married."

"Ever been close?"

He paused but didn't look away. "There was a girl once. Felt like the real deal, but the timing was off. I think if we'd gone forward it would have ended badly. It was a pretty long time ago, though. I haven't thought about it much since then."

"No?"

He set his beer on the porch. "No, not really. Do you know what I have been thinking about a lot lately, though? Like, incessantly?"

"What?"

He took her beer and set it next to his.

"Kissing you." He moved closer. "Sacramento, San Antonio. Tag. Lilly. I just don't care about any of that stuff." He brought a hand up to cup her jaw. "I'm not sure what happens next week, Emily, or next month, but what I am absolutely certain of is that I like you. I like being around you, and I definitely like kissing you, very much."

The list of obstacles and reasons and consequences evaporated from her mind at his words and his touch. Ryan was right. None of those things mattered in the moonlight here on the porch. Details could be sorted out later, because right now she needed him. She hadn't felt this way since . . . ever.

His hand was warm on her face as he leaned closer, brushing his lips across her cheek. "Just one little kiss," he whispered, but she didn't want just one. She wanted him to kiss her over and over again. And then some more. The porch swing swayed and creaked as they moved closer. His hands slid up to tangle in her hair, as if he wanted to capture the moment in his grasp, and finally he kissed her. His breath was warm, his lips soft but insistent, and Emily gave in to all of it. The delicious anticipation, the satisfaction of pulling him close, the pleasure of just *being* with him.

Kisses and caresses, sighs and whispers. Emily was enthralled as it continued. The swing protested again, but they ignored it, pushing pillows off to give them a little more room.

"There, now I can reach you better," he said, laughing against the curve of her neck.

She had one arm around his shoulders and the other near his jaw. She rubbed her palm against the little bit of stubble, loving the scratch against her skin. He kissed her neck and she giggled, so he kissed her lips again, and teasing turned to tantalizing. His hand drifted to her breast, and she pressed herself forward, encouraging, inviting, and a soft moan escaped her.

Emily heard a door close, although it took a moment for her mind to register the sound. She was *that* distracted, but then the kitchen light turned on, the beam blasting across them through the window like a deputy's flashlight. They bolted upright and apart, the swing creaking loudly.

"Hello?" Chloe called out, and Emily nearly groaned in frustration.

"It's just me, honey," she called out. "Go back to bed."

"What are you doing?"

"Nothing." *Nothing except being exquisitely felt up.*

"There's a spider in my room. He is legit ginormous."

Ohmygosh, seriously? She looked over at Ryan. His smile was full of disappointed understanding.

"Can't you kill a spider by yourself?" Emily called out.

"I can't reach it. He's on the ceiling, and if I go to sleep, he'll drop down on my face and lay eggs in my hair."

Ryan chuckled softly, whispering, "Do you want me to get it?"

Emily shook her head. "No, but I'm afraid we have to call this a night." She turned back toward the window. "I'll be right in, Chloe."

Ryan's forehead tipped forward to rest against hers. "Okay," he breathed. "But can we do this again tomorrow? I happen to have a pretty nice room down at the Rosebush Hotel. I wouldn't mind showing you."

Emily smiled and reluctantly stood up. "That is a very tempting offer, Mr. Taggert. Very tempting, and I'd like to oblige, but here in Trillium Bay, we take our courting slowly."

He sighed, deep and heavy, running his hands down her arms until they caught with hers. "I suspected as much, but the invitation stands. Think about it."

"I suspect I will think of little else. But in the meantime, I have to go kill a ginormous spider."

"Okay, and I will go jump in that ice-cold lake." He leaned forward, giving her one last fast kiss, and she felt her body wanting to surge forward. She felt as if she was seventeen again, only this was so much better because she knew it wasn't just the kissing that was wonderful. It was the kissing *Ryan* that was so wonderful.

Finally, he stepped back. "Okay. I really have to go now. Which way is that lake?"

Chapter 24

"Morning, Mom," Chloe said as Emily walked into Gigi's kitchen, bleary-eyed and searching for coffee. She hadn't gotten much sleep last night. After killing what was legitimately a huge-ass spider, she'd lain in bed and thought about Ryan, and kissing Ryan, and touching Ryan, and being completely and totally naked with Ryan. Then she'd thought about all the reasons that was impractical and unwise. And inevitable.

She stopped short at the sight of her daughter, up, dressed, and apparently ready for the day.

"What are you doing up so early?"

"The boat races. Remember? I told you. I'm going to the boat races with Susie and the gang, and guess what?"

"What?"

"It's going to be *yachts* of fun." Chloe waggled her eyebrows, and Emily groaned.

"New rule. No puns before I've had my coffee." She picked up her phone from the counter. There was a text from Ryan that had come in at one in the morning. It just said, THINKING ABOUT YOU.

She smiled and turned her face away so Chloe wouldn't see her blush.

The other message was from Jewel: CALL ME. AND TELL CHLOE THAT I MISS HER FACE.

"Jewel wants me to call. She said she misses your face."

"Tell her I said I miss her face, too." Chloe popped up from her chair and grabbed the knapsack sitting on the table, then put her empty cereal bowl in the sink. "I do miss her, but do you know what's kind of strange, Mom?"

"The fact that Gigi always wears exercise clothes but never exercises?"

Chloe giggled. "Besides that. I thought I'd miss San Antonio like crazy, and I totally don't. I definitely think we should do summers here, and maybe come sometimes in the winter, too, because I'm dying to see some real snow, and Leo says driving over the ice bridge is better than a roller coaster."

"I did love winters here," Emily said. She missed the changing seasons and the fellowship of the neighbors during long snowy months. It hadn't felt isolated. It had felt comfortable, but she'd forgotten that during her time away. Coming home this time had been like sinking into a favorite sofa.

Emily pulled Chloe in for a hug. "I'm very glad to hear you're enjoying it here, sweetheart. I really am. I'd love to come home more often, too."

"Maybe we should just move here."

It was way too early in the morning for radical comments like that. Emily tilted back to look at her daughter. "Move here?"

"Yeah. I don't know. I just really like having so many nice people around. Not one single kid has called me a giraffe, and my friends from back home don't seem to really notice I'm gone. At first we were texting each other all the time, but that's sort of, I don't know. Stopped?"

"But what about Jewel?"

Chloe smiled. "She could come, too." Then she leaned in for another squeeze, and Emily counted it as a blessing that her twelve-year-old daughter hadn't decided yet that she was too old for hugs.

"Have yachts of fun at the boat races," Emily said, tugging Chloe's braid.

Chloe laughed. "Thanks, Mom. I'll see you later."

Emily filled her coffee cup and sat down at the kitchen table to call Jewel. *Please have good news. Please have good news.*

Jewel's voice was breathless as she answered. "Hey, sweetie. You just caught me at the end of my workout, but I'm glad you called. I've got some good news and some other news that is crazy good news, but you might not think it's entirely good news. Although it is, it's just not going to make you totally excited. I mean, I think you will be totally excited on some level, but on another level, well—"

Jewel was never one to get straight to the point, and her breathlessness made it even harder to understand her. "Jewel, I've only got sixty-five percent battery on my phone. Could you just spit it out, please? What is it you're trying to say?"

There was a long pause followed by a couple bigger breaths. "Let me drink my water a second."

Emily tapped her fingers on Gigi's kitchen table, listening to Jewel glug her water.

"Okay," Jewel finally said, "we'll start with the totally-good good news. We have an offer on the Disaster-ville house. It's not an awesome offer, but it's okay. It's good enough."

"What's the offer?"

Jewel told her, and Emily's heart sank like a boulder tossed into Lake Huron. It was enough to cover all their renovations and closing costs and leave Emily a small cushion between solvency and disaster. The amount could tide her and Chloe over for a while, but the only way they'd be able to afford another flip was if Jewel was willing to put in extra.

"But they're preapproved with a great credit rating, so we should be able to close pretty soon," Jewel was saying. "Like in just a few weeks. Can you get home for that?"

"I guess. I'll have to look into flights." And spend the money on airfare. At least she could do a fast round-trip flight and leave Chloe with Gigi. Leaving Tiny in charge of her current renovation was not ideal. Quite likely nothing productive would be accomplished while she was away, although his square dancing might improve. Then again, she could ask Ryan to keep an eye on things. Maybe.

"I think we should take the offer, Em. There's been very little buyer interest in this house, and I think the sooner we unload this monstrosity, the better off we'll all be. Normally you know I'd say we should counteroffer, but I also know they're ready to pull the trigger on another house if they can't get this one at the price they're offering."

Emily was as eager as Jewel to put the house in her rearview mirror. It was a financial hit, but who knew when another buyer might show up? That house had been doomed since the day they'd gotten the keys.

"Okay. Let's take it before the roof caves in or the place gets infested with locusts. I'll see how soon I can get there. What's the other news?" She found herself squinting, as if bracing for impact, and Jewel took a couple deeper breaths.

"Well, I was going to wait until you got here for the closing, but I can't keep this a secret."

Definitely bracing for impact. She could tell by the tone of Jewel's voice this was something significant.

"Kevin and I are getting married! Can you believe it?" Jewel's voice went supersonically loud, and her words were followed by squeals so shrill they pierced right into Emily's eardrum. Wow, that really hurt. Was there blood? Her ear might actually be bleeding right now. But that was nothing compared to the shock jolting through her chest. Married? Jewel was getting married? To Kevin the electrician?

"You are?" Her own voice was nearly as loud, nearly as squeaky. Excellent. Now both her ears were bleeding. "How the hell did that happen? I mean . . . oh my gosh! That's . . . that's fantastic?" It wasn't, though. It wasn't fantastic at all. Jewel hardly knew him! "Um, so tell me everything." That was the polite question, but what she really wanted to ask was *Have you lost your fricking mind?*

"I know, isn't it? We've been spending practically every day together since you've been in Michigan, and this just feels so right. I'm so happy."

"Honey, I'm happy for you, too. I really am, but are you sure about this? I mean, you haven't been dating very long."

"We haven't been officially dating for long, but I've known Kevin for over a year. I work with him a lot more often than you do, and it turns out he's had his eye on me for all that time. He was just too shy to say anything. And his proposal was the cutest thing ever."

"Do tell." That was another polite question because at the moment, Emily's mind had jumped ahead to *Crap, oh crap, oh crap, how does this affect our living arrangement?*

"It was adorable, really. Last night we were in the produce section at the grocery store, and I was looking at the red peppers and Kevin was acting kind of weird, and I was actually starting to get annoyed because he kept saying, 'Don't you want some carrots?' And I kept saying, 'No, we don't need any carrots.' And he kept saying he was sure I wanted some carrots, and I finally turned around to say we didn't need any damn carrots, and there he was down on one knee, holding out the ring. He said, 'I love you, babe. Marry me and you can have these karats to wear for the rest of your life.'"

Emily tried to breathe. That proposal sounded . . . cute. A little dorky, but cute, and certainly better than the proposal Emily had gotten from Nick. His had been more postcoital in nature and not very well thought out. They'd drawn her engagement ring on her finger with a magic marker. Once that shit washed off she should have cut and run, but at the time it had seemed incredibly romantic.

Love makes you so stupid. No, change that. Love is great, but sometimes *sex* makes you stupid. She should embroider that on a pillow.

And give it to Jewel.

"So adorable," Emily said. "That's, um . . . so adorable." She really wanted to be a good and supportive friend right now, but Jewel didn't actually want her true opinion. "Have you made any definite plans yet?

A long engagement?" *Please?* "Have you set a date?" Emily braced for impact one more time.

"August thirtieth."

Breathe. Breathe.

"Next August?" *Please be next August. Please be next August.*

Jewel's voice was full of sympathy, for all the good that did. "No, honey. This August. We're just really excited to start our new lives together."

Where is a paper bag? Does Gigi have a paper bag? Emily was about to hyperventilate. "Wow, that's really . . . soon!" *Wow, I am so up shit creek right now.*

"I know, but all the pieces are just falling into place. We're getting married out at Kibbe Ranch. Kevin's sister works there and was able to lock in the banquet barn for us. And Em, there's something else you should know."

"Oh my God. There's more?"

"I got a job. A real job at an office."

Did Wenniway Island have volcanoes? Because it seemed like the ground was shaking, and certainly that wasn't just because of this earth-shattering news. Or maybe it was.

"You got an office job? I didn't even know you were interviewing." Emily reached out and grabbed the back of the chair next to her for stability.

"I wasn't, but this opportunity came along and it was just too good to pass up. I'll be working at the same place Kevin works. I know this is bad timing for you, Em, but maybe it's a blessing in disguise. This last flip was such a nightmare, I'm not sure I have it in me to try another one. I was going to tell you that even before Kevin proposed. I've realized I'm not cut out for house flipping. It's too risky, and I want a job that has benefits and stability. I'm sorry."

This was one of those times when being a good friend required faking it. "You don't have to be sorry, Jewel. I totally understand. I'm bummed, of course, because I loved working with you. And . . ." Emily couldn't stop the catch in her throat as tears threatened to overwhelm her. "And I really liked living with you, too. I don't mean to sound insensitive, but have you thought about that? About the house? I guess Chloe and I will have to move out, huh?"

Jewel's voice quivered, too. "I guess I kind of need you to. I don't want you to, but I just . . ."

"I know. I get it. And I understand. You've been so great to Chloe and me, letting us stay there all this time. We've been so lucky." Her mouth said the words and mostly she meant them, but in the back of her mind she couldn't help but panic. Jewel owned that house, fair and square, and she charged Emily a pittance in rent to live there. That had been a real blessing, but now she was being evicted with just a few weeks' notice. Where was Emily going to find a place to live in that same school district that wouldn't charge her three times the rent? And how was she going to deal with that when she was committed to staying in Trillium Bay until Gigi's cottage was finished?

"I can help you find a new place," Jewel said. "I'll start looking right away. Well, I mean, when I'm not busy with wedding planning stuff. That might be kind of time-consuming. But I will totally help you pack up your stuff. Or I can even do it for you and put it into storage since I realize I'm giving you, like, no time to plan."

No, she sure as hell wasn't. No time and no warning. Getting engaged was one thing, but getting married in just a matter of weeks was . . . well, maybe it was sweet and romantic, but maybe it was foolish and shortsighted.

"Jewel, are you sure about this? Why rush into it? Can't you be engaged for a while?"

"I don't need to wait, Em. I'm sure about this. Like I said, I've known Kevin for almost a year. Be happy for me."

"I am. If you're happy, then I'm happy." Emily took a big, deep breath. This was Jewel's life and her decision to make. She'd already spent enough energy trying to dissuade her sister and Tag from being involved with each other, and the truth was, Emily wasn't all that immune, either. She'd kissed Ryan just a handful of times, but her heart was already halfway in. "I think Kevin is a smart guy and very lucky to marry you, but I have to admit, I'm going to miss you like crazy."

"I know. I'm going to miss you, too, but we'll still see each other all the time. You know we will."

Sure they would, but everything would be different.

"And in case it isn't obvious, I want you to be my maid of honor."

Maid of honor. Wow. That should be such a thrill. Really it should, and under any other circumstances Emily would be elated, but right now all she could think about was that meant more money. A bridesmaid's dress for her, an outfit for Chloe, maybe a shower or bachelorette party for Jewel. All while she was trying to work on the island and find a new place in Texas. Holy. Shit. Shit. Shit.

"Really? Me? That's so awesome," she lied. "I'm honored to be your maid of honor."

"I wouldn't even consider asking anyone else. The ceremony is going to be very small, of course, since we don't have much time to plan."

They talked for another few minutes as Jewel rattled on about looking for a dress and what colors she wanted and how cute Kevin had been last night at a party introducing her to everyone as his fiancée. Emily wanted to be pleased about this, but it was so sudden. She'd been on cruise control for the last few weeks, just working on Gigi's cottage, biding her time until the San Antonio house sold, thinking she'd evaluate her options then. But suddenly most of her options were gone. It was like standing at the edge of a diving board, mentally preparing for a very complicated dive, and having someone rush up from behind and push you in before you were ready. Now Emily was in free fall, just waiting to hit, splat, against the water.

"I'm so excited for you, sweetie." She'd finally had enough and interrupted Jewel. "I'd love to talk more, but I really have to get to my own job here. I'll call you again later."

They said a few more goodbyes, and finally the called ended. Not a moment too soon, because the reality of it all was hitting Emily hard, and she needed to go have a little cry. What the hell was she going to do? Jewel was getting married and had gotten a job. So now Emily had no house to go back to. No business partner to rely on. No money. As soon as this remodeling job of Gigi's was over with . . . she would have no place to go and nothing to do. Except worry. Holy. Shit.

~

When Emily arrived at the cottage an hour later, she found only Georgie.

"Hey, where is everybody?" she asked as she walked into the kitchen, which was full of brand-new cabinets with the exact-right finish. Unfortunately, none of these cabinets were attached to any of the walls. She'd thought that would have been completed yesterday.

Georgie reached up and scratched her head, making that topknot of her hair fall to one side. "Um, that's sort of an interesting story."

"It's always an interesting story. What happened this time?"

"Tiny was using the old ladder to get up on the roof to fix that loose shingle. You know which ladder I'm talking about?"

"Does it matter which ladder?"

"I guess not, except for if you knew which ladder I'm talking about you'd know for sure that there was no way in hell that ladder was ever going to hold up under Tiny, but he was so happy this morning about spending time with Gloria that he thought for sure he could just scamper on up that ladder before it even knew it was being climbed. Then he figured he'd fix the shingle and just scurry on back down."

"Seriously? And you guys let him climb that ladder?" Now she knew which one they meant. She wouldn't have let Chloe use that ladder, and she weighed two hundred pounds *less* than Tiny.

Georgie shrugged and scratched her head again. "Well, he's the foreman, and plus he was pretty convincing. He said it could hold him."

"Okay, so what happened?"

"Turns out he was wrong."

Emily crossed her arms. "I gathered that. Is he okay?"

"Not sure. He got to about the sixth rung and the whole thing just gave way, and he came bouncing down with it. Whatever rungs he didn't break with his feet, he broke with his head. The whole ladder split in two. It was really kind of cool to watch. Except for when Tiny landed he twisted his ankle pretty bad. He didn't think it was broken, but Matt said he really ought to go have it checked out at the medical center."

On Emily's list of things to do? Double-check workers' compensation and liability insurance.

"Yes, I'm glad Matt told him to do that, but that doesn't explain where everyone else is."

"Tiny couldn't walk, and it took all the rest of the guys to carry him."

"They carried him? Did it occur to anyone to call a horse taxi or a dray or something?"

Emily watched as the thought registered on Georgie's face. "That would've been a really good idea."

"Yeah, no kidding. So they are all down at the medical center?"

Georgie nodded, scratching her head one more time, knocking that topknot back to the other side.

"What time was that?"

"About an hour ago, but honestly, I doubt they made very good time. He's mighty heavy."

The day continued on downhill from there. It took hours for the crew to get back from the island's medical center even though Emily texted every single one of them and told them to hurry. Horsey, of course, had to take a detour because his mother needed milk, eggs, and hemorrhoid cream from O'Doul's grocery store. Matt thought everyone should do some centering yoga after the stress of seeing Tiny fall, not to mention the back strain of having to carry him, and Georgie, not surprisingly, had cramps.

Tiny showed up late in the afternoon, at least having the good sense to take a taxi, and now sat in the middle of the main room on a red velveteen sofa that Emily had ordered for one of the guest rooms, calling out instructions. He wore an enormous protective boot. The doctor said it was just a sprain, thank goodness, but that still meant he had to stay off of it for a few days. At least the sprained ankle wasn't the one with the tether on it.

By four o'clock, Emily had about had it with the lot of them and sent everybody home. She just wanted to be alone in the house to try and get her bearings. She needed to process all the moving parts of her life that had turned it into a not-remotely-well-oiled machine. All day she'd been thinking about Jewel's phone call, and Chloe's comments about moving, and Ryan's kisses, and what it all meant. Big changes. That's what it meant. Good or bad, the changes were going to be big, and she didn't feel as if she had control over any of them.

She opened the screen door to go sit on the porch for a few minutes and just *think*. The hinge was loose, and this, at least, was something she could handle. She could fix this herself. At least she thought she could, but the damn thing didn't cooperate. The screw was stripped, the angle was hard to get at, and the door slammed on her finger not once but twice when she tried to tighten the screw using a different screwdriver. Clearly the damn door was taunting her, so she retaliated by punching it. Funny thing about having a fistfight with a screen door, though. The screen usually surrenders. And then you have a torn screen.

"Fuck," she said, slamming the door again, just to show it who was boss. And then three more times just to really prove her point. "Fuck, fuck, fuck!" Slam. Slam. Slam.

"So . . . what did that screen door ever do to you?" Ryan's voice floated up from the base of the stairs . . . and she burst into tears.

He trotted up to the porch and put his arms around her, and she let him, although it was a personal philosophy of hers to never, ever let anyone see her cry. She just couldn't help it, and he was so big and strong and it felt safe in his arms. "Hey, hey, hey. What's the matter?"

She didn't want to tell him. She didn't want to unload all those troubles on him. She'd already admitted to having borrowed money from Gigi, but she didn't want him to know how much, and she didn't want him to know that she had no place to go back to, but she couldn't hold it in. All the truths came tumbling out, along with more tears.

He'd pulled her inside at the first sign of waterworks, and now they were sitting on the velvet sofa. To his credit, Ryan held up pretty well. She knew most men were not great during these types of emotional crises, but he just listened and nodded and pushed her hair back from her face when it fell forward. Then he went and got her some tissues from the bathroom when she needed to blow her nose.

"I must be a mess," she said, feeling more than a little embarrassed now that the tears had finally ebbed.

"You look fine. Just a little . . . pink and puffy."

"Awesome."

She stood up and went into the bathroom to see for herself in the mirror. "Ouch. More than pink and puffy. I look like I've been attacked by bees."

Ryan came up behind her and gently turned her around, leaving his hands resting lightly on her shoulders. "Do you know what you need?"

"Half a million dollars and a new work crew?"

He chuckled and slid his palms upward until his hands cupped her face, and he ran his thumbs slowly along her jaw. "Well, yes, but I don't happen to have that. What I do have, however"—he leaned his body forward, capturing her between the bathroom vanity and the broad expanse of his chest—"is a really nice hotel room."

She leaned her torso back a few inches, looking up at him. "Ryan Taggert, are you trying to take advantage of me when I'm in such a vulnerable state?"

He looked thoroughly unapologetic. "I suppose that's a matter of perspective, because what I think I'm trying to do is make you feel better. The fact that I will also be making myself feel better in the process is just a perk." He kissed her temple softly. "So how about we go back to my very nice hotel room, have a few drinks, talk about some potential solutions to those problems, or we could just sit on the balcony and enjoy the nice evening breeze. Doesn't that sound good?"

"Drinks on the balcony? That's what you're suggesting?"

He shrugged. "Or whatever. You know. Your call."

This had been one doozy of a day. Chloe's desire to move, Jewel's crazy news, Tiny nearly breaking his ankle, the attack of the killer screen door, and all the stress of what to do with her future—it was all just too much. Ryan was right. Emily needed a break. A release. Good Lord, did she ever. One year and seven months was far too long to wait. And besides that, she liked him. A lot. He made her feel good, and if she let him, he could probably make her feel even better.

"I can't go to your hotel room, Ryan."

His optimistic expression fell. "You can't?"

She slid her hands up his thick arms and looped them around his neck. "No. I can't wait that long." She leaned forward, reaching up on her toes until her face was nearly level with his soulful eyes and wistful smile. "I can't wait any longer at all." She pressed her lips to his and kissed him with all the longing that had been building up inside her for weeks. Ryan groaned low in his throat, wrapping his arms around her waist and hauling her up tightly against him.

"I like the way you think."

"I like the way you do a lot of stuff," she murmured against his cheek.

"Oh, you have no idea the stuff I have planned for you."

He backed out of the bathroom and into the living room, not letting her out of his embrace. It was clumsy and silly and deliciously arousing to be pressed against him as he moved. He was all angles and hard planes where she was soft and curvy, and yet they fit together perfectly. He sat back down on the velvet surface, pulling her with him so her legs went on either side of his hips, and his . . . enthusiasm was obvious.

It left her feeling breathless and exhilarated and entirely feminine in all the best ways.

He bounced a little, releasing his hold on her to press on the seat cushions, and then he shook his head. "That thing is too narrow and not nearly strong enough for what I have in mind." Her laughter caught in her throat, and her eyes widened as she saw the intensity in his. She'd thought he was kidding. Now she wasn't so sure, but that was just fine. They'd revved up the engines while kissing on top of that lighthouse. They'd kicked the tires on her porch swing the other night. Now it was time to go for a ride. A fast ride. And she was so ready.

His hands moved up her legs to her hips, his fingers spread wide, his thumbs tracing along the inside of her thighs. He paused the movement just as he reached the hemline of her shorts, and those thumbs of his were dangerously close to touching her just where she wanted to be touched.

His gaze locked with hers. "Are you sure about this? I don't really want to take advantage of your vulnerable state."

"I'm sure. So very sure. But . . ." Her voice trailed off.

"What?"

"Um, protection?"

His smile was equal parts smug and grateful. "Gotcha covered. Or, got myself covered." He leaned to the side, taking her listing with him as he jostled the wallet out of his back pocket and pulled out a foil packet.

"You just happen to have that?"

"I do. I've been waiting for this for weeks."

"For weeks? You have?" Her skin flushed all over.

He nodded fast. "Pretty much since the first day I met you. I'm an optimist."

"I can't tell if I should be flattered or feel like I've fallen into a trap."

"Flattered. By all means feel flattered."

She was flattered, and she was going to make the most of this. Chloe was running around with friends, Gigi was playing bingo at the community hall, the work crew was long gone, and no one was expecting her anyplace anytime soon, so the next hour was going to be all for her and all for Ryan. She leaned forward and kissed him, clutching the fabric of his shirt and tugging it upward, breaking the kiss just long enough to pull it over his head and off of his arms. His breath hitched and he sat up straight when her hands came into contact with his skin and ran over his shoulders. He was smooth and muscular, steel wrapped in velvet under her palms. Yes, she was definitely going to make this count.

"Do you know what you are, Emily Chambers?" He breathed against her throat. "You're the kind of woman a man wants to make promises to."

"Good," she said. "Then promise me this is going to be awesome."

He chuckled, deep from his chest. "I promise. It's going to be awesome."

Chapter 25

"After paying closing costs on the Disaster-ville house, paying you back, and then paying off my other debts, I figure I'll have enough left over to take care of Chloe and myself for about six or eight months. Assuming I can find a decent place to live."

Emily and her grandmother were sitting in Gigi's kitchen sipping their morning coffee, and she was filling her in on all the latest happenings. Well, not *all* the latest. She didn't mention anything about Ryan, of course, but told her all the stuff about Jewel and the San Antonio house.

"Jewel was charging me a ridiculously low rent, so those costs are going to triple. Plus utilities and taxes and such. I'm definitely going to have to get a different job because I can't afford to buy another flip, and Chloe might even have to transfer to a different school."

"That would be awesome!" Chloe said, peeking her head around the corner of Gigi's kitchen. "I hate my school."

"You are not supposed to be eavesdropping." Emily had thought Chloe was still asleep.

"I'm just saving time. You know there are no secrets on this island. I'd find out eventually." She had them on that. It was general knowledge that most *secrets* on this island were general knowledge.

"Can we move here, Mom? I would love to move here." Chloe was practically bouncing in her fuzzy slippers and Harry Potter pajamas.

Gigi grinned. "Of course you can move here. Problem solved. Martini anyone?"

"That does not solve my problems, Gigi. I can't move back here. Chloe, we can't move back here. Gigi, you may not have a martini at eight thirty in the morning." Had everyone gone crazy?

"Why can't we move here?" Chloe said. "You don't have a job, we don't have a place to live, and if I have to change schools anyway, I may as well transfer here. It would be really cool to go to the same place you went. And Aunt Brooke would be my science teacher, unless she becomes the mayor. And I could see what it's like here in the winter. I have always wanted to try winter."

"But what about your friends in Texas?"

"Um, the ones who call me giraffe and make fun of my freckles? Those friends? Yeah, I'm okay leaving them behind."

"Well, then, what about my friends?" Emily said.

Chloe paused for a moment, looking back at her as if she didn't quite know how to break this news. "Um, I don't mean to be mean or anything, Mom, but who are your friends? I mean, I know you go out sometimes, but mostly it seems like you just work and do stuff with me and Jewel."

"Are you suggesting I don't have any friends? I have friends. There's um . . . let's see. There's . . . well, okay, so I don't have a ton of super-close friends, but I have a vast network of superficial acquaintances."

"You have friends here," Gigi said. "Gloria and the drunk puzzle girls, and you have your sisters and me and your cousins. I think it's all settled."

"It's not all settled. Please, Gigi, don't make this harder."

"I'm not trying to make it harder. I'm trying to make it easier. There are six bedrooms in this house and just me living here. I have more than enough room. Plus, I want you to renovate the rest of my cottages."

"Oh, see, Mom? Now you have a job here. Just consider it, please. You said you wanted me to like it here, right? You succeeded. Well done!

I like to hike and bike. And eat fudge. You like fudge, right?" Chloe nodded and lifted her eyebrows.

Emily smiled. "I do like fudge."

"Excellent. It's decided," Gigi said. "Now I can really show those Mahoney sisters that I'm the rental queen. Not to mention the fact that Bridget O'Malley was not looking that great in church last week. She cannot be long for this world, bless her decrepit old heart. We could pool our money and buy her place. I'd love to add another rental to my roster. And I won't even have to marry anyone to do it!"

Emily felt herself filling up with gratitude, but also filling up with caution. "Oh, Gigi, that is so generous. It really is, but I can't let you support me that way. I need to be supporting Chloe and myself . . . by myself."

"You will be doing it by yourself. I'd be hiring you, not offering charity. You think I could get anyone else I trusted and who would put so much blood, sweat, and tears into one of my places? You've been doing a wonderful job at that cottage over the past month, and so far, you're doing it fast and on budget. I have to be honest, kid. I had my doubts, but now I'm sure you can handle the job."

"You didn't think I could do it?"

"Nope, but I'm always willing to bet on you."

There was a compliment in there someplace. Maybe. "Well, don't go counting those chickens, Gigi. The place isn't finished yet."

"I am not the least bit worried, and listen, Delores Crenshaw was looking a little frail at church last week, too, and her cottage is right next door to the place you're working on now. You know, it occurs to me that I could be your business partner. I won't do any actual work, of course, but I can tell you who seems likely to die next so we can be first in line with an offer."

"Wow. That's morbid yet clever," Emily said, standing up. "You guys have given me a lot to think about, but right now I have to get over to the cottage and see how my crew is doing. Yesterday, they wasted an hour trying to get a faucet to work before realizing Horsey had turned off the water supply to the house to do some plumbing upstairs."

Gigi's confidence might be misplaced. There was still plenty to do on that cottage renovation. And Chloe's desire to move here was most certainly influenced by the fact that she'd been on *vacation* for the past several weeks. She might change her tune when the harsh weather hit and she was back in school. Still, it was worth considering.

Wasn't it?

Chapter 26

"Will we be witnessing your skills with the greased pole, Mr. Taggert?"

It was Independence Day on Trillium Bay, and Vera VonMeisterburger was in charge of fun and games. A fact which Ryan found ironic because nothing about her said fun, and nothing about her said games. Except maybe the Hunger Games. She seemed like the type who would thrive in a dystopian society pitting little children against each other.

"Here is a sign-up sheet," she said, waving a clipboard at him. "There are also contests for watermelon seed spitting, hot dog eating, and pie eating as well. Or if you fancy carnival-type games, we have several, as you can see." She gestured toward Trillium Pointe, which was full of striped tents, kites flying, banners waving, and so much red, white, and blue that there was no mistaking what day it was.

Ryan looked around, hoping to spot Emily. His chest whumped at the thought of her, and after their last few romantic encounters, he was getting suspiciously close to understanding how his father felt about Lilly. Something about those Callaghan women was simply irresistible. They'd found a few stolen moments over the past few days and had made the most of every one of them, and damn, if he didn't start thinking about something else soon, he'd be pitching a tent of his own.

Off toward the library, Ryan saw the beekeeper playing an accordion next to a man playing the banjo. A patriotic little dog sitting next to them had been dyed with red and blue stripes, and all around him were kids running and playing, adults smiling and laughing. It was a slice of pure Americana.

"The greased pole, Mr. Taggert," Mrs. VonMeisterburger said again, tapping his forearm with the clipboard. "I'm sure we'd all very much enjoy seeing you scale that mighty rod."

"What? Oh, no. Sorry, no pole climbing for me today." He walked toward a hot dog stand and saw Brooke and Gigi sitting at a picnic table. They smiled and waved. There was Yoga Matt, throwing softballs at a target while half a dozen young women cheered him on. June Mahoney and her sisters walked by and pretended not to know him, while old Bridget O'Malley sat on a bench wearing wraparound sunglasses that were as big as ski goggles.

Fifteen minutes of wandering around and still no Emily, but he did finally find his dad. They said their hellos, and Ryan couldn't help but notice his dad looked fatigued.

"You feeling good, Dad? You look a little tired." He rested a hand on Tag's shoulder.

Tag shook his head. "Just up late with Lilly."

"Oh, got it. No specifics, please."

"No, it's not that. We had a fight. She still doesn't want to tell her father about us because Emily has her so convinced that Harlan is never going to speak to her again. I think the longer we wait, the worse it will seem. It's not as if we're doing anything wrong."

Ryan felt his face scrunch a bit. "Well . . ."

Tag frowned. "Okay, ageism aside, Lilly and I are two responsible, single adults. All this sneaking around is ridiculous, and I don't like keeping secrets from people. It's just not in my nature."

"I know it's not, Dad, and if it makes you feel any better, I don't think it's much of a secret. My impression here is that everyone knows except Harlan."

"They do? Well, that does it then. I'm telling Harlan today."

"Today? With all these explosives around? You might want to rethink that." Ryan looked around, counting how many nearby items Harlan could use as a weapon of Tag destruction.

"No." Tag's tone was adamant. "I don't want to rethink it. We've tried it Lilly's way, and all it's done is make me feel deceitful and a little foolish. You know, I've played poker now for three weeks in a row with Harlan, and I can't mislead him anymore. I have too much integrity for that. Plus, I like him."

"You like him?" Ryan looked back at his father.

"Yes."

"Harlan Callaghan?"

"Yes."

"Chief of Police Harlan Callaghan?"

"Yes. Stop it. I know who I'm talking about."

"Okay then." Ryan shook his head. "I hope you like him well enough to be his son-in-law because there is a good possibility he's going to want you to do right by his daughter. This is where I feel compelled to remind you he has a gun."

"I know he has one, but he never carries it."

"That works in your favor then. It'll give you time to get away when he goes to load it."

Tag did not seem to appreciate his humor. "You're obnoxious. Have I ever told you that?"

"Yes, but I think I'm also right this time. Go ahead and tell him if you want to, but maybe don't do it when he's trying to monitor all the Fourth of July stuff and all the extra tourists. He's pretty busy today, and I think that might be kind of a sit-down-over-cigars-and-whiskey kind of conversation."

Tag looked frustrated, but Ryan could see him working through the various scenarios. "I suppose you're right," he finally said. "It's gone on this long. I guess a few more days won't matter."

"Right, and in the meantime, we can spit some watermelon seeds. Doesn't that sound fun?"

"Mom, we should take Grandpa a snow cone," Chloe said, pointing to the top of the hill where Harlan stood surveying the festivities. "He looks kind of hot, don't you think?"

Emily shielded her eyes and looked in his direction. He was in one of his favorite locations, standing at the crest of Leelanau Hill, leaning against the fence. She knew that from that vantage point he could see most of the park and keep an eye on all the people and the happenings, like a guard in a watchtower.

She didn't really want to hoof it all the way up that hill, but it wouldn't hurt to make an effort to do something nice. He had stopped by Gigi's cottage the other day and almost, very nearly said she was doing a moderately acceptable job.

"Okay, let's do it," Emily said. They stood in line for five minutes while Mrs. Bostwick explained to the poor teenager scooping the ice that her son, Reed, worked for the governor and was terribly important. Finally, they got a turn, ordered their cherry snow cones, and while Emily paid for them, Chloe got a better offer.

"Mom, Susie Mahoney says I should meet them by the popcorn stand. She's with everybody. Can I go?"

"I thought you wanted to take a snow cone to Grandpa?"

"Can't you take it to him?"

"By myself?" Even Emily realized how pathetic that sounded.

Chloe frowned at her. "He's not so bad as you say, Mom. I think he's kind of nice. Give him a chance. Isn't that what you always tell me? Give people the benefit of the doubt?"

Did she say that? It seemed like good advice to give a kid, but not such great advice when talking about Harlan. But now she had two snow cones in her hands, and Chloe was poised to sprint. "Oh, fine. Go find your friends."

Emily headed toward the hill, feeling stupidly nervous about being alone with her own father, and she realized that for this entire visit, it had never been just the two of them. The Cold War had continued, but maybe it was time to try once more. Plus, any minute now Lilly was going to tell him about Tag and lose her favorite daughter status, and that would boost Emily up to at least second place. She needed to take advantage of that while she could.

Nearing the crest, she called out, "Hi, Dad. I bought you a snow cone. Chloe thought you looked hot."

"Thanks." He took the cone from her hand.

"You're welcome." She really wanted to head right back down the hill and go find Ryan, but she felt rather obligated to visit with her dad for a few minutes, so she climbed up on the fence next to where he was leaning, and they nibbled their snow cones in silence.

"How's your day going?" she finally said.

"I've had better. I had worse."

Excellent. That was very helpful. Way to keep the conversation rolling, Dad.

After what seemed like a full minute, he finally said, "How's your day going?"

She was having a fabulous day, because for the past few days, she'd been having fabulous sex with Ryan. "I'm pretty good," she said.

"Uh-huh." He paused for another moment, then said, "I know about the Taggert fella."

Emily swallowed a chunk of ice big enough to sink the *Titanic*. How did he know about Ryan already? Maybe, hopefully, she'd heard him wrong. "What's that you say?"

"I know about the Taggert fella."

Yep, she'd heard him right. But she and Ryan had been very discreet. Incredibly discreet. Except for the lighthouse. Shit. So much for secrecy around here.

"I want you to know, Dad, he's a good person, and I'm so much wiser now and very careful."

"What? You? I'm talking about your sister and that John Taggert guy. What are you talking about?"

Oh good grief. She was so used to being scolded by him she'd nearly confessed before getting caught. She stuffed the snow cone in her mouth and mumbled, "Me? Um, nothing. What are . . . what are you talking about?" Time to play dumb, which was apparently going to be no challenge whatsoever.

He tossed the paper cup from his snow cone into the nearby trash can and crossed his arms, looking stern. Then again, he always looked stern. "I know Lilly has been keeping company with that man. Tag," he scoffed. "What kind of a grown man goes around using a nickname?"

"I don't know. Chief." She pressed her lips together, wondering if he'd catch her sarcastic slip.

"It's indecent, that's what it is. He's my age. He should be ashamed of himself. And what is it with you girls? Why can't any of you settle down with someone from a nice island family?"

"Um . . . I can't speak for Lilly, Dad, but keep in mind, we're related to half the population, and the other half are Mahoneys. We don't really have much to choose from."

He tapped at a tuft of grass with the heel of his shoe. "What about that Reed kid? He was a good boy. He works for the governor now, and he's terribly important."

Mrs. Bostwick must have bent her father's ear.

"Reed was a good boy, and now he seems to be a nice man. A much better man than Nick turned out to be. I shouldn't have run away like I did, Dad. It was wrong. I know that now, and I'm sorry."

Another moment passed. Harlan uncrossed his arms and slid his hands into his pockets, and Emily thought the conversation might be over, but it wasn't.

"You know, there are certain days in a man's life that he looks forward to. Days he knows are significant. Graduating. Getting married. Seeing his children for the first time." He sighed and looked off into the distance. "I still remember the day you were born. Coldest winter we'd had in years, and there was Mary, in labor and bundled up to the hilt as we walked to Dr. Pine's house. She wouldn't let me get her a sled. She said she wanted to walk. Then you came along and you were kind of orangey all over, squalling like nobody's business. You looked so mad, I couldn't help but laugh."

He paused and shook his head and actually chuckled. But then he sighed again. "And I remember it as clear as if it was yesterday. I held you on my chest, and I thought to myself, *You know, one day I'm going to have to walk this precious little girl down an aisle and hand her off to another man.* But the thing is, Peach, you never gave me that chance. You stole it from me. You just took off with that punk, a kid who didn't even respect you enough to come and ask me for your hand like a real man would have. And the thing that still bothers me the most? The thing that hurts me to this very day? It's that you seemed okay with it."

Emily felt as if the sun had moved a million miles closer and she was burning from the heat. It was more words than her father had spoken to her in a lifetime, and this was what he said? It was honest and raw, and if she hadn't been sitting on the fence, she would have crumpled to the ground from the burden of it.

"I'm sorry, Dad. I really am. I never meant to hurt you, and honestly, by the time I left with Nick, I didn't really think you'd care. I thought it might be a relief."

He turned to look at her, actually appearing surprised. "A relief? To know you were out there where I couldn't protect you? That was my job." He pointed to his chest. "I promised your mother I'd take care of you, and then I didn't. I couldn't because you'd left. All those times you got in trouble growing up, that's all I was trying to do. Keep you safe. It was the only part of being a parent that I thought I might be any good at." He scoffed and turned to stare forward again. "I didn't do very well by you, though, did I? And now it seems I haven't done too well by your sister either. She's going to take off with that Taggert fellow, and it'll be years before I see her again, too."

Emily felt tears scalding her eyes. This was so much more than she'd bargained for when she'd climbed up this hill with a snow cone. She'd seen things from her own side and never thought much about his. The pattern of his disapproval was so ingrained during her teenage years, and she never thought there could be more to it. But now she was a parent herself, and she understood the inherent fear that came with it. The constant worry that never fully went away. The need to protect your child at all costs.

"I don't know what to say, Dad, other than to tell you I wish with all my heart that I could go back and fix the stuff I broke. Running away was a mistake. Nick was a mistake, but Chloe is my everything, and I don't ever want her to wonder if I regret having her, because I don't. We can't change what's behind us, but if you want to, maybe we can turn in a new direction for the future?"

He pressed his lips together, and Emily could see he was actually choked up. Emotion under all that gruff exterior. Finally, he nodded. "She's a good kid, Emily. You've done all right. You might be better at this parenting thing than I was."

Did Harlan Callaghan just admit to a flaw?

"I know I've made mistakes," he said, "but all I know now is that I don't want to drive Lilly away like I did with you."

Emily thought about patting him on the back, but it just seemed like too much. She didn't want to overwhelm him, so she kept her hands on the fence. "Well, the thing about parenting, Dad, is that it's for life, so you might not get a do-over, but that doesn't mean you stop trying. It's up to you to decide how to handle things with Lilly. As for me, you're stuck with me, too, so if you want to try to salvage something, I'm willing to try. That's why I'm here."

"Here on this hill, or here on this island?"

"Both, I guess."

He looked over at her and then reached up and patted her knee, and she almost fell off the fence from that robust demonstration of his affection. "I'm glad you're here," he said.

Her heart bloomed like a lilac in the spring sunshine because that was as much of a declaration of love as she might have ever hoped for.

"I'm glad I'm here, too, Dad. On the island and right here on this hill with you."

Chapter 27

"Hey there, Peachy-keen! Happy Independence Day," said Gloria Persimmons, waving enthusiastically.

Emily and her dad had come down the hill together soon after their conversation ended. He'd gone off to find Judge Murphy and Father O'Reilly, probably so they could reminisce about the good old days when they were the ones causing trouble, and Emily had made her way toward Ryan. Now they were sitting at a picnic table watching Tiny, Garth, and a handful of other guys competing against each other in a pie-eating contest. For a skinny guy, Garth sure could snarf down a banana cream.

Emily looked up at Gloria's call and struggled to maintain her composure. Her friend was decked out head to toe in a stars-and-stripes ensemble that Uncle Sam would have considered too patriotic, from her red sparkly tennis shoes all the way up to the miniature flags sticking out from each ponytail. That was some outfit. Tiny stood next to her using the world's biggest, sturdiest crutches because of his sprained ankle.

"Same to you, Gloria. Tiny, how's that ankle?" Emily said.

"Not so bad. I've got Glo-Glo here to help me forget about the pain. She's my angel."

Gloria giggled and bumped against him, nearly knocking him off his crutches in her enthusiasm, but just as quickly wrapped her arms around his middle to catch him.

"And you're my naughty devil."

He beamed at Emily over the top of Gloria's head and mouthed the words *thank you.*

Emily smiled back, but her mind was uttering *Glo-Glo*? One square dance and they were already to the pet-name stage? What was it with people these days? Tag and Lilly falling hard and fast. Kevin and Jewel falling even faster. And now Tiny and Gloria? Was she the only one with any sense of caution? Then Ryan pressed his thigh against hers underneath the table, and she realized she was just as susceptible as the rest of them.

It was wonderful and terrible at the same time. Wonderful because it felt so damn good to experience the rush and the tumble of a new romance. Wonderful because Ryan was everything she would look for in a partner. Smart, funny, handsome, generous. Sexy. And did she mention sexy? But it was terrible, too. Because Tag and Lilly were still going strong, and if the four of them continued on, good heavens, their family tree could end up more gnarled and twisted than that one-hundred-year-old lilac tree down the hill from Gigi's cottage. What if Tag and Lilly had a son? It would be Ryan's half brother and Emily's nephew. And what if things continued on with Ryan and Emily and one day they had a son? He would be Tag's grandson and Lilly's nephew. And how would those two kids be related to each other? It was all just a little too Greek tragedy for her, and all things considered, they might actually be breaking laws in some states.

Then, of course, there was the not-so-little matter of geography. Emily was very seriously considering moving back home to the island, and Ryan would go home to Sacramento. Too far apart to be workable. There was Chloe to consider, too, of course, but she'd been thoroughly Team Ryan for weeks, so somehow Emily didn't think she'd mind.

So many things to consider, so many angles to look at this from, but today was Independence Day, and tonight there would be fireworks. Fireworks of all sorts, she hoped.

"So, guess what?" she whispered to Ryan after Gloria and Tiny had ambled away.

"What?"

"Chloe is sleeping at Brooke's house, so I'm completely kid-free for the entire night."

"Are you now?" He lowered his sunglasses to peer at her.

"Yes, and guess what else?" She was already enjoying this.

"What?" he asked, his voice husky with anticipation.

"Gigi sleeps like a tranquilized elephant and never has any idea what time I come home."

His eyebrows rose at her scandalous intentions. "Why, Miss Chambers, are you suggesting that we stay out past curfew?"

"I am. I would like to exercise a little independence of my own on this Fourth of July holiday. So how's about a little star-spangled romance at your hotel?"

"I like the way you think."

"And as I've mentioned before, I like the way you do a whole bunch of stuff."

~

"You are so smart, Emily Chambers. You were absolutely correct. Private fireworks are far superior to public fireworks," Ryan said with a satisfied smile as he rolled over in his hotel bed, pulling Emily with him. She was soft and warm and so delicious, he could already feel his body stirring again, but first, a bit of rest. That had been quite a workout.

She stretched like a cat in the sun next to him. "I am smart, and I especially liked that grand finale."

"Thank you. I tried to include a little something extra since it's the Fourth of July."

"How very patriotic you are," she said with a giggle.

"I am all for the raising of the flag."

Lying in a hotel bed, tangled up with Emily in his arms, Ryan was feeling all kinds of wonderful. Being with her was so natural and easy. Not the *take it for granted* kind of easy, but rather, the *honey, I'm home* kind of easy. Maybe it was just all the public displays of affection he'd seen today, or maybe it was because he'd been without a relationship for a long time, but deep down this felt . . . right. He also knew, deep down, that it wasn't because of either of those other things. And it wasn't just from positive associations, and it wasn't just random chemicals zooming around in his head. It was Emily. It was her laugh and her smile and her enthusiasm for her work. It was the way she interacted with her daughter. It was simply everything about her. Ryan was an opportunities guy, and if his mother were alive, she'd say, "Ryan, you should marry that girl before she gets away." Of course, it was far too soon to be thinking such things, but he was thinking them anyway.

"Emily?" he asked softly, wondering if she'd drifted off to sleep. The room was dark except for the glow of some streetlamps. They'd left the windows open, and a soft breeze set the curtains to dancing a slow waltz back and forth.

"Hmm?"

"I like you."

He felt her chuckle more than he heard it, but she lifted her head from his shoulder and smiled down at him. "I like you, too."

"I seem to like you quite a bit."

She nodded. "Same."

"I'm not sure what to do about that. About . . . us. I just know I'd like there to be . . . some kind of us. You know?"

Her smiled faded and her expression matched the emotions he was feeling. Uncertainty about their odds, but earnest in their hope to make it work.

"Same."

He could feel her heart beating against his chest as he pulled her over on top of him, like he wanted to be surrounded by her in every possible way. Her hair fell around his face like a curtain, keeping them hidden from the world.

"There's something I should mention, probably." She stared down at him in the dim light. "I'm thinking about moving back here. To the island."

"You are?"

"Chloe wants to. I seem to be in kind of a nice place with my family, which I haven't had in years, and Gigi wants me to renovate more of her cottages. We even talked about buying that cottage down the hill from where I've been working."

He knew which one she meant. He knew instantly, but she kept talking.

"Mrs. O'Malley, the fossil who owns that little pink house, hasn't been looking so well at church lately, and Gigi thinks we could pool our money and buy it as another rental for her, but I don't know. It's just an idea."

She couldn't buy that place because Taggert Property Management already owned it. He should tell her that right this minute, but he had clients to consider. And Emily moving home wasn't contingent on that one place. If it was, then certainly he'd tell her. He knew a solid plan from a fanciful speculation. Like she'd said, it was just an idea.

Even so, he felt a little guilty. He wanted to tell her, but he couldn't. A contract was binding. He'd figure something out, some way to explain it to her, but not right now, because right now, Emily was smiling down at him, her expression full of invitation.

"In the meantime," she said, "until we figure out what to do about us, I suggest we just keep doing this."

Then she kissed him, and he agreed.

Chapter 28

"So the cat's out of the bag, the fox is in the henhouse, the shit has hit the fan," Ryan said to Bryce over the phone. "I'm not sure which of these phrases suits the situation best, but the bottom line here is that Chief of Police Harlan Eldred Callaghan now knows that our father is banging his daughter."

"Dude," Bryce said, his voice scratchy from sleep. "Do you have any idea what fucking time it is here?"

Ryan glanced at the clock on his nightstand. It was 7:00 a.m. "Oh shit. Sorry. Forgot about the three-hour time difference. Good morning. Thought you'd want to be the first to hear the news. Well, actually you're the first person who isn't physically on this island to hear the news. As far as the people around here go, I think everyone now knows."

"Dude, seriously, could we talk about this later? I'm in REM sleep."

"Can't talk later. I've got to shower, and then I'm taking Chloe and Emily out for breakfast before we go see the reenactors at the fort."

"Who is Chloe?"

"Emily's daughter."

"Who is Emily?

"Lilly's sister."

"Who is Lilly?"

"The gold-digging bimbo. Did you take an Ambien? What the hell is wrong with you?"

"It's four o'clock in the morning, you asshole, and you woke me up. That's what's wrong with me. What the hell is wrong with you? You're wide awake and way too cheerfu—oh shit. You're doing it with the bimbo's sister, aren't you? The chick from the airport. I knew it. I knew I couldn't trust you."

That should be insulting, but Bryce was right. Ryan was cheerful, and he *was* doing it with the bimbo's sister. In fact, he'd just walked her home, sneaking around through shrubberies and along the back side of hotels so no one would spot them. It was like a college walk of shame all over again, only this time he didn't feel any shame. He just felt good.

"Relax, Bryce. It's not a problem. Everything is fine."

"Fine? So that means you've convinced Dad not to retire?"

"No, he's still retiring, as far as I know, but at least so far the chief of police hasn't thrown him off the bridge."

"Go back to sleep, honey," Bryce said softly to his wife. "It's just Ryan, and he's high on dopamine. What? No, not dope. Dopamine. Never mind. Go back to sleep."

"Tell Trish I'm sorry I woke her up," Ryan said.

"You should be sorry, and you should also be sorry that you haven't talked any sense into Dad. I'm going to send Jack out there."

"No, you don't need to. Listen, Dad is nearly finished with this Clairmont Hotel job, and once that's over, he'll be mostly done here anyway. I think he and Lilly have some trips planned or something. He was sketchy on the details."

"Of course he was, but there's still the Mahoney job. That's going to take months. Are you planning to stay for that? Or go back and forth, or what?"

This was the part Ryan didn't want to get into, but realistically, the sooner Bryce knew, the better. "I think there is a distinct possibility that the Mahoney deal is a no-go. We've run into some complications."

"What? Why? You said it was a slam-dunk." Ryan could hear Bryce get up out of bed, and then he heard the sliding glass door open and close. His brother must have walked out onto their balcony.

"The spot they want to put that bed-and-breakfast is a prime location, but a three-story building will ruin the view for the cottages behind it."

"So, that's up to the people in those cottages to deal with. Not our problem as long as the zoning is in place, and you said that was already handled. You said the hundred-and-ten-year-old lady had already signed to make the sale."

"She's a hundred and two, and yes she signed, but I just don't feel right about it."

"What is it you're not telling me?"

Bryce knew him too well.

"Look, Emily has been renovating this cottage for her grandmother. She's put a lot of work into it, and if we build a bed-and-breakfast in that location, the value of Emily's place is going to plummet. It'll go from having an unobstructed view of the lake and the bridge to being a view of the back side of someone else's property."

"Are you telling me that you want to let this lucrative deal fall through just because you got a case of the feels for some woman?"

"That's ironic coming from a guy who's been married three times. Are you telling me you didn't do that, three times, because you had a case of the feels?"

Bryce coughed. "Sure, I got married, but I never gave up any business deals. I'm not an idiot. You need to look at this strategically. You said that place behind the B and B is a rental anyway. It's not like you're ruining the view for someone's house, and you said she was a flipper, so she probably doesn't have any attachment to the place anyhow. If she's as smart and savvy of a businesswoman as you've said, she'll understand that this is just business. You're overreacting."

Ryan was starting to feel defensive. He didn't want Bryce to talk him out of this. He owed it to Emily. "I'm not. I'm telling you this contract with the Mahoneys needs to go away. Emily wants the property for herself, and she needs it more than we do."

"What? How do you figure that?"

"She and her grandmother want to buy it. Emily's going to renovate it, and they'll turn it into another rental cottage."

"But we've already bought it for our own client. Ryan, if you back out of this deal, those Mahoney women could sue us. Besides, I've looked over the specs, and this is a great project. You'll be in and out in a few months, and then we're free and clear. Just tell your bed buddy to buy a different cottage. I'm sure that place isn't the only one. She'll understand. Now, it's four fifteen and I've got about forty-five minutes to sleep before the baby wakes up, and then I'll have to wake Trish up to take care of him, and that always makes Trish grouchy, so I'm hanging up now. I'll call you later, and do not under any circumstances cancel that Mahoney deal."

Ryan started to argue but realized he was talking to air. Bryce was gone. That conversation went pretty much the way he'd expected. The business side of his brain agreed with his brother. The deal was too good and too easy for Taggert Property Management to give up for such a flimsy reason. The other side of his brain, the side that was all clouded with images of Emily in the bed beside him, had him all turned around. He needed to tell her about the contract, and soon, because she was flying back to San Antonio any day now to close on that other house. He'd talk to her about it tonight. Bryce was right. She was smart and practical. She'd understand. It wasn't a personal thing. It was just business.

Chapter 29

All the memories of sneaking around as a teenager came back to Emily as she ducked her head and walked through the lobby of the Rosebush Hotel. It was nearing dinnertime, and they'd decided to have, as Ryan had termed it, *room service and romance*, so she now found herself standing outside his hotel room door. She lifted her hand to knock, but the door opened and he pulled her in, slammed it shut, and pressed her against it.

She gasped at the pressure. "Why, hello, Mr. Taggert."

"Hello, Miss Chambers," he said, smiling. "I've heard it said that courting here on Trillium Bay tends to go at a slower pace, but you're in *my* room now. I don't think those rules apply."

"That's awfully bossy of you." She put her hands on his hips and pulled him close.

A low, satisfied groan came from his throat. "Maybe, but something tells me we're on the same page here."

"I believe we are."

"Good, because I have been thinking about you all damn day."

"Me too. Same page."

The door thumped in its frame as he leaned forward to kiss her, sending shock waves of pleasure pulsing through her body and scattering her thoughts.

He was so very good at this.

She pushed at him, and he looked startled, until he realized she was pushing him toward the bed. His gaze turned hungry as he pulled his shirt up and over his head.

Damn, she'd never get tired of seeing that, seeing the planes and valleys of his torso. He dropped his shirt on the floor and pulled her toward him.

"I like that dress," he said.

"Do you?" She reached up and pushed one tiny strap off her shoulder.

"Yes. Very much."

"That's nice." She flicked the other strap off her shoulder and let it slide down. It caught on her hips, and Ryan watched, mesmerized as she hooked her thumbs and eased it the rest of the way down.

"Damn," he breathed, and Emily felt both powerful and powerless under his gaze. So many obstacles could ultimately pull them apart, but all of them were meaningless because of all that pulled them together. Ryan wrapped his arms around her, and as they tumbled to the mattress, Emily Chambers realized she wasn't just falling into bed. Damned if she wasn't falling in love.

~

"I think we need that room service now. Are you hungry?" Ryan asked sometime later as they lay entwined, bedsheets twisted around them.

"After that? I'm famished."

He laughed and kissed her again, nearly setting off a chain reaction that would have delayed food another half an hour at least. She pushed at his chest.

"Seriously. I'm legit starving. I need some food."

"Okay, okay, I'll call right now." He leaned over the side of the bed to find his phone from somewhere in that pile of clothes. Emily looked over so she might fully appreciate the fascinating way Ryan's muscles flexed as he did that. At last he found the phone, tugging it from the pocket of a pair of jeans. "Hey, my brother called. I was supposed to get in touch with him this afternoon, and I'm sure he's in a frenzy. Do you mind if I give him a quick call back after I order us some food?"

"Of course I don't mind. Would you mind if I jumped in the shower?"

"Not if you don't mind if I join you."

"I'm never going to get to eat, am I?"

"I promise I will let you eat. What do you want?"

"Surprise me," she said as she pulled on his T-shirt and walked toward the bathroom.

"I love a woman who lets me be in charge," he called after her.

"Don't get used to it," she replied before shutting the door.

The bathroom was tiny, and the big floral pattern of the wallpaper made it seem smaller still. The shower was hardly big enough for her, let alone her and Ryan, so Emily decided to just rinse off quickly and then let him have his turn. She was in and out in five minutes, and she could hear him on the phone as she toweled off. She glanced in the mirror, wondering how much effort it was going to take to make herself presentable. She needed to get dressed and get back to Gigi's place without her grandmother, and especially her daughter, realizing what she'd been up to.

"I tried to tell you that earlier, Bryce, but you were zoned out on Ambien. They're just little old ladies. I think I can handle them," she heard Ryan say. It seemed an odd statement, and she couldn't help but lean closer to the door to hear what else he was saying. And then she wished she hadn't.

"No, Dad's drawings are for a three-story bed-and-breakfast right in front of the place Emily is working on." He laughed at something his brother said, and added, "Yeah, the pink house with the old lady in it, but that's why these Mahoney sisters are so anxious for us to build on it. I've talked to them myself, and they'd be willing to lose money if it would screw over the Callaghans. Some sort of old island rivalry."

Emily's heart, which only moments before had been thumping so happily at thoughts of Ryan, suddenly dropped down to the floor. What did he just say? A bed-and-breakfast right in front of Gigi's cottage? The Mahoney sisters?

She had to be wrong. She must have misheard.

She finished drying herself off and wrapped the towel around her. Ryan was quiet for a few minutes, listening to his brother, and then she heard him speak again. "Yes, we already bought the property. Quite frankly, I can't believe it's still a secret, the way these islanders gossip. That's why the Mahoneys are so insistent we not let anyone in Trillium Bay know that they're our client. It's all very cloak-and-dagger."

He laughed again, and they continued with the conversation. Emily hadn't heard wrong. He was working for the Mahoneys. How could he not tell her that? He knew she was interested in that cottage, but judging from what he'd said, his company already owned it. That didn't make any sense. It didn't make any sense at all. Humiliation washed over her like the hot water of the shower, and her breath went shallow. He'd completely misled her, and she could not think of one defendable reason why he might have done that. So all she could think about now was getting out of that room.

She came out of the bathroom, and he looked her way, his smile mischievous as he noted her towel. He was sitting in the chair near the window with his feet up on the sill. He had put his shorts back on, and she suddenly felt very vulnerable and very naked.

"I have to go now, Bryce. Better things to do than talk to you. Yeah, we'll work out those details later." He tossed the phone to the bed and stood up. "Hey, sorry that took so long. Bryce always wants to talk business." He stepped toward her and kissed her neck, and she wanted to slap his face away. He should have told her about that property. Why would he not just tell her? But maybe she was still wrong. She had to be wrong. His words went round and round in her head as she struggled to come to any other conclusion.

"I know you Taggerts are all about business," she said, noting the flat tone to her own voice. She couldn't hide it.

Ryan stepped back and looked at her. "You okay?"

"Yeah. Fine. The shower is too small for two. I need to get dressed."

"Okay, yeah. I'm just going to hop in there, then. Make yourself at home, and I'll be out in a flash. I ordered us enough food for five people. You'll need the energy." He smiled again, but she just nodded. His smiled dimmed a bit. "It should arrive pretty soon. You sure you're good?"

She nodded vigorously. She should just ask him, but she knew what she'd heard, and she didn't want to listen to him spin it. She didn't want to listen to him justify why it wasn't personal. It was just business, but it felt personal to her. He knew what she'd poured into that remodel, and he was going to ruin it? Just so the Mahoney sisters could have a bed-and-breakfast? She had to be wrong.

She offered up a lame smile. "Yes. I'm good. Go take your shower."

He closed the door behind him, and she pulled on her clothes as quickly as she could, her mind racing over random possibilities. She looked at the desk in the corner of the room. It was covered with papers, right out in the open. So what would be the harm in looking? She pulled her shoes on and found her feet walking her in that direction. There were some drawings of the interior of Gigi's place with ideas he hadn't shown her, and there were some sketches of the outside with a few modifications.

Some papers from the bottom of the stack were dog-eared and torn at the edges, as if they'd been carried around in a binder that wasn't quite big enough. She thought of Ryan's overstuffed computer bag and all the papers that had been sticking out of that when he'd walked into the Wawatam airport. She pulled them out to get a better look, and the stone that had been in her gut for the past fifteen minutes grew sharp claws. These were drawings of a three-story bed-and-breakfast, sitting right where the pink cottage was now. There were landmarks on the drawings, like the old lilac tree she'd pointed out to Ryan from the window of Gigi's rental. There was no mistaking it.

She needed some air. She needed some distance to think. She pulled open the drawer of the nightstand to find a pen and some paper and quickly scrawled Ryan a note.

Sorry. Something's come up. I had to head home. I'll catch up with you later.

It was the coward's way out, and she hated that. She was a face-it-head-on kind of woman, but right now she had to step away from the scene of this crime to even decide how she felt before discussing it with him. She left the note next to his phone and quietly left, shutting the hotel room door with a significant click.

~

Where the hell was she? Ryan looked around the small room for a minute before seeing the note on the bed. *Something's come up?* He hoped it wasn't serious. Or something having to do with Chloe. He dialed Emily's phone, but it went straight to voice mail.

"Hey, it's me. I hope everything is okay. Call me back when you can."

Room service knocked on the door, and Ryan resigned himself to eating alone. He was tempted to go over to Gigi's house just to make sure everything was all right. Why hadn't she at least knocked on the bathroom door to tell him she was leaving? Unrest swirled in his gut.

They'd just had a really good time together, right? A really good time. They'd been enjoying each other's company for weeks now, and each time he saw her, he wanted her more and more. He thought he'd made that abundantly clear.

So why the abrupt departure? Why leave without saying goodbye? He read the note a few more times, but it was nothing much to go on.

He looked around the room, searching for clues, but nothing caught his eye. It was just a regular hotel room with all his regular stuff. His suitcase, his clothes, his computer and computer bag, the stack of papers and the drawings from his dad. Nothing unusual to explain why she might have left here.

There was nothing much he could do about it from here, and odds were good that it was nothing more serious than Chloe being legit upset about something minor or Gigi needing somebody to make her a martini. Emily would call him later, or she would call him tomorrow.

He ate his dinner, and then he ate hers, and he wished she was there. In fact, he pretty much always wished she was there. All the time. If she moved back to this island, well, that wasn't terribly convenient. Truthfully, neither was San Antonio if he lived in Sacramento. And he couldn't leave Sacramento. That was *his* home. It's where his brothers were and his friends. He didn't want to leave all that behind. Sure, he traveled more days than not, but it was still *home.* Then again, maybe home had less to do with location and more to do with who you were with. And all he knew right now was that whenever Emily was in his arms, that felt like home to him.

Chapter 30

Emily slumped over the kitchen table nursing a martini that Gigi had made for her. It was bitter and harsh and suited her mood perfectly. She'd left Ryan's hotel room and gone straight to Bridget O'Malley's house to ask about the sale of her little pink cottage. Now Emily almost wished she hadn't.

"So, just so I'm clear," Gigi said, "Ryan told Bridget O'Malley that his company purchased her land to build a bed-and-breakfast there, and they intend to call it the O'Malley House?" Gigi was on her second martini, but being a professional drinker, it didn't seem to alter her personality that much. Emily, on the other hand, was feeling the effects from just a few sips. Maybe that was because Ryan had never fed her. The liar. The trickster. The bastard.

"Yes, Gigi. Mrs. O'Malley even showed me the drawings, and they were almost identical to the ones I saw in Ryan's room."

"Do we need to talk about what you were doing in Ryan's room?"

"I'd rather not."

"I thought as much. Well, nonetheless, are you sure he mentioned the Mahoney sisters? Bridget would never sell anything to them. I once saw her refuse to sell April a rice crispy treat at a bake sale."

"Yes, I distinctly heard him mention the Mahoneys. Ryan told me that lots of their clients like to remain confidential to avoid situations just like this, so I have to imagine that's why June hired them. She knew

Bridget O'Malley wouldn't sell to them, and she also knows that putting a three-story building in that spot will completely ruin the view from your rental cottage. This is a double-whammy from those dia-fucking-bolical Mahoneys." Emily was finally starting to understand her grandmother's extreme dislike of them. She was feeling an extreme dislike of them, too. And an extreme dislike of the Taggerts as well. "I just can't believe Ryan wouldn't mention it to me when I said we were thinking about buying the house for you. He never breathed a word of it."

"Why don't we just tell the Taggerts not to build on it?" Chloe asked, peeking her head around the corner. Emily really did need to talk to her daughter about eavesdropping, but the kid came by it naturally.

Emily stood up and hugged her instead.

"We could try that, honey, but money is very important to men like the Taggerts. Ryan and his brothers are dedicated to making it and keeping it." She sat back down with a depressed thump. "I guess the one bit of good news is that Jewel called me earlier to say the closing for the San Antonio house is the day after tomorrow. Gigi, if you don't mind keeping an eye on Chloe for a few days, I'll fly to San Antonio on the next available flight."

"Of course I don't mind. Chloe and I will have fun. We'll take some selfies."

"I just feel like we don't have all the information we need, Mom," Chloe said. "I mean, how did you find out about this deal anyway?"

Secrets. Secrets. Secrets. At least Chloe wasn't asking why she was in Ryan's room. She must not have heard that part. "Um, I was with Ryan and I heard him talking to his brother on the phone, and then I saw the drawings he made."

"But did you ask him? You should ask him."

Chloe was probably right. Emily should ask him, but right now she felt angry and hurt. It just seemed like he could have told her he was working for the Mahoneys somewhere between the *Hi, I'm Ryan*, and the *I just have to kiss you.*

Gigi stood up, draining the last of her martini. "Well, my darlings, we can talk about this some more tomorrow. I need to get my beauty rest." She leaned over and kissed Chloe on the forehead, and then she came around to the other side of the table to kiss Emily's forehead, too. "Don't worry about this too much, honey. Things have a way of working out, and I'm sure this will, too."

Emily's phone buzzed for the third time since she'd left Ryan's hotel. Same text message, slightly different wording. He'd left her a voice mail, too.

Hey, I'm kind of worried. Hope everything is okay. Call me back.

She didn't want to talk about this on the phone, and she didn't want to have the conversation by text, either. She just wanted to ignore him.

Ryan Taggert was an asshole. He had deliberately misled her. He'd misled a gullible 102-year-old woman, too, and he did it just to make a buck. He was not at all the man she thought he was.

Emily leaned over to grab her laptop from the counter, flipping it open so she could look at flight times. "Chloe, you should head on upstairs. I just need to make some plane reservations, and then I'm going to bed too."

"Okay, but I still feel like if we just ask Mrs. O'Malley not to sell it, then she won't. Or if she has sold it, I really think we just need to ask Ryan and Tag not to build there."

Emily patted her arm. "I hope you're right, honey. I'll ask them about it when I get back from San Antonio."

"How long will you be there?"

"Four or five days. I have to pack up all our stuff at home, I mean, from Jewel's house, and put it in storage until we figure out where we want to live."

"Would this be a good time to mention that I want to try living here? Maybe not for forever, but for a year or so? Just until my boobs grow in and then we can go back to San Antonio and I can tell Anastasia Whitcomb to kiss my butt."

Emily smiled for the first time in several hours. "Do you really think you want to live here?"

Chloe came up and hugged her. "I think it would be fun. We could help Aunt Brooke become the mayor, and I could ride horses all year round. I really like my new friends, too. Susie Mahoney is like my best friend in the world."

Chloe looked so earnest and hopeful. What was Emily fighting against? She had everything she needed right here. Eventually Taggert Property Management would finish their jobs and get the hell off her island. She was the one who had a right to be here. Not them.

"Probably, honey. I can't give you an answer tonight because I'm kind of confused about some stuff, but I promise I will think about it."

"Do you want to know the other reason I like it here?"

"Why?"

"People have started calling me Niblet. I think that's kind of cute."

~

"Thanks for giving me a ride to the boat docks, Dad," Emily said as she sat next to her father in the police wagon early the next morning. "You really didn't have to."

"I know I didn't have to, but once in a while maybe you could try to let me do something nice."

"Okay, I will. In that case, can I ask you for a favor?"

"Of course."

"Will you stop by the cottage I'm renovating once or twice a day and make sure my crew is actually working and not doing yoga or square dancing or just generally wasting time?"

"I can absolutely do that. Will you do something for me?"

"I can try."

"Okay. I won't tell you to move home because I don't think that's my business. You have to do what you think is best for you and Chloe, but I want you to promise to come visit more often. And if you decide you do want to move here, I could sure use some updating at my place. Nothing too fancy, but it might be time for me to get a dishwasher or replace the green appliances."

"Are you offering me a job?"

"A job, a place to stay, whatever you need."

Emily turned her face away to brush off a tear. If Harlan saw her crying, he'd regret saying anything at all. "I think maybe I would like to move home, Dad. Maybe not permanently, but long enough so Chloe can see what she thinks of a Michigan winter, so maybe we could stay for a year and see how it goes?"

"I like that idea. I like that idea a lot."

She smiled. "Me too."

There. That was one decision made. She was going to pack up her stuff in San Antonio and ship it here. She'd miss Jewel like crazy, but since her friend now had a new job and a new fiancé, realistically she wasn't going to have much time for Emily for a while anyway. She'd just have to come to Trillium Bay for a summer vacation.

"Can I ask you something, Peach?" Harlan said a few minutes later.

"Of course."

"What do you think I ought to do about that Taggert fella and your sister?"

He was asking her opinion. That was a pretty big deal.

"I don't really know, Dad, but one thing I suggest is that you don't freeze Lilly out. You might not realize this, but sometimes you're a little hard to talk to."

She saw the slight twitch of his lips. That was the Harlan Callaghan version of LOL, so she was satisfied.

"That might be true, so I'll try. But this is a hard one. It was bad enough when you took off, but at least I could understand the attraction. But this? Her and him? He's my age. Do you know how wrong I'd feel spending time with someone her age? It's indecent."

"I'm not sure what to tell you. It doesn't make a lot of sense to me, either, but it's Lilly's life, and she has to learn to deal with the consequences of her decisions, just like I had to."

Apparently Emily was still learning that lesson, because by all accounts her judgment in men had not improved much in the past fifteen years. She wasn't likely to meet anyone on the island, either, but at the moment, that felt like a blessing.

"Here we are," her father said, pulling on the reins. The horses shuffled to a lazy stop, and Emily grabbed her bag from the back.

"Thanks again, Dad." She felt another tear coming and flicked it away. "I'll be back in five days. I'll see you then."

"I look forward to it."

She climbed down from the buggy and smiled up at him. "Me too, Dad." And she actually meant it.

Chapter 31

The first thing Emily Chambers noticed five days later when she stepped off the ferryboat and walked down the dock toward Main Street of Trillium Bay was Dmitri Krushnic in his beekeeping hat sitting out front of Joe's Cuppa Joe enjoying some version of coffee that included whipped cream and sprinkles.

"Hiya, Peach. Good to have you back. How was San Antonio?"

She shrugged and readjusted the travel bag slung over her shoulder. "It was okay, I guess, but can you keep a secret?" She knew he could not.

He put his hand over his heart solemnly. "I'll take it to the grave."

That was a risky promise to make, knowing his track record. "I've decided to move back home. Here to the island."

His smile broadened, exposing that gap between his two front teeth. "Why, that's wonderful news. Just wonderful, and I promise my lips are sealed. No one will hear it from me."

She sincerely doubted that, but no matter. Peach had come home to stay, and telling Dmitri it was a secret was certainly the most expedient way to spread the word.

She kept on going, her tennis shoes making little squeaks against the pavement as she walked. Most of her summer clothes were already at Gigi's, and during her stay in San Antonio, Emily had packed up all of her worldly possessions and arranged to have them shipped to the island. She'd had a lovely, bittersweet visit with Jewel. They'd hugged and cried and made promises to always, always keep in touch, and Emily knew they would. A friendship like theirs could survive the distance.

In Emily's wallet was a cashier's check made out to Margaret O'Reilly-Callaghan-Harper-Smith for the full amount of the loan, and another cashier's check with the balance of Emily's money to be deposited into the Trillium Bay Savings & Loan. It felt very good to be paying her grandmother back, and it had felt very, *very* good to close on that disaster house. And it felt *very, very,* very good to be back home on Wenniway Island.

During her long day of travel from San Antonio to Michigan, Emily had time to think and plan and strategize about her future. For all the good that would do. Life had a way of shifting under her feet like quicksand, and she had learned to just make the best of it. Like Gigi always said, "When God closes a door, he shoves you out the window." Emily knew this lesson better than anyone, so making long-term plans was probably pointless, but one thing she knew for certain about her future? Ryan Taggert wasn't going to be in it.

He'd tried to call her twice while she was gone, but she didn't even listen to the messages. What could he possibly say that would make up for the fact that he'd tricked an old lady into selling her land to Taggert Property Management when she was really selling it to the Mahoney sisters? That was despicable, and it was a clear demonstration of his priorities. Business came first. People and their feelings came second.

The truth was, he'd all but lied to Emily, too, and that betrayal cut deep. Not because Mrs. O'Malley's property was that important to her, but because his dishonesty revealed the core of who he was: a man more concerned about money than integrity. And the fact that he was willing to build something right in front of Gigi's cottage, laughing with his brother about how it would ruin the view for Gigi's place? A place he knew Emily had put her heart and soul into renovating? Well, that revealed exactly where she fell on his list of priorities. At the bottom.

For all she knew, he'd build that three-story bed-and-breakfast and put the trash dumpsters right behind it so everyone sitting on the porch of Gigi's freshly remodeled cottage would smell nasty, foul old garbage instead of lilacs and fudge. That stunk, and so did he. And so did her broken heart. She'd let herself fall for him. For the soulful gazes and wistful smiles. For the muscles and the kissing and the amazing sex. She'd let herself believe it was real when she should have known better. It wasn't real.

But she wasn't going to let that stop her now. Her broken heart would mend. She didn't need a man in her life, and she certainly didn't need one like Ryan Taggert. And she'd figure out some way to keep the view from the cottage pretty, too. Tall trees, pretty flowering shrubs, something. And if she couldn't buy Mrs. O'Malley's house, she'd buy some other cottage. Delores Crenshaw was looking none too healthy, after all, so Emily had options. She'd figure out a way. She always did, and she and Chloe would be just fine.

Thinking of Chloe, Emily picked up her pace. She was eager to see her daughter but needed to stop by the cottage first to see if any progress had been made in her absence. She trusted that her dad had kept his word and stopped by, but that didn't mean much had gotten accomplished. Her crew had all the supplies they needed to get most everything finished, but, well, she knew how often things went wrong when she was *there*, so she could only imagine what had happened while she was *gone*.

It was nearly six in the evening as she walked up the steps and heard voices, laughter, and the sound of work. At this time of day? Either that was a good sign or a very, very bad sign. She opened the door and was amazed, like Dorothy landing in Oz. Her crew had made tremendous progress! The kitchen cabinets and counters were installed, the floors gleamed, the light fixtures hung in just the right spots, the broken tiles around the fireplace had been replaced, and even the furniture had been arranged. What. The. Hell? The place looked amazing.

“Miss Chambers!” Tiny said. “Welcome back. What do you think?” He spun slowly in a circle, arms outstretched, and she couldn’t help but notice he was wearing neither his leg splint nor his electric dog collar, and he had on a new clean shirt. He looked like a whole new man. That Gloria Persimmons was having a very positive effect on him.

“I’m shocked, Tiny. In the best possible way. Everything looks wonderful.”

“Hiya, boss lady,” Horsey said, strolling through the room with painting supplies in his hand. “Glad to have you back. We were just cleaning up.”

“Namaste,” Georgie said as she and Yoga Matt followed close behind him. Matt smiled and gave her a nod.

“Wyatt and Garth already left for the day, but all the wiring is finished. Just a few switch plates left to install and a few other things. I left the punch list on the kitchen island if you’d like to take a look,” Tiny said.

“I am speechless, Tiny. I can’t believe how much you’ve all accomplished in just five days.”

“Well, we had a little help.”

She looked back at her foreman. “Help from whom?’

“From the Taggerts. They’ve been here the past couple of days and even brought over a few guys from the Clairmont. More hands sure make things go faster. Especially hands that know what they’re doing.”

Ryan’s hands certainly knew what to do, but she didn’t want to think about that right now because she was mad at him. Very, very mad. “Ryan and Tag have been helping? Why?”

Tiny’s face was guileless. “I don’t know, ma’am. I guess you’d have to ask for yourself. Tag’s not here, but Ryan’s upstairs replacing some windows.”

He was here? Ryan was here? She wasn’t really ready for that confrontation. But why on earth had he done this work? Guilt? Some pointless apology? It was too late for that.

"If you don't mind, we were just heading out for the day," Tiny added, "but we'll see you bright and early tomorrow morning." He picked up the enormous tackle box that served as his lunch box and made his way to the front door. The others followed, calling out their goodbyes and smiling broadly at her as they passed. They were proud of themselves, and she smiled back, because she was proud of them, too.

But Ryan was upstairs, and she was too curious to resist. She set down her travel bag and made her way up the steps. Slowly, though her heart was thumping as if she'd sprinted all the way from the boat dock. She heard some tapping in the bedroom on her left, so she walked in, and yep, there he was in faded jeans and a white undershirt, putting a glob of spackle on the wall with his finger. His back was to her so she got to admire those muscles for a second before he turned around and she'd have to remember why she was mad at him. Because she was mad. Very, very mad.

"Um, hello?"

He turned around at her words, and she was right. There were all those muscles on the front side of him, too, and damned if she didn't have to work extremely hard to remember why she was mad. Oh yes. That's right. He was ruining her view. Ironic, really, since the view she had right now of him was pretty enjoyable.

"Hey. Welcome back." His voice seemed a little huskier than usual.

"Thanks."

They stood there awkwardly, staring as he wiped his hands with a work rag. "You ran out on me," he finally said. "That wasn't very nice."

Now she scowled. "It wasn't very nice to buy the property right in front of this cottage without telling me, either. Seems like you might have mentioned that when we were talking about it in bed. And it wasn't very nice for you to trick an old lady into selling you her house, either."

"Chloe said that's why you were mad, and you were absolutely right to be." He shook his head, a rueful smile barely tilting the corner of his mouth.

"You talked to Chloe?"

"Yeah." That smile turned sheepish. "While you were in San Antonio, she and Susie Mahoney demanded a meeting with me, my dad, Gigi, and June Mahoney. It wasn't easy getting those two old women in a room together, but the kids were adamant. Lilly helped, but it was all Chloe's idea. That's some clever girl you've got there. She'll make a great business manager someday."

"What are you talking about?" Chloe *called a meeting?*

He tossed the rag onto a nearby table. "Well, it seems that when Chloe and Susie Mahoney compared notes and realized what we so-called adults were up to, they decided to put an end to this feud once and for all. Susie told her grandma June that if she built a bed-and-breakfast in front of Gigi's cottage, Susie would never speak to her again. And Chloe told Tag and me that if we built it, she'd make sure that neither you nor Lilly ever spoke to him or me again. She was quite persuasive, and having Lilly on her side didn't hurt." He slowly walked toward her, all soulful eyes and wistful smile, that bastard.

"But Peach, none of that was necessary. If you'd just answered my phone calls, I would have told you everything. I started having second thoughts as soon as I was here with you and saw what the Mahoney plans would do to Gigi's view, and once you'd told me you were interested in that pink house, I told Bryce the deal was off. I just couldn't tell you that yet, because we had a confidentiality clause in the contract, and I didn't feel like getting sued." He came closer still, with all the muscles, and pulled both of her hands into his. "I don't know what you think you heard on the phone, but that was me telling my brother I'd have to renegotiate with the Mahoneys, and I've done that. I gave them an alternate plan to consider, and although they were not easy to convince, I finally got everyone to agree. You'll keep your view."

Her breath went deep as her heart lifted high. "You did? I will? How?"

"Come downstairs a minute. Let me show you something." He pulled her with him and she followed, still in a bit of a daze. *So they weren't building a bed-and-breakfast?*

In the kitchen, on the newly completed island, was a drafting notebook. Ryan opened it up and took out several pages that were already detached and spread the drawings out. They were versions of Bridget O'Malley's little pink house, but with some exterior upgrades, like a new front porch and larger windows. There were some other sketches, too, mostly empty interiors that Emily recognized as the inside of that same house.

"I don't understand," she said, looking at the drawings spread out over the counter.

"The Mahoney sisters were willing, reluctantly, to sell the land back, but Mrs. O'Malley decided she'd rather keep their money. Apparently she charbroiled a tray of snickerdoodles last week, so the fire chief finally convinced her to move to the retirement community since it's closer to a hydrant."

Emily chuckled and felt a moment of relief on behalf of Mrs. O'Malley. And the fire department, but that didn't really solve her problem.

"But that means the Mahoneys still own the land, doesn't it?"

His smile was warm, nearly as warm as a tray full of snickerdoodles.

"Yes, they do," he said. "I'm sorry I couldn't get them to agree to sell it to you and Gigi, but I told them my company could not, under any circumstances, build them a bed-and-breakfast due to a conflict of interest. Not that Susie or Chloe would have let that happen anyway. But here's the better news. I managed to convince them to leave the pink house. I told them it would make far more sense to remodel it, and I said I knew of an excellent and reliable someone who might be available to take on that project."

He couldn't be serious. None of this could be real. "You think the Mahoneys are going to hire me to remodel Mrs. O'Malley's house for them?"

He nodded and gazed down at her with optimistic expectation in his eyes. "The job's yours if you want it. Gigi said it was okay, by the way. The feud is officially over, although I don't think she and June are ever going to be pals."

Emily's mind was spinning at a dozen different speeds and in a dozen different directions. "I'm so confused, Ryan. Why would you do all this? Not just because of me."

He chuckled and pulled her into his arms. "Yes, of course because of you. Do you not remember the part where I said I liked you? Like, liked you a lot?"

She did remember him saying that, but those words were mixed in with all the other stuff that had happened in the last few weeks, and now it was hard to put all the pieces together into any kind of coherent thoughts. Especially when his body was pressing up against hers, making it officially impossible for her to stay upset with him.

"I like you, too, Ryan, but I thought business always came first? Isn't your company going to lose a lot of money if they don't build that bed-and-breakfast?"

His nod was casual. "Yep, we're losing all sorts of money, and Bryce is none too happy about that, but Peach, that's just business. This is personal, and I realize now which is more important." He leaned down and kissed her lips, soft and sweet. It was a tender kiss, full of apology and promise, and she moved against him, wrapping her arms around his shoulders and returning his kiss with all the hope and forgiveness she had inside.

Ryan hugged her tighter, then lifted his head to gaze down at her, his eyes searching hers. "I'm not sure what happens next for us. This is all so new, but I just know for certain that I want us . . . to be *an us*. Because when I said I liked you, I wasn't being completely honest. The truth is, I seem to have fallen in love with you."

Emily's heart fluttered and rippled and sang the "Hallelujah" chorus. "Me too. Same. I think I've fallen in love with you, too, but you live in Sacramento, and I'm moving back here."

His expression said, *I have more good news.* "Yeah, about that. As luck would have it, Tag has found another hotel on the island in need of my consulting expertise. The place is a mess. So it looks like I'll be sticking around the island for a while. Sacramento will just have to do without me."

"Sticking around? For how long?" *Please be a long time. Please be a long time.*

His shrug was coy but very encouraging. "It's going to take me *months*, maybe even *years* to get that place back in shape."

His answer made joy burst inside her chest like a firework because it was the best news she'd heard since . . . since forever. She rose up on her toes to get closer to those lips of his. "It gets mighty cold here in the winter. I'd be willing to keep you warm, if you're interested."

"Oh hell yes to that. I am. I'm very interested."

He scooped her up, carrying her over to the red velvet sofa and covering her face and neck with tickling kisses until laughter overtook them.

She smiled up at him, happiness flowing through her body. She was home. Back with her family. She had a place to live, a job to do, a wonderful daughter, and a man to love. Life was good. She reached up and traced her fingers along his jaw. "I can't believe you've done all this for me," she said softly.

His eyes were full of tenderness. "I'd do anything for you, Peach. Anything and everything. Except, maybe . . . square-dance."

AUTHOR'S NOTE

I hope you enjoyed your visit to Trillium Bay! Some readers may recognize similarities to Michigan's Mackinac Island, which was the inspiration for the setting of this series. Naturally, I took some creative liberties with the details since Wenniway is a fictionalized island. Nonetheless, Michigan natives may find clues to well-known landmarks and island activities, and I offer my thanks to the many Mackinac Island families who shared their experiences with me.

ACKNOWLEDGMENTS

To my tribe of awesome women who supported me through each day of writing this book. Melody Guy, thank you for being on Team Tracy. Your support and expertise guided me. Kelli Martin, thank you for your continued support, for always bringing me joy, and for joining me on spa day. Nalini Akolekar, thank you times infinity for holding my hands when days got tough, even if it meant you had to hold them over the keyboard.

Thank you to Webster Girl and Tenacious D for believing in me, for bringing me waffles, and for lighting up my life every single day. But I can't believe I let you talk me into getting a Great Dane.

Thank you Catherine Bybee and Tiffany Snow for laughing with me (and at me) and for your listening ears and helpful advice. Love you, girls, and all your rock-star ways.

Thank you Kimberly Kincaid, Alyssa Alexander, and Darcy Woods for all the encouraging calls, emails, texts, smoke signals, and carrier pigeons. Knowing you have always been in my corner helps me come out of it once in a while. I heart you big. So big.

To my dear friend Jane, for reading, rereading, and then rereading again. You are the shiny gemstone in the tiara of my life. Or rather, you would be if I had a tiara. Which I don't, but I should. And so should you.

And finally, to my wonderful, supportive, energetic readers. You are the reason I do what I do. I hope this story brings a smile to your face, a single tear to your eye, and a few hours of blissful escapism. If you keep reading, I'll keep writing!

ABOUT THE AUTHOR

Photo © 2012 Allie Gadziewski

Tracy Brogan is an award-winning, bestselling novelist who writes fun and funny stories about ordinary people finding extraordinary love, as well as lush historical romances full of royal intrigue, damsels causing distress—and the occasional man in a kilt. She is a three-time nominee for the prestigious RITA Award from Romance Writers of America for her Bell Harbor Series: *Crazy Little Thing*, *The Best Medicine*, and *Love Me Sweet.*

Brogan loves to hear from readers, so visit her website at www.tracybrogan.com or visit her on Facebook at www.facebook.com/AuthorTracyBrogan.